AND THEN SHE WAS GONE

A DETECTIVE JACK STRATTON NOVEL

CHRISTOPHER GREYSON

Novels featuring Jack Stratton in order:

AND THEN SHE WAS GONE
GIRL JACKED
JACK KNIFED
JACKS ARE WILD
JACK AND THE GIANT KILLER
DATA JACK
JACK OF HEARTS
JACK FROST

Also by Christopher Greyson:

PURE OF HEART

THE GIRL WHO LIVED

AND THEN SHE WAS GONE

Find out more about the author and upcoming books online at www.ChristopherGreyson.com.

ISBN: 1-68399-003-X
ISBN-13: 978-1-68399-003-1

This book is dedicated to my wife. She not only saved my life but brought me to a wonderful place. To her I am forever indebted.

CONTENTS

1

WHERE HAVE ALL THE HEROES GONE?

"HELP ME!" The old woman's desperate plea rose above the din of the afternoon traffic. Bystanders moved away from the trouble; in the rough neighborhood of Hamilton Heights, you kept your head down and your eyes shut if you wanted to make it home alive.

The junkie yanked on the woman's handbag. His lanky forearms, riddled with scabs, stuck out from his filthy red hoodie as he attempted to twist the leather strap from her hands. "Let go, you old hag."

A small crowd formed, watching the struggle from a safe distance. No one offered assistance. One man took out his phone but didn't call the police. He pressed the video record button instead.

Age and poverty had worn the Hispanic woman's shoulders into the shape of a wishbone. "No money." She clung to the strap of the handbag like a drowning child clutching a rope. "Jus' medicine."

The junkie's eyes widened at this welcome news, and he jerked harder, pulling the old woman forward. Her legs buckled and then her knees crashed down on the pavement. He planted his feet and dragged her forward, scraping her legs along the jagged concrete while her fingers tightened on the leather.

"My husband needs it," the woman begged.

"Give it up." He smashed his foot down on her fingers. The junkie's dilated pupils darted erratically toward the growing audience, but he didn't see anyone rushing to stop him.

"Please—"

The strap broke, and the woman landed with a sick thud on the sidewalk. The thief bolted with his prize clutched under his arm.

As the indifferent crowd parted to let him through, two young men stepped out of Ma Barker's Mini Mart—straight into the thief's escape route. He slammed into the first man—Chandler, all six foot six and two hundred ninety pounds of him—and bounced right off. Chandler didn't budge.

The junkie swore and scrambled to his feet as Jack Stratton pushed past Chandler to get a better view down the sidewalk, where a tiny, bent woman with disheveled hair and bloody knees shouted and pointed.

"Please, stop him!" the woman begged, limping toward the two young men. "He stole my purse!"

The old woman, toddling determinedly toward them, looked straight into Jack's eyes, pleading, *Do something!*

Without asking for a second opinion from his brain, Jack flew after the red hoodie.

"Jack, stop!" Chandler called out, too late.

The old woman's cry for help rang in Jack's ears. Her face flashed through his mind—desperate, helpless. A victim. Jack had been a helpless victim, prey, in the past. Not now. Jack was the hunter now. The adrenaline surging through his body was like rocket fuel. *I've got this.*

The wiry thief cradled the purse like a football. He had a lead and picked up the pace, but he wasn't in shape and Jack's legs quickly ate up the distance. The junkie weaved between pedestrians or shoved them aside.

But Jack wasn't just in shape, he was close to his athletic peak. For over a year, he had been training with the same focus as an Olympian—his objective not a gold medal but a gold shield. His quarry suddenly changed direction and zigzagged to the other side of the street. Jack wasn't thinking with his head but with his feet, and he cut in front of a car so close that his hand brushed the car's hood and the rear bumper passed within an inch of him, but he didn't even register the sounds of the aggrieved driver yelling at him or the horn or squealing brakes. Anger simmering just below the surface propelled Jack forward. Less than ten yards separated them now.

"I'm not stopping!" Jack shouted as he flew forward.

The junkie cast a desperate glance over his shoulder, gasping for breath. Losing steam, he cut down an alley.

Jack barely slowed as he rounded the corner. Trash littered both sides of the narrow utility alley. Its graffiti-covered brick walls trapped the summer heat like a furnace, and the stench of garbage and urine hung in the stale air. A rat, searching for its next meal, scurried under a dumpster.

The alley came to a dead end, and the junkie had nowhere to go. Cornered, he turned to face Jack.

Jack skidded to a halt. Figuring the junkie had had enough, Jack expected the guy to give up.

"Hand over the bag."

A thin smile curled across the junkie's cracked lips. Then he hurled the handbag at Jack's head.

Jack snagged it with one hand. "Now that wasn't so hard, was it?"

But the creep had one more trick up his filthy sleeve, and a sudden flash of light turned out to be a knife in his hand. The serrated blade was short, about four inches, but long enough to kill.

"Whoa!" Jack dropped the handbag to the side and raised his arms. The junkie seemed unsure how to press his advantage and took a step forward.

Jack cursed himself. Once again his need for justice had short-circuited his instinct for self-preservation. Should he bolt and leave the handbag, or stay and fight?

The junkie decided for him, lunging straight at him, slashing with the knife toward Jack's vulnerable face, neck, and abdomen. Jack jumped back, but not quite fast enough—the blade sliced through the front of his shirt, grazing his skin.

The junkie thrust again, and all of Jack's training took over. He pushed off with his right foot and twisted sideways. His right hand swept down in a scoop block, and he used the momentum to knock the junkie's jab to the side.

It was about self-defense now, as Jack quickly sprang forward. His right elbow connected with the thief's face, just under the nose. A groan and sounds of the druggie's teeth rearranging themselves in his jaw echoed off the bricks in the narrow alley. Jack watched the knife fly out of the junkie's hand and skid along the asphalt. The thief was thrown into the wall and he slid down in a heap.

Jack picked the purse up off the ground and brushed the dirt off it.

"Freeze!" The sharp order came from behind Jack. He turned toward the opening of the alley.

"Don't move!" the policeman yelled. His gun raised, he moved forward. "Put your hands over your head."

"Who, me?" Jack stared at the cop in disbelief as he realized that the order was directed at him. "But…" He looked at the purse in his hand. "Wait a minute—"

"Put your hands above your head," the policeman ordered again.

Jack raised his hands while the junkie rose to his feet and slyly stepped closer to the opening of the alleyway.

Jack moved toward the junkie, but the policeman barked, "Freeze!"

Seeing that the cop's attention was focused on Jack, the junkie bolted past the cop and toward the street.

"*That* guy's the crook!" Jack pointed at the fleeing thief.

"Hands in the air. Now."

"He's getting away." Jack's voice was filled with indignation.

"You're the one with the purse. Now show me your hands."

Jack did what he was told.

"Drop what's in your left hand."

Jack started to lower his arm.

"Drop it."

"It's that old lady's purse. Can I set it down?"

"*Drop it!*"

Jack released the purse.

"Keep your hands in the air and face the wall," the policeman ordered. "Feet out and spread 'em."

"I'm the good guy," Jack grumbled as he put his hands on the brick wall and set his feet wide apart. "Can we hurry this up so you can catch the real thief?"

The policeman holstered his gun as he moved up behind Jack. "Do you have any weapons on you?"

"I don't. But that guy did. A knife. It's over there." Jack nodded in the direction of the blade.

"Why were you beating him up?" the policeman asked in a low, authoritative voice.

"He stole a woman's handbag outside Ma Barker's."

"That doesn't explain you bashing him into the wall."

"He pulled a knife on me. What was I supposed to do—ask him if he'd like some tea and crumpets?"

Chandler, panting heavily, thumped to a stop at the front of the alley and yelled, "Jack!"

"Stay where you are!" The policeman kept one hand on Jack's shoulder and pointed the other at Chandler.

"What happened?" Chandler asked.

Jack grinned. "I'm getting frisked."

Chandler shook his head. "That's not a good thing, Jack. *Why* are you getting frisked?"

Jack shrugged as the policeman patted him down. "He thinks I was beating up that junkie for no reason and I stole the old lady's handbag."

Chandler frowned and walked forward.

"You too"—the policeman stepped back and pointed at Chandler—"against the wall."

"Yes, sir." Chandler joined his friend, upraised hands against the wall.

"Why are you treating *him* like a criminal?" Jack asked. "Because he's black?"

"Shut up, Jack," Chandler snapped. "You're going to get us arrested."

"For what? We're the good guys."

"Both of you shut up and face the wall."

Jack kept his hands on the wall and craned his neck to get a better look at the cop. Young guy, no evidence of a sense of humor, but then, maybe he was just as scared as Jack and Chandler.

The cop directed his next question to Chandler. "Now what's your story?"

"We were coming out of Ma Barker's on D Street when this junkie stole an older woman's handbag," Chandler politely explained.

"Is she all right?" Jack asked quietly.

"Her knees were all bloody, but I think she was okay. All she talked about was her husband's medicine. She'll be happy you got it back."

"Did you see the other man steal the handbag?" The policeman finished patting Jack down.

"Neither of us did," Jack said over his shoulder, "but the lady was screaming, 'He stole my bag,' and that junkie didn't exactly look like the purple handbag type." He figured this explanation would surely exonerate him and started to turn around.

"Keep facing the wall. You too," the cop reminded Chandler.

Chandler, who hadn't moved a hair, said, "Yes, sir," to the brick wall.

"He didn't do anything," Jack persisted.

"Shut up!" the policeman snapped. He patted Chandler down, then stepped back and looked back and forth between them. "Names," barked the cop. "You first." He scowled at Jack.

"Stratton. Jack Stratton."

"And you?"

"Chandler Carter, sir."

The policeman reached for his shoulder radio. "This is Officer Denby. Have there been any reports of a situation around D Street and Forty-Third?"

As the officer called it in, Chandler whispered to Jack, "How about trying to get us out of this?"

"We didn't do anything. We're fine."

"No, we're not. Have you forgotten what it's like in the hood?"

"No. I never forget." Jack gave Chandler a meaningful look. "What took you so long to get here, anyway?"

"I…er…I wanted to make sure the old lady was okay."

Jack frowned. "You haven't been exercising, have you?"

"I have," Chandler muttered.

"Yeah, right." Jack cocked an eyebrow toward Chandler's belly and said in his best imitation of a drill sergeant's growl, "You've got three months to lose fifteen pounds, *soldier.*"

"Ten."

"That was last month. You've gained."

"I plateaued."

Jack chuckled.

The policeman's radio beeped, and they heard the dispatcher: *"Officer Jenkins is on scene. Possible mugging."*

"Eat less, run more," Jack said.

"Just keep your big mouth shut or neither of us will have to worry about my weight," Chandler grumbled.

"Why?"

"Because we'll be disqualified before the weigh-in."

The policeman spoke into his radio. "Officer Jenkins? This is Officer Denby. Do you copy?"

Jenkins' voice came through the speaker: *"Copy."*

"Can you give me a description of the perp?"

"Tall. Thin build. Wearing a red hoodie."

"Was anyone with him?"

"No. But two teenagers chased after him. One African American, one Caucasian, both male."

Jack kept his hands on the wall and looked over his shoulder. "And one of them is tall and really good-looking, right?"

"That would be me." Chandler grinned and raised himself up to his full six foot six.

"I'm with them now," Denby said.

Over the radio came the voice of the old woman. *"My purse, where is my purse?"*

"Hold on, ma'am," Jenkins said. *"Did you recover the handbag?"*

Jack smiled broadly.

Officer Denby responded, "That's affirmative. We did."

Jack glanced over at Chandler and mouthed, *We?*

Chandler shook his head and mouthed, *Stop.*

"I'm driving the victim over to you. What's your location?"

"I'm in a dead-end alley between J and K. Cross-street is Forty-First."

Denby clicked his radio off and ambled toward Jack and Chandler. "Okay, you two can turn around." He somewhat begrudgingly added, "I know you thought you were doing the right thing, but you should have called the police."

"I didn't want him to get away," Jack said.

"He won't. We'll pick him up." Denby took a small notebook and pen from a pocket on his shirt. "Anything you can tell me about him?"

"Approximately five foot eleven. One hundred forty, maybe fifty pounds. Newer white Nikes, ripped blue jeans, grubby red hoodie. Medium-length sandy hair. Oh, and a Grim Reaper tattoo on his neck."

The cop's eyebrows traveled in different directions.

"And he's missing at least two front teeth." Jack topped off his performance with his signature grin. At which Chandler lowered his eyes and shook his head.

"What?" Jack shrugged.

"How did you remember all that?" Denby asked.

"I'm studying to be a cop."

Denby radioed in the enhanced description of the perp, then nodded toward the weapon on the ground, pulling a plastic evidence bag from his pocket. "This is the knife the guy had on him?"

"Yes, sir."

Chandler pointed to Jack's side. "Did you tear your shirt?"

Jack looked down at the slice in his T-shirt and groaned. "Oh, no, it's one of my favorites."

Chandler almost-yelled with concern, "Did he stab you?"

"No." Jack pulled back. "It's just a scratch."

"A guy almost slices you up and you're more worried about your T-shirt?"

"Well, I look really good in it."

Chandler shook his head. "You need to call the cops. Simple math. Bad guys have knives. Cops have guns."

"I got the handbag, didn't I?"

Denby stood to the side, tuning them out to write up his paperwork.

"Don't you get it?" Chandler said. "Nothing's worth getting killed over, Jack. What would your father say?"

Jack ran his hand through his thick brown hair. "Don't bring my dad into it," he said in a low voice. "That's crossing the line."

"Ha!" Chandler said. "Your dad would flip out and he'd be right."

"Whatever. I got the purse back."

"You pull any of that hero stuff in the Army and I'll shoot you myself." Chandler shook his head, but grinned.

Sensing that the cloud of testosterone and adrenaline had somewhat dissipated, Denby picked up the purse and began walking toward the street. "You boys enlisted?"

Jack nodded, in step beside Denby. "Yes, sir. We go to basic in three months. Serve two years. Pay for college with a GI bill, and then off to the Police Academy."

"I went through Fort Benning."

"We don't know where they're sending us yet," Chandler said.

A police cruiser stopped at the end of the alley, the old woman peering out the back window.

Denby handed the purse to Jack. "You can do the honors."

Chandler nudged him forward. The woman opened the window and leaned out, her hands gripping the frame.

Jack held out the purse. "Here you go, ma'am."

"Oh, thank you." Her bruised hand trembled as she unzipped it. When she saw that the pharmacy bag was still inside, she clutched it to her chest and her deep brown eyes searched Jack's face. "Thank you. Thank you, young man." She reached out for Jack's arm, light as a bird, and patted him. She waved them closer, then squeezed Chandler's hand too. "You boys are my heroes."

"It was our pleasure, ma'am." Jack felt like he was about to float into the sky—like he could do anything, fly maybe, or lift the police car up with one hand, with the officer and the lady in it.

"We're just happy to help, ma'am." Chandler tipped his head to the woman, then to Denby, and he and Jack headed down the street.

When they were out of earshot, Jack swaggered like a cowboy and in his best John Wayne Texan drawl said, "Just happy to help, little lady," tipping an imaginary ten-gallon hat.

Chandler was quick to bring his friend back to earth with a punch in the arm. "Quit joking around. That cop was right—you should have called the police."

Jack just walked faster. "What was I supposed to do? When I saw her, all scared and helpless, I had to do something."

Chandler grabbed Jack's arm and pulled him to stop. "Seriously. I know you've had a hard life, and you want to help others. But you can't help everyone."

"I'm not trying to. Believe me, I stick my neck out for nobody."

Chandler jogged a few paces to catch up. "Someday you're going to find someone you can't help, Jack. Not everyone can be saved."

"Yeah, yeah, yeah," Jack said, but as he walked toward home, a pit began to grow in his stomach.

2

A BRIGHT FUTURE

All was silent around Stacy Shaw's little cubicle. The last of her coworkers had gone home over an hour ago, but just to be sure, she raised herself up on the arms of her chair and peeked over the cubicle wall at the maze of cubbies. Only when she was certain she was alone did she dare to break one of the standing rules at H. T. Wells Financial and, with a little gasp of pleasure, slip her aching feet out of their high-heeled prisons. Wiggling her toes, she settled back in her stiff office chair and let herself enjoy her mini-rebellion.

The serenity was broken when her phone beeped, announcing yet another text from her mother. She glanced at the screen. Her mother had forwarded her an advertisement for a Taser. *Personal Protection Guaranteed*, the ad promised in giant type. In the picture, a white-haired grandmother posed like Rambo.

Stacy didn't reply to this, the fourth similarly themed text in the last few days, suggesting pepper spray, guard dogs, even a gun safety class. It all started after her mother read an article about a rash of purse snatchings in Fairfield. In spite of Stacy's insistence that their new home was in a quiet bedroom community, and that she and Michael already had friends in the neighborhood, her mother still worried.

"Stacy." Her boss's deep, slightly irritated voice broke the silence. Startled, Stacy jumped out of her chair, banging her knee on the desk drawer. So she wasn't alone after all.

"Do you have a second?" her boss called out.

Ouch, ouch! "Yes." She tried to put a smile in her voice. "I'll be right there."

Apparently that wasn't good enough for Leland Chambers, director of finance, who now stepped out of his posh corner office to summon her like a boorish customer flagging down a waitress. "I need to speak with you."

Stacy jammed her feet back into her shoes and rushed down the empty corridor after him.

"Here." He dumped a stack of folders into her arms, then cocooned himself in his high-back leather chair behind his wide mahogany desk. "I'm taking a long weekend on the Vineyard. I'll need those done by Wednesday."

"Yes. Certainly, Mr. Chambers."

"Call me Leland."

Stacy nodded, but had no intention of honoring the request. Leland Chambers was upper management and she was a worker bee who badly needed a job. The haves and have-nots didn't mix—not if they wanted to stay employed.

Stacy Shaw was a mid-level financial analyst. Everything about her dress matched her position—plain and practical, from her gray silk blouse, classic black skirt, and narrow leather belt, to the simple (yet uncomfortable) black heels to compensate for her diminutive stature. Her makeup was light and natural, her blond hair neat, her only jewelry a pair of pearl stud earrings. All compliant with HR's dress code; all designed to make her blend in, or rather, not to stand out in any way.

"Do you need anything else?" she asked. "I'd planned to work late tonight."

"Won't your husband be upset?"

Is he implying something? Gross! "He's out of town on business." Stacy self-consciously held the pile of papers to her chest.

Chambers swiveled slightly in his chair and sized her up. "I'm surprised he leaves your side."

Double gross! She pretended to read the top folder in an attempt to hide her disgust at the shallow come-on. "He has to, for his job."

Chambers snapped his fingers. "Now I know who you look like. I've been trying to nail it down since you came on board."

"Who?" she asked, and immediately regretted doing so, fearing who she was about to be compared to.

"Jennifer Lawrence. A lot shorter, but your smile is spot-on."

Stacy lowered her eyes as her hand tucked an errant strand of naturally blond hair behind her ear. "Thank you," she mumbled, and turned to make a hasty exit.

"Hey, wait a minute." He jumped up and followed her. "I'm heading down to O'Flaherty's. Accounting just wrapped up the end of the quarter, and they're celebrating."

He stopped with one foot inside her cubicle and angled his shoulders. From his tasseled leather loafers and pleated khakis to his fitted white shirt and perfectly groomed goatee, Mr. Chambers' style seemed carefully lifted from a *GQ* magazine. Even his fingernails were expertly manicured. He seemed to be striking a pose. It wasn't the first time in her short tenure at H. T. Wells that Stacy had wanted to strangle him with his own silk tie.

After he had showed both profiles for her adoration, pretending to survey the hallways, his gaze settled on her. "Would you care to join me?"

Stacy shook her head. "Thank you, but I want to finish up a couple of things." She sat down.

"That works out well for me." A suggestive smile spread across his broad face. "I'm going for a quick run around Hamilton Park first, while it's still light out. It's a beautiful park—during the day." He twirled the key ring to his Porsche Carrera 911. "That gives you an hour. By that time, the accountants will have enough drinks in them that maybe they won't be so boring. C'mon, it'll be fun. All work and no play …"

"Actually …"

"You've done enough time in the mines for one day. Besides, the buck stops with me. I'll adjust your time card." This gem came with an over-the-top, slow-motion wink.

"I couldn't let you do that." She smoothed her skirt and rested her hands on the hem so it was as long as possible, covering as much of herself as she could, and scrunched up in her chair.

"But *I* can." He leaned against the cubicle wall. "Think of it as a 'welcome on board' bonus."

She crossed her arms tightly.

"What's it been, almost three months now? Happy anniversary."

He opened his hand as if he were giving her a gift, and she flinched—just the tiniest bit, but he saw it, just as she saw the hot flush of male rejection that rose up his thick neck.

He took a moment to clear his throat loudly and adjust his tie. He resumed, frostily now, "It's only an hour, and you're doing great work. I believe in rewarding a job well done."

Maybe it was his choice of words—*Happy anniversary*. Her thoughts immediately shifted to Michael, and she missed her husband so intensely she had to close her eyes to keep tears from forming. But when she looked up again, Leland Chambers was still standing there, his *GQ* slouch replaced by an aggressive pit bull stance.

"Thank you," she said, too loudly, "but I really have to be heading home. I'm just going to finish up the Right-A-Way Shipping report and call it a night."

"What?"

"I noticed they were spending a large amount of money on insurance."

"Right-A-Way Shipping?"

"Yes. At my last job, this same level of coverage was a quarter of this amount—"

"That report is done." His tone had changed yet again. He stepped forward and glared at her monitor. "What are you doing with it?" His thighs pressed against her chair, pinning her in place.

She'd gotten a glimpse of his "other side" before—everybody knew about it—but it had never been directed at her. "But I'm supposed to review the report and—"

"No," Mr. Chambers snapped. "You're supposed to review your section of the report, and you assured me that you had. Are you changing what you submitted?"

She cleared her throat. "No. But I found a discrepancy with—"

Mr. Chambers banged his hand down on the desk. "No! You should have nothing to do with that. I've already reviewed and approved the report myself."

"Umm …" She shuffled some papers around on her desk, her hands trembling and suddenly ice-cold.

"Is this why you're working late? When I approved your overtime, I thought you were catching up on tasks, not just making busywork for yourself so you can get paid time and a half."

"I'm not! I was just—"

He thrust a finger at the monitor. "Close the file and send me what you've done to it."

Stacy nodded. She opened the mail program. "I haven't changed anything." Her mouth was so dry, it came out almost a croak.

Mr. Chambers spun his keys around his finger again, like an outlaw gunslinger twirling his pistol. "I'll take a look at it in the morning." His voice softened somewhat, but he still stood with both feet planted wide just behind her chair. "You couldn't know, but once these reports are submitted, it's a nightmare to make corrections. I'd rather get a public flogging than have to request to change it."

"I…I only highlighted the line. I didn't alter the report."

His keys chimed as they spun round again. "I'll review it later. No harm, no foul. Like you said, you didn't change anything."

Stacy nodded, but didn't turn around.

"Are you sure you won't reconsider? O'Flaherty's makes a heck of a Long Island Iced Tea."

Are you kidding? No way, Mr. Hyde. "No, thank you." She made a point of taking out her pocket calendar and a pen. "Have a good night."

"Well, I'm sure we'll be at O'Flaherty's for a while if you change your mind. If not, I'll see you tomorrow."

Feeling like a prisoner in a cell, Stacy listened to his keys jingle as he walked away, tapping each cubicle wall as he passed it. She closed her eyes and tried to calm her breathing, slow her heart. She wanted to call Michael, but she wasn't sure if he was free or having dinner with clients. He had called earlier from his hotel room to let her know that he'd arrived and that their old car had held up on the long journey. And considering nothing had really happened, she figured there was no reason to get Michael upset, too.

She pushed the incident with Mr. Chambers aside and got back to work. She dealt with the requests in her inbox quickly and finished all her reports within forty-five minutes. After clicking the last report closed, she triumphantly sent it off. Now, with her focus off her work, she heard the deep hum of a vacuum cleaner in the distance.

As she shut down her computer, her eyes fell as usual on the framed picture beside the monitor. Their honeymoon in the Bahamas. She was lying on a lounge chair next to Michael, her husband of three blissful days, with the glittering sand and shimmering sea behind them. Had it really been seven years already? Everything was changing so fast. New house, new job, and now … She gently laid a hand on her stomach. "My little miracle," she whispered.

Longing and need and anxiety—a familiar cluster of emotions lately—washed through her. She had to get home and under the covers and call Michael, *now*. Her escape was close enough that she had a little giggle, imagining herself snarling like a rabid dog at anyone foolish enough to interrupt her in her mission.

She pushed in her chair and grabbed her favorite handbag off the floor. It was damp, and she smelled the pungent scent of carpet cleaner. *Oh, shoot. Hope it dries okay.*

But this small setback was quickly forgotten in her elation at leaving the office. On her way out, almost skipping through the corridors, she passed her coworkers' cubicles, bedecked with photos of happy families, smiling kids, and hugging couples. Week by week, as she got to know her coworkers better, she was growing fonder of them. She was certainly not alone in disliking Leland Chambers.

The air conditioner had already turned off for the evening, and an airless heat had settled through the offices, but a strong shudder ran through her. She could almost feel her hormonal balance shifting, yet again. One second she was hot, the next her teeth were almost chattering and she had goose bumps.

But it wasn't just the hormones, it was the thought of the silence, the cold stillness, she faced at home without Michael. She had grown up a latchkey kid in a quiet house with no brothers or sisters, her parents always gone. Some kids grow up to relish solitude, but Stacy hated being alone. She suddenly felt so, so tired as she punched the elevator button one more time and the industrial roar of the vacuum cleaner came closer.

What looked like a small Zamboni rounded the corner up ahead. At first, the burly custodian kept his eyes focused on the area directly in front of the machine, but then he noticed her and turned the machine off.

"Hello, Mrs. Shaw," he called from about ten feet away, with an awkward wave. His eyes darted all around, never meeting hers, as he came closer.

"Hi, Jeremy." She always tried her best to make polite conversation with Jeremy; he had few friends, and was clearly a little challenged mentally in some way, but he was very sweet. Most of the women in the office tried to avoid any contact with him, but even though Jeremy towered over Stacy, she'd never been afraid of him.

She spoke carefully. "You're working late."

"Like you." Jeremy smiled lopsidedly. He spoke deliberately, but his speech was slurred and hard to understand. He wiped his hand on his coveralls.

She nodded. There was something she wanted to ask him, and after a moment, she remembered what it was.

"Jeremy, did you clean my carpet again last night?"

His eyes brightened. "You saw?"

"Yes. But…didn't you just clean it on Monday?"

"I cleaned your office extra." Jeremy looked at the ceiling. "You like it? It smells nice?"

Stacy sighed. She didn't want to hurt his feelings. "Yes. But next time maybe you can just vacuum?"

"Okay. T'ank you. I'll do that."

"Well, have a nice night, Jeremy."

Finally, the elevator chimed its arrival. Jeremy awkwardly offered his hand to shake. As she shook it, she tried not to recoil at the touch of his rough calluses and thick fingernails.

"See you tomorrow," Jeremy said.

"Good night."

Jeremy watched her until she disappeared through the door. She heard the vacuum cleaner turn back on, then quieter and quieter with each floor as the elevator descended.

Outside, the warm, moist summer night air felt wonderful on her skin. The sun had set, and faint stars peeked out from behind dark clouds that were rolling in. Every step put the office further behind her, and just as suddenly as it had come on, the anxiety of loneliness was whisked away by the exhilaration of freedom. She'd get used to this roller coaster. It wasn't so bad, after all. She was free and alive and pregnant and sweaty (okay, the body temperature thing was pretty annoying) and in love with her life. She wanted nothing more than to take off her bra, slip into one of Michael's T-shirts, and curl up on the couch with a pint of ice cream.

A voice behind her made her jump.

"Is the job making you crazy yet?"

Stacy's hand flew to her chest.

"Sorry. Didn't mean to scare you." Betty Robinson crunched her cigarette butt under her heel and walked over. "Did Mr. Happy Pants chain you to the desk, or are you working late, fixing one of his mistakes that he's blaming you for?"

Stacy chuckled. "Chased me around the desk would be more accurate."

Betty was on the north side of fifty and looked like she'd probably always been tough. Stacy couldn't help but wonder what it would feel like—as a woman—to be so tall and … *imposing* might be the best word. In heels, she loomed over Stacy. And she sure did like high heels, usually boots, unlike five-foot-two Stacy, who pretty much had to add a couple of inches just to be treated as an adult but would have preferred slippers if she could have gotten away with it. When she first met her, Stacy wondered why Betty always wore outfits that seemed to draw attention to her height and huge feet and thick shoulders. After she came to know her a little better, she realized that Betty dressed to intimidate.

"You haven't asked any questions for a few days," Betty said. "Does that mean the torch has been passed?"

"Hardly," Stacy said. "I think it'll take me another three months to get the hang of everything you were doing. How's upstairs?"

"Living the dream." Betty smiled coyly. "Make sure you keep up on the Henkle filing or the end of the summer will be killer for you."

"I will." Stacy cleared her throat. "Hey, did you work on the Right-A-Way Shipping report for Mr. Chambers?"

Betty slipped a cigarette out of the pack. "I still work on it. Don't tell me something's wrong with the report or I'll scream."

"You work on it now?" Stacy asked, confused.

"I approve the PO section. Leland does the insurance." With a click of her lighter, she was all business. "Is there an issue?"

"No. But I did notice we overpaid the insurance premium again, and from my records check, it was at least the second time it's happened."

Betty let a stream of smoke drift from her mouth, then exhaled through pursed lips. "Hmm. It happens. They've shifted the payment dates before. As long as the insurance doesn't lapse. That would be a complete nightmare. Do me a favor and forget about it. If you touch it now, five people have to sign off on it again, including me."

She looked down at Stacy's stomach. "You're going to be showing soon. When are you going to make the announcement?"

"Soon. My obstetrician says everything looks good, but please don't say anything. Michael wants us to wait until after the first trimester just in case something goes wrong. You're the only one who knows."

"I won't say a word. But no complications?"

"None. Our own little miracle."

"With everything that happened before, that's wonderful news."

Stacy nodded emphatically. There'd been times when she'd wondered whether it was a good idea to confide in Betty about the past, but right now she felt very lucky to have her as a friend.

An older blue BMW pulled up to the curb and the taller woman gave Stacy a quick squeeze. "Do you need a lift?"

"No, thanks. My car's right in the company lot."

"Bruce and I would love to have you two over for dinner again," Betty said as she got in the car. "Wouldn't we, Bruce?"

Her husband, a tall man with a friendly grin that softened his square face, leaned across the front seat. "We'd love to. We can get something delivered and I'll get a decent meal. How about tomorrow?"

Betty smacked his arm. "Bruce! You could cook once in a while, you know."

"She won't want to come if I cook."

"It'll have to be next week," Stacy said. "Michael's coming home tomorrow."

"Michael's out of town?" Betty asked.

"For work."

"Oh, is he…" Bruce said.

Bruce and Betty exchanged a quick glance.

"If you're free"—Bruce kept his eyes on his wife until she nodded—"then why not just come tonight?" He reached a long arm over the seat back to open the back door. "How about a low-key, intimate dinner for three? How does Chateau de Mama Mia's Pizza sound?"

"If you want the company," Betty added.

Stacy pictured the lonely, echoing house and almost jumped in the backseat. But she had a home to-do list two pages long.

"Not tonight. Actually, I'm trying to take advantage of the time to myself, so I was looking forward to doing some tidying up before Michael comes home. And I'm beat."

"The job's making you crazy," Betty cautioned as she clicked her seat belt. "Or you're nesting. Don't overdo it."

"I won't."

Stacy waved as they pulled away from the curb, then walked around the corner of the building to the nearly deserted company parking lot. There were only a couple of cars there and her Civic was one of them.

The door squeaked as she opened it. She mentally added *Lube car door* to her honey-do list. Michael had suggested they get her another car, but Stacy knew they couldn't afford it. Right now, every penny was going into the savings they would have to tap in a few months.

She turned the key, but absolutely nothing happened. Not even a click.

She turned the key again. Nothing.

"Oh, no. Not now." She pushed on the gas pedal and turned the key again. The engine didn't so much as sputter.

Fighting back tears, she laid her head against the steering wheel. If only she had gone with Betty and Bruce, she could be ordering pizza toppings now. Her phone rang, and she jumped. *What now?* she wanted to scream, but when she saw the caller ID, her smile returned. "Are you psychic?"

"That's right. Let's see … you're about to tell me that you love me," Michael joked.

"I do love you. And I'm *so* glad to hear your voice."

"Why? Is everything okay?"

Stacy hesitated. *No,* she wanted to say, but she knew that would only worry him, and he was already a bundle of nerves because of the pregnancy. "Everything's fine." The car was stifling and she opened the door for some air.

"Oh, okay. You sounded a little upset. Rough day?"

Maybe he really is psychic. "Nothing I can't handle. Really, I'm fine. You're the one with a big day tomorrow. Is everything ready for your presentation?"

"Yup. I just spent an hour at the copy store making handouts," Michael said. "I'm hoping that if I throw in a few boxes of doughnuts, they'll stay for the whole presentation."

"I'm sure you'll knock their socks off." Stacy took the keys out of the ignition. "You sound tired."

"Actually, I am. The long drive was brutal," Michael admitted. "It's been an exhausting day. Tomorrow looks like a beast too."

"Then go get some rest. I'll see you tomorrow night. I love you." Stacy blew a soft kiss into the phone.

"Love you too. 'Night." Michael hung up.

Stacy slumped back into the seat and stared across the road to the park. A warm breeze blew through the open door; it was a beautiful night. She took a deep breath, enjoying the balmy summer air.

If she cut through the park, it was only a twenty-minute walk home. She could leave the car overnight, then Michael could fix it when he got home and they'd save the money for a tow. Satisfied with her plan, she grabbed her handbag, locked the car, and crossed the street.

The entrance to Hamilton Park was marked by a beautiful stone archway. Modeled after Roman architecture, the twin stone columns towered fifteen feet on each side, forming the base for an ornately carved arch. The thick, pitted iron gates were always open.

Inside the grounds, old-fashioned streetlamps lit the paved main paths. A web of smaller unlit paths also crisscrossed the park, but Stacy elected to stick to the lighted areas. As she walked, she went down the list of all the things she would need to buy over the next few months: nursery furniture, baby clothes, one of those instant thermometers. She pretended that Michael was beside her, on one of their lunch breaks they took in the park.

"In a little while, we can buy an affordable car. Reliable. Maybe a minivan. If we get a used one…"

She felt a little ridiculous talking to herself, and suddenly realized that beyond the sporadically lit path it was completely dark. Her happiness dissipated as she remembered Mr. Chambers saying, "It's a beautiful park—during the day."

During the day …

Stacy was passing by a monument, a neoclassical column that stood twelve feet high. The top of the column was decorated with four busts facing in each of the four compass directions, four men scowling at her in stony, silent judgment as she passed.

The park felt different now. The rolling hills and groomed grounds no longer reminded her of families strolling and children playing. Now they reminded her of a cemetery.

The faster she walked, the louder her heels rang on the concrete, and the tap-tap-tap of her shoes matched the rapid pace of her heart. A bench ahead drew her attention. At first it looked like her couch on laundry day, covered in a mound of clothes. But as she drew closer, the mound moved.

A homeless man sat up and glared directly at her. He had apparently laid two filled trash bags over himself, and as he rose, the contents of one of the bags spilled onto the walkway.

Instinctively, Stacy moved to the far side of the path. The man crouched low over his bags, like a raccoon protecting his trash treasure, his eyes barely visible behind bushy eyebrows, his yellow teeth poking out from his unkempt beard. He cursed under his breath as he watched her pass.

Stacy took a deep breath and upped her pace. Her mother's warnings and cautionary tales replaced the baby's shopping list as she hustled toward the park exit closest to her street.

The lovely park's tall oaks and flowering shrubs turned restless in the wind. A dead tree's branches clawed at the sky like skeletal fingers. Just a few yards off the path, everything was murky and shrouded, and the shifting shadows played tricks on her mind. Branches groaned and creaked, leaves rustled, an unseen creature scurried along the undergrowth.

She was almost jogging now. The heel of one of her leather shoes had dug a deep blister into the back of her foot. As she crested a hill, she stopped to get her bearings. Up ahead, the path dipped down again—into darkness. She could just barely make out another of the old-fashioned streetlights, but it was unlit, as lifeless as a dead tree. *Just a little bit farther now.*

She started forward, her skin prickling. She found herself holding her breath as she hurried through the darkness, forcing an exhale now and then. With every step, shivers crawled down her spine. When she heard the rush of water from a fountain up ahead, she knew she was almost out of the darkened area. And then she saw the next streetlight through the trees, shining like a welcome beacon. She breathed a sigh of relief.

"I can make it," she reassured herself.

A muffled sound made her turn to the side. Not far away, along the tree line atop the hill, a darker shadow stood apart from the others—a hulking silhouette emerging from the woods.

The figure rushed toward her.

Stacy shrieked incoherently and bolted.

Her pursuer's footsteps rang loudly off the concrete behind her, heavy and fast. Tears blurred Stacy's vision, but she cast one fleeting glance over her shoulder. Like a bear crashing down from a mountain, her pursuer was gaining on her fast.

The figure was still shrouded in darkness, and the only detail Stacy could make out clearly was a ski mask.

As she ran, Stacy searched desperately for her phone in her handbag. Tight bands circled her chest as she gasped for air. Her heart thumped and thrashed like an unbalanced washing machine.

She felt the phone but her assailant's long fingers seized her belt and yanked her back painfully.

"Let me go!"

She flung her handbag as far into the woods as she could. "Take it. Just take it! There's money in there!" she screamed.

But the attacker ignored the bag and kept hold of her belt, and Stacy's scream turned into a guttural wail. She felt like she was swimming through a riptide, desperate to make it to shore, as her hands clutched at the air.

She glanced back. The front of the ski mask was painted with a skull—a skull with a twisted, evil grin.

She raised her leg and drove her heel down onto her attacker's foot as hard as she could. There was a growl of pain, and the fingers grasping her belt let go.

Stacy stumbled and then took off, screaming for help, but the only person who heard her was the one she was escaping from. The light was still too far away, and mere light wouldn't protect her now. Her only chance was to lose her attacker in the darkness. She kicked off her shoes and ran off the path, the wet grass slick beneath her bare feet.

She still had her phone in her hand, and once again she tried to dial. But her attacker had recovered quickly and closed the distance. Pushed from behind, she pitched forward and landed hard on her chest. The phone flew from her hand and landed softly in the grass in front of her, the numbers 911 illuminated on the screen. She just needed to press the call button.

But it was too late. A hand grabbed the back of her neck. Long fingers wrapped around her belt and yanked her up.

She screamed and grabbed at the hands, but they only tightened their grip. A muscular arm circled her waist from behind and dragged her toward the woods. Her arms thrashed, but she could only beat helplessly at the air. She kicked backward, and her foot struck flesh, but her attacker didn't slow.

Fear turned into abject terror.

She dug her feet into the ground, trying to slow their progress. A rock sliced deep into her heel, but still she fought and kicked.

Finally her attacker must have decided they were far enough from the path, as Stacy was flung roughly to the ground, face up.

"Please, no—"

With one last burst of strength, she clawed at her attacker's face. Grasping the ski mask, she wrenched it off.

Her eyes widened with recognition of the last face she would ever see.

A fist slammed into her face. She tried to think, but her mind fogged. "Please—"

Then the fist struck again, and everything went black.

3

CAN'T YOU SEE THE RESEMBLANCE?

Jack had been waiting in the line for a passport at the post office for almost an hour. As the line crawled forward, his reservoir of patience inched downward, and he was running on fumes. Now the man in front of him was chatting with the woman behind the counter as though they were old friends.

The government office looked as if someone had mashed together a bank and a deli. Speckled gray and black linoleum tiles covered the open floor. A counter divided the room in half. There were five sections where clerks could assist people, but only one window was open. Jack stood with about a dozen other people in a roped-off section that made him feel like a rat in a maze. For the hundredth time, he willed the line to move forward.

"Enjoy the rest of the afternoon." The woman smiled at the man she'd just helped.

What's left of it, Jack thought to himself. He stepped forward and handed her his passport application.

The woman set his papers on the counter, adjusted her glasses with one hand, and patted her short, coffee-colored hair with the other. Using her finger as a guide, she checked that each box of the form was correct. When she lazily reached for her coffee cup, Jack wanted to scream.

He read the brass name plate on her desk. "Deborah, as you know, that form's ten pages long. There's no reason to double-check every item again. I'm getting a passport before I enlist in the Army. I checked the form, my recruiter checked it, my father checked it, and my mom went over it with a magnifying glass. Let's say we speed-read this, and you can have an early lunch?" He gave her one of his roguish grins.

Deborah's wrinkles deepened. "If there's a problem, they'll kick it back and you'll have to do everything all over again."

"I'm not leaving for three months. Besides"—Jack leaned closer—"I'm sure you know this form so well that you can give it a quick scan and we'll both be out of here."

Deborah tipped her chin down and leveled her gaze over the rim of her glasses. "If you're going in the Army, get used to dotting your i's and crossing your t's. All right, Mr.—Jack Alton Stratton. Short for John, right?"

"No, ma'am. It's Jack." He didn't explain that he had given himself the name Jack, and it stood for everything about him: present and past, pride and humiliation. Probably too much information for this nice lady on this beautiful afternoon.

But she didn't press for more details, and he'd known very few situations where politeness and a smile weren't at least worth a try—especially where the ladies were concerned.

"Hair?"

"Brown."

"Eyes?"

"Two."

She frowned.

Jack flashed a handsome grin. "Brown."

She looked down but the corners of her mouth ticked up. "Six foot one and one hundred eighty pounds?"

"Sure am."

"Age?"

"Seventeen. For the next couple of days, anyway."

"Yes, I see you have a birthday coming up." Her finger stopped at the box for birthplace. "What town were you born in?"

Jack's back stiffened. He hated filling out paperwork; it reminded him of all the basic things he didn't know about himself. What was his real name? Who was his birth father? Where was he born? Facts most people took for granted, Jack ached to know.

He lowered his voice. "I don't know. It says 'unknown.'"

"Enough with the comedy routine." She pointed with her pen to remind him of the line of people waiting behind him—people who, her eyebrows seemed to be implying, all had real names and families and hometowns. "Birthplace?"

"I'm not kidding. I don't know. My mom thought we should write something instead of just leaving it blank."

"Your mom doesn't remember where she gave birth to you? Not even the state?"

Jack bit into his cheek. "I was…abandoned by my birth mother." Jack hated that word, *abandoned.*

Her cheeks blushed a pale pink. "Oh. I'm sorry."

Jack stood up straight. "It's all right. The truth is, I don't know the answers to half the questions on that form."

"I am truly sorry." She cleared her throat, and when she spoke again, her tone had softened. "And this is your present address?" She clearly felt bad, and that was the last thing Jack wanted. He'd had his fill of pity.

Jack pointed at the address. "That's the happy ending to my story." He worked up a smile. "After a few years in the foster care system, I got adopted. Which was a bit of a miracle, considering I was eleven."

"Miracle?" She looked confused.

"I was past the expiration date. Most people want to adopt babies."

She nodded.

"But I ended up with the best parents a kid could have."

She returned his infectious smile.

Jack had called the Strattons Mom and Dad from the moment they took him in. His parents loved him, and he loved them back. But the scars of his past had never completely healed.

Deborah quickly skimmed the remaining pages. "Your mother did a great job filling out this form. Okay, stand there." She pointed to a spot on the floor in front of a tripod camera.

Jack hurried over. "Do you have a mirror?"

She looked at him quizzically. "What for?"

Jack fussed with his thick, dark brown hair. "To try to look semi-decent."

Deborah chuckled. "Darling, you're as handsome as a movie star. Trust me, you don't need a mirror."

Jack's chest puffed out and the flash popped. "Thanks. When will—"

"Two to six weeks." She slipped Jack's photo, check, and paperwork in an envelope, printed off the mailing label, and dropped it on a stack.

Jack gave her a little salute as he headed for the door.

"Jack!" she called out before he reached the exit. A flurry of emotions crossed her face before she solemnly said, "Thank you for serving."

Jack straightened his shoulders and lifted his chin. He nodded politely and thanked Deborah for her help.

As he walked out of the old post office, he stopped in front of a large mural that he must have passed by hundreds of times in his life without really seeing it. Four World War I soldiers in their doughboy helmets charged up a hill, ready to face death. As Jack stared into the eyes of the young soldier in the front, the full impact of his decision to join the Army started to sink in. In three months, he would be going to basic training. After that, Afghanistan, or possibly Iraq. Even though they'd serve a hundred years apart, he and the soldier were now inexorably linked.

When he pushed open the door into the bright June sun, he smiled. *I have three months. One last summer.* All his worries about his future blew away in the summer breeze, and he knew exactly what he wanted to do after getting the passport application out of the way. He walked across the outdoor courtyard and headed for his pride and joy.

His 1978 Chevy Impala. He'd worked one whole summer for the parts and another summer to make the body pristine. He'd gotten some help from the guys at the high school auto shop. Jack's dad helped, too. They'd both spent days at a time under the hood, or pulling dents and sanding rust. To Jack, the Batmobile or even the Millennium Falcon had nothing on his ride.

And, oh, that heavenly shade of blue. But there was still a long list of stuff on the internals Jack knew he needed to fix: the piston rings were worn, the water pump was grinding, and it needed a valve job. The outside was mint, but the inside was messed up.

Just like Jack.

He hopped in and rubbed the dash. "Hey, baby." Talking to the car wasn't superstition, it was a greeting. He gave her another pat and started her up. To save some money, one of the guys in the school auto shop had suggested he use an old motorcycle muffler they had out back. As Jack's foot hit the gas, the car sounded like someone had mated a monster truck with a Jaguar.

Traffic was light for the middle of the day. It took only ten minutes to drive over to Hamilton Park, where he and Chandler had planned to meet. The park was the centerpiece of downtown Fairfield. A jogging path surrounded the eleven hundred acres, thick with trees. A wide, paved walking trail studded with benches formed a figure eight through its gentle slopes, and at its center was a stately four-tiered fountain.

As Jack drove down Main Street, he saw a line of police cruisers and several unmarked Ford Crown Victorias parked in front of the H. T. Wells office building. Jack sat up in his seat to get a better view of what was happening. There were no fire trucks or ambulances, which ruled out a bad traffic accident or a medical emergency.

Two men in suits followed by a patrol officer escorted a pair of sobbing women to one of the Crown Vics. Jack scanned the area around the building but saw no police tape marking the scene of a crime. He wondered what it was all about—as always, already mulling over several potential scenarios.

Farther down the road, on the southwest corner of Hamilton Park, were a large, run-down parking lot and a couple of aging basketball courts. Jack pulled in and shut the car off. In this area, an addict was liable to smash your windows looking for loose change, but Jack knew if they didn't see anything valuable, typically they would leave the car alone. Still, he popped the door panel out with a snap, dropped his favorite sunglasses inside, then snapped it shut. If someone did break in, they'd take whatever was in the glove compartment—nothing of value—while Jack's secret compartment was as safe as the Batcave.

He headed toward the basketball courts, where about twenty people sat on aluminum bleachers, watching a pick-up game. It was easy to spot Chandler's light-green T-shirt and the *Army Strong* slogan stretched across his massive chest; even sitting, he towered over everyone.

He waved Jack over. "You're late!"

"You can't be late for a pickup game."

"Where were you?"

"Applying for my passport."

Chandler shook his head. "You're late for that too—I got mine last week."

"Well, it's a good thing I have you to mother me." Jack fist-bumped his friend.

Chandler gestured to the attractive girl with long, dark hair sitting next to him. They'd been going out for a few weeks, and since Chandler seemed pretty taken with her, Jack had engineered a double date with them for tonight so he could meet her.

"This is Makayla." Makayla extended a slender hand. Her high cheekbones accentuated her big brown eyes. "Makayla, this is my brother, Jack."

Makayla shot a puzzled glance Chandler's way and seemed to hesitate, thinking of what to say, before finally settling on, "I've heard a lot about you."

"Don't believe a word of it." Jack shook her hand and sat on Chandler's other side.

Makayla leaned closer to Chandler and whispered, "He can't be your brother."

"Yep. Jack's my brother."

Makayla folded her arms and lifted her eyebrows.

"What?" Chandler shrugged.

"Clearly he is not your brother." Makayla peered around Chandler to look Jack in the eyes, then leaned closer to Chandler.

Chandler's eyes danced. "Why do you say that? Don't you see the resemblance?"

"But he's—he's—"

"What?"

"He's white!"

Jack opened his eyes wide in comic surprise, then frantically patted at his arms. "I'm *white*?" he squeaked, jumping up and down.

The mostly African American spectators turned around to look, though most of them had seen the two friends—and some of their antics—at previous games.

Chandler pulled Jack back down and said to Makayla in a mock-serious whisper, "We've never told him."

"So you're … adopted?" Makayla asked.

Jack's mouth fell open. "Chandler? Is this true?"

"We never told him that either," Chandler said with a straight face. "Leave it to my Aunt Haddie. We must be the only poor black family that goes and adopts a white kid."

"Shut the front door. You're playing me." Makayla gave Chandler a hard push. Jack and Chandler smiled at each other. Since they were seven, they'd pulled this joke dozens of times.

"Technically," Jack said, "I'm his foster brother. I lived with Chandler, his sister, Michelle, and Aunt Haddie—you've met her, I guess—for four years before the Strattons adopted me and I moved out."

"In my mind, Jack's blood," Chandler added. "I hate foster labels or any of that junk. Jack's as much family to me as Michelle. Not a foster or anything else."

Jack put his arm around his friend's massive shoulders and made a goofy face. "Can you see the resemblance now?"

Makayla laughed. "Now I can. Even though you two are as black and white as yin and yang."

"That's no big deal. Look at the size difference." Jack patted Chandler's stomach. "We've got to get Chandler here to jog."

Chandler knocked his hand away. "Funny."

"I'm not kidding." Jack raised an eyebrow. "Did you run this morning?"

"Sort of."

"Sort of? Come on, Chandler. You're supposed to be running every day."

"Who's being the mother now?"

"Touché."

"I thought you were going to stop by and we'd both go for a run." Chandler draped his arm across Makayla's shoulders.

"I was tied up with the passport. You should have gone anyway."

"I'll go running tonight."

"Really, when? We're all going out tonight, remember? Bowling."

"I'll go right after this game."

Makayla pouted. "You said you'd take me for an ice cream."

Chandler rubbed his close-cropped head. "I can't win."

"Sure you can." Jack crossed his arms. "Take her for ice cream at Wilbur's, right near the school, but don't get one for yourself. She can eat the ice cream while she watches you run laps at the track."

"Works for me." Makayla smiled.

"I don't have my jogging sneakers."

"Oh, boo-hoo. We're going to be running in boots soon. It'll be good for you."

Chandler sighed, conceding defeat.

Makayla waved at a girl on the other side of the bleachers. "My sister's here. I'll be right back." As she got up, she added, "Nice meeting you, Jack. See you tonight."

When she was out of earshot, Jack said, "She's a keeper, bro."

"Yeah, I hope so." Chandler stretched his legs out. "So, who's your date tonight?"

"Kelly."

"That girl you met at the galleria?"

"Yes."

Chandler made the sound of a bomb falling and then blowing up. "Kelly, whoa. I don't know if I'm ready for that."

"What? You've never even met her yet." Jack kicked a bottle cap off the bleachers.

"It's just…you've talked about her some, and—"

"I never said anything bad about her."

"She just doesn't seem like your type."

"My 'type'?" Jack's shoulders rose. "I don't have a type. But if I did, blond cheerleader with a great bod is a good type to have, don't ya think?"

"I'm talking about the super-rich part—drives Daddy's BMW, lives in Knob Hill—that type."

"You don't like her because her family has money?"

"No …" Chandler stretched the word out. "It's not her. It's you. You're not a country club, polo horse type of guy."

Jack laughed. "You got that right. Let's see how she feels about bowling."

Chandler leaned back. "Look, I know you. Under your tough exterior, you got a big heart. You fall hard. This girl is gonna want fancy restaurants and exotic trips, not ice cream and b-ball."

Jack shrugged. "Maybe she's different."

"Maybe …"

They watched the game for a bit, then Chandler said, "Pick us up at six thirty?"

"Yeah."

"You'll be late."

"Five bucks says I'm not."

Chandler reached for his wallet. "Though it's hardly a bet if the outcome is guaranteed. And it's a guarantee you'll be late. Easy money."

"Shut up." Jack stood.

"We on?" Chandler held out five bucks.

"No."

Chandler laughed.

As Jack walked to his car, a police cruiser rolled into the parking lot, followed by a dark brown Crown Vic. Two officers hurried out of the cruiser, one male and one female.

Jack stopped when he saw the grizzled man riding shotgun in the Crown Vic: Detective Clark. When Jack was twelve, his adoptive father set up a couple of police station tours and ride-alongs. The detective took a liking to Jack, answered all his questions—and Jack had a lot of them—and gave him a real picture of what law enforcement was like, warts and all.

The car door opened and Clark got out, spoke to the uniformed cops, and handed them some papers. The two officers nodded and followed the other detective over to the basketball courts.

Detective Clark noticed Jack and strode over. His short gray hair was a few shades lighter than his suit. He gave Jack's hand a firm shake. "Jack Stratton. How are you?"

Jack grinned. Clark's voice sounded like a cement grinder chewing up rocks.

"I'm good."

"I heard you're headed into the Army. Why not go straight to college?"

"I thought the Army would be best."

Detective Clark's expression remained unchanged.

"My dad's having to take early retirement because of his health," Jack said. "It's his heart. I didn't want him to have the stress of paying for my college too."

Detective Clark gave Jack an approving nod. "Well, the Army is a good way in. GI enrollment. *Then* college though, right? And after that, the police academy?"

"That's the plan. I still have that shirt you gave me."

"I never thought you'd grow into it. That thing had to be four sizes too big when I gave it to you."

Jack briefly smiled. He had always known he would grow into it someday.

"Smart plan, Jack. That's what my partner did." Detective Clark watched one of the officers talking to a few people in the bleachers. "Just remember to stay out of trouble. Any kind of disciplinary record can kill your chances."

"I will." Jack followed the seasoned officer's watchful stare. "What's going on? I saw a lot of police cars down by H. T. Wells."

Clark raised an eyebrow. "Observant." He took out a cigarette.

His eyes, with dark circles under them, looked even grayer than usual, like the sky before a storm.

"Something happened last night," Clark said. He handed Jack a flyer and lit his cigarette while Jack read.

MISSING

> Stacy Shaw. Age 26. White female. Blond, blue eyes. 5'2". 110 pounds. Last seen wearing a gray blouse and a black skirt, and carrying a tan handbag with gold swirls. Stacy is a diabetic and may need immediate medical attention.

The picture showed a petite woman with shoulder-length honey-blond hair. Her bangs made her bright, cornflower-blue eyes and wide smile stand out in her heart-shaped face. The way she angled her head made her seem shy. She reminded Jack of a teacher he had a crush on once.

"What happened?" Jack asked.

"The young lady works over at Wells. We found her car a mile outside of town, in a ditch, at Ford's Crossing last night. She went off the road, down the embankment, and hit a tree. We're looking for anyone who may have seen her."

Jack pointed to the cruisers. "Why so much manpower?"

Clark took a long draw on his cigarette. "I can't say, but believe me, it's critical we find her as soon as possible." He looked at Jack. "Do me a favor—ask around, okay?"

"Yes, sir. Can I keep this?" Jack held up the flyer.

"Sure. Tell your old man I said hi. Nice to see you, Jack." With a parting pat on the back, Clark turned to go.

Jack walked to the Impala. As he got into his car, he said aloud, "Someday…Detective Jack Stratton."

As he was exiting the parking lot, he saw a policeman rush over to the detectives, followed by two teenage girls. Clark held the flyer out. One of the girls pointed at the picture and nodded. Clark reached for his notebook.

Jack hoped the detective had just gotten a good lead.

4

DOMINOES

Jack tucked in his short-sleeved, black, button-up shirt that fit as though it was custom-made and studied himself in the mirror. *Maybe this one?*

Jack was not a big fan of the rituals and expectations that went along with a first date, and in this case, instead of enjoying the anticipation of spending time with Kelly, he was concerned about her parents' opinion of him. They sounded like they were kinda snobby, and he wouldn't have a chance with her if he didn't get past the parents first. He looked at the large pile of shirts on his bed and groaned.

Jack's father, at his desk across the hall, leaned away to call out, "You look pretty enough. Get your butt in gear."

Jack reluctantly settled on the black shirt. Nothing fancy, but it fit.

"Yoo-hoo! Jack?" his mother called from the bottom of the staircase.

Jack pulled on his sneakers and hurried down the hall. "What time is it?" He thundered down the stairs of their modest Cape Cod-style house.

"Five forty-two." His dad followed him and tapped his watch and tilted his head as if to say, *You wouldn't have to ask if you wore the watch I gave you.*

"I'm late!"

His mother was waiting at the bottom of the stairs. "No speeding. You can be fashionably late." She brushed off a piece of lint as he passed and tucked a twenty-dollar bill in his front pocket. "It builds anticipation!"

A small, slender woman with hazel eyes, Laura Stratton had wanted the best for Jack from the first time he walked through the front door wearing a terrified expression, Chandler's hand-me-downs, and shoes two sizes too big. The last thing he'd wanted was to leave Chandler, Michelle, and Aunt Haddie, but Laura had earned his trust.

He touched his pocket and winked at her. "Thanks."

His father followed him down the stairs and patted him on the back. "Midnight, Cinderellie." His blue eyes peered past his round glasses up at Jack. Short and heavy-set, Ted Stratton's presence drew your attention. Jack didn't know whether it was the years of teaching math or the way he carried himself, but when his father was in the room, the focus always shifted to him.

"Two o'clock?" Jack grinned.

"Eleven?"

"You're going backward!"

"You should have gone for one o'clock." His mother rubbed Jack's shoulder as she cast an arbitrating glance her husband's way.

"Midnight it is." Jack's father's tone left no room for haggling.

"Fine." Jack leaned down and kissed his mom's cheek. She grinned at him like a proud mother smiling at a newborn baby. He expected her to pinch his cheek like she usually did, but instead she stretched up and kissed it.

"You're picking up Chandler too?" his dad asked.

"Yeah, he's bringing his new girlfriend, Makayla."

Jack's mom dashed away. "Ooh—let me get my camera."

"Mom, it's just a date."

"It's the first time you're taking Kelly out. First dates are important."

Jack looked to his father, who just shrugged.

"You look fly, son."

"Thanks, Dad." He had to fight not to laugh whenever his parents tried to use slang.

"There's something we should talk about. You should—"

"Uh-oh…Is this the beginning of a be-careful speech?"

"Well…"

"Dad, I'm good."

His father, who over the years had put thousands of rebellious teenagers in their place, was not to be deterred.

"Sorry, but there's a lot at stake now. You're about to enter the Army, and I know you wouldn't do anything to mess that up. As your father, it's my job to remind you that life is like dominoes."

"I thought it was like a box of chocolates but without the little map on the cover," Jack joked. "So be careful or you'll end up with a goopy-centered one that tastes like old licorice."

His father's eyes narrowed in his teacher stare, and Jack knew he'd better at least pretend to listen. After making sure he had Jack's attention, Ted Stratton said, "Dominoes. You knock one down and the rest fall. Now, if you do well in the Army, you'll go to college and move right into law enforcement. But one night's foolishness and bad decisions and the dominoes could fall the other way. You need to think every choice through. Let's just say you're out and someone gets their hands on some booze—"

"Dad, I'm not going to—"

"Let's just say. You're underage. You have one drink and you get pulled over by the police. There goes the Army. That's one domino. Without the Army, how are you going to afford college? Another domino down. How are you going to get on the police force with no Army, no college, no job, and a DUI on your record? See? One bad decision can bring the whole thing down."

Jack nodded. He saw it all right, a long snake of dominoes falling silently, nothing to stop it. On top of that, he had a bad feeling that his dad was going to find out about his brush with the law and the junkie in the alley. His father would see it pretty much like Chandler did—as one of the best examples of a domino they'd ever seen.

Ted put a hand on Jack's shoulder. "Hey, why am I saying anything? I trust you. You know all this."

Jack had just a second to reassure his dad, with a look, that he'd absorbed the message and acknowledged its good sense, before Laura rushed back into the room with her old-school camera.

"Okay. Stand together."

Jack stood with his father for a picture, then his dad took the camera and his mom moved next to Jack. The camera flashed a few more times.

"Now that Laura's made sure a record has been preserved for posterity," Jack's dad said, giving her a peck on the cheek, "you're free to go."

Jack grabbed his keys. As he headed for the door, he caught a glimpse of Detective Clark's face on the silent TV, and doubled back to grab the remote off the couch and turn the sound on.

"Hey, it's Derrick Clark," his dad said.

"Yeah. I saw him at the park this afternoon. He said to say hi." Jack turned up the volume. The shot switched to a young female reporter sitting at the news desk. Beside her was a screen showing the same photo of Stacy Shaw used in the flyer.

"Fairfield Police are asking for the public's assistance in locating a missing woman thought to be in danger. Her name is Stacy Shaw. We join Channel 5's Paula Thompson, reporting live from police headquarters."

The camera cut to a young woman holding a microphone. "Thank you, Amy. I'm told that there will be an announcement momentarily."

The shot switched back to the news desk. "Paula, given the amount of police involvement, do they suspect foul play?"

"Well, if they do, they're not saying. All they will say is that Mrs. Shaw has a medical condition and that it's imperative she be located as soon as possible." She glanced behind her. "Hold on, I think they're entering now."

The camera panned to a doorway in the back of the room, from which a man in a gray suit emerged. He was short and barrel-chested and looked like a drill instructor who'd become a civilian: buzz cut, neatly pressed suit, tan skin, dark brown eyes.

"That's the new detective, Tony Vargas," Jack's dad said. "You'd like him. He's ex-Army."

Detective Vargas was followed by a man and a woman, both visibly distraught. The man's sandy-colored hair was mussed and his face was contorted in anguish. The woman next to him looked like a younger, female version of him—sister, perhaps?

Detective Vargas strode up to a podium and immediately began speaking. "I'm Detective Vargas of the Fairfield Police." He nodded to the gathered reporters. "Thank you for assembling on such short notice. I appreciate your help in getting the word out to our communities."

He cleared his throat. "By now you've all been informed of the disappearance of Stacy Shaw. Her abandoned car was found at Ford's Crossing, where it went off the road and struck a tree. Stacy may be injured and disoriented and in need of medical assistance. Stacy is a diabetic and may have suffered an episode before the incident. It's imperative that we locate Stacy as soon as possible. I'm here to ask for the public's assistance. If you have any information about Stacy, please contact the police immediately."

"Shouldn't he refer to her as Mrs. Shaw?" Jack's mom asked. "It sounds disrespectful."

"They do that on purpose, right, Dad?" His father nodded. "They use the first name, in case…something else happened to her."

"What do you mean?"

"In case she's been kidnapped and whoever grabbed her is watching the press conference…" He trailed off. His mother had moped and drooped for weeks after

Jack told her he wanted to join the Army, and often became distraught watching the news. He didn't want to upset her right now.

His father finished for him. "They use the victim's first name over and over, to try to humanize her."

"Oh, I see." She fiddled with her cross necklace.

Vargas was being interviewed. A reporter stepped forward. "Detective Vargas, given the rapid escalation of responders, do you suspect foul play?"

"No," said Vargas. "Right now this is strictly a missing person case." He moved to the side and motioned the man forward. "Stacy's husband, Michael Shaw, who has been cooperating in the search, would like to make a statement for the family."

Michael Shaw stepped up to the podium and spoke directly into the camera. "My wife…" His voice broke. He bowed his head and his shoulders seemed to be shaking. Then he held up a framed photo of Stacy. "My wife is missing, and I want to ask anyone who may have seen her…to call the police. We love Stacy and…and she's…" He broke down crying.

The woman next to him wrapped an arm around his shoulders.

"That poor family," Laura said, and her husband put his arm around her protectively. The clock on the mantel chimed.

"I've gotta run!" Jack hurried to the door.

"Remember, don't speed." His mother straightened his collar. "Have fun."

As Jack ran for the Impala, his father yelled, "Not *too* much fun!"

5

THE HAVES AND THE HAVE-NOTS

Jack rolled up the long, circular driveway to the front of the Dawsons' home and double-checked the address. The sprawling, brick-face house commanded the highest point in Knob Hill, one of the richest neighborhoods in Fairfield. Jack parked the Impala in the driveway next to a shiny Mercedes, which was parked next to a sleek BMW, and glanced at the clock—6:14. It would be tight to get to the bowling alley by 6:30.

"I should've left right after the photos," he muttered, jogging up the granite steps to the massive oak front door. Jack looked at the oversize black knocker mounted dead center, like something out of the Middle Ages. He exhaled and tried to gather himself. Just as he reached out for the huge piece of metal, assuming he should give it a few thunks to announce his presence, he spotted a doorbell discreetly mounted beside the door. Before he could press it, the front door was whipped open.

Kelly Dawson, in designer jeans and a pink top with matching lipstick. For a moment he could only stand there, blinking. The hallway chandelier behind her sparkled like flashbulbs.

When he was able to breathe, he mumbled, "Wow. You're gorgeous."

She chuckled. "I had help. My mom and I had a girls' day out to get me ready."

"Seriously, you belong on a runway, not in a doorway." Kelly beamed, and he saw an opportunity to test the waters.

"A whole day shopping? A date with me is that special?"

Kelly blushed. *Good sign. She likes you, buddy boy.*

He glanced over her shoulder. *No parents. Bonus.* "Ready?"

"Yes." She grabbed her jacket. "Let's go."

But before they could make their escape, a woman appeared in the hallway, rich, manicured, and regal, even in a casual lounge outfit. The resemblance left Jack with no doubt that she was Kelly's mother. The tall, slender blonde placed a hand on Kelly's shoulder while extending the other out to Jack. "Jack. It's a pleasure to meet you. Nancy Dawson."

"Nice to meet you too." *Mrs. Dawson? Ms.? Nancy?* His parents had taught him to be polite, but he didn't want to sound hopelessly old-fashioned. Or overly friendly.

"Kelly?" a male voice called from inside.

Kelly rolled her eyes. "I'm just leaving, Dad."

"Wait there a second."

Kelly bit her bottom lip.

There was a heavy sound of heels across what sounded like a vast tile floor, and then Mr. Dawson strutted around the corner and up to the doorway, his phone in his hand. Even with Jack one step beneath him, Jack was still taller—a fact that seemed to bother Mr. Dawson, judging by the way he held his chin up, shot out his arm, and squeezed Jack's hand—hard.

Jack didn't flinch. "Nice to meet you, sir. I'm Jack Stratton."

Mr. Dawson nodded, just barely. "Phil Dawson." He eyed Jack up and down. "Where are you two headed?"

"Bowling. It's a double date."

"That sounds fun. With whom?" Kelly's mother asked.

"My best friend, Chandler, and his girlfriend, Makayla."

Mr. Dawson's expression soured slightly, and Mrs. Dawson's smile flickered. "Are they friends from your school?" Mrs. Dawson asked.

"Yes," said Jack warily.

"What school is that?" asked Mr. Dawson.

Kelly jumped. "Oh, look at the time." She tsked. "I don't want to miss our reservation." She quickly kissed her father on the cheek.

Mr. Dawson opened his mouth to say something more, but Kelly grabbed Jack by the hand and hurried down the steps.

"Don't be too late!" Her mom's voice was noticeably strained.

"I won't." Kelly threw her parents an over-the-shoulder wave.

Kelly's parents stood on the top step, watching them, as Jack opened the passenger door for her, then hurried to the driver's seat. Mr. Dawson didn't look pleased.

Jack struggled to get the keys out of his pocket. When Kelly's father started to walk down the steps, she whispered, "Um, we'd better go…"

Jack finally ripped the keys free of his pocket and slammed them into the ignition. The Impala's engine roared to life. In his haste, he jammed the gas pedal down to the floor, a big mistake. The Impala's gas pedal was so sensitive that the difference between starting at ten miles per hour and a hundred and ten miles per hour was about a quarter of an inch. The car shot forward, whipping Kelly back against her seat. Then Jack quickly tapped the brakes, and she jerked forward like a cowboy riding a mad bull.

Mortified, Jack muttered, "Sorry," managed to find a normal speed, then, once clear of the driveway, he sped back up. "I take it your family doesn't bowl much?"

"Never. How'd you know?"

"You don't need reservations." Jack chuckled.

Kelly wrinkled her nose. "You don't?"

Jack wanted to ask whether she'd ever been in a bowling alley, but he bit his tongue.

"I apologize about my father. He wasn't happy when I told him you didn't go to Westmore Academy."

Jack's smile faded. "I take it he's not a fan of public schools?"

"That would be an understatement."

"Is that why you didn't want to tell him I went to Fairfield High?"

She sat up straight. "I'm not my father." Seventeen years of frustration were crammed into that one sentence.

"That's good." Jack gave her a little wink. "It'd be kinda weird to take him bowling."

His joke broke through the awkwardness, and she leaned back comfortably in the vintage bench seat—so much better when on a date than bucket seats.

"Are we meeting your friends at the bowling alley?"

"No." Jack looked at her as much as he could while driving. "We're picking them up at my Aunt Haddie's."

Kelly pulled down the visor and frowned when she saw it had no mirror. Jack made a mental note to buy one of those clip-on mirrors when he got a chance.

After fanning out her hair and straightening her blouse, she turned back to Jack. "Do I look okay?" She searched his face.

Jack casually stretched his arm across the seat back and shook his head with mock regret. "Well, all I know is, this car's gonna need some serious fireproofing." She looked adorably confused. "It could burst into flames at any moment, you're so hot."

"That line is *so* over-the-top." She lifted her chin in a wide arc, but Jack could tell she liked it. She sat back, and her body relaxed. The more they talked, the more her stiffness eased.

As they crossed through town, the McMansions with landscaped grounds gave way to modest suburban plots, and then to duplexes and tenements. The yards grew smaller and smaller until most had nothing but a sliver of grass.

Kelly shifted uncomfortably. "Your aunt lives here?"

"Aunt Haddie? She's more than my aunt. She was my foster mother for four years. Now she's my second mom, for life."

Jack pulled down a little road and parked in front of a big two-story house. Aunt Haddie tried her best to keep the place up, but that cost money she didn't have. Jack had to smile, seeing the mismatched windows and the door he and Chandler had picked up on the side of the road. The house always made him smile. It was scruffy and patched together, but it was home.

He hopped out of the car and went to get Kelly's door, but she was already getting out.

"Sorry," she said. "You don't have to get my door."

"I know. But I want to. My dad drilled it into me." He closed her door and offered her his arm.

"I have a feminist English teacher who'd flip out if you held a door open for her."

Jack shrugged. "She doesn't have to walk through it."

"She'd consider it chauvinistic," Kelly continued.

"If it really bothered her, she could close it and open it herself. Look, I know you know how to open a door."

"Then why do you do it?"

Jack stopped. "I asked my dad that when he ran out in the rain to get the door for my mom. He said he did it for three reasons. One, it lets the other person know my focus is not on me; it's on you. Two, it says what we're doing, we're doing together. Three, it shows any other guys watching that you're with me and I think you're special." He shrugged. "Call it whatever, but that's why I do it."

"Your dad sounds nice."

"Best dad in the world, but don't tell him I said that."

They headed toward the back, where a wooden staircase led up to a small porch. Through the brightly lit windows, he could see Aunt Haddie's tidy kitchen.

Jack opened the door and started to go through first, but Kelly stopped on the landing.

Jack paused. "Don't you want to come in?"

"Oh, yeah, of course, but…now you're *not* getting the door for me. After your speech, I kinda hoped you would."

Jack stood with one foot inside and one outside. "I'll always get the door for you. Like I said, it's your choice if you want to go through. But I thought you'd be more comfortable if I went first into a stranger's house."

He rubbed the back of her hand with his thumb and led her inside to the kitchen, where a tall teenage girl was already coming their way.

"Jack!" The girl stopped short when she saw Kelly. Jack gave her a quick hug and stepped aside to introduce Kelly.

Michelle, Jack's foster sister, was dark-skinned, with a bright, pretty face and a lean runner's body. Her large brown eyes seemed even bigger because of her glasses. She brushed back her curly black hair and stood up straight.

"Hi, Jack. Chandler and Makayla are in his room." She spoke politely, as if she'd been to finishing school, though her impish eyebrow waggle gave an unmistakable glimpse into the mind of a fifteen-year-old girl. In a way, she had been to a finishing school. Aunt Haddie was a stickler about manners and eye contact and first impressions, and all the children who came under her care had a similar quiet confidence and poise.

Jack pulled Michelle to his side. "Kelly, this is my sister, Michelle. Half-Pint, Kelly."

Michelle wiggled an arm free. "Nice to meet you." She smiled at Kelly as she elbowed Jack in the stomach. "Hey, I'm almost as big as you."

"You'll never be as big as me." His standard response, but he wasn't so sure anymore. Michelle was already very tall, and showing promise in track and field. Maybe she'd outrun him someday too, as she'd been threatening to do since she was a little girl.

Kelly smiled. "Hi, Michelle. Nice to meet you, too." She was just about to ask Michelle another question, to keep the conversation going, when Chandler and Makayla walked into the kitchen.

"Why don't you ever use the front door?" Chandler grumbled.

"Chandler and Makayla, this is Kelly."

Chandler's enormous hand gently shook Kelly's. "I'm Jack's brother."

"Oh, no, don't start that again!" Makayla gave Chandler a lighthearted poke in the ribs.

Any questions Kelly might have had were cut short when a heavyset woman came through the open kitchen door, laden with grocery bags. Aunt Haddie.

"Who's letting all the flies in?" She wore a simple dress and her hair was pulled back neatly. The energy that seemed to follow her into the room could have lit a city block. Michelle hurried over and grabbed the bags from her hands.

A warm smile spread across Aunt Haddie's face when she saw her "Jackie," and she came over and pulled him into a big hug. Then she turned to Kelly and loudly whispered, "He always left the door open when he was little, too." She and the miscreant in question exchanged affectionate smiles. "I'm Haddie Williams, but just about everyone calls me Aunt Haddie."

"Kelly Dawson. Nice to meet you." They shook hands.

"Do you need a hand with the rest of the groc—" Jack started to say, but just then three young teenagers came pouring through the kitchen door, each lugging a couple of bags.

"Nope." Aunt Haddie winked. "We have a full house lately. Many hands make light work."

Didn't Jack know it. The kitchen was small, but Aunt Haddie ran it like a ship's galley. He'd seen her put together three meals a day for eight hungry kids, and by the time they were done, the countertops were clean and there wasn't a single dish in the sink.

"Sweet." Chandler clapped his hands together, and everyone jumped. He laughed. "Let's go. I won't be late." He kissed Aunt Haddie's cheek and led Makayla toward the door.

"Is your cousin Lori meeting you there?" Aunt Haddie asked Makayla.

"No. She decided not to come. She's really upset. Have you guys heard about that missing woman, Stacy Shaw?"

Everyone nodded.

"Well, Lori's the receptionist at H. T. Wells, where Stacy works."

"I pray she's okay." Aunt Haddie—no stranger to tragedy—gave Makayla's shoulder a comforting squeeze. "All of you be extra careful tonight." Aunt Haddie fixed her gaze on Jack. "You all need to stay away from trouble."

"Okay." Jack held up his hands in mock surrender. "But is there a reason that *I'm* the focus of your attention here?"

"Yes," Aunt Haddie said. "Would you like me to provide a list?"

Just the thought of Aunt Haddie running down a list of Jack's past exploits in front of Kelly was enough to stop him cold. "No, ma'am."

She wiggled a finger at him and reached up to give him a peck on the cheek.

"It was nice meeting you," Kelly said as they walked outside.

The four of them were halfway to his car when Aunt Haddie called from the doorway. "Jackie!"

He cringed and felt the color rise in his cheeks. Aunt Haddie was the only person who still called him Jackie.

She called again and waved him back. "Just one second. I have something for Laura. I need to speak to you a minute."

Kelly nodded toward the Impala. "I'll wait in the car with Chandler and Makayla."

"Thanks."

Jack ran past Aunt Haddie's latest group of teenage charges, who were heading back to grab another load of groceries, and followed Aunt Haddie into the little hallway. When she turned around, Jack saw her raised eyebrow and groaned. He knew what was coming.

"Don't go giving me that look, Jack Alton Stratton."

Jack's shoulders hunched up. "I haven't done anything wrong."

She held up a finger. "And you'd better keep it that way. Chandler told me that you applied for a passport."

Not what he'd expected. "That's me being responsible. How is that cause for a talk?"

"Because now you're a short-timer. You're going to be going overseas soon. People make all sorts of bad choices when they rush into things because they only have a little bit of time. That girl you're going out with tonight is going to see that special something I saw in you when you first walked through my door eleven years ago, and she may not want to let it go. And when the two of you realize that you're leaving soon…"

"It's just a date."

She reached out, put her hand on his chin, and peered right into his eyes. "You have a sensitive heart."

Jack tried to pull away, but she held him fast and gave his chin a little shake.

"You need to guard your heart. You love deep. You'll hurt deep. Go slow."

"You sound just like Chandler. It's just a date!"

"That's right. So keep it that way. Here." She pressed a thank-you card into his hands. "Tell Ted and Laura how much I appreciate them."

Jack nodded. His parents had never come out and said so, but Jack knew they gave Aunt Haddie a little money whenever they could.

She kissed his cheek. "Love you."

"Love you too."

Jack made his getaway through the kitchen, where Michelle was directing a whirlwind of motion as the teenagers put away groceries.

"See you!" Jack waved, then whipped open the door and ran onto the porch—straight into a teenage girl straining to carry four bags at once. She stumbled back, miraculously dropping only one bag.

"Watch it!" she snapped. The brown ponytail on top of her head shook back and forth.

"Sorry, kid." Jack bent down to get the bag at the same time she did and they bumped heads. He rubbed his forehead. "You've got a hard head."

She grabbed the bag, and he could tell she was about to blast him, but she froze when her blazing green eyes met Jack's. Her eyes widened and her mouth fell open.

Jack checked the bag and saw that nothing was broken. He held it out to the girl, but she just stared. He rattled the bag in front of her. "Are you okay?" he asked.

She blinked a couple of times and pressed her lips together in an awkward, shy grin. She started to shake her head, but it quickly turned into a nod. The result was her head wobbling all around her shoulders.

Michelle came out onto the porch. Jack looked to her for help, awkwardly holding his hand out in the direction of the girl. Michelle sized up the situation and giggled. She took the girl by the hand and grabbed the bag from Jack. "Have fun!" she called over her shoulder, tugging the girl toward the house.

"See ya, Half-Pint!"

"It's six thirty-two!" Chandler crowed triumphantly as he got in the car.

Jack was defending himself with the expected affectionate insults and mock indignation as they pulled out onto the street—and saw an unmarked police cruiser coming toward them, with two men in front. Jack recognized one of the men in suits as Detective Tony Vargas.

Chandler pointed. "It's never good when the suits show up."

6

WHEN THE SUITS SHOW UP

They turned onto the road that ran alongside Hamilton Park and pulled up at the light. A young man swaggered down the sidewalk. He wore his pants low and his baseball cap backward and at an angle.

In the backseat, Makayla wrinkled her nose. "Why do guys do that?"

Kelly looked out the window at the young man and took a deep breath. "Do what?"

"Wear their pants down around their ankles. Don't they know how unattractive that looks?"

Chandler leaned forward and tapped Jack's shoulder. "Hey, is that J-Dog?"

Jack stiffened. "No. It's Two Point." His hand gripped the steering wheel tighter.

Kelly looked back and forth between Chandler and Jack. "Two what?"

"Chandler thought that guy across the street was J-Dog," Makayla explained. "But it's his brother, Two Point."

"J-Dog and Jack don't mix," Chandler said.

Two Point glowered at the Impala. He gave Chandler a curt nod but glared at Jack.

"Looks like Two Point and Jack don't mix either," Kelly said, gripping her purse tighter.

Jack took a right.

"I can't believe Nina is dating him," Makayla said.

"What?" Chandler turned to her. "Since when?"

"I saw them at the movies last night," Makayla said. "Then Nina posted all about it on Facebook." She lifted her hand over her head dramatically. "She likes to announce every detail of her life in real time."

"Why do they call him Two Point?" Kelly glanced back over her shoulder.

"It's short for Two Point Oh," Makayla explained. "His real name is Tommy. He's a year younger than his brother, Jay—that's J-Dog's real name. They look alike and act alike, so people started to call him Jay Two Point Oh, but that nickname's too long."

"Do you have a nickname, Jack?" Kelly asked.

"Jackie!" Chandler called out.

"No." Jack held his hand out like a militant school crossing guard. "Only a few older people call me that now."

Chandler smiled. "We also call him Jack-O. Jackster. Jack-a-reeno. Crazy Jack."

Jack shook his head. "Don't listen to him. It's just Jack."

"Oh, oh, oh." Chandler pounded the seat. "You got a new one yesterday. Super Jack Flash!"

"Super Jack Flash?" Kelly's voice went high.

"He ran like the Flash and swooped in like Superman." Chandler stretched his long arms over the seat like a little kid pretending to fly. "And he saved this little old lady's handbag."

"You were there too."

Jack didn't know whether he broke into a sweat because of embarrassment or because of the way Kelly gazed at him.

Chandler scoffed. "*I* didn't do anything. You're the one who chased the junkie down. He almost got stabbed," he added dramatically.

Kelly's eyes widened. "The guy had a knife?"

"It was just a small knife."

Kelly leaned in so close that her breath lightly touched his neck.

A car horn blared. Jack quickly swerved back into his lane.

"Keep it between the buoys, Captain Jack." Chandler sat back and broke into a wide grin. "Hey! That's another one—Captain Jack."

Jack just shook his head and bathed in the glory of being young and alive on this summer night, in the Impala, joking with friends. And to top it all off, sitting just the space of a wish away from him was a beautiful girl whose hair smelled like water lilies.

* * *

They ate at the Burger Hut and then headed over to the bowling alley. Once it became clear that Kelly had no idea how to bowl, Jack offered to get the manager to put up the bumpers for her, but she was a good sport about rolling gutter balls all night. Jack won, and Makayla came in second—a fact Jack planned to rib Chandler about later that night. It was a huge success; Jack and Makayla got along like a house afire, and Kelly, though hopeless as a bowler, proved adept at keeping score and giggling at the guys' clowning, which won points with Chandler.

When the bowling alley closed and kicked them out at ten o'clock, they headed back to Aunt Haddie's. Chandler leaned forward in the backseat. "You did great for the first time, Kelly."

Kelly blew a raspberry. "That was harder than it looks." She crossed her arms and mock-pouted. "I stank."

Chandler leaned toward Jack and stage-whispered, "This is the part where you say, 'No, you didn't.'"

"You gave it a great try," Jack said.

Kelly looked taken aback.

Chandler groaned.

"Say she *did* great," Makayla said.

"I said it was a great try."

"That's not the same," said Chandler.

"I'm not going to lie and just say she did great."

"Jack!" Makayla slapped her forehead.

Chandler rubbed his temples. "You're a real sweet talker with the ladies, bro."

"Wait a minute." Jack pulled down the rearview mirror so he could see Chandler. "People lie to each other all the time when they should be honest." He looked at

Kelly. "I'm not doing you any favors by lying to you. What if you picked out a dress that made you look fat?"

Chandler snorted. "You're digging the hole deeper here."

"Jack, you're so wrong." Makayla leaned up against the back of Kelly's seat and placed a hand on her shoulder in solidarity.

Kelly nodded.

Chandler raised his hand. "Unanimous."

"It's not a vote." Jack stopped at a red light and put the car in park.

"Jack, we're at a light," Chandler pointed out.

"One second." Jack turned in his seat so he faced Kelly. "I tell the truth. Straight up. Tell me how different this feels." He cleared his throat. "You did awesome at bowling. Wow. Really good. By the way, you look great, I mean, *really* great tonight."

Kelly scowled.

Jack lightly touched the back of her hand. "Or I could tell you the truth, like this. As far as bowling went, you can't hit the broadside of a barn with a bowling ball. But it doesn't matter, because I never saw the pins. I couldn't take my eyes off you."

Makayla and Kelly both said, "Awww…"

"The light's green, Romeo," Chandler said.

Jack put the car back in drive. He glanced at Kelly. "I'd rather you know that I'll tell you the truth no matter what. I want to be a guy people can trust."

Kelly smiled. "You're right. I like it better when you tell me the truth. I change my vote."

"Me too!" Makayla raised her hand. She sat back, crossed her arms, and frowned at Chandler.

"What?"

"You could say something like that to me."

"How? You beat me." Chandler made a face. "But I still did awesome." He pointed at himself. "I got three strikes in a row." Chandler flexed his arm.

"And at least ten gutter balls," Jack pointed out.

"Oh, now we'll just have to check the replays for that statistic, folks. Anyway, I'm going to give Makayla a sincere compliment now." He leaned against Makayla to whisper in her ear.

She giggled and wrapped her arms around him.

They cuddled in the backseat and Jack took the turn onto Aunt Haddie's street. Jack started telling Kelly a story about another bowling night, but his voice trailed off at the unnerving sight of red and blue police lights flashing off the houses.

He sped up. Four doors down from Aunt Haddie's, three police cruisers were parked with their lights on. A small crowd had gathered on the street, and a news van with a satellite pole fully extended was parked on the grass of one of the vacant lots.

"What do you think's going down?" Chandler asked.

Jack pulled up to Aunt Haddie's. "I don't know. The cops are at the Martins'."

As they got out of the car, Aunt Haddie's door flew open, and Michelle and four foster kids scrambled out. Michelle ran over to Jack and Chandler.

"What's going on, kid?" Jack asked Michelle.

She shrugged. "No clue."

Aunt Haddie appeared in the doorway and called out, "Michelle!"

"Yes, ma'am?"

"Get inside. Everyone get inside." Like a mother hen gathering her chicks, Aunt Haddie scooted her rubbernecking charges back into the house.

"I'm gonna check it out," Jack said.

"Chandler and Jackie." Aunt Haddie's voice rose. "You, too. Inside. Right now."

Chandler and Makayla followed Michelle up the back steps, but Jack grabbed Kelly by the hand and hurried toward the police lights.

Aunt Haddie motioned him to come over. "Jackie!"

Jack gave her a quick wave and then cupped his hand to his ear like he couldn't hear her. He caught the change in her expression but kept going.

I'm going to get it for this.

Jack and Kelly waded through the circle of people until they stood beside a short, plump girl Jack knew. "What's going on, Shawna?"

Shawna shook her head back and forth, the beads on the ends of her braided hair clinking together. "There're a dozen cops inside and a few suits. They've been in there almost an hour."

"Why?"

Shawna shrugged. "No clue."

"Two Point must've really stepped in it this time," Jack said.

"Then he's toast," Shawna said. "He's still on probation."

The TV crew flooded the sidewalk with light, and a news reporter walked in front of the camera. When he gestured to the small crowd, the camera panned, capturing the onlookers. Jack wrapped a protective arm around Kelly as the crowd shifted around them.

The front door of the Martins' house opened. The cameraman swung the lens around as the crowd pushed forward. Two policemen emerged, each carrying a large, clear plastic evidence bag. Inside one was a white jacket with red stripes. The other held white, high-top basketball shoes. J-Dog followed next, in handcuffs, with Detective Vargas close behind him.

"It's J-Dog they're arresting?" Jack blurted out. "I thought he'd gone straight."

Shawna made a snapping sound with her lower lip. "I didn't see that coming."

J-Dog's mother appeared in the doorway, crying. Jack couldn't hear what was being said, but he could tell she was begging.

Detective Vargas, a restraining hand on J-Dog's shoulder, shook his head as he walked down the steps.

J-Dog's eyes searched the crowd. Jack saw despair hidden beneath the tough-guy mask. His shoulders slumped as he got in the car.

"It's never good when the suits show up," Shawna said. "He's so screwed."

"Let's get out of here," Jack said. He took Kelly by the hand and led her through the crowd back toward the car. But before they reached it, Michelle popped out of the house and rushed over.

"What happened?"

"They arrested J-Dog. Where's Chandler?"

"He's getting an earful about how irresponsible you are." Michelle snickered. "I'd beat feet unless you want a big talking-to."

Jack held up his hands. "You'd better get inside, Half-Pint. Tell him to call me."

She nodded, waved, and ran around to the back door.

Jack and Kelly hopped in the Impala just as the police car drove by with J-Dog in the back, his head in his hands.

"Are you friends with the guy who got arrested?" Kelly asked.

"Friends? With J-Dog? No. Never. I can't stand him."

"Didn't you grow up with him?"

"Yeah." Jack watched as the cruiser drove away. "And we didn't like each other then, either. He always rubbed me the wrong way. We're like oil and water."

Kelly nodded.

"After I got adopted and moved, I heard he got worse. Jay turned into J-Dog and he deserved the nickname. He's as mean and crazy as a junkyard dog." Jack rolled down his window. "His mother's real nice, though. Seeing her crying like that…"

"I'm sorry."

"Me too."

"Where do you want to go now?" Kelly asked.

Jack glanced at the clock. 10:44 p.m. "How late can you stay out?"

"One."

Thanks, Dad.

Jack racked his brain for someplace else to go. The list of places in Fairfield where a seventeen-year-old could go at eleven o'clock at night consisted of a couple of convenience stores, the laundromat, and the Waffle House. Or…

"There's a little park that overlooks the bay on the way to your house," Jack said. "It has a great view."

Kelly's face lit up. "That sounds awesome."

Jack pulled out and drove fast.

Bay View Park was popular with runners because it sat on a wide plateau. It was also popular with kids who wanted privacy, because the parking lot was shielded by trees and the police visited infrequently.

Tonight the parking lot was empty.

Jack eased the Impala into a spot away from the streetlights and turned off the car.

Kelly's hand shot out and clicked her seat belt release. She turned to Jack but suddenly frowned.

"What's wrong?"

"Nothing." Her eyes shifted down, and her finger traced an invisible outline on the seat. "Did you really mean all that?"

Jack's mind raced as he tried to figure out what "all that" could be. He reached his hand along the back of the seat and lowered his voice. "All that?" he repeated, hoping for clarification.

Her cheeks flushed. "About not being able to keep your eyes off me because…" Her pearl-white teeth bit her bottom lip.

"Because you looked so beautiful?"

She slowly nodded.

Jack stroked the back of her hand. "Yeah. I meant all that."

A stray strand of hair fell across her cheek. Jack reached over and tucked it behind her ear.

She leaned closer.

So did Jack.

He slid his hand behind her head. Kelly's lips pressed together. Jack leaned in, pulled her close, and kissed her. A tender, gentle kiss.

When he pulled back, Kelly's big blue eyes were peering out from under her lashes. "Wow. I didn't expect that."

Jack grinned.

She looked up longingly. "Only one?"

Jack leaned in again and let her take the lead this time. She pressed her soft lips to his, and this kiss lasted longer. Jack stroked her cheek lightly with his thumb. With each touch, the tension between them slipped away.

Kelly's hand glided along Jack's arm. She traced his hand and stopped at the rough scar that circled his wrist. He pulled his hand away.

"How'd you get that?"

Jack stiffened. "It's nothing."

"I thought you always told the truth."

Jack sat back in his seat, rolled his head away, and stared out the window. "You don't want to hear it."

Kelly's fingers reached out for his hand. "I do." Her voice was soft.

Jack exhaled.

Kelly tilted her head and waited.

Jack was honest to a fault, if that's possible, but right now he wanted to lie. Something inside screamed, *Pretend you were joking. Say you just cut yourself on a can, or fixing a bike*—anything but the truth. Another part of him wanted to share what really happened.

Jack took a deep breath. He wanted her to know about his past, and not run in the other direction. He turned to face her. "Before I came to Aunt Haddie's," Jack said, "I stayed in some pretty bad places."

"Foster homes?"

"No." Jack reached out and put a hand on the steering wheel. "No. Before that. Motels that rent by the hour, crackhouses, whorehouses. Places like that."

Kelly smiled awkwardly as she waited for the punch line that wouldn't come.

She has no idea. He'd have to ease in. "Okay, when I was little, I loved the show *Cops*. You ever seen it?"

She shook her head.

"I thought cops were the best. One night, there was this party going on with druggies and prostitutes. I was alone in the kitchen. It was one of those galley kitchens." Jack pulled his hands apart as if he were stretching taffy. "Like one narrow hallway with a stove, a sink, and a little window at the end."

Kelly nodded.

"Well, I was looking out the window when some cop pulled over a car on the street below. It was just like the show. I got so excited, I ran into the party and yelled, 'COPS!'"

Kelly just kept her eyes glued to him.

"I wanted them to come look with me, but the druggies went nuts. Everyone freaked and ran for the door. At the time, I thought it was funny. So… after everyone had calmed down, I did it again. I yelled 'COPS!' and they started running for the door again."

Kelly moved closer.

"Then this ghoulish-looking guy came over to me and asked, 'Do you want to play cops and robbers, kid?' I never had anyone to hang with. So when someone finally asked, I was all excited. He took me into the kitchen and pulled out a set of handcuffs. Real ones. I wanted to be the cop, but he told me that I was going to be the robber. I just wanted to play with someone. Anyway, the guy cuffed me to the radiator. One of those old bare-metal types. It didn't take long to figure out he wasn't coming back anytime soon."

"That's horrible." Kelly's fingers traced the scar. "But how did you get the scar?"

The memory of that sensation hit Jack like a Mack truck. "It was winter. It got cold out, and the radiator came on."

Kelly's fingers stopped moving.

"They were metal cuffs. That old radiator got as hot as a blast furnace and the heat traveled straight through the chain to the metal cuff. Burned my skin." He inhaled. "Seared it."

"Oh, Jack."

He exhaled. "I finally figured out how to pull my shirt over my head and then down my arm. I tucked it between the cuffs and my skin."

Kelly's eyes glistened with tears.

Jack clicked his tongue. "He put the cuffs on me at two minutes past midnight. There was a clock on the stove. Candi, she was a hooker at the party, she found me at eleven twenty-two."

"You spent all night chained in the kitchen?"

Jack shrugged and looked up at the roof.

"How old were you?"

"Five."

"Who was watching you?"

"She was passed out in the next room, too."

"Who's *she*?"

Jack's hand tightened around the steering wheel. "The lady who gave birth to me."

"Your mom? She was *there*?"

Jack peered out the window at the trees silhouetted against the night sky. "That was home. For that week anyway."

"But you said the party was all druggies and prostitutes. Why would your mother have people like that over?" Kelly's question faded into awkward silence.

Jack debated about just saying his mother was a drug addict. That was partly the truth. "Because she was one of them. She was a hooker. And an addict."

Kelly pulled her hand back.

Jack stiffened. *So much for the truth, the whole truth, and nothing but.*

Kelly sat for a long minute, staring out the window.

Jack knew this was a lot more than most people could handle, and tried to break the tension. "I can just picture your father's face when you tell him that one."

Kelly snapped out of her daze, reached over, and took Jack's hand. "Like I said, I'm not my father."

Jack searched her face. He expected to see scorn, but there was none. His fingers drummed the dashboard. "You don't think less of me?"

"Do you think less of me because of the way my father acts?"

"No."

She squeezed his hand.

"Seriously, I hope this wasn't too much of a buzz kill," he said, trying to lighten the mood.

Kelly slid over until her body pressed against his. She leaned against his chest. "No. It hurts to think that you had it so bad."

"Lots of people have had it worse." He put his arm around her.

Kelly murmured, "So you rescued a little old lady?"

Jack's breathing clicked up a notch. He nodded.

"You chased the guy and almost got stabbed?"

He raised his hand as if he were taking an oath. "All true."

He thought for a moment of his father's speech, his mother's warning, and Aunt Haddie's words, but then he looked into Kelly's blue eyes and he felt like Superman, and Kelly was matching his heat with a smoldering stare. For a moment they couldn't take their eyes off each other.

He felt for the small scratch on his side just above his waistband, the one he'd hidden from Chandler and his parents. "Actually…" He grabbed the bottom of his T-shirt. "I think the knife may have nicked me." He lifted up his shirt so she could see his side.

"Oh, Jack," she purred with concern as she searched for signs of injury. She gently touched above the scrape.

His skin tingled at her touch.

"Does that hurt?" she asked.

He shook his head. "No. But maybe you should feel… all around. You know, just in case."

Her eyes sparkled with mischief. Slowly, she ran her fingers along his chest muscles. Every trail her fingers traced sent electricity rippling along his skin.

His chest rose and fell faster as her eyes locked with his. Then she leaned in and kissed him.

A ripple traveled from the crown of Jack's head to his feet, and his veins surged with warmth; he felt wanted.

Her kisses were long and slow. Jack slipped his fingers into her hair. The wispy blond strands felt like silk. As they kissed, he tasted her lip gloss—cherry. Jack had a new favorite flavor.

After a few minutes, Jack felt something vibrate. He opened one eye and noted with amusement that the windows had fogged.

Kelly pulled back and smiled shyly. "My phone." She pulled it out of her pocket, pressed the silence call button, and tossed it on the floor.

Jack pulled her close. "You taste like cherry mixed with spring."

"You smell like musk."

Musk? That doesn't sound good. What the heck is musk?

Kelly's phone vibrated again. "What now?" Kelly moaned, fearing the worst. She grabbed her phone off the floor, scrolled through her texts, and cringed. "My father's freaking out."

Jack looked at the clock. "Why?"

Kelly swallowed. "He saw us on the news when they took J-Dog."

That couldn't be good.

She turned to Jack with an I-don't-want-to-but-I-have-to-go look.

Jack hoped his forced smile didn't betray his extreme frustration. "I'll take you home."

"I'm really sorry."

"It's okay." Jack started the engine and backed out of the parking lot.

Kelly texted her father back as Jack drove her home. When they pulled into the driveway, it looked as though every light inside and out of the Dawson home had been turned on. Jack parked the Impala, but before he'd even shut the engine off, the front door flew open and Mr. Dawson stormed down the steps, followed closely by his wife.

Mr. Dawson pointed toward the house. "Get inside, Kelly. Now." His order was just below a shout.

Begrudgingly, Jack got out of the car. He didn't know whether he was crazy or brave, but he felt he had to face her father. "Mr. Dawson—" Jack started to say, but Mr. Dawson stormed around the car and cut him off.

"How *dare* you?" Mr. Dawson jabbed his plump finger in Jack's face.

Jack looked down at the red-faced man and fought to control his own temper. He understood the man was upset; he realized that he was a father with a beautiful daughter and clearly something had set him off.

"You took my daughter to *Washington Heights*?"

Of all the possible offenses Jack thought he was going to be accused of committing, taking her to Aunt Haddie's wasn't even on the list. "What?"

"Get the smirk off your face before I knock it off," Mr. Dawson snapped. "Don't try to deny it. We saw you on the news."

"I'm sorry, sir. I wasn't going to deny it. I grew up there and—"

"Now my daughter's picture is plastered across the TV for all my friends to see. She was surrounded by all those—" He ground his teeth together as though he were gnawing on the word he really wanted to use.

Jack straightened up. "All those what?"

My family. When Aunt Haddie and the Washington Heights community brought him in, he'd been living like a feral child for seven years, he couldn't speak in sentences and was used to sleeping in the corner on the floor. When Aunt Haddie brought him in, he'd bonded with her in a way few could understand. Jack didn't see prejudice like Mr. Dawson's as an opinion, he saw it as an attack on his family.

Jack stepped forward. "Say what you're thinking. Sir."

Before Mr. Dawson had time to answer, Mrs. Dawson intervened. She put her hand on her husband's arm and urged him back.

Mr. Dawson took a deep breath and stepped away from Jack. His purple face looked dangerously close to popping.

"Those *people* are my family and friends," Jack said.

"Don't make this a racial thing," Mr. Dawson said.

"I think you just did."

Mrs. Dawson stepped next to her husband. "We were concerned for our daughter after seeing her on the news." Jack looked over at Kelly, who had ignored her father's command to go inside and was standing on the steps, doing a silent cheer. *Give me a J! Give me an A! …*

"I think we've all had our fill of excitement for the evening," Mrs. Dawson continued. "Why don't we call it a night?"

Mr. Dawson spun around and stomped up the steps past Kelly.

Mrs. Dawson watched her husband disappear inside. She closed her eyes and exhaled. "Good night, Jack," she said. She walked over to her daughter and put an arm around her shoulders, and the two of them started inside.

Jack jumped into the Impala. He looked over at Kelly, but her back was already turned away. He fired up the engine, dropped the car into drive, and slowly rolled down the hill.

When he reached the street, he hit the gas.

7

DRIVING AUNT HADDIE

Jack pulled into Aunt Haddie's driveway the next morning. As he walked up to the house, Michelle danced outside, followed by the shy girl with the ponytail on top of her head and emerald-green eyes. What was her name, anyway?

"What's up, my brother?" Michelle hammed it up and gave him a high five.

"Hey, Half-Pint."

"Chandler's not here."

Jack stopped short. "Where is he?"

"He had to help Mr. Emerson get a refrigerator."

Jack groaned. "I was hoping we'd work out."

"You shoulda called first," Michelle said in a singsong voice.

"The big creep could've let me know he was going out."

The girl with the ponytail stepped toe to toe with Jack and thrust her chin out. "Don't call Chandler a creep." Her eyes narrowed as she glared up at him.

Jack swallowed a laugh. "Whoa. Easy there, killer." He held up his hands. "I'm just busting on him."

"Well…" She wrapped a curl from her ponytail around her finger. "Don't."

Michelle put a hand on the girl's shoulder. "Jack, this is Replacement."

Jack grinned at the odd nickname. "Hey. Nice to meet you…Replacement. Hard head you've got there." He felt a little throb in his forehead, remembering their encounter on the landing the night before.

Replacement huffed, but didn't step back.

Jack turned back to Michelle. "Is he coming back anytime soon?"

"Not for a couple of hours."

"Let him know I was here. Tell him to get two miles in today." Jack turned to go.

"Hey, don't go yet. Aunt Haddie wants to see you. She called your house this morning. Your mom said you were coming, so she's expecting you."

Jack sighed. *Here comes the lecture about going down to see who got arrested last night.* He trudged into the kitchen, debating whether to look humble and apologetic or stand up straight and take it like a man.

"Jackie." Aunt Haddie hurried down the hallway, her handbag bumping against her hip with each step. "I'm so glad you're here. Would you mind giving me a ride?"

"Sure." Jack exhaled, relieved. "But I have to be back by noon. Kelly's having a cookout and, amazingly, I'm invited. Kelly had to beg her mom to let me come, so I have to be there."

"We'll be back before then," she assured him.

"Actually, I'm not eager to attend. It's weird her father okayed my invite. Where do you need to go?"

"Long Bay."

Jack's smile dropped. "Long Bay Prison?"

Aunt Haddie nodded. "With Mrs. Martin."

"To see J-Dog?"

"Don't use street names," Aunt Haddie chided. "As you are certainly aware"—she stuck out her chin and leveled a laser stare—"Jay got arrested last night. They are holding him at Long Bay until he's arraigned. Mrs. Martin needs to see her son."

"They put him in the Bay?" Jack asked. "What did he get arrested for? Was it something to do with the Stacy Shaw disappearance?"

Aunt Haddie's brow wrinkled. "I'm certain he had nothing to do with that poor woman."

"But it was Detective Vargas who arrested him. He's the lead on that investigation." Jack tipped his head to the side. "That's a big jackpot if he's involved."

"He's not. Jay just found the woman's wallet. It's a misunderstanding."

"*Found* it?" Jack scoffed. "You don't get arrested for finding a wallet. Is that what they took out of the house?"

"It is, and I think that's enough questions for now. If you're going to give me and Mrs. Martin a ride, let's get on with it. And I'm sure Jay will be glad to see you too."

Jack snorted. "Jay doesn't want to see me."

"I know you two have had your differences, but he'll want to see a friendly face."

Jack pointed at himself. "When it comes to this face and Jay, there's no 'friendly' involved. I can't stand him, and he hates me right back."

Aunt Haddie inhaled slowly and once again leveled her gaze at Jack.

Jack swallowed. Not even his father could match Aunt Haddie's stern look. Her stare pinned him in place and he didn't even think about trying to look away.

"I'm sure he doesn't hate you," Aunt Haddie said. "I know Jay went through a troubled patch, but he's been trying very hard to fly right since his father passed on last year. I want you on your best behavior."

Jack's shoulders slumped. "Yes, ma'am."

A sweet smile stretched across Aunt Haddie's face, and she squeezed his hand.

They walked out the door. Michelle and Replacement sat talking on the steps. Aunt Haddie stopped in front of Replacement. "Please watch out for Michelle until we get back. It could be a couple of hours."

"I will, ma'am." The girl nodded and squared her shoulders.

Jack shot a puzzled look at Michelle, which she answered with a wink. Jack followed Aunt Haddie to the car and held the door open for her.

The Martins lived only four doors down. He pulled to a stop in front of the Martins', but instead of getting out, he angled his thumb back toward Aunt Haddie's. "You're putting that kid in charge of Michelle?"

"Don't you remember how good it made you feel to have responsibilities?"

"Is that how you remember it?" Jack chuckled.

"Every child needs structure. Replacement's a born protector."

"Replacement? I thought you shouldn't use street names."

Aunt Haddie pinned him with her eyes again. "There are exceptions to some rules. Her real name is Alice, but right now…right now she'd prefer to be called something else."

"But Replacement? For a second there I thought Michelle called her Placemat."

"Don't tease, Jackie. Besides, Chandler picked out the name for her."

"Figures," Jack muttered.

"Oh, don't be silly, it's sweet. And the important thing is, she likes it."

"What's wrong with her real name?"

Aunt Haddie folded her hands on her lap. "Her given name is Alice. When she first came here, every time I spoke to her, she'd start to cry. For the life of me, I couldn't figure out why. Chandler solved that riddle. Alice was named after her mother, who died. Every time she heard the name Alice, it cut her to the quick."

Jack nodded. "Okay, but why Replacement?"

"Her first night here, she ran into a closet and wouldn't come out. I tried to talk to her and so did Michelle, but she wouldn't budge. We couldn't believe it when she let Chandler in. He sat down on the floor with her. He knew what she was going through because he lost his parents too, you know. He understood her, and she got him. They talked for almost an hour. Then he gave her a nickname to make her feel like she belonged."

"I don't get how being a 'replacement' makes her feel like she fits in," Jack said.

"You would if you'd let me finish," Aunt Haddie said sternly. "Chandler said to her, 'I'm going in the Army, and I need someone to fill my shoes. You'll have to watch over Aunt Haddie and keep an eye on Michelle until I get back. But while you're doing that, everyone's going to treat you how they treat *me*. You'll be *my* replacement. Do you know what that means? No one will pick on you, because you're my replacement. It means all the kisses and hugs Aunt Haddie gives me, she'll give you. It means all the cool stuff my sister Michelle does with me, she'll do with you, because you're my replacement.'" Aunt Haddie's voice filled with pride. "After that, she'd only respond to her new nickname. That poor little angel. She's been through hell, so don't you go teasing her. Understood?"

"Yes, ma'am."

They got out of the car and approached the Martins' house. It had seen better days. The paint was peeling and the lawn needed to be mowed. Jack could just picture what Mr. Martin's reaction to that would have been if he were still alive. Mr. Martin had been the opposite of Jay. He wasn't the type to start yelling; he'd just go grab a paint can and get the job done. He was the kind of man who was always working on his house. The paint was always fresh and the lawn groomed. He put on a light show every Christmas and displayed flags for the Fourth. Life had been hard for Mrs. Martin since his passing.

She came out the front door as Jack and Aunt Haddie walked up. A petite woman with graying hair, she stood on the top step, clutching a small purse.

"Morning, Mrs. Martin," Jack said.

"Good morning, Jackie." Her voice was soft. "Thank you for doing this. It's very nice of you."

"It's no trouble at all. Jackie's glad to help." Aunt Haddie let go of Jack and took Mrs. Martin's arm.

"Thank you so much, Haddie. I'm just worried sick. Do you think Jay's okay?"

"I'm sure he's fine," she said reassuringly. She steadied Mrs. Martin as they walked to the car.

Jack opened the back door and Mrs. Martin got in. Aunt Haddie sat in the backseat next to her friend.

Mrs. Martin's smile was thin. "I hope he's been getting some sleep." Her voice was just above a whisper and her bottom lip trembled. "He's always been such a light sleeper. When he was small, I had to get his father a different alarm clock because the ticking would wake my little boy up."

Aunt Haddie rubbed Mrs. Martin's back. "He'll be okay."

"You go sit in the front, Haddie. Jackie will be uncomfortable chauffeuring us around like this."

"Nonsense, Charlotte." She patted the woman's hand. "You don't mind, do you, Jackie?"

Jack shook his head. "It's like *Driving Miss Daisy* in reverse." He tipped his head as he slid into the driver's seat and slipped into his best Morgan Freeman impression. "We'll get going right away, ma'am. You two just sit back and try to relax."

* * *

The ride to the holding facility at Long Bay Prison was painfully slow for Jack. In the backseat, Aunt Haddie tried to comfort Mrs. Martin, and Jack could hear a muffled sob now and then.

Aunt Haddie held on to Mrs. Martin's hand and prayed. "The Lord will work it out, Charlotte."

"I know, I know," Mrs. Martin said.

"How's Tommy taking this?" Aunt Haddie asked.

"Badly. He didn't come home last night. I called over to Nina's and all his friends', but no one's seen him. I'm so worried about him. It's strange—before their father's death, Tommy was so well behaved. Jay was the one who was always getting into trouble. But after Aaron passed… well, Jay's gotten his life together. He got a job, he worked hard and got a promotion. He's a delivery driver now. But Tommy, it's been just the opposite. His father's death just…just knocked him off the tracks, you know? Like flipping a switch. He won't listen to anyone. And now this."

"I'm sure Tommy will come home soon," Aunt Haddie said.

Mrs. Martin sniffled. "But what about Jay? They're going to charge him."

"What's he getting charged with?" Jack pulled down the rearview mirror so he could see Mrs. Martin.

"Fraudulent use of an ATM card, larceny, and identity theft."

Jack turned ninety degrees in his seat. "Seriously?"

"Jack." Aunt Haddie raised a hand. "Eyes on the road."

Jack straightened out the car.

"The police said he stole that missing woman's wallet and then tried to use an ATM card that wasn't his. He didn't get any money out of the account, but they said that doesn't matter, he tried to use the card. But he didn't do it." She gripped Aunt Haddie's hand. "I know Jay. He said he found that woman's wallet."

"Do they believe that part at least?" Jack asked. "Or do they think he's somehow involved in the Stacy Shaw disappearance?"

"They think he knows where Mrs. Shaw is," Mrs. Martin said, her voice shaking. "But he couldn't have been involved. He's never hurt anyone. You know him, Jackie. Have you ever seen him have a temper?"

Jack crooked his head to the side. The truth was, J-Dog's temper was notorious. Jack had seen him start fights a handful of times—and each time, it was a lopsided victory for J-Dog.

Jack chose to ignore the question. "So that's why they're charging him with all those felonies," he said instead. "They're leaning on him to get information on Stacy Shaw." He turned to look at Mrs. Martin.

Aunt Haddie pointed forward. "Pay attention to your driving."

"Sorry," Jack said. "Where did the police find the wallet?"

"In Jay's jacket. When they searched the house. I think Jay was going to try to figure out who it belonged to so he could give it back. I'm certain he didn't steal it like they said…" She broke down and sobbed.

Jack opened his mouth to speak, but Aunt Haddie shook her head.

Mrs. Martin cried quietly as Aunt Haddie rubbed her back. They spent the rest of the ride in silence.

When they pulled into the prison parking lot, Jack got the door and the two women got out. Aunt Haddie patted Jack's arm.

They walked down the long concrete path to the prison. Jack had been out here once before as part of a police ride-along. He'd been accompanied by a group of burly police officers, but even so, it was unnerving.

As they headed to the entrance, they could see the prison exercise yard in the distance. Several layers of fences crowned with barbed wire separated them from the prisoners. They called the exercise yard at the Bay "The Beast Pit," because all the weights and illegal steroids turned guys into creatures that only vaguely resembled humans. Right now, a dozen men snarled and growled as they tossed massive steel weights into the air like they were beach balls. The prisoners looked at the guards like wolves trapped in cages, with contempt and loathing.

It all put Jack on edge, from the cold, indifferent tone of the guards to the prisoners who glared at him with nothing but hate. The place had the antiseptic smell of a hospital mixed with the stale air of a tomb, and although the concrete and tiles looked as if they belonged in a university, to Jack it was like walking into a morgue.

When the first heavy metal gate clanged shut behind them and the unseen lock sealed it with a loud click, Jack recalled what he hated the most about this place: he was trapped. Locked behind steel doors and concrete.

Jack flexed his hands and his breathing sped up. Panic rippled through him as flashbacks from his childhood hijacked his brain. It felt as if the floor was rolling out from under him. Everything inside screamed at him to turn around and run—to tear down the door and barrel outside. Sweat ran down his back and the room spun. He stretched his hand out and felt cold concrete.

Get out! yelled a voice in his head but his feet didn't move. He watched Aunt Haddie and Mrs. Martin walking down the corridor ahead of him, the two old women holding each other up.

He couldn't leave them alone in here.

His fist smacked the wall and the pain helped a little to stop the spinning and wake him out of the nightmare. He hurried to catch up.

* * *

After showing their IDs several times, enduring two pat-downs, and handing over their bags and everything in their pockets, Mrs. Martin, Aunt Haddie, and Jack were silently escorted to a long, stark room. The cinderblock walls were painted a drab gray and green, and with no exterior windows, the air smelled stale and musty. Warning posters were everywhere, informing prisoners that biting, spitting, or throwing of bodily waste would result in thirty days added to their sentence.

This was the visiting room.

The space was cut in two by a metal and glass divider partitioned into five individual sections. Each section consisted of two metal stools cemented to the floor on the visitors' side, one stool on the prisoners' side; between them, a thick Plexiglas window atop a waist-high metal counter. No phone, no speakers, just small holes drilled through the glass. Speaking through the holes forced people to raise their voices to a level that enabled the guards and everyone else to hear their conversations.

Mrs. Martin was directed to the visitors' section at the far right. She took a seat on one of the metal stools and waited anxiously. Jack and Aunt Haddie stood by the wall, behind the yellow line painted on the floor.

There was no doubt in Jack's mind that if he were ever in here for any length of time, he would go mad. His chest tightened. Everywhere he looked, all he saw was pain. At the far-left visitors' section, a prisoner in a bright-orange jumpsuit sat on the edge of his round metal stool. The tendons in his neck stood out as he jabbed a finger toward the emaciated girl on the other side of the Plexiglas. Each time his hand thrust, she winced. Hot bile rose in the back of Jack's throat.

He turned away, but his new view was no easier to watch. A young mother held up a toddler to the partition. Curious little hands reached out toward the man on the other side, who had tears in his eyes. His enormous hand pressed hard against the Plexiglas as the toddler's fingers traced its outline.

Jack wondered whether the boy and his father had ever actually touched, skin to skin. He fought the urge to scan the faces of the men in the room to look for similarities to himself. Jack didn't know anything about his own biological father. No name. No details.

Two guards escorted J-Dog into the room on the other side of the glass. J-Dog normally walked with his chin up, looking down his nose at everyone, but today he kept his chin tucked down. With one hand moving back and forth as though he was pulling himself forward with it, he strutted over to the metal stool.

When J-Dog raised his head, Jack was shocked and Mrs. Martin's hand flew to her mouth. His face was bruised, his right eye swollen shut. His upper lip was fat and cut; his right hand was bandaged.

"Oh, baby..." Mrs. Martin's voice broke.

"I'm fine."

"Who did that to you?"

"Some of the welcoming committee. It was nothing. I can handle it." He leaned close to the window and peered out with his left eye. "I told you not to come here."

"I spoke with your lawyer."

"Lawyer?" J-Dog scoffed. "The court-appointed guy's a dumb old white guy. He's an idiot. He's already trying to get me to take a deal."

"Mr. Carlson believes you should cooperate with the police."

"They can keep on me. But I'm not sayin' nothin'."

"But Jay, they think you had something to do with that woman who went missing."

"Like I'd go anywhere near a white woman. Too much trouble." Jay glanced at the beefy, pale guard standing in the corner. "I didn't have nothin' to do with it. I didn't know her."

"The police say you met her. They say you delivered baby furniture to her house."

"So what? She didn't even look at me. That's not meeting someone."

Mrs. Martin shook her head. "Jay, why won't you just tell the police where you found the wallet? That young lady is missing. If you tell them where you found it, they said they'd consider reducing the charges."

"You can't believe a word the cops say. That Detective Vargas tricked me." Jay's nostrils flared. "He lied. He said the lady just wanted the wallet back and since I had no record I'd get probation, and even that would go away if I kept my nose clean. He said all I had to do was just admit I found it. He lied. He never said she was missing, or anything about an ATM."

Mrs. Martin put her head in her hands. "Jay…they have a picture of you at the bank."

J-Dog turned his face away from his mother. His lips pulled back and he bared his teeth, but he didn't say anything.

"They also found blood. On your shoes. Is it that woman's? Jay, did…did you have something to do with it?"

Jay glared at the ceiling. "No. I didn't." His lip curled back and the muscles of his jaw throbbed.

"Oh, Jay." Mrs. Martin reached out and placed her hand on the Plexiglas. "Please talk to Attorney Carlson." Her shoulders shook as a small sob jolted her slender frame.

His mother's tears extinguished the fire in Jay's eyes. The anger burning there flickered and died. "Shh, Momma. Everything's gonna be good. You always say that. Everything's gonna be good. We'll figure it out." He leaned down and angled his head so she would look at him. "I got a little money. In my bureau, the top drawer. In a white envelope. You gotta use it for the bills."

"I'll use it for your bail."

"It's only enough for bills. I'd never have the money for bail."

"I'll put up the house."

"No! I won't let you."

"But Jay…" Mrs. Martin held her hand over her mouth to cover another sob.

"It's good, Momma. Everything's gonna be good."

She nodded, and J-Dog's eyes met Jack's. Jack expected to be on the receiving end of a nasty sneer, but instead, the eyes that looked back at him were hollow. J-Dog was broken, and Jack knew it. He'd seen that same dead look on his own face in a mirror a thousand times.

For a split second, Jack remembered when they were kids, and an innocent young Jay riding his ten-speed bike in the parking lot behind their elementary school flashed in his mind.

Then the door behind J-Dog opened and a guard led in another prisoner. The man looked like an experiment gone wrong, trying to cross a linebacker and a Russian super-soldier. Tattoos covered half of his bald head, while a jagged scar wrapped upward around his neck and then down the other side. A chunk of his top lip was missing, resulting in a permanent snarl.

J-Dog sat up straighter, and a tiny bead of sweat formed on his forehead. The other prisoner's eyes locked on J-Dog as he was led over to his own window. Even as he sat down opposite a pregnant woman, he was glaring at J-Dog with murder in his eyes.

"Jay, please talk to them," Mrs. Martin begged.

J-Dog's eyes shifted back and forth between the enormous man and his mother.

Aunt Haddie reached out and squeezed Jack's hand.

Jack knew child molesters, rapists, and men accused of violent crimes against women were typically kept isolated in prison—for their own safety, since general population wasn't exactly kind to that sort of criminal. But J-Dog had been put in general population in the Bay, and Jack realized why: the cops were putting pressure on him to talk.

J-Dog's dead if he had anything to do with a missing lady.

Jack glanced back at the musclehead seated four sections away. He wouldn't want to fight the monster in an open field with a bat, let alone in a concrete cell, and that mutant was just one of many in here who might want a piece of J-Dog.

Jack shuddered. How long did they have to stay here?

Mrs. Martin folded her hands in her lap and stared at her son. Her shoulders pulled back and she lifted her chin. When she spoke, it was deliberate and steady, with no lurking tears. "Your father would want you to tell the police the truth."

J-Dog shut his eyes and shook his head.

Mrs. Martin sat motionless, saying nothing.

"Momma, I didn't have anything to do with that missing lady. I swear it on Daddy's grave."

The oath slammed into Jack. J-Dog loved his father. In fact, Jack had been jealous of their relationship when they were kids. J-Dog had followed his father everywhere; he was Jay's hero. They had a falling-out when J-Dog was a teenager and got in trouble with the law, but when his father died, J-Dog was inconsolable.

"I believe you." Mrs. Martin looked around the room and her shoulders slumped again. "I just don't know what to do." She rubbed the back of one hand with the thumb of the other. She took a deep breath. "Jay, there's something else. Tommy hasn't come home since you were arrested." She passed a tired hand over her forehead. "He hasn't even called. I phoned his girlfriend, but Nina hasn't seen him." She looked up at Jay. "Do you know where he could be?"

J-Dog leaned back. His initial look of confusion was quickly replaced by a flash of anger. "Momma, don't look for Tommy."

"What?"

"I need you to leave Tommy alone right now. Leave him be."

"Why?"

"You just do. Don't stir the pot."

"I can't. He's my boy too." Mrs. Martin looked distraught. "Maybe I should file a missing person report?"

A guard strutted forward and barked, "Time."

J-Dog jumped up. "Tommy's fine, wherever he is. Don't get the police involved."

The guard stepped forward.

"Do you know where he is? Is Tommy in trouble? Jay? Jay?"

J-Dog stepped back. "Just take care of yourself."

"Jay?" Mrs. Martin called out as she touched the window. "I'll get you help."

J-Dog looked at his mother. There seemed to be a brief flicker of optimism, but it was quickly extinguished, and in the ashes all that remained was hopelessness.

As J-Dog was escorted from the room, Aunt Haddie stepped forward and wrapped her arm around Mrs. Martin's shoulders. "It's okay. It'll be okay."

An impatient-looking guard opened the door for them, and they headed back the way they'd come. Jack felt like a diver who'd stayed underwater too long and his oxygen was running out. He wanted to sprint for the exit, but he forced himself to keep the slow and steady pace set by the women.

When the fresh air outside finally hit his face, Jack drank his fill. Just the atmosphere of the prison had felt crushing, and now he was free. He flexed his hands and stretched. But he could see that Mrs. Martin was having trouble. She was breathing so heavily, Jack worried she was going to hyperventilate.

Aunt Haddie stopped. "It's all right, Charlotte. Everything will be all right."

J-Dog's mother covered her face with her hands. "Did you hear him? Why would Jay say that? Did you hear what he said?"

"What, Charlotte?"

"Not to look for Tommy. What does that mean?" She shook her head. "Where is Tommy? I'm so worried about him, Haddie. Maybe he's thinking of doing something foolish? He'd do anything for Jay."

Aunt Haddie said soothingly, "I'm sure Tommy will show up."

"But I don't know where else to look." Mrs. Martin's hand shot out and grabbed Jack's wrist. "You're his friend, Jackie. You grew up with my boys." Her grip was tight. Her eyes pleaded. "Please, Jackie. Please find Tommy."

"I'd like to, Mrs. Martin, but I don't know where he would go."

"You know his friends. You can find him."

"I don't even know where to start looking."

Mrs. Martin stared up at him. "You're smart. You'll think of something."

Jack looked at Aunt Haddie and then into Mrs. Martin's big brown eyes, filled with tears. He knew that you don't always get the missions you want.

"I'll sure try, ma'am," he said.

8

THE GAME

After dropping off Aunt Haddie and Mrs. Martin, Jack drove straight to Kelly's. There were so many expensive cars lining the long driveway, he had to park at the end, behind a Porsche Boxster. He left at least three feet in front of him to avoid even a remote chance of dinging its smooth red paint.

As he walked up the driveway, Jack glanced back over his shoulder at his Impala. All the other vehicles—BMWs, Audis, and Mercedes gleaming in the afternoon sun—looked like they had just come off a dealership's lot. Jack's car was as out of place as a sumo wrestler in a ballet.

Don't ever be ashamed of who you are. Remembering one of Aunt Haddie's lessons, Jack stiffened his backbone.

Kelly and a girl with sandy hair walked down the driveway. When she saw Jack, Kelly stopped, clasped both hands behind her back, and rose up on her toes. "Hey." Her cherry-red lips, only inches away, spread into a warm smile.

Jack also smiled, remembering those lips. "Sorry I'm late." He offered his hand to Kelly's friend. "Jack Stratton."

Kelly turned to her friend. "This is Courtney."

Courtney eyed Jack up and down. "You're a brave man."

Kelly shot her a look, then turned to Jack. "I tried to call and warn you this was turning into a shindig."

"I wasn't home. I had to visit someone in prison."

Courtney's eyes widened. Kelly's expression was a mix of shock and excitement. Courtney mouthed, *Bad boy*, but Jack pretended not to notice.

"I should have known my dad was up to something when he gave in too easily," Kelly said. "He told my older brother to invite some of his friends."

"That's fine. Let's go say hi," Jack suggested.

Kelly hesitated.

"Is there something else?"

Kelly twisted back and forth. "My ex is here too. He's friends with my brother."

This just keeps getting better.

Jack hid his apprehension, leaned closer, and whispered, "You're the only one I care about seeing." A crooked grin crossed his face. "It'll be fun."

The three of them walked up the driveway and around the side of the house. Jack held open the gate to the backyard and let Kelly and Courtney through. Kelly took his hand.

The backyard was huge—and beautiful. It appeared as if a ground crew had spent days working on it. The grass was green, lush, and meticulously edged, bushes were shaped and trimmed, and the flowers were in full bloom, carefully arranged in beds of fresh wood chips. Behind that, an in-ground pool, twice the size of a standard one, glistened aquamarine blue. Well-dressed people milled about.

Courtney hurried over to a group of five girls who eyed Jack like a panel of judges at a talent show. They pointed and talked and pointed again until they collectively nodded their approval and surrounded Courtney, eager for more details about Kelly's new boyfriend.

Mrs. Dawson noticed them from where she stood chatting with several women in a gazebo flanked by twin Japanese maples. She nodded at guests sitting at rows of tables set up under a large white tent, then strolled over to them. She smiled warmly, but there was a tightness around her eyes.

"Jack. I'm so glad you could make it."

"Thank you very much for inviting me. It's a beautiful day for a barbecue."

"It is. Have you been enjoying it?"

"No, I just got here. I was…" Jack cleared his throat. "I was sort of trapped inside all morning."

"I know what you mean," she said. "It's such a beautiful day, you feel like a prisoner being inside on a day like this."

"You can say that again. Is your husband here?" Jack asked. "I'd like to thank him for the invitation."

Mrs. Dawson considered for a moment. Jack had the distinct impression she was deciding whether she should try to talk him out of that course of action.

Jack waited confidently.

Mrs. Dawson waved her hand toward the house. "He's up there." The tight smile on her lips conveyed to Jack that this was a meeting she really didn't want to happen.

Mr. Dawson stood on the top step of a slate-covered patio like a king in command of his court. He had a cocktail in one hand and gestured expressively with the other at eight men on the steps below him. When he joked, they all laughed at once. He paused, and they nodded with introspection. And when he started to speak again, they smiled and looked on with rapt attention. It was a puppet court, and Mr. Dawson was the one pulling the strings.

Jack's back tightened as he strode across the grass. As he approached, the conversation on the steps abruptly stopped. Clearly there was some invisible barrier between these men and everyone else—and Jack had just shattered it. Silence descended on the group. Even a golden retriever that had been running around the yard stopped and watched.

Jack marched up the steps to Mr. Dawson, smiled, and held out his hand. "Thank you for the invitation, sir."

Mr. Dawson swirled the ice cubes in his glass thoughtfully, and his court jesters stood ready to receive a cue that they understood. Jack hadn't waited for the king to call, a clear breach of etiquette that had caught the king off-guard. He forced a smile across his face and gripped Jack's hand. "Glad you could make it." He turned toward the other men. "This is an acquaintance of my daughter's. Jack…?"

"Stratton. Jack Stratton." Jack briefly met the men's vacant stares. "Thanks again." He nodded at Mr. Dawson, and then, while still in charge, turned to go. Mr. Dawson's lips twitched.

Jack wondered how much the loss of control bothered him. Mr. Dawson was used to running companies and manipulating people. He called, they came—and they stayed until he said that they were allowed to go. That was how everyone in his world operated.

But not Jack.

Out of the corner of his eye, Jack noticed the side glances of the other men and kept a controlled pace across the yard. The brief greeting had gone just how Jack had wanted. In, "thank you," and out. Nice, quick, and polite.

He felt like a pirate king as he strode under the white marquee where Kelly was waiting for him. Courtney whispered something to her, and Kelly's eyes widened. Then they both broke into a giggle.

"I'd sure like to know what you just said," Jack said to Courtney.

"I was just thinking aloud." Courtney crossed her arms. "You must have—"

"Courtney!" Kelly gasped.

"I was kidding!" Courtney grinned impishly.

Kelly took Jack's hand. "Let's get a drink."

Jack headed over to a table covered with assorted bottles and drinks and poured himself a glass of iced tea.

"That was impressive," Kelly said, fixing herself a drink. "My father's about as approachable as a porcupine. Thank you for doing it." She swirled the soda in her glass and looked up at him through curled lashes. "Do you have plans for Friday night?"

"What's the matter with tonight?"

She lit up, then huffed. "I have to go out with my mom."

"Then Friday night it is." Jack lowered his voice and his glass. "Now that we have the uncomfortable part behind us, how about we head over to…" Jack trailed off when Kelly's startled gaze shifted to something behind him.

Jack turned to face three guys walking up. Tall, blond, fit, well-groomed clones.

"Preston," said the one in the red polo shirt. He stuck out his hand. "So you're my baby sister's new boyfriend?" He squeezed Jack's hand, hard, and tilted his head toward his companions. "These are my friends Warner and Archer."

Jack had to fight off a smirk when he looked at the distressed jeans Warner and Archer wore—identical in their factory-made imperfections. *It says a lot about a guy if he has to pay to have someone break in his pants for him.*

Jack stepped forward. "Nice to meet you."

Warner's eyes shifted between Jack and Kelly and settled on Kelly, his thin lips pressed into a slight sneer as he ogled her. She made just the slightest movement closer to Jack, and Warner tipped his head back and his small blue eyes stared down his angular nose at Jack. "Jack, huh?" He tried to crush Jack's hand as he shook it.

"That's me." Jack tightened his grip. He'd taken an immediate dislike to the guy.

Warner winced and let go.

Archer just nodded casually at Jack and appeared uninterested in the entire interaction.

Preston set his drink down on a table and eyed Jack. "We're having a little touch football game in a minute, in the field across the street. We're one guy short. Care to help us out?"

"We were just about to take off," Kelly said.

"No, you're not," Preston said. "You're going out with Mom after."

"It's only light contact," Warner said pointedly to Jack. "If you're worried, we can go easy."

Jack looked at Kelly. "Do you mind?"

Kelly gave him a you-don't-know-what-you're-getting-yourself-into look and shrugged. "Go ahead."

"I'm up for a game," Jack said.

Warner stepped on Archer's foot.

"You can be on my side, Jack," Archer offered quickly.

As the boys and Kelly walked down the driveway, five of Kelly's girlfriends followed behind. Jack could only catch bits and pieces of their conversation, but it all focused on one thing: him. There seemed to be a universal consensus that he was making a big mistake by playing in the game.

When they reached the large grassy field across the street from her house, Jack handed Kelly his wallet and keys. "So, which one's your old boyfriend?"

Kelly looked a little embarrassed. "Warner."

Jack winked and then turned back to the field. In addition to the three guys he'd met, a few other boys had gathered—not all of them tall and blond, Jack noted, but all carrying themselves with the same air of well-bred, ingrained superiority. Archer waved him over. As Jack jogged across the grass, Preston and Warner exchanged a sideways wink and nod.

"As you can see, it's four on four. Light contact," Archer reminded them after they had broken into teams. "I'm usually quarterback, but if you want to…?" He held a hand out to Jack.

Jack shook his head. "No, thanks."

They lined up, and for the next hour, Jack was tackled, bashed, elbowed, and repeatedly stepped on. Jack's teammates kept setting him up to take a beating, stopping or even stepping aside when they should have blocked for him, leaving him an easy target. And Warner hit the hardest. They tried to make their cheap shots look accidental, and of course they went out of their way to be polite in front of the genteel onlookers, making a big show of helping Jack off the ground each time they knocked him down.

But Jack gave as good as he got. Preston elbowed him in the face, and on the next play Jack "accidentally" kneed him in the thigh. Warner stomped on Jack's ankle, and as Jack stumbled, he just happened to hit Warner hard in the solar plexus.

Jack was just getting up from a hard tackle by Preston when Warner slammed into Jack from behind and Jack crashed to the dirt. Preston immediately offered him a hand up and a smug smile.

Jack's hands balled into fists.

A shrill whistle cut through the air. Kelly ran forward, a bright-pink whistle between her teeth and a big glass of lemonade in her hand. "Refreshment time-out!" She brought the glass to Jack.

"We're in the middle of a game," Preston whined.

"You can take a break," she called over her shoulder, heading back toward the house and hoping Jack would follow her. He took the hint, ignoring the disgruntled preppies.

"Are you okay?"

"I'm fine. Thanks for the drink. And the time-out."

Kelly held up the whistle. "Cheerleading." She flicked some dirt off Jack's shoulder. "Sorry. Those guys are jerks. You can stop."

Courtney ran up with her phone in her hand. "Move together."

"Will you stop taking pictures?" Kelly said.

Courtney pouted. "I have nothing on my Facebook wall. You got all dressed up and you two are adorable."

Kelly slid close to Jack.

Three photos later, Courtney winked and stuck her phone in her back pocket with the fluid motion of a samurai sheathing his sword.

"Come on, Kelly!" Preston yelled. "We wanna play."

Jack finished the lemonade in one gulp. "Thank you." As he handed Kelly the glass, he stared at Courtney. "Where are you posting that?"

"Facebook. I put everything on my page."

"Wait a minute," Jack muttered. "That's it."

"What's it?" Kelly asked, confused.

"Come on, Stratton!" Warner called. "Or are you wimping out?"

Jack ignored him and spoke to Kelly. "I just thought of something. I have to go."

"Now?"

Jack looked back to Preston. He hated to leave in the middle of a fight. "I've gotta take off," he yelled.

The guys on the field jeered; Warner the loudest.

Kelly took Jack's hand as he headed for the Impala. "Is everything all right?" Her blue eyes sparkled and her cheeks were flushed.

"I'm good. A friend of mine needs help. You're cool with that?"

"Yeah. I'm sorry about those jerks."

"I don't care what they think. This has nothing to do with them."

Kelly handed Jack his wallet and keys.

He tossed the keys up in the air, then caught them again with a loud jingle. "Are we on for Friday night?"

"Yes." She kissed him. It was a quick kiss, but long enough for her fingertips to brush down his forearm as lightly as a snowflake.

"Wow."

She smiled.

As Jack climbed into the driver's seat, he had to grind his teeth together to keep from groaning in pain in front of Kelly.

Seven guys came jogging over together in a pack. "Hey, Jack!" Preston called out. "Now that you know how we play, next game we can go a little harder."

"Sure. Anytime." Jack waved him off.

Archer grinned slyly. "We play most Saturdays. Tell you what, why don't you get a team together? Bring some friends."

Jack tried not to make a face. "Sounds like a blast."

"If it's too rough for you," Warner said, strutting forward, "I'll let you ref. I'm sure Kelly will let you borrow her cheerleader whistle." He laughed, and the others joined him.

Jack was about to get back out of the car—he was already reaching for the door handle—but Kelly leaned in the window, pulled him close, and kissed him. This was a much longer kiss. Her hand slid to the base of Jack's head, and he slowly moved his own hand so it caressed her neck and ear.

When she pulled away, Jack just gazed at her, only barely aware that Archer and Preston were struggling to hold Warner back.

"Guess that'll have to hold me awhile," Jack finally said with a smile.

Kelly's breathing was ragged. "Call me?"

"I will." Jack started up the car. He knew all eyes were on them. He tipped an imaginary hat to the boys, who could only glare as he backed out and drove away.

***

Twenty minutes later, Jack was in Washington Heights. He parked in front of Aunt Haddie's, pulled a gym bag from his trunk, and headed around to the back door. He stopped at the bottom of the stairs when he heard the old pickup truck pulling up in the driveway.

Chandler jumped out of the cab, grease and oil on his clothes, hands, and face. He looked like a mechanic who'd operated on a car that didn't survive the procedure. Chandler waved back at the driver. "See ya, Mr. Emerson."

Mr. Emerson, an old man with white hair and even whiter teeth, flashed an enormous grin. "Couldn't have done it without you, son. Thanks!"

As Mr. Emerson drove off, Chandler turned to Jack, wiping grease off his hands on an old rag. "Don't tell me you're here to work out, because I just spent three hours breaking my back."

"I thought you were just delivering a refrigerator."

"I was." Chandler held up four oil-smeared fingers. "Fourth floor. I had to lug the thing up strapped to a dolly. Then the used refrigerator Mr. Emerson got wouldn't fit. So I had to swap out the motor and install it, then take the one we brought up back down all those stairs." He again stuck up four fingers for emphasis.

"That's better than what I had to do. I drove Aunt Haddie and Mrs. Martin to Long Bay."

Chandler laughed. "Was there a riot? You look like you got jumped."

Jack looked down at his dirty, grass-stained clothes. "Oh, this is from Kelly's barbecue."

Chandler puffed a derisive snort. "That sure is some kind of barbecue those rich folks throw."

"Knock it off. There was also a pickup football game," Jack said. "And no one told me that I was the ball."

Chandler laughed again. "Class warfare up on Knob Hill. Oh, yes, I can see it."

"You want to give me a hand finding Two Point?" Jack asked.

"Not really. Why do you want to find him?"

"I promised Mrs. Martin. And Aunt Haddie." Jack didn't need to add the last part. He knew Chandler would go with him. He held up the gym bag. "You mind if I take a quick shower first?"

"Sure. After me." Chandler looked Jack over. "You need it. Looks like you're gonna need a *lotta* showers if you wanna keep going to those barbecues."

"Oh, yeah? You look like you lost a fight with the Swamp Monster."

The back door opened and Aunt Haddie came out onto the porch. She took one look at Chandler and Jack and put her hands on her hips.

"They're work clothes!" Chandler called up.

Aunt Haddie's shoulders bounced up and down, then she burst out laughing. Her laugh was deep, big, and bright.

Chandler spread his hands out. "I earned these stains with honor. I lugged a refrigerator up and down—"

"Jewels in your crown in Heaven. For now, you boys will have to settle for meatloaf and mashed potatoes."

Chandler's face lit up.

"I'll fix you both a big plate, but you'll need to wash up first." She disappeared into the house, still laughing.

As they headed up the steps, Jack asked Chandler, "Can I get on your computer?"

"Sure. It's your old computer."

"I just need to look something up on Facebook. I thought of something at Kelly's and want to check it out. Also, can you ask Makayla to call Nina and see if she's heard from Two Point?"

"Sure. What's all this about, Jack?"

"J-Dog wasn't lying," Jack said. "He didn't steal Stacy Shaw's wallet. But I think I know who did."

9

THE HUNT FOR TWO

Jack scrubbed the dirt out of his hair and tried to crack his shoulder. His lip stung, but the burning from the scrape up his side hurt worse.

He leaned his head down and let the hot water wash over him. It felt like only a second later when he heard familiar thumping: Aunt Haddie, banging out her familiar warning to take a quick shower. He clicked the water off. Aunt Haddie didn't have much money, and it was expensive to heat that old hot water tank.

Jack watched the water spiral down the drain. "When I get my own place, I'm taking showers until the water runs cold."

After he toweled off and changed into clean pants, Jack stepped into the hallway, still pulling on his T-shirt. Michelle opened her bedroom door and rolled her eyes.

"Normal people get dressed *in* the bathroom."

"Be quiet, Half-Pint."

She giggled. "Are you sleeping over?"

"I think so. Where's Chandler?"

"In the kitchen."

Jack headed downstairs. Chandler sat at the kitchen table, about to bite into an Oreo that he quickly hid beneath the table.

"Let's go." Jack didn't break stride as he headed out the door.

"Hold on a minute, Sherlock." Chandler thundered down the back steps after Jack. "So where are we headed?"

"Did Makayla call Nina?"

"Yeah, but Nina's not answering."

"Well, let's head over there anyways." Jack opened the trunk of the Impala and tossed in his gym bag. Before closing the trunk, he took out a Boston Red Sox baseball cap and pulled it on.

"You're willing to cover up your precious hair with a hat?" Chandler put on a horrified look.

"You're the one who's always messing with your hair, primping and preening."

"You know it. So would you if you looked this good." Chandler threw his big arms out and posed like a *GQ* model.

Jack laughed.

"You're going to cry when the Army shaves your curly locks, Rapunzel," Chandler said.

"I don't mind short hair."

"We're not talking shorta—we're talking none."

Jack shrugged. "It'll grow back. I'll cut it as short as they want for as long as they want, as long as they let me serve."

Chandler stood by the Impala's passenger door, but Jack walked right past it. "We're not driving?" Chandler asked.

"Nah, let's walk. It's not far. And you need the exercise."

"Don't start with that again."

"Don't act like you weren't eating that cookie a minute ago."

"You saw?"

"I saw. Plus…" Jack pointed to his own front teeth and Chandler ran his tongue over the front of his. "A little more between those two." He pointed.

The screen door banged open and Replacement appeared in the doorway. She waved to Chandler. He waved back. She gave him a thumbs-up, and Chandler nodded. Then she vanished back inside.

"What was that all about?" Jack asked as they started walking.

"She's just letting me know that everything's cool."

"What's she, your watchdog?"

"Be nice. Some people had it different than you coming here," Chandler said. "You had it bad before, so coming here was a good thing for you. Michelle and I had it real good until my folks died. So did Replacement. Her whole family died in a car accident. She lost everything. Then she went into the system."

"Her whole family?"

"Yeah. Her mom, dad, and two little brothers."

They walked a few steps in silence. Chandler kicked a rock. "She and I are a lot alike."

Jack pictured the petite white girl standing next to his huge black friend. "I guess you don't have to look like someone to be like them."

"She's a good kid. She just—well, at her foster home before this one, she had it *real* bad."

Jack's jaw clenched. He'd grown up with foster kids. Their lives generally started rough and went downhill from there. He didn't want to think about what "real bad" could mean.

Jack tried not to think of his own past. The numerous therapists he'd seen over the years always told him he should talk about his past, get everything out in the open and deal with it—but Jack insisted on doing the opposite. Whenever old wounds opened back up, he would just shut down. He couldn't kill the past, so he'd buried it. He was determined to cage the demons that raged inside him and lock them away so they could never get out.

Chandler punched his arm—hard.

Jack stumbled sideways. "Hey!"

Chandler made a goofy face.

"Why'd you do that?" Jack snapped.

"You looked like you wanted to kill someone."

"So you hit me? That's brilliant."

"I wanted to get you thinking about something else." Chandler grinned. "It worked."

Jack stared at Chandler's smiling face and his temper cooled. His friend was right. "Idiot."

"But you just called me brilliant!" Chandler's smile widened.

Jack shook his head, and they walked in step again. He didn't want to admit it, but Chandler was probably the biggest reason he stayed sane. The pull of hate and anger inside Jack was strong, and he found himself frequently drawn to the darkness. But Chandler always had a way of coaxing him back from the edge. What might Jack have become without all those years of his friend's help? He shoved Chandler's shoulder, and his big friend laughed.

Jack had never understood how Chandler and Michelle had turned out so normal. They'd lost their parents when they were both little, yet they didn't seem to bear the scars Jack did. He felt like a jigsaw puzzle with a bunch of pieces missing. But they seemed happy all the time.

As they neared the end of the street, Chandler asked, "Are we cutting through the park?"

"Yeah. I want to check the basketball courts. Two Point hangs there, so maybe somebody saw something."

"Too bad we can't ask Victor." Chandler looked around. "I bet he knows where Two Point is."

Jack stopped. "Victor Perez?"

"Yeah." Chandler stopped too. "Two Point's part of the D Street Crew—Victor's gang. You knew that, right?"

"No. But you're right, the gang leader would know. If Nina's not around, we should definitely talk to Victor."

Chandler looked at Jack as if he had three heads. "Are you out of your mind? Talking to Victor's no joke. You risk a bullet in your head just by being near him."

Jack shrugged. "I just want to talk to him, not fight with him. Besides, I know Victor."

"Maybe a long time ago you did," Chandler said. "Trust me, Victor is bad news. Everyone in his crew is packing. It's bad all the way around."

Jack kicked a rock across the road. Following the path of the rock, he noticed a ponytail poking out from behind a large elm tree. Replacement. "Your watchdog followed us," Jack whispered.

Chandler smiled but didn't let on that they'd seen her. "She does that."

Jack angled his head back toward the tree. "She shouldn't go where we're headed."

"Listen to your own advice. We shouldn't go there either," Chandler grumbled. But he turned around and whistled.

Replacement immediately popped out from her hiding spot. Without a word, Chandler pointed back to the house. Replacement's shoulders slumped, but she obediently turned and started jogging back toward Aunt Haddie's.

Chandler turned back to Jack. "Are we really gonna do this?" he asked. "I don't feel like getting shot."

"You don't have to come," Jack said.

"Yes, I do. I don't want to. I don't think you should go. But if you go, I go." Chandler held up a large hand. "But let me be clear. I'm just going to watch your back."

"Then let's go."

10

A FAVOR

Jack and Chandler entered Hamilton Park through the west gate—the side that bordered the projects, where the main power lines entered town. The three-story-tall electric towers cut a wide green swath away from the park like a river of grass that stretched into the distance until it eventually wound its way north.

They walked past the old baseball diamond and playground. The diamond had been abandoned by park maintenance years ago, and the playground was in no better shape. The V-shaped metal supports for the swings were still standing, but only a few rusted chains dangled down. Overlooking it all, on a little hill, sat a single picnic table. Since the table afforded a 360-degree view, it was the spot of choice for people who wanted to see who was coming.

Four men sat at the table. Shirtless, with more tattoos than bare skin, the three who faced Jack and Chandler's direction all had the same sneer. As Jack and Chandler approached, they rose and swaggered forward. The fourth man, Victor, remained seated with his back to them.

"This is an *extremely* stupid idea," Chandler muttered to Jack. "When was the last time you talked to Victor, anyway?"

"When we played baseball."

Chandler mashed his lips together. "That was in middle school."

"And that was the last time I talked to him."

Chandler's nostrils flared.

As Jack scanned the men up ahead, he was grateful to have Chandler with him. "Thanks for coming."

"Just ask him about Two Point and let's get out of here."

The tallest of the three men walked forward and stopped in front of Jack. He looked like half the guys Jack had seen in the prison's exercise yard. The muscles in his chest flexed as he clenched and unclenched his hands.

"Whatcha want?" he asked, seeming eager for a flippant answer as an excuse to fight. His mouth stayed open after he spoke, revealing a line of gold teeth.

"I'm Jack Stratton. I'm here to talk to Victor."

"Jack Stratton?" Victor got up and turned around.

It had been years since Jack had seen Victor up close. The thin, gangly kid Jack remembered bore little resemblance to this hardened man with lean muscles covered in tattoos.

"Hey, Victor. Long time. You got a minute?"

Victor strutted forward. From the bulge under his shirt, it was clear he was packing. Jack's pulse quickened. *Just ask about Two Point and get out of here.*

Victor stopped a couple of feet in front of Jack, crossed his arms, and tilted his head back. "What you want from me, little white Boy Scout?"

The other guys laughed.

Jack let the rip go. "A favor. You got a second?" Jack pointed with his thumb over to the old swing set. He didn't want to talk to Victor in front of his crew.

Victor smoothed down the ends of his thin mustache, debating for a second. Jack hoped it was all an act to show who was in charge.

"I just need a favor," Jack said.

Victor nodded to his posse and started walking, but he stopped when Chandler followed. Chandler's eyes went back and forth between Jack and Victor. Jack gave Chandler a quick nod. He hoped that let him know he wasn't happy about the situation, but it was best to do whatever Victor wanted.

"I'll wait here," Chandler grumbled.

When they were out of earshot, Victor spoke. "Ask." He eyed Jack suspiciously.

"You hear about J-Dog?"

"Hear about him? They pulled me in too when that lady went missing. Is that why he got arrested?"

"The cops talked to you?"

"Yeah, whatcha think?" Victor spat. "They know I'm in charge of Hamilton, and she worked near here. A fly farts in the park and they think I got something to do with it." He crossed his arms, and the muscles in his forearms rippled the dragon tattoos. "I don't talk to you since middle school and now you show up asking questions? I heard you wanna be a cop. You workin' for 'em?"

Jack's mind raced. This wasn't how he imagined the conversation would go. "Aunt Haddie is friends with J-Dog's mom," he said. "I'm just helping out."

Victor's eyes narrowed. "You wearin' a wire?"

Without hesitation, Jack pulled his shirt off over his head.

"You really are a Boy Scout, huh?" Victor took out a cigarette. "Helpin' your foster mom and savin' little old ladies' handbags?"

"You know about that?"

Victor gave Jack a look. "I know everything that goes on in my part of town." He lit the smoke. "I believe you. Put your shirt back on. So, what's this favor?"

Jack pulled his shirt over his head. "I'm looking for Two Point. Have you seen him?"

"No, but that squid better not be around here. I kicked him to the curb for the stuff he was pulling. Him boosting from cars got me dragged into the pigpen."

"He was mugging people?"

Victor scoffed. "Two Point's spineless. He's no dog—he's a weasel. He doesn't have the nuts to jack a nun. I caught him boosting from cars in the parking lot, so I bounced his sorry ass." Victor looked back up the hill. "Stealing's bad for business. It brings the cops down on the area. I don't want the heat around. So nobody steals."

"If you see him, will you let me know?"

Victor smoothed out his stubble. "I will. But then we're even."

"Even? For what?"

"It's a small world, Boy Scout. That lady who got robbed outside Ma Barker's? She's my *abuela*."

Jack racked his brain trying to remember his Spanish classes.

"If I hear something, I'll reach out." Victor tapped his chest with two fingers. Then he headed back up the hill.

Jack waved Chandler over and started walking away. Chandler jogged up beside him. When they were out of the park and out of Victor's sight, Chandler punched Jack's arm. "I told you those guys were bad news," Chandler growled in a low whisper.

Jack rubbed his arm. "That killed."

"Sorry. It was a little harder than I intended."

"A little? It felt like you hit me with a telephone pole."

"Yeah, well, you deserved it. The small guy with the big skull tattoo was packing."

"So was Victor."

"I hate being around gangbangers with guns. Who knows when someone's gonna start shooting? So, did Victor tell you anything?"

Jack looked back over his shoulder. The men returned to sit around the table again, one standing sentinel. "He kicked Tommy out of his crew for breaking into cars in the parking lot. He hasn't seen him."

"You believe him?"

"Victor's telling us straight. He doesn't know anything."

"How can you be so sure?"

"You know the old lady with the handbag?" Jack grinned. "She's Victor's *abuela*."

"His grandmother? No way."

Grandmother. I knew it was something like that.

Chandler kicked a rock. "So basically we don't know anything."

"Actually, I've got a plan to flush Two Point out."

11

YOU'RE NOT MY DATE

Jack held open the door to Tullie's Café, but Chandler didn't go in.

"What, you want a coffee now?" Chandler asked.

"No. Nina will be here soon."

Chandler stepped aside so a woman could exit. "How do you know that?"

"Makayla said Nina posts every detail of her life on Facebook. So I checked her page. She 'liked' Tullie's milkshake special and commented that she's getting one after work today."

"So she *might* be here. You could have told me that earlier," Chandler muttered as he walked in.

Inside the café, a few regulars sipped coffee, read, or chatted away. A long counter and stools ran the length of the front window, and six round tables the size of extra-large pizzas dotted the middle of the room. In the back was a counter where three teenagers waited for a customer to interrupt them from whatever they were doing on their phones.

They headed to the back counter. One of the three teenagers glanced up from her texting.

Jack turned to Chandler. "Get what you want. It's on me."

"No."

"I'm dragging you all over the place. The least I can do is get you a coffee."

Chandler peered into the glass counter and waved his hand. "No. The least you could do is get me an extra-large vanilla milkshake, a chocolate fudge bar…" He straightened up and added with a boyish grin, "And a strawberry-frosted sprinkle doughnut."

Jack held up a hand to the teenager. "Don't get him that." To Chandler he said, "Why don't you get a coffee and a breakfast sandwich, so you at least get some protein?"

"Because it doesn't taste as good."

"You're not getting all that junk."

"You're not my date. I can order for myself."

Jack leaned back. "Fine. Blow your weigh-in. I'll send you a postcard from Germany."

Chandler scowled.

The barista shifted uncomfortably, her eyes moving back and forth between them.

Chandler huffed. "Fine."

Jack pulled out his wallet. "I'm still paying."

Chandler ordered a coffee and a breakfast sandwich. Jack got a coffee and a biscuit.

"Counter or table?" Chandler asked.

"Table in the far corner," Jack said. "I want to keep an eye on the door."

"Smart. Where'd you learn that?"

"Clint Eastwood." Jack sat down and did his best *High Plains Drifter* impersonation. "You never put your back to the door, you keep your eyes on it."

They took their food, thanked the barista, who mumbled, "Have a good one"—not looking up from her phone—and went to the corner table. Jack nodded to the door. "Perfect angle."

Chandler took in the scene. "Yeah, that works." He turned to face Jack. "You're not turning into Dirty Harry, are you?"

Jack started to take a bite of his biscuit, but Chandler rapped Jack's knuckles with the handle of a fork.

"Ow." Jack shook his hand. "What was that for?"

"You didn't pray." Chandler bowed his head. "Dear Lord, please watch over our families while we're serving. Protect them here. Thank you for this food. In Jesus's name, amen."

"It's a biscuit," Jack said. "You don't have to pray for a snack."

"I'll tell Aunt Haddie you said so." Chandler unwrapped his sandwich.

"You're not going to do that at every meal when we go overseas though, right?" Jack asked.

"I most certainly am."

"Why? You're not going to be a chaplain."

"I'm just saying thank you. It's polite."

As they ate, Jack kept an eye on the door. They were quiet while Chandler finished up his sandwich, but when he was done, he nervously tapped the table. "What're we going to do, Jack?"

"What are we going to do about what?"

Chandler flicked a sugar packet across the table, using a fork like a hockey stick. "When we're overseas. I don't know what I'd do if something happened to anyone at Aunt Haddie's."

"I didn't think about that. I guess the Army would get us home."

"I can't even think about it. If something happened to them…"

"Hey." Jack flicked the sugar packet back, and it hit Chandler in the chest. "Have some faith."

"Yeah. I suppose." Chandler took the cover off his coffee and frowned. "You know this isn't going to taste anywhere near as good as a milkshake."

"Fifty calories versus a bazillion. Simple math."

"Speaking of math, you'd better watch how much money you're spending."

"I am."

"You killed yourself at that hardware store every weekend. Don't go blowing it on dates with uptown girls."

"I won't. I've got more than enough to make it to basic and enjoy the summer. And, hey, I like Kelly, so back off a little."

"Hmph. Okay, message received. Still, saving some is a good idea." Chandler ripped open three sugar packets and emptied them into his coffee. As he stirred, he kept his eyes on the cup. "You know…when I called your house, your mom kinda hinted at something."

"Spit it out."

"Well, she sorta asked me if I could ask you…"

Jack had a bad feeling about Chandler's hesitation.

"Can she bake you a birthday cake?"

"No," Jack snapped. "I hate Garbage Day."

"Stop calling it that. Come on, she really wants to."

"I know. I get it." Jack lowered his voice. "But it's *not* my birthday. It's the date the social workers put down on my file. Sorry, but I just can't stand the whole day. I hate it. I'm not going to celebrate it."

Chandler held up a hand. "Okay, okay. I understand. I'll let it go."

They waited in silence. Customers came and went, but no sign of Nina.

Jack finished his coffee. "Listen, if something were to happen overseas, you know, to one of us—"

"Nothing's gonna happen. I got your back." Chandler drained his coffee and grinned. "That was good."

Jack stared at his big friend and waited. He knew part of Chandler's secret to happiness—reduce everything to bare essentials: the food is good, I got your back, pray before every meal—but he still marveled at the quick turnaround from the subject of possible dangers ahead of them.

"What?" Chandler said.

Jack shrugged. "Was it good? Did you get enough to eat?"

"Yeah, that hit the spot. The turkey bacon rocked."

"I'm glad."

Jack waited again. The pause grew, along with Chandler's smile.

"You know I paid, right?" Jack said.

Chandler nodded. "Yup. You sure did."

Jack waited some more.

Chandler continued to smile.

"Well, are you going to say thank you?"

"What?" Chandler angled his head and made a face. "Do you want me to thank you every time you give me something?"

"Oh… I get it. The whole prayer thing," Jack said.

"It's polite."

Jack chucked a sugar packet at his friend. "You don't have to do it every time."

"Okay, I won't thank you every time."

Jack was going to say something more, but just then Nina came through the door. "She's here," he said.

Nina was known for her fashion, and she didn't disappoint, now in cuffed skinny jeans, black peep-toe booties, and a teal cross-front oversize tee. Another thing about Nina: if she wasn't bopping and moving to a music track in her head or talking—and she was pretty much always talking—she had to be moving, gesturing wildly with her hands or something. She was snapping her fingers when the door shut behind her.

Jack waved. Nina gave a quick nod that sent her large silver hoop earrings jangling, then headed to the counter. Jack and Chandler got up and joined her.

"Hi, Nina," Jack said. "How's it going?"

"Jack, haven't seen you in a while. What are you guys up to?"

"Actually, we're looking for Two Point," Jack said. He leaned one hand on the counter. "His mother's looking for him. Have you seen—"

"Nope," she answered curtly. "Not since Thursday." She turned to the clerk. "I'll have an extra-large vanilla shake."

Chandler frowned—whether about Two Point or Nina's order, Jack couldn't tell.

"His mom really needs to talk to him, Nina," Chandler said forcefully. "She's worried. Have you heard from him at all?"

"I haven't heard from him and I don't want to hear from him. You can tell him that when you see him. Nobody blows me off after a date. But nobody."

Nina went to pay, but Jack beat her to it. He handed the cash to the clerk and spoke to Nina. "He hasn't talked to you since Thursday? Hasn't even texted? What a jerk."

"Yep." She popped the *p*. As she stuffed her cash back in her faux-leather bag, she tilted her angular face and smiled politely. "Thank you. At least some men know how to treat a lady."

"No problem. We'll see you later." Jack took one step toward the door, then stopped. "Oh, I can't believe it. I forgot to call my mom. Give me your phone, Chandler."

Chandler looked puzzled. "I don't have a phone."

"Oh, that's right." Jack's eyes fell on Nina. "Nina…do you mind? I have to call my mom. Can I borrow your phone? Just for a second."

"Sure, hon."

As Nina handed Jack the phone, Jack winked at Chandler. A look of understanding spread across Chandler's face, and he turned to Nina. "Hey, I've been meaning to ask you. Makayla's birthday is coming up. Any suggestions for where I should shop for her?"

Elated, Nina steered Chandler to a table, prattling off a list of shops, malls, and boutiques—and her opinion about each of them—while Jack, just as elated, for different reasons, walked toward the back of the café and pretended to make a call. After a couple of minutes, he returned to the table to rescue Chandler.

"Thanks for the phone."

"Anytime," Nina said.

"C'mon, Chandler," Jack said. "Let's bounce."

As they walked outside, Chandler asked, "Where to now?"

Jack smiled. "To meet up with Two Point."

* * *

Jack and Chandler stood in the doorway of a shuttered nail salon and watched the apartment building across the street. Nina's apartment building.

"Why would Two Point come here now?" Chandler asked. "Nina's still at the coffee shop."

"He'll be here." Jack leaned against the wall.

"Why are you so sure?"

"Nina asked him to come." Jack smiled. "When I borrowed Nina's phone, I texted Two Point: *Parents out of house. Want some sugar? Come now.*"

Chandler grinned. "Oh, in that case…he'll be here, all right. Very smooth, Jack Stratton. I've taught you well."

They grinned at each other.

Ten minutes later, Two Point rounded the corner. He strutted down the street, one hand in his pocket, the other tapping out some beat on his thigh. Jack and Chandler jogged across the street to intercept him, but he bolted when he saw them coming.

Jack sprinted after him. Two Point was fast, but it was no contest. Two Point's shorts hung past his knees, limiting his stride, and Jack quickly closed the distance in a few long, powerful strides. *And that's why they call me Super Jack Flash.*

Two Point cut down an alley lined with trash bins and littered with garbage. A chain-link fence topped with barbed wire blocked passage about halfway down the alley. It had a gate, but it was padlocked shut. Two Point wasn't getting away.

Jack caught up, grabbed his shirt, and pulled him to a stop.

"Why are you running, Two?" Jack pinned him to the wall.

Two Point struggled. "Screw you, Stratton."

"I asked you a question. Why'd you take off?"

"Stop…" Chandler panted as he ran up "…running."

Two Point tried to bolt again, but Chandler grabbed his arm.

"What?" Two Point pushed Chandler, with no effect whatsoever. Chandler's eyes narrowed. Two Point stopped struggling. "What do you guys want?"

"Why'd you run?" Jack asked again.

"I heard you were looking for me."

"So you ran?" Chandler tightened his grip.

"Let go of me. I'll call the cops."

"Call them." Jack got in his face. "Listen, I know you know about J-Dog."

"What about him?"

"He got arrested," Jack said.

"For stealing a wallet and using it at the ATM," Chandler added.

"That's bull!" Two Point yanked his shirt free. "J-Dog didn't do nothin'."

"I know." Jack crossed his arms. "*You* did."

Two Point froze for a second, then his fake swagger came rushing back. "Me? I wasn't even there, man."

"I have proof," Jack said.

"You buggin'. What proof?"

"A picture."

Chandler and Two Point looked equally puzzled.

"You're lying," Two Point said.

"No. See, girls like to take pictures on dates." Jack pulled out a piece of paper from his pocket. "And girls also just love to post on Facebook. You took Nina to the movies Thursday night, correct?"

"What of it?"

"I figure you wanted to impress Nina Fashionista, so you had to dress up. And since you have no taste or style, you borrowed your older brother's jacket and shoes."

Two Point smacked his hands together. "That stupid…" He shifted his weight to his heels and glanced down the alley.

Jack held up the picture he'd printed out. Two Point was standing next to a smiling Nina in front of the movie theater, wearing a white jacket with red stripes, and white basketball sneakers. "This is the jacket I saw the police carrying out in their evidence bag when they arrested J-Dog."

Two Point looked up and down the alley. Chandler blocked the exit back to the street.

"I don't know what you're talking about," Two Point repeated. "Did J-Dog find a wallet? If he did, it's nothin'. He's got no record. They'll slap his wrist and let him go."

Jack slowly shook his head. "Did you read that name on the ATM card you tried to use?"

Two Point stared at Jack.

"Stacy Shaw ring a bell?"

Two Point hiked up his shorts so they didn't droop anymore. "Who?"

"She's that lady who's missing," Jack said.

Two Point went pale.

"The cops put J-Dog in the Bay because they think he had something to do with it. He got roughed up pretty bad the first night. Your mother is going out of her mind."

"So?"

Jack grabbed Two Point's shirt and yanked him forward. "I'm trying to help your brother, and you're screwing around, lying to me. *You* borrowed his jacket, and it was *you* who put the wallet there. The cops found it. J-Dog knew it must have been you who took it, but you're on probation, so J-Dog said he found it to cover for you."

Two Point looked bored. "So?" he said again.

"Your brother's in prison because of you!" Chandler stuck a huge finger in Two Point's face. "What's wrong with you?" he shouted. "He's watching out for you, but you're just going to let him take the blame? He's your *brother*. Your father would be so disappointed, so upset. You should see how bad your mother looks."

Two Point's glare softened. "Okay. I'm not saying I found it…but what if I did."

Jack let go of his shirt. "Say you did."

"I didn't, but let's just say…" Two Point kicked a crushed can down the alley and started to pace. "What good's it gonna do if I tell the cops that?"

"An innocent guy, *who happens to be your brother*, who happens to be trying to do the right thing, is going to get out of prison, for one!" Chandler yelled.

Two Point tapped his own chest with a long finger. "And I'd be in. They'd put *me* in the Bay."

"Not if you tell them the truth," Jack said. "How did you get the wallet?"

"I found it." Two Point grabbed the handle of a trash bin and shook it. "And you think the cops would believe that?"

"Yeah, I do." Jack looked down at the picture still in his hands.

"They'd believe a lily-white kid like you, Stratton, but there's no way they'd even hear me out."

"That's bull—"

Two Point shoved a trash barrel at Jack, turned, and sprinted toward the locked gate. Jack was taken by surprise for only a moment, then bolted after him.

"You're not going anywhere!" Chandler called out as Two Point ran.

Two Point grabbed the gate and yanked. The padlocked chain was wrapped around it loosely, and Two Point's slender frame was able to slip through.

Jack tried to squeeze through after him, but his chest was too broad. He couldn't fit. His hand grasped at the air as Two Point scrambled away.

"Ha!" Two Point taunted, jogging away backward.

"You can't run forever!" Jack kicked the chain link in disgust.

Chandler walked up behind him. "Don't worry about it," he said. "He has to go home sometime."

12

THE RED WHISTLE

"What a slimy piece of garbage," Jack grumbled as they crossed the road to cut through Hamilton Park.

"So, J-Dog was telling the truth after all," Chandler said. "It makes sense now. Why else would Jay not say anything? He'd do anything for Two." He shook his head. "But taking the rap for stealing from an ATM?"

"Jay's been trying to step up since his dad died. When he confessed," Jack said, "he didn't know anything about this missing woman or Two Point trying to use her ATM card. He wouldn't have known just how much he was confessing to. He probably assumed Two just boosted a purse. He thought he was pleading guilty to petty theft, just a misdemeanor."

"And Two Point's on probation, so Jay figured he'd take the hit," Chandler said, shaking his head. Jack and Chandler were both having a lot of trouble swallowing the brother-on-brother betrayal.

"Yep. And now it's too late. Even if he told the truth now—which he won't, because he would never flip on his brother—no one would believe him. It's his word against Two's."

"What about the Facebook picture?" Chandler asked, looking for an optimistic twist. "Can you show it to that detective you know?"

"Detective Clark. I'll try."

They were walking toward a little man-made pond about the size of a kidney-shaped football field. Beside it stood a white wooden pavilion, and inside, a woman paced back and forth from railing to railing, muttering to herself and jerking her head. They gave her as wide a berth as possible as they passed, but Jack kept glancing over his shoulder to look back.

Chandler gave him a little shove. "Don't stare."

"Do you see her bag?"

"Yeah."

"It's tan with gold swirls."

"So? Let's go." Chandler nudged him.

Jack walked back toward the pavilion.

"What are you doing?" Chandler muttered. "She looks crazy. Let's just go."

Jack ignored his friend and headed for the pavilion. Before he reached the steps, the woman stopped pacing and spun around to face him. Her face was thin, and her scraggly hair was wispy. In the pale light it looked like a dandelion that was missing chunks of its fluffy seeds. Jack could see clear through to her scalp. Her hand flew to the big red whistle on a chain around her neck.

Jack held up his hand as if he were approaching a frightened animal. "Hello." He softened his voice and posture as he stopped on the bottom step. The wood creaked. "I was wondering if I could ask you a question."

The woman clutched her whistle tighter and looked sideways at Jack. "You're not a policeman."

Jack nodded. "You're right, I'm not a policeman. But I was wondering where you got such a pretty handbag."

She clutched the bag tight. The whistle rattled in her hand. "It's mine."

"I'm sure it is." Jack smiled. "I thought it looked so pretty that I should get one for my girlfriend."

"It is pretty." The woman's finger traced along a gold swirl on the side of the handbag. "I like your cap. Red, like my whistle."

"Thank you. Do you know where I could get a bag like that for my girlfriend? Where did you get yours?"

She shook her head, and the wisps of hair fluttered. One hand went to her head to tamp down the flyaways. "I don't know where to buy one. Who are you?" she asked.

"I'm Jack. What's your name?"

"Robyn."

"That's a nice name." Jack looked closely at the bag. "Where did you *find* that handbag, Robyn?"

"Number thirteen."

"Thirteen?"

Robyn pointed toward the benches that lined the path through the park. "I count them. I don't like thirteen so I won't sit there. I like your hat."

"Thanks. Thirteen benches down from where?"

"The fountain."

"Thirteen benches from the fountain heading to Main Street?"

She nodded.

Jack paused. He wanted to ask Chandler to do something, but if he broke eye contact with Robyn, she'd probably dart away like a frightened bird. "Where was the handbag? On the bench?"

Her whistle rattled when she shook her head. "In the woods." She clutched the bag again. "Someone threw it away. Now it's mine."

"Yes, it's yours. Did you see who threw away the handbag?"

"No. I found it."

"Why were you in the woods?" Chandler asked.

"I had to pee."

"Okay…" Jack tried not to make a face. "So you went into the woods?"

Robyn nodded and said, "Your hat's red like my whistle. My whistle is real loud. Do you want to hear it?" She lifted it toward her lips.

"NO," Jack and Chandler said in unison.

"If I blow it, my friends will come. We watch out for each other in the park. It's really, really loud."

"I bet it is. Did you find anything else in the woods?" Jack said.

"Nope." Robyn shook her head vigorously. "My whistle's red." She held it up. "Like your hat."

Jack took the cap off. "Would you like my hat?"

"I'll take it!" Her hand shot up like a little girl who knew the answer in her favorite class. "It matches my whistle."

"Well, I'm not sure I can give it up." Jack looked down at the hat in his hands. "What about if I trade you for it?"

Robyn eyed him suspiciously and darted backward. "I don't have anything to trade."

"How about that bag? It's tan and it doesn't match your whistle."

"It doesn't." She nodded, but not too enthusiastically.

"What about my red hat and ten dollars?" Jack took a ten out of his pocket.

Robyn nodded rapidly. She reached into the handbag and took out a plastic shopping bag.

"Was that plastic bag in the handbag when you found it?" Jack asked.

"No. It's mine. I didn't take anything out of the handbag. Those things belong there. Things should stay where they belong."

Jack put the ten in his baseball cap, set it down on the floor of the pavilion, and stepped back. "I'll just leave it here."

With three quick steps, Robyn darted forward, put the handbag on the ground, grabbed the hat, and hurried away. Like a bird with a bit of shiny string, she flitted to the far side of the pavilion, admiring her prize.

"Thank you." Jack picked up the handbag.

As Jack and Chandler walked away, Chandler looked at Jack. "Isn't that your dad's hat?"

"What?" Jack spun around. "Oh, no! No way. Are you sure? I must have put the wrong hat in my gym bag."

Robyn was walking back and forth in the pavilion, muttering to herself again. Sure enough, Jack could see now that she was wearing his dad's Special Edition Red Sox cap. It was similar to Jack's, but Jack could tell the difference, and his dad certainly would.

"I'm an idiot," Jack grumbled as he turned back around. "That's his favorite fishing hat. I'm a dead man."

Chandler patted him on the shoulder. "He'll get over it. So why did you make that trade anyway?"

Jack held up the handbag. "I think this is Stacy Shaw's. The missing person flyer said she had a tan handbag with gold swirls."

Jack opened it and looked inside. He was careful not to touch anything, but by shifting the bag around he was able to see all its contents. There was a glasses case, a set of keys, lip balm, half a package of antacids, a compact, some hair clips and elastics, a hairbrush, hand wipes, two pens, a black case the size of a thick book, a bottle of prenatal vitamins, and two business cards—one for Luisa's Luxe Hair Studio and one for a fertility clinic.

"You really think it's hers?" Chandler asked.

"Maybe. It's quite a coincidence if it isn't. Especially since there's a diabetic alert tag on the key ring. Come on." Jack headed back into the park.

"Where are we going now?"

"The fountain. Then we need to go thirteen benches down."

13

THIRTEEN BENCHES

"Thirteen," Chandler announced. The bench sat at the edge of the walking path between two hills, at the bottom of a little valley. Jack jogged up the slope behind the bench. At the top, a large grassy field stretched away until it connected with another path in the distance. With no bushes or trees, it was a perfect spot for picnicking or playing Frisbee.

Chandler caught up with Jack, huffing and puffing. "Now what?"

Jack headed back down the slope. "Come on." He motioned for Chandler to follow. "Robyn found the handbag on the other side."

Chandler exhaled loudly. "How do you know where she found it?"

"She said she found it when she was peeing in the woods. This side looks like a golf course, so it has to be the other side."

"You should have asked her to come and point out where she found it."

"She never would have come with us." Jack briskly walked past the bench and up the slope on the other side.

"Why are you hustling?" Chandler said.

"Stacy."

"What? You think she's here? Her car was found at Ford's Crossing."

"And her bag, if this is her bag, was found here. Look, if Stacy left town or something, she would have taken her purse. My dad says a woman never leaves her purse anywhere. Remember Victor's grandmother? She held on to her handbag like her life depended on it."

Chandler nodded. "Sure, but you really think Stacy could be out here, alive?"

"Maybe she was trying to get back home and ended up here somehow. She was in an accident and she's diabetic. Vargas said she could be disoriented. She could be injured or hurt somewhere nearby. It's a big park, a lot of woods."

They reached the top of the hill and stopped again. The sun was low in the sky and the shadows stretched long across the ground. The grass here was wild and unmowed. Scrub undergrowth was mixed with trash. The ground sloped away quickly, but a hundred yards distant, they could see the corner of the pond and cattail reeds at the edge of the marshy area.

To their right, the ground sloped back up a bit and the brush and reeds gave way to maple and pine trees, creating a small stretch of forest.

Chandler pointed to a trail that cut into the woods. "There's a path over there."

Jack pointed to a different spot. "See those two small spruce trees? Perfect potty."

"Gross. I'll wait here."

"Germaphobe," Jack muttered.

Jack walked toward the trees, scanning the ground as he went. The scrub brush at the edge of the grass was full of litter that probably ended up here after being blown by the wind. Plastic bags and discarded fast-food wrappers waved like small flags in the breeze.

Jack checked the area around the two spruces. The spot was shielded from sight, but nothing stood out among the remains of old beer bottles, their jagged bottoms protruding from the ground like punji stakes. He looked back to see where Chandler was, and saw him studying something in the scrub brush.

"Did you find something?" Jack jogged over.

Chandler pointed in the direction of the pond. "I think someone went that way. Look, these branches are broken."

The stubby pine Chandler pointed to was dead, but brown needles still clung to the branches like ribs on a skeleton. Several of its lower branches were snapped off, and the tall grass in front of the bush had been crushed down in the direction of the pond.

Jack cupped his hands to his mouth. "Stacy!"

Silence was the only reply.

They picked their way through the underbrush toward the pond. The scrubby plants changed to cattails, and then they came upon a two-foot-wide section of crushed and broken reeds. Someone had obviously trampled through.

"I'm getting the heebie-jeebies right about now," Chandler said.

Jack peered down. The ground was spongy, but not wet. The reeds were dry and snapped off easily in his hand.

"Maybe it was some kids going fishing."

They kept walking. The trail of crushed reeds ran in a straight line to the pond. A short muddy bank with rocks spotted by dark-brown algae led to the water's mucky edge. This area, too, was littered with trash. Nearby, the remains of a rusted bike frame were chained to a scrawny maple. The seat, handlebars, and tires had long since been stripped away. At Jack's feet, the tire from a lawnmower stuck halfway out of the muck. He poked at it with the heel of his sneaker, and a rotten, wet compost stench rose up.

Jack's lip curled as he looked at the murky water. Lily pads and weeds choked the surface. The handle of an abandoned shopping cart rose out of the water ten feet from the shore.

Discouraged by the scene and by the dead-end search, Jack said, "If she did come this way, she must have turned back around."

"I think it had to be a fisherman who made this path," Chandler said. "It ends right at the bank."

A swarm of gnats discovered Jack and clustered around his face. He waved them away. "Who would fish in this water?"

Somewhere back the way they'd come, a tree branch snapped. Jack spun around and peered into the woods, and Chandler jumped.

"Stacy?" Jack called out.

The brush and trees moved in the slight breeze. A squirrel darted along a branch and disappeared into the leaves. But something felt wrong. The hairs on the back of Jack's neck rose.

Chandler started to move, but Jack held up his hand, signaling him to stop.

"What?" Chandler asked.

"Apart from that snapping branch, did you hear something else?"

"Are you trying to freak me out? You don't need to. I didn't hear anything besides me wetting my pants."

Jack couldn't shake the feeling that someone was watching them. He looked around, but saw no one.

"I think it was just the— Look!" Chandler pointed.

Jack looked toward the rusted bike frame. Just beyond it, a green trash bag lay open on the ground, with something sticking out. Jack couldn't see what it was in the fading light. Then the wind blew the plastic, and it fluttered closed. Jack walked toward it. Chandler followed just behind him, matching each step.

When they reached the bag, Jack grabbed a fallen branch and crouched down. The stick felt wet but not rotted. He stuck the branch in the opening of the bag. Slowly he lifted the plastic to see what lay underneath.

A worn brown boot stuck partway out.

"It's just a boot." Jack exhaled and stood back up. "Let's go check that other path. It's getting dark."

They had both started back the way they'd come when Chandler suddenly stopped and held his arm against Jack's chest.

"Don't tell me you found the other boot?" Jack said.

Chandler didn't reply. His fingers grabbed the front of Jack's shirt and tightened involuntarily.

Jack followed Chandler's gaze to a short, twisted holly tree. As a slight breeze blew down the hill, the strings of a hanging spiderweb reflected the light against the dark green holly leaves.

Except the web wasn't gray or white. It was golden.

Coils of dread tightened around Jack's chest. His breath stalled.

It wasn't a spider's web.

"Oh, snap. It's hair." Chandler turned away in horror.

Jack looked back up the hill. From this angle, it was easy to see the destruction that someone had made along the way. A direct path from the broken branches, past the holly tree—and the golden blond hair—to the pond.

Jack turned back toward the pond and Chandler followed.

The sun poked out from the evening clouds, bringing out the greens in the lily pads. The light danced on the water, but now that Jack was looking for it, he saw one spot, only a few feet from the muddy bank, that sparkled slightly differently from the rest.

Cold sweat ran down his back, pinning his shirt to his skin. His throat tightened. He picked up a fallen branch and moved over to the water's edge.

"What do you see?" Chandler asked.

Jack heard the question, but his focus was on the water. He squatted down, reached out with the branch as far as he could, and slowly pushed away a couple of lily pads.

Just under the surface lay Stacy Shaw.

"Damn."

14

MY OWN LYING EYES

Jack sat alone at a cold metal table in the police department interrogation room. After driving them to the police station, they had split up Jack and Chandler and now Jack stared blankly at the empty chair across from him.

The stench of the bog had seeped into his clothes and he couldn't get the odor out of his nostrils no matter how many times he blew his nose. Even his skin seemed different—cold—and he felt hollow inside.

The door to the room swung wide, and Detective Clark stuck his head in. "You okay, Jack?"

Jack wanted to lie and say yes. He knew horrible crime scenes were part of the job of being a policeman. But when he looked up at the old detective, he didn't say anything. He just cocked his head slightly to the left, his right shoulder rising with it.

"Appalling, isn't it—death?"

"Yeah."

"How about something from the soda machine?" Clark gestured for Jack to follow him. "Some sugar will help with the shock."

"I remember my first DOA," Clark said as they walked down a back hallway to an alcove with a vending machine. "It was an elderly gentleman. He had died at a ripe old age of natural causes, but it still bothered me for weeks." He pressed the only button on the soda machine that didn't have a red light on. He handed Jack a can. "Has this put you off a career in law enforcement?"

The cold liquid felt good on Jack's dry throat. He stared into the can and thought about Clark's question, then took another long sip. "If it wasn't me who found her, it would have been someone else, right? So, no. I'm not rethinking it."

A uniformed officer peeked his head in. "Detective Clark, got a second?"

"I'll be right back. If you need to use the men's room, it's right there." Clark pointed at a door down the hallway and stepped away with the officer, leaving Jack alone in the alcove. The soda machine hummed, the air conditioner buzzed, and the overhead lights made a faint clicking to add to the electrical chorus. Jack knew he was in the middle of a police station surrounded by police officers and firepower, but the hallway seemed cavernous. He felt raw and exposed. He pushed his back tight against the wall and closed his eyes.

Jack pictured the golden light on the pond and the horror beneath the water. He could see Stacy there, hovering just beneath the surface—floating like a ghost. Her beautiful blond hair drifted around her angelic face like tendrils.

He closed his eyes and tried to calm his breathing. He willed himself to change the picture in his mind, but somehow he could only see her face. He was used to nightmares—but he wasn't used to not being able to escape the terror when he was awake.

Jack's eyes flashed open. Hanging on the wall directly across from him was a missing person poster for Stacy Shaw, her eyes bright and so full of life.

He felt sick.

A door opened down the hallway, and a woman's voice said, "Detective Vargas?"

"Superintendent Finney, come on in."

They lowered their voices, but because of the echo in the narrow corridor, Jack could still clearly hear them.

"I have the ME's report," the superintendent said. "Manual strangulation. He couldn't give us an exact time, but he puts preliminary time of death between seven and eleven Thursday night. He also confirmed she was pregnant, eleven weeks along."

Jack had feared that would be the case because of the prenatal vitamins in Stacy's purse.

"Any evidence of sexual assault?" Vargas asked.

"Inconclusive."

"Well, the time of death fits with what we know. She worked late that night. Her manager"—papers shuffled—"Leland Chambers said he last saw her a little after seven, and the custodian saw her about forty-five minutes after that. Another employee, Betty Robinson, spoke with Stacy when she left the building at quarter till eight. Her husband, Michael, called her from his hotel in Schenectady, New York, and spoke to her at seven fifty-two p.m. He called again at nine, but got no answer. Her phone was on the same cell tower for both calls." More papers shuffled. "Not a surprise. The Morse Hill cell tower covers both her work and Ford's Crossing, where her car was found."

"Her phone was found in the car?" Finney asked.

"On the front seat. Keys were still in the ignition."

"When did the state trooper find the car?"

"Ten fifteen."

"So she was killed sometime between eight and ten."

"Yes. Small window."

"If she was attacked and killed in the park," the superintendent said, "why would her car be a mile away?"

Vargas coughed. "We don't know. Maybe the killer took her car for a joy ride."

"Have you pulled all the video surveillance cameras between the two locations?"

"We started pulling them when she went missing. So far there's nothing." Vargas let out a long breath. "But we did get a hit on Jay Martin's sneakers. The blood on the edge of the sole—it's Stacy's. The blood samples found on the rocks at the top of the hill are Stacy's as well. He must have dragged her across the rocks. She had a deep laceration on her heel."

"Well, that puts a bow on it. Nice work." A chair slid back.

"Thanks. I just wish it had ended differently," Vargas said. Another chair scraped against the floor. "Well, I've got to go interview those two guys who found the body."

"Keep me posted."

A door clicked closed, and Jack heard the superintendent's heels move down the hallway in the opposite direction.

He stared at Stacy's picture on the wall. *They think it's Jay. They're pretty certain of it. But it wasn't. Someone killed you, but not him.*

Stacy's eyes seemed to meet his, and more than anything, he wished he could ask her one question. "Do you know who killed you?"

* * *

The stoic police officer standing at the interrogation room door moved to the side when Jack entered, and Detective Vargas smiled. Vargas may have been wearing a neatly pressed business suit with highly polished shoes, but he still had the bearing of a soldier. He strode over to the other side of the table, across from Jack, and pulled a chair back, but didn't sit down. Instead, he placed an evidence bag with the tan and gold handbag on the table.

"So you're Jack Stratton?" His hard, dark-brown eyes studied Jack's face.

Jack nodded.

"Well, Jack, I need to ask you a few questions." His tone was much harsher than it had been with the superintendent.

Jack nodded again.

"Let's start with this handbag." Vargas held it up.

The overhead light glared on the evidence bag and made the gold swirls sparkle. The image of Stacy's golden hair glittering under the water flashed into Jack's mind. He felt sick to his stomach.

"Do you recognize this?"

Numbly, he nodded then looked away.

"I need your verbal confirmation. Look at it again, please." Vargas gave the bag a little shake.

Jack forced his eyes up. "That's the bag I found."

"Can you please tell me how you came to find it?"

Jack explained how he saw Robyn with the bag and recognized it from the description in the flyers, and then how he got it from her.

"Wait a minute. You paid this homeless woman for evidence?"

"No... She had the bag and I didn't think that she'd just give it to me, so I traded her for it."

Vargas frowned. "Why didn't you contact the police when you saw her with the bag?"

Jack sat back. Chandler had wanted to go to the police, but Jack hadn't listened to him. "I guess because I didn't know for certain that it was Stacy's."

"But you recognized it because of the flyer? Where did you get this flyer?"

"Detective Clark. He was handing them out at the basketball court in Hamilton Park."

Vargas sat down and folded his hands on the table. "I heard you know Detective Clark."

"He's a friend of my dad's."

"So Clark gave you one of these flyers a couple of days ago?"

"Yes, sir."

"And you remembered the description of that handbag. That's some seriously good police work."

Jack wanted to accept the comment as a compliment, but there was something about the detective's undertone that made Jack question whether he was sincere.

"I also heard you want to be a cop," Vargas continued.

"Yes, sir. I'm going into the Army first."

"I did that too. The Army was good to me. I did six years, then I moved right into law enforcement. San Antonio."

"I'm doing two years, then college."

"Why not go right to college?"

"Money."

"That's why I didn't go." Vargas leaned back in his chair. "Your parents aren't helping you out?"

The question bothered Jack. "My dad has to retire early. Health issues. This is his last year teaching. I don't want him to worry about my school."

"Very considerate." Vargas's praise didn't match the look in his dark eyes. "You told the responding officer that you didn't touch any of the items in the handbag, is that correct?"

"Yeah. I just looked inside."

"Why?"

"To see if it was Stacy's. I saw the medic alert tag. That's when I figured it was hers."

Vargas crossed his arms. "And you didn't call the police then?"

"I planned to, but Robyn told me where she found it and I wanted to check that out."

"But you said earlier that you didn't call the police when you first saw the bag because you weren't sure it was Stacy's. You looked inside. Now you're sure. I think you would have called them at that point." Vargas planted his feet on the floor and rocked back in the chair. "You knew it was hers then, right? You said so. Tan with gold swirls and a diabetic medic alert tag inside." Vargas looked at the cop at the door, and they both nodded as if they had come to a mutual understanding. "So after you… *traded* for this handbag, you went to…" Vargas flipped open a notebook and scanned the page. "You went thirteen benches down from the fountain. Thirteen benches? That's pretty specific directions this homeless woman gave you."

"Robyn's superstitious. She doesn't sit on the thirteenth bench."

"And then what? You went straight to Stacy's body?" Vargas's tone had changed. There was an edge to it.

"No. I got to the bench—"

"Just you?"

"No. Chandler was with me, but he just came because I asked."

"So, you're at the bench, what then? Did Robyn tell you that she found it on the east side?"

"No, but she did say that she found it when she was going to the bathroom in the woods. The east side, if that's the side toward the pond, has trees. The other side is open grass."

"What made you go to the pond?"

"Well, we saw some branches were snapped and we followed them."

"That led you to the body?"

"No, we turned around to leave and then we saw…" Jack swallowed. "Saw some blond hair on this holly bush."

"How far away were you from the hair when you saw it?"

"Chandler saw it first. He was close, a few feet maybe. It stood out. It's blond and the holly leaves are dark green."

"That's still pretty far away from the pond."

"The reeds were broken—the path was obvious."

Vargas steepled his fingers. "The reeds were broken? Reeds?" He exchanged a quizzical look with the policeman near the door. "I thought reeds bend. But either way, are you a hunter?"

"A hunter?" Jack asked, confused. "No. Why?"

"I'm trying to figure out how you became a tracker."

"You don't have to be a tracker to see that path. It was clear that someone went that way. Perhaps dragged a body. They were those dry reeds that break when you touch them. Chandler thought a fisherman made the path but—"

"But you didn't call the police?"

"To tell them that I found a path?"

"To alert us that you found the handbag and all that you suspected. You want to be a cop, right? What would a uniformed officer be required to do?"

"Call it in," Jack conceded. "But—"

"So you trampled down the path and contaminated a crime scene?" Vargas grumbled.

Jack held up both hands palms out. "I didn't know it was a crime scene. I still hoped she was alive. I was just trying to help."

"Help?" Vargas stuck his tongue in his cheek. "Oh, that's right, you want to be a cop. But I'm trying to figure out who you're *really* helping. You see, we have a suspect in Stacy Shaw's disappearance. His name's Jay Martin. We put him in the Bay until he decides that he wants to cooperate. Make him sweat and tell us what happened to Stacy. That, and I wanted to see who he'd talk to."

Jack straightened up.

"And someone did come to speak to Jay." Vargas dragged his finger across his notebook page. "I see that Jack Stratton is listed on the visitor log of Long Bay Prison. And you visited Jay Martin."

"Yeah, but, but," Jack stammered, "I drove his mother there."

"So you're a friend of Jay Martin's?"

Jack tried to hold his tongue, but restraint lost out to youthful indignation. "Friend? No. Actually, I can't stand the guy."

"You want me to believe that? Sure. You're just a Good Samaritan. Is that why you were in the park?"

"I was cutting through. I saw the handbag—"

"And then you just happened to go straight to where the body was. Next thing I know, you're going to tell me that Jay isn't the real killer."

"He's not. Jay's telling the truth."

Vargas let his head roll to the side. He looked at the uniformed officer and laughed. "Didn't I just tell him he'd say that?"

The cop nodded.

Jack's stomach churned. "No. It's not like that. Jay's brother borrowed his jacket and shoes. For a date. I can prove it. I have pictures." Jack patted himself down, trying to remember where he'd put them.

"So do I." Vargas flipped open a folder to show a picture of a black male at the ATM. It only caught a sliver of the man's face, but Jay's distinct jacket was clearly visible.

Vargas's finger bent when he jammed it down on the picture. "There's an old saying, Jack. Who am I gonna believe, you or my own lying eyes?"

"That's Two Point," Jack stammered. "Tommy Martin. Jay's brother."

"Ha!" The word popped from Vargas's lips. "You want to know what I think?" He put his elbows on the table and his brown eyes bored holes in Jack. "I think you're screwing with my investigation so you can help out your friend Jay Martin."

"No…"

"Clark thinks that you're just some wide-eyed kid who wants to be a detective someday, but I'm not buying it." Vargas crossed his arms. "I think you're a punk, helping out someone in his crew. You went to the prison and met with Jay. He told you where he dumped Stacy Shaw's body. That's how you went right to it. You didn't 'find' it. You knew exactly where it was."

Jack rubbed his temples. He felt as though his head was about to explode. "I was trying to help and—"

"Why should I believe you?"

Jack's mind raced as he struggled to figure out a way to prove his innocence. "How could I have known in advance the homeless lady had the handbag? And if I did, why wouldn't I just leave an anonymous tip? That would lead you to the handbag and then to the body. If I was trying to help Jay Martin, then why say it was his brother and not 'someone framed him' or something? There's a million different scenarios. If—"

Vargas held up a hand. "Well, the facts say otherwise, but out of respect for Detective Clark, let's just say I give you the benefit of the doubt and say you really were just trying to help out."

"I was."

"Then make no mistake about it, Nancy Drew: from here on out, stay the hell away from my investigation." Vargas took his gold badge off his belt and held it in Jack's face. "Do you see this? It's a detective badge. See what it says? *Detective* Vargas." He put the badge on the table and tapped it. "Do you have one? No. Because you're not a detective. You're not an officer. You're nobody. Get that through your head. If I catch you within ten yards of that park or anyone with anything to do with my investigation, I'll charge you with obstruction so fast your head will spin." He looked at the cop and gestured to Jack. "Get him the hell out of my sight."

The policeman motioned to Jack. Jack stood and looked down at Vargas. He didn't glare. He didn't smirk. Just stared.

"You want to say something?" Vargas picked his badge up and buffed it on his sleeve. "Don't dig your hole any deeper."

Jack clamped his mouth shut and stalked out of the room.

15

UNLOVABLE

Jack and Chandler were sitting at the kitchen table, waiting for Aunt Haddie, when she finally walked in, after eleven. She looked exhausted. Everyone knew her for her smile and the twinkle in her eyes. Tonight, she almost didn't look like the same woman; both boys saw the deep lines of concern on her face, the gray in her hair, and the slump in her shoulders. For the first time in his life, Jack realized she was getting old.

Jack decided it was best not to tell her what Vargas had said to him at the police station. He stood and got her a ginger ale.

"How's Mrs. Martin?" Chandler asked.

Aunt Haddie rubbed her eyes and smiled thinly at Jack as he handed her the glass. "Not good. They're going to charge Jay with murder."

Jack leaned against the table. He had known it was coming, but it still rocked him. Vargas's words haunted him now. *Who are you gonna believe…*

"Is there anything we can do?" Chandler asked.

Aunt Haddie sighed. "Pray. That's a start." She patted Jack's shoulder. "It's late. Why don't you stay over, Jackie? Your old bedroom's open."

Jack nodded.

Aunt Haddie kissed Chandler's cheek and the top of Jack's head. "Thank you both for trying." She shuffled down the hallway.

"Do you think Two Point did it?" Chandler asked Jack, once she was gone.

"I don't think so," Jack said. "Stacy Shaw was strangled. Remember when Two Point broke his wrist trying to go down the library stairs on his bike? His left hand is still all screwed up. I don't think he'd be physically able to strangle anyone, even a small woman, with one hand."

"I forgot about the hand."

"Besides, he's a pansy. You know how Bobbie G calls him Tommy Two Feet because he runs away if someone says boo. Stealing and running? Yeah, that I'd buy, but not murder."

"Yeah," said Chandler. "I agree. He's gone down a bad path, but this … yeah. It's not Tommy."

The two friends talked for a bit more, then Chandler excused himself to go upstairs to bed.

Jack was tired, but he knew he couldn't fall asleep, and he wasn't in a rush to go lie down and stare at the ceiling. So he just sat there at the kitchen table, listening to the sounds of the old house. It was familiar. It was comforting.

He turned toward the sound of footsteps in the hallway. Aunt Haddie worked her way down the hall.

"Do you have a second, Jackie?"

Jack sat up straighter when she pulled back a chair and sat down.

"Mrs. Martin wanted me to thank you."

"Thank me? A lot of good I did. I got Jay looking at a murder charge."

"But you tried." She reached out and patted his hand.

"Well, at least I'm done messing up."

"No. Now Jay needs your help even more."

"*My* help?" Jack looked into the old woman's eyes. She had no idea how close he and Chandler had come to getting arrested. "The only person who can help Jay is Tommy."

"No, Charlotte finally heard from Tommy today. I hate to say this, but he's not going to do anything. Tommy said Jay is on his own."

"Yeah, that's what Tommy told us too. I can't tell you what I think of him…" She shot him a look that might not have been totally disapproving of whatever insult he was about to level at Tommy. "But in that case," he continued, "Jay needs to talk to his lawyer. Or the police. And I told Jay that."

"He did speak with his lawyer. They don't believe him. Jackie… no one else is going to step up."

"There's nothing I can do. I already stuck my neck out—not for Jay but for his mom's sake—and what did it get me? I thought they were going to arrest me for a minute. I don't like Jay anyway. He's done enough bad stuff in his life that he never paid the price for. What goes around comes around. I can't help him."

Aunt Haddie pointed at the kitchen door. "Ever since the first time you walked in here, you told me that one day you're going to be an officer of the peace."

He nodded but kept silent, to let her make her point.

"Well, what kind of policeman do you want to be? Are you only going to help white folk?"

Jack's mouth dropped open and his eyes went wide. "*What?*"

"No need to raise your voice."

"Seriously?" Jack pointed at himself. "No way you're saying I'm a racist!"

"Of course not." Aunt Haddie held up a hand. "Now lower your voice, or better yet, listen. You wouldn't think twice about the color of someone's skin. I know that about you as certainly as I know the sky is blue. But how can you draw a line on who you'll help? And where do you draw that line? Are you only going to help little old ladies whose purses get stolen?"

"That's different. She needed my help."

"*Jay* needs your help. You and I both know he didn't do it. But no one else believes him."

"The little old lady was nice," Jack muttered.

"Oh, so you're only going to help *nice* folk. What about rich folk? How about plump middle-aged ladies like me? Or are you only going to help young skinny girls?"

"Wait, Aunt Haddie, please. Do you know why they call him J-Dog? It's short for Junkyard Dog. He's—" Jack exhaled. "Do you know why I hate him? I had a pin. It was a cheap silver pin, half of it looked like it got run over by a car, but at the top it said *Hope*. My birth mother gave it to me. She said my father gave it to her. It was the only thing I had from either of them. I took it off when we went swimming, and guess what? A little later, I caught J-Dog in the act of stealing it. And instead of giving it back to me, he threw it in the pond."

Aunt Haddie looked both confused and angry. "Why?"

Jack shrugged. "Because he's mean. I doubt he even knows why he did it. Aunt Haddie, some people are born mean."

Aunt Haddie's voice softened. "And some people change."

Jack huffed.

"Black, white, rich, poor, or mean as a dog—a carpenter's son I know came to help everyone, even those who don't change. And that's what we're supposed to do. Love the unlovable."

Jack looked away.

"You don't know why a person acts the way they do. There's still some good in that boy. I know it. And even if I didn't, it doesn't matter. Doesn't matter at all. If you're a police officer, you help everyone."

Aunt Haddie waited until Jack looked her in the eye.

"You need to ask yourself a question before you put on that badge, Jackie. Who are you going to protect and serve? If the answer isn't everyone, you'd better think twice about becoming a policeman."

Jack winced.

"Right now, Jay needs your help." Aunt Haddie reached out and took his hand.

"But Aunt Haddie, what can I do? I'm not a cop." He shrugged. "Right now, I'm just... Jack."

"Do me one favor? Pray on it. You'll do that for me?"

Jack rolled his eyes. "That's not fair. I can't say no to that."

Aunt Haddie squeezed his hand and winked. "Get some sleep." She eased herself out of the chair and patted his shoulder. "I'll go make up your bed."

Silence fell in the kitchen. Jack sat with his head in his hands, trying to drive the image of Stacy Shaw out of his mind. *She died looking her killer in the eye.*

Jack finally stood up. He locked the back door and made sure the rest of the house was secure, then headed upstairs. At the end of the hallway, he opened the last door on the left. It was like running into an old friend. He'd spent four years calling this room his own. Aunt Haddie had made the bed, and the little room was neat and tidy. *His room.*

Inside he hurt, but the corners of his mouth turned up.

He still remembered when he first stood here in the doorway and Aunt Haddie said those words: "This is your room." Jack had felt as though he'd won the lottery and gotten his own castle.

He took off his sneakers and set them down neatly near the door. He didn't even think about just kicking them off and leaving them scattered; Aunt Haddie ran a tight ship, and he would never lose those lessons. He pulled off his shirt, lay back on the bed, and interlaced his fingers behind his head.

The glow from the streetlight shone in the window. One of those stickers from the sheriff's department was stuck to a corner of the glass, to let firefighters know it was a child's room. The light hit the sticker and cast a shadow of a sheriff's star on the ceiling. Jack stared at the outline, as he had countless times. He used to imagine it was his own signal, like Commissioner Gordon calling Batman. Somewhere out there a person was in trouble, and it was up to him to rush out into the night and save them. He just never thought the person who would need him would be Jay Martin.

But Jack knew Jay didn't kill Stacy Shaw. He was just watching out for his brother. And now he might spend the rest of his life in prison.

Jack looked over at the globe on the desk in the corner.

Seven billion people on the planet. Out of that, only six people know Jay's innocent. Jay, Tommy, me, Chandler, Aunt Haddie, and Mrs. Martin.

Jack shut his eyes.

Seven: the person who really killed Stacy Shaw.

His chest tightened.

He looked back to the sheriff's star silhouetted on the ceiling. Some people called it a badge; Jack thought of it as a shield. When you're a kid and a victim, a shield's a good thing. When Jack was little, he wanted someone to protect him. The first night in this bed was the first time Jack had really felt safe.

Over the next months and years, Aunt Haddie had often talked about layers of defense. He remembered her saying that in her house, she was his protector. The Fairfield police protected the town. More police protected the state, and even more soldiers protected the country. And Jack had always wanted to protect people too. He was outraged that monsters thought they could slink around in the shadows and hurt other kids. He wanted to hunt the monsters. Catch them and put them someplace where they could never hurt anyone again.

He looked at his reflection in the window. He wasn't a kid anymore; he was a man. He wasn't helpless; he could fight back. He had the power to fight not only for himself but for people who couldn't. He would protect Aunt Haddie now, and Chandler if he had to, and...people who needed his help. Even if no one believed them. Even if they were... unlovable.

Jack got out of bed. He walked over to the desk, opened a drawer, pulled out a pocket notebook, and fanned out the pages to make sure it was blank. Then he wrote FACTS at the top of the first page.

He began his list: *Jay Martin is innocent.*

16

SO HAS MRS. FRANKLIN

Ford's Crossing was an underdeveloped area of Fairfield a mile northwest of Hamilton Park. Jack parked at the side of the road where the main electric high-tension wires that ran into town cut across. The street was wide and deserted.

Chandler shut the Impala's door and asked, "So, what are we doing here? You didn't tell me to wear running clothes, so I'm assuming it's something more interesting than early-morning torture."

"Torture? I should tell you to drop and give me fifty." Jack gave Chandler a playful punch, though he was dead serious about their mission. "This is the last known place Stacy was. I figured we'd start here."

Jack walked down the grassy slope toward a thick old oak tree. A yellow ribbon had been tied around the trunk. "This must be where they found Stacy's car." He pointed at a two-foot section where the bark had been broken away and fresh wood was exposed. Pieces of broken glass and plastic lay on the ground.

Chandler picked up a piece of plastic and turned it around in his hands. "But she was killed near her office. Why's her car here?"

"Good question. If she wrecked her car, why head back to work?"

"Maybe to get a ride home?"

Jack squatted down and smoothed out an area of sand with his hand. Using his finger, he made a large rectangle. "This is Hamilton Park." He marked the basketball courts down at the bottom-left corner and then, above that, the baseball field at the west entrance. He picked up a rock the size of an egg and placed it just below the bottom center of the rectangle. "That's H. T. Wells." He made an *X* well outside the upper-left corner of the park outline. "We're way up here somewhere." He grabbed an acorn and held it up. "This is Stacy's house." He placed it just above the upper-right corner of the park outline.

"How do you know where she lives?"

"I Googled it," Jack said. "She lives in Morton's Hill. It's that house next to where we'd go sledding."

"The little yellow ranch with the tall bushes?"

"Yeah."

Chandler pointed at Jack's dirt map. "So it would have been faster for her to walk due east and head straight home than go back south to her office?"

"I agree."

"Then why did we find her body in the middle of the park?"

Jack shrugged. "That's the million-dollar question."

Chandler sighed. "Look. I don't think we should be doing this. No good can come from us sticking our noses where they don't belong. Please, can't we leave it to the cops?"

"I would, except the cops aren't looking anymore. They think Jay is guilty. Once they charge someone, they're done looking."

"Then that's Jay's problem. I'm not getting jammed up because of him," Chandler said.

"That's why I told you to stay home."

"Not gonna happen. You go, I go."

Jack stood up. "I want to check out her work. Did you call Makayla's cousin? Is everything cool?"

"Makayla called her, but I don't think this is your smartest idea. Lori's just the receptionist. She didn't work with Stacy or anything."

"I only want to talk to her. We'll take her to lunch. What's the worst that could happen?"

* * *

Built in the 1960s, the brick building had been recently remodeled to house shops on the first floor, with the four floors above dedicated to office space. H. T. Wells had the top two floors to themselves. It must be a nice place to work, Jack thought, pulling up to the curb in front—great views of the park.

Chandler craned his neck out the window to look up at the building. "Why don't we wait until she's off work?"

"Let's just go up and ask her if she wants to go to lunch. That way we get a look around inside, too."

"No. There is absolutely no way. I promised Makayla we wouldn't get Lori in trouble. Besides, I hate to break this to you, but you can't look around inside. Not even if you were a cop, and you're not."

"I'm not pretending to be a cop—"

"Then why did you put on your police academy shirt?"

Jack looked down at his blue and white T-shirt with the police academy logo. "It's the only clean thing I had in the car. It was in my gym bag."

"You could have borrowed a shirt."

"Thanks, I'll remember that next time I need a pup tent. I look good in this." Jack turned in his seat to face Chandler. "Don't worry, I've got this. I've been reading and watching cop shows since I can remember."

"So has Mrs. Franklin next door, but she's still a little old grandmother. Not a detective."

Jack stared out the windshield. The silence in the car became thick.

Chandler rapped his knuckles against the door panel. "I know you—you keep going and you don't quit. Sometimes…that's not a good thing. Most of the time it just ticks people off and gets you in trouble."

"I'll be right out. Fifteen minutes."

Chandler's eyebrows went in opposite directions; one dropped heavily on the lid while the other arched high. "Are you even listening? And why are we risking this? For J-Dog? I thought you can't stand him."

"I can't."

Chandler huffed. "You know the rules, Jack. You get in trouble and we're screwed as far as the recruiter goes. One call to the cops could make them take a second look at us."

"Stay here."

"That's not happening."

"I'm serious. It would look weird both of us going in anyway."

"I'm not waiting here. You go, I go. That's the deal. Besides, I promised Makayla."

Jack opened the door.

"Hey." Chandler grabbed Jack's arm. "Don't do anything stupid."

"Come on. It's me you're talking about." Jack got out of the car.

"That's why I'm saying it."

They took the elevator up to the fourth floor. The doors opened onto a luxurious reception area. Jack noticed a hallway leading off to the right; to the left was a waiting area with leather couches and marble coffee tables covered with glossy magazines. A vase of summer flowers in full bloom added life and color to the impressively long teak reception desk. Jack wrinkled his nose at the odd odor—fresh flowers mixed with the synthetic smell of some kind of cleaner.

The receptionist, Makayla's cousin Lori, stood behind the desk, and three men in suits were taking turns signing their names in a ledger. When she saw Chandler, Lori held up one finger and pointed covertly to the waiting area. Jack and Chandler moved to the side.

Lori handed lanyards to the men in suits. On the front of each card, the word *Visitor* was printed in bright-green text. The men chatted with Lori until a thin woman in a sharp gray suit strode down the hallway. She greeted the men, and they followed her back down the hallway.

Now that Lori was alone, Jack was about to approach the desk, but just then a beefy custodian in navy-blue coveralls pushed a rolling recycle bin down the hall to the reception desk. His small, close-set eyes, set in a round, ruddy face, stayed focused on the ground, and his mouth hung open in a slack way. "Do you have any recycling, Lori?" he asked.

She picked up a white container and handed it to him. "How are you today, Jeremy?" she said with a smile.

He shrugged and dumped the container. "Still sad."

She patted his arm. "It'll get better."

"It'll get better," he repeated.

"Jeremy?" Lori pointed down at the floor. "Can you use less carpet cleaner next time?"

Jeremy nodded quickly. "Sorry. Someone spilled. I had to get the stains out. Sorry." Jeremy tipped the heavy bin back and wheeled it toward the elevator.

When he was gone, Lori waved Jack and Chandler over. They walked to the desk as she scooted around.

Medium height, a little on the curvy side, and in her early twenties, Lori looked every bit the business receptionist—charcoal slacks, pale blue top, her long, dark hair swept up in a low chignon. She grabbed Chandler's hand as though they were old friends.

"Look at you!" She grinned at Chandler. "I can't tell you how grateful my aunt is for that refrigerator."

"That's on Mr. Emerson." Chandler blushed. "He's the one who fixed it."

"Mr. Emerson didn't bring that refrigerator up four floors. Anyway, she's tickled pink, let me tell you." Lori squeezed his hand.

As Chandler and Lori chatted, Jack glanced down at the visitor sign-in log and his eyes widened. *Detective Anthony Vargas.* Under "purpose of visit," he had written "Review security footage." The checkout time was blank. Jack's heart beat fast.

"Makayla called me," Lori said. "What's the big favor?"

"It's, uhh…" Chandler cleared his throat and looked at Jack.

Jack tore his eyes from the log. "We were wondering if we could take you out to lunch. Right now. Not here."

"Sure. Why?"

Footsteps came down the hall, and Jack held his breath. But it was just two women walking to the elevator, engaged in a quiet conversation.

Jack exhaled. "I want to ask you a few questions about Stacy Shaw."

Lori cast a nervous glance at the women, who were getting on the elevator, then checked the clock. "I have to wait for my cover to get here. I'll meet you downstairs in, like, ten minutes, or you can

wait—"

"Great." Jack moved for the elevator. "We'll wait out front. Outside."

Jack's head was on a swivel as they walked. When they reached the elevator doors, Jack pressed the button four quick times.

"Hold up a second," Chandler said.

"What?"

"I have to use the restroom." Chandler winked.

The elevator doors dinged and opened. "No." Jack practically dragged Chandler inside the elevator. "We gotta go."

Jack reached out and rapidly pressed the bottom button.

"I don't get you." Chandler frowned. "You wanted to look around, and I come up with a great idea so we can do it but—"

Jack repeatedly mashed the button to close the doors. "That detective is here."

The doors closed, and Chandler's eyes widened. "Now? Vargas?"

Jack crossed his arms and leaned against the wall. "Yeah. So I figure we'd better beat feet. Did Vargas say anything to you about staying away from the investigation?"

"No. He told me to stay away from *you*," Chandler huffed. "Like I said, you rub some people the wrong way. Did Vargas tell you to stay away from this?"

"Yeah, but I don't think he'd really arrest me. Still, you should wait in the car."

"Arrest you?" Chandler stomped, and the whole elevator shook. "You need to get serious. Don't mess this up. Did he use that word? Arrest?"

"Can you not do that in here, Stampy?" Jack glanced at the weight capacity of the elevator. "I won't screw anything up."

The elevator dinged. Jack and Chandler faced the doors they'd entered through, but it was the doors behind them that opened. Embarrassed, they turned and walked out of the elevator.

Jack looked around, puzzled. They weren't in the lobby. The dark concrete room they found themselves in led to a loading dock. The large corrugated roll-down door at the end was closed, and five recycling bins were lined up in front of a dumpster against the wall. A concrete hallway lay to their left. The deep thrum of machinery reverberated off the bare walls and ceiling.

The elevator doors closed behind them.

Jack spun around and pressed the button. It didn't light up.

They heard the elevator going back up.

Chandler pointed to the elevator button panel. "You need a key. What button did you press to get us here?"

"The bottom one," Jack said.

"You mean you pressed B? B's for basement. Not for the lobby."

"I wasn't looking at the letters, I just pressed the bottom button. Sorry."

It felt like a cave—humid, stale, and musty. "Let's cut through here," Jack said. He walked over to the loading dock door. He tried the door handle but it didn't budge. There was a badge reader next to it.

"Great," Chandler grumbled. "I bet we're not allowed down here."

"Calm down," Jack said, half to himself. "Let's see where the hallway goes."

The elevator behind them dinged. A moment later, the custodian they saw earlier wheeled the recycling bin out and headed toward the bins along the wall.

Chandler hurried toward the elevator, but Jack started toward Jeremy.

"What are you doing?" Chandler's voice was filled with caution, as if Jack was getting too close to a cliff.

"He's the custodian. If he worked that night, he might have been the one who saw her before she left."

Chandler grabbed his arm. "Vargas is in the house, man." The elevator doors beeped and started to close. Chandler's hand shot out and stopped them.

"You go," Jack said. "I just need a couple of minutes."

The elevator doors beeped.

"I'll meet you outside," Jack said. "Go."

"I'm not leaving." Chandler yanked his hand away from the doors and let them close. "Aw, no, I'll wait. Hurry it up."

Jack nodded.

As they walked over to Jeremy, Chandler whispered, "And please don't get this guy upset."

"I won't."

Jack waved at Jeremy. "Hello."

Jeremy waved back. "Hi." He hefted the heavy recycling bin up in one quick motion and dumped the paper out into the dumpster.

"I'm Jack. You work upstairs at H. T. Wells?"

"Yes." A big smile crossed Jeremy's face. "You were just there. Both of you. Didn't you see me?"

"I did." Jack nodded. "I was wondering if I could ask you some questions."

"Okay." Jeremy wiped his nose with the back of his thick hand and loudly sucked in the snot dripping into his sinuses. Chandler turned away, gagging.

"Did you know Stacy Shaw?"

"Yes." Jeremy slammed the lid on the recycling bin. His brows drew together and his small eyes became dots. "I talked to the police."

"You talked to the police? About what?"

"When Mrs. Shaw went home." Jeremy wheeled another bin over to the dumpster.

"Oh, you saw her leave?"

"Yes." Jeremy jerked the bin up and dumped it in a fluid motion. Paper poured out into the dumpster. He let the bin land with a loud bang.

"How did she look?"

Jeremy's smile rose and fell, as if he couldn't make up his mind how the memory made him feel. "Pretty."

"I mean, how did she seem? Was she happy or tired or…?"

Jeremy shrugged. "Happy."

"What time did she go home?" Jack asked.

Jeremy's head jerked to the side and his arm twitched. The sudden, spastic movement made Jack step back.

Jeremy held up his watch. "Eight."

Jack looked at the battered silver watch. "That's an interesting watch. What are those marks?"

"My mother put them on there." On the face were three colored marks—green at twelve, blue at five, and red at nine.

"What time do you start work, Jeremy?" Jack spoke slowly.

"Twelve o'clock. Four days a week."

"When do you go home?"

"Nine."

Jack pointed at Jeremy's watch. "That's smart of you to use the colors."

Jeremy rubbed his watch. "My mom did it."

"Was anyone else here besides you and Stacy that night?"

"She was nice. She's not coming back." He grabbed another recycling bin and wheeled it over to the dumpster.

"I'm sorry about that. Was anyone else here?"

"Mr. Chambers." Jeremy said the name as though it left a bad taste in his mouth.

"You don't like Mr. Chambers?"

Jeremy looked away. "He's not nice."

"To you?"

"No. Mrs. Shaw. He got mad." Jeremy hefted the recycling bin up and banged it against the dumpster. A waterfall of paper poured out. "But she's nice."

"Do you know why Mr. Chambers got mad?" Jack asked.

"Because right away."

"Mr. Chambers wanted something right away?" Chandler asked, confused.

Jeremy shrugged.

"Do you know what he wanted right away?" Jack asked.

Jeremy shrugged again and grabbed another bin.

"Who was the last person to leave before Stacy?" Jack asked.

"Mr. Chambers."

Jack shot Chandler a quick look. "And what time did he leave?"

Jeremy looked down at his watch. "Before Stacy."

"What time?" Jack repeated.

Jeremy frowned. "A couple of minutes." He started to lift the recycling bin, but this time he strained and grunted loudly.

Jack grabbed the other side of the recycling bin to help Jeremy, but found himself struggling with the weight too.

Jeremy shifted his legs, and together they raised it enough to tip it. Jack exhaled as they set the bin down. "Wow. These are heavy."

A broad smile stretched across Jeremy's face. "I'm strong." He flexed both arms like a wrestler who had just won a match.

"You are," Jack agreed. "Did anyone come in after Mrs. Shaw left?"

Jeremy nodded. "Mr. Chambers came back. I think he forgot something."

The loading dock door rattled loudly and lifted upward. Light streamed under the rising door.

Jeremy started to walk away. "I have to tell David UPS is here."

"How was Mr. Chambers when he came back?" Jack asked.

Jeremy shrugged.

"Was he happy?"

Jeremy shook his head.

"Can you describe what he was like?"

Jeremy stopped. He rubbed a hand on his overalls. "Sweaty?" He looked at Jack expectantly. "He went to the park. You shouldn't go to the park at night."

The UPS driver beeped.

"I got to get David." Jeremy hurried away.

Jack and Chandler headed for the open loading dock door. Jack pulled a small notebook from his back pocket.

"You brought a notebook?" Chandler asked.

"Yeah. I don't want to forget anything. And I didn't. Look." Jack tapped the page. "Leland Chambers was Stacy's manager."

Chandler's eyes widened. "No way."

Jack and Chandler exited the building through the loading dock, then circled around to the front. They got there just as Lori hurried out the revolving door. "Can we do the food cart?" she asked. "They make great burritos." She pointed across the street to a bright-green food cart with a huge banana-yellow umbrella over it.

"Sure." Chandler smiled.

"I can take you someplace where we can sit down if you want." Jack's eyes settled on the plain, dark-green sedan he'd parked behind. It hadn't meant anything to him before, but now it screamed *unmarked police car.*

"This is fine." Lori walked across the street. "I only have a half hour and I had to stop by the restroom, so the clock's ticking."

"You can say that again," Jack muttered to himself.

They ordered their food—Jack paid—then moved toward a shady bench. Jack left his burrito wrapped up and took out his notebook. "Did you know Stacy Shaw?"

"A little. She just started maybe three months ago. She was really sweet."

"What did she do here?" Jack asked.

"She worked in finance. She's an analyst, I think."

Jack wrote that down. "Who would she be friends with?"

Lori pondered as she ate. "Betty Robinson. Betty trained Stacy, and they went to lunch together a lot."

"Was there anyone she didn't get along with?"

Lori shook her head. "Nothing I heard about—and I get all the gossip, believe me. It's like I'm a bartender. Everyone comes out to the front desk and tells me their secrets."

"No one said anything about her?"

"Nothing bad. She didn't really go out after work with the regular crew."

"Did you know her husband?"

"I met him a couple of times. He's a salesman for a software company, Connect IT, I think. He seemed really nice." She slowly lowered her burrito. "I feel so bad for him. He called the office from New York that day. We chitchatted about his job, then I transferred the call to Stacy. It was close to five, so I almost didn't pick it up because I wanted to go home." She paused and looked down at her burrito. "That could have been the last time she spoke with him." She stopped chewing and looked up. "It makes you think about life. You know?"

Chandler nodded.

Jack flipped back a page and read the name written there. "Do you know a Mr. Chambers?"

"Leland Chambers? Yeah. He works in finance. He was Stacy's boss. He was the last person to see her, I think. Well, besides Betty."

Jack started writing again. "Is that Betty Robinson?"

"Yes. Betty was outside waiting for a ride when Stacy left."

"Did they talk?"

"I guess. Or at least that's what I overheard in the break room. I have no idea what about."

"What can you tell me about this Leland guy?"

Lori scanned the area for any fellow employees and leaned close. "He's slime in a suit. I have to stand up when he comes over to the desk, if you know what I mean? Leland hits on anything in a skirt. I'm surprised HR hasn't done something, but of course it's run by a man, so I guess I'm not shocked."

What a scumbag. "Chambers was Stacy's supervisor?"

"Yes. He's the manager in Finance. I know the police interviewed him." Lori looked at the time on her phone and groaned. "I have to go." She finished her soda and tossed it in the recycling bin.

"Would it be okay if I used a restroom in the office?" Chandler asked.

"Sure."

Jack looked askance at Chandler. As they crossed the street, he whispered, "You can't go back in there."

"But this time I really have to go," Chandler whispered back.

"Vargas is still in there." Jack pointed at the sedan. "Hold it."

Chandler scowled.

"Do you know who else the police interviewed?" Jack asked Lori.

"Lots of people, but especially Leland, Betty, and Jeremy. Oh, there's a detective meeting with Peter Guppy today. He came in just before you."

"Really?" Jack tried to sound surprised. "What does Peter Guppy do?"

"He's IT and security. They were talking about reviewing the security cameras."

"When did they interview the others?"

"Right after Stacy went missing. They interviewed me, too. Actually, the detective is still here if you want to speak with him."

"Uh, no, not right now, thanks." Jack avoided looking at Chandler. "Is there any way you can set me up to talk with Stacy's boss or Betty Robinson?"

"I don't know about Chambers, but I'm sure my friend Betty will talk to you."

"You're sure Betty will talk about what?" said a tall woman smoking near the corner of the building. She put out her cigarette, sauntered over, and smiled at Lori.

"Ah, hi, Betty." Lori swallowed. "This is my cousin's boyfriend, Chandler Carter, and his friend Jack Stratton."

They all shook hands.

"And, uh... Jack was the one who found Stacy's body," Lori added. "Jack's heading for a career in law enforcement. He'd like to help."

"Oh..." Betty looked troubled.

"I just have a couple of questions," Jack said. "Do you have a few minutes?"

Betty hesitated.

Lori leaned in. "For Stacy's sake."

Betty lit another cigarette. "I have a little time."

Jack turned to Lori. "Thank you." Then he gave Chandler a look that he hoped conveyed, *Take a walk*.

Right on cue, Chandler said smoothly, "Lori, I'll catch you later." And softly, to Jack, "I'm gonna use the restroom in the coffee shop." To Betty he added, "Nice to meet you, ma'am." He followed Lori to the door, gave her a quick hug, then made a beeline for the coffee shop at the end of the building.

Jack took out his notebook. "Lori tells me you trained Stacy?"

"Yes, I trained Stacy to take over my responsibilities when I was promoted."

"Do you know if Stacy had any issues at work?"

"No. She was as quiet as a church mouse and about as threatening as one. She got along with everyone."

"Even her new manager?"

"Leland?" Betty took a long drag of her cigarette and let the smoke slowly drift out of her mouth. Jack felt she was editing her thoughts. "He got along well enough with her."

"Were you friendly with Stacy outside of work?"

"We were getting there. She'd been to my home and I'd been to hers."

"You spoke with Stacy the night she disappeared?"

"My husband was late to pick me up. We spoke right here." She pointed down. "Then my husband dropped me at home and went to run a few errands."

"How did Stacy seem?"

"Fine. Upbeat. Actually she was quite happy because her pregnancy was going so well, which was a miracle after the botched procedure she went through."

"You knew she was pregnant?"

Betty looked guilty. "Yes. I knew. But she hadn't told anyone else at work yet. She was afraid of how people would react—you know, start a new job and then get pregnant almost right away. She was hoping to prove her worth first, before breaking the news. Besides, it was still pretty early."

Jack nodded. "So she wasn't unhappy about anything?"

"Well, Leland was busting her chops a little, but that's just Leland pretending he's a big boy."

Betty was proving to be quite open, so he asked a question he had been waiting till the right moment to ask. "What's your opinion of Leland? What's he like to work with?"

Betty didn't edit herself this time, and almost seemed relieved to have been asked. "In my opinion, Leland is a jackass taught to walk upright. He's difficult to work with; we've all felt it from time to time."

"Do you know what he was busting her chops about?"

"Just work stuff. It was nothing. I told Stacy that, then I invited her over for dinner. But she declined because her husband was away for his job. She said she was going home to clean instead."

"Clean?"

"Her house. She said she wanted Michael to come home to a clean house," Betty said forlornly.

Jack cleared his throat. "Where was her car parked?"

"There's a company lot to the left." She pointed down the street, but the building blocked the view of the lot.

"You didn't see her get in her car?"

"No. When we pulled away, she was walking to the lot."

The front door whipped open. Jack flinched, half expecting it to be Vargas, but it was just another stranger in a suit.

"Did you see her talk to anyone?" Jack asked. "Was there anyone else around?"

"Nope. Some foot traffic, but no one stood out." She took one last drag on her cigarette and stubbed it out. "I'm sorry, but I've got a one o'clock meeting." She took a card out of her pocket. "If you have any other questions, you can give me a call."

"Thanks." Jack stuck the card behind his notebook. "I really appreciate—"

"Speak of the devil," Betty said, pointing across the street. "You asked about Stacy's boss—that's him right there, the sweaty guy in the neon-green sneakers."

Jack looked where she was pointing. Waiting among the crowd for the crosswalk light was a tall man wearing running gear and green sneakers that looked like they would glow in the dark. He looked to be in his mid thirties. From his wide shoulders and thick chest, it was obvious he not only ran but lifted weights as well.

The crosswalk light changed, and Leland jogged forward.

Betty waved him over, and before Jack could stop her, said, "Leland, do you have a minute? This is Jack Stratton. He found Stacy's body and he has a couple of follow-up questions for us."

Jack was aghast. Why would Chambers answer questions from a kid? Especially if he had anything to hide. This might get him into even more trouble with Vargas. But though he made it clear from his manner that he was a busy man who had lots of better things to be doing, Chambers glanced down at Jack's police academy shirt and nodded. "What do you need?"

Jack looked down at the logo on his shirt and realized that Leland thought he was a cop. He'd just been presented with an opening he'd never even dreamed of. Like some switch flipped inside him, Jack felt like a policeman. He squared his shoulders, lowered his voice, and focused. "Thank you. It'll only take a few minutes."

"I hope so. I'm on a one o'clock call. Betty is too."

"You have time," Betty said. "The Right-A-Way Shipping guys are always a few minutes late. And I'll stall for you." She gave a wink. "Like I always do," she added before walking away.

Leland put his large hands on his hips and faced Jack, his impatience hardly masked. "Well?"

Jack flipped to a new page of his notebook. "Mr. Chambers, Stacy was working late the night she disappeared. Was that her regular schedule?"

"Yes. Thursday night was her late night. I was giving her some overtime."

"Stacy left work while you were out for your run?"

"Yes. I got ready for my run around seven. She was finishing up on some work. We chatted and I left. That was the last time I saw her."

"Do you remember what you talked about? Did she mention if she was going out after work?"

"No. I try not to be too chummy with people under me. It was more of a how's-the-weather type of conversation. Then I left."

"Did you see her in the park during your run?"

Leland looked Jack up and down. "No. The last time I saw her was before I went out jogging. Are you as young as you look?"

Jack ignored the observation and kept going. "What route did you run in the park?"

"The outside loop. It was just a quick run to blow off steam."

"And when you came back, was there anyone here?"

"No. The place was deserted." Leland smiled smugly. "First to arrive, last to leave, but I make the sacrifice."

Jack tapped his notebook. "There was no one else in the building? What about cleaning staff?"

"There's usually a janitor or two. I thought you meant real employees." Leland looked down at his watch. "I need to be at that meeting."

"Certainly." Jack saw his window of opportunity closing fast, so he went for it. "You said you went for a run to…" Jack scanned his notes. "Blow off steam. Why did you need to blow off steam? Was that because of the argument you and Stacy had?"

Leland's expression didn't change. "Not at all. Stacy and I didn't argue."

Jeremy had said that Leland and Stacy argued, and Stacy had hinted about it to Betty. Jack didn't have enough time to flip back through the notebook, so he had to rely on his memory. Jeremy had said Leland wanted something right away?

Leland tapped his watch with a long finger. "Time's up. I've got a meeting to catch." He turned to go.

Jack remembered Betty's saucy wink as she left him and Chambers together. The Right-A-Way Shipping guys, she had said. And it hit him: Jeremy had heard them wrong. Chambers didn't need something *right away*; they had argued about Right-A-Way Shipping.

"Mr. Chambers," Jack called after him, following him to the door. "The night Stacy went missing, you two had a disagreement over Right-A-Way Shipping. What was that about?"

Leland's mask cracked, and his upper lip twitched. "Oh, that. It was nothing. Stacy was working on the Right-A-Way Shipping report. It's part of her job. She was… delayed." As he spoke, he seemed to be selecting each word with careful effort. "Yes, that's right—she was late in getting the report back to me and I have strict deadlines." His face relaxed. "She was new to the job, and it was just a minor infraction. I let it go. Where did you hear—" Leland stopped himself and smiled coldly. "Well, if you would excuse me. Have a good day."

Jack looked up from his notepad, prepared to press Leland on the issue, but he froze when, through the glass doors, he saw the elevator. And stepping off that elevator was Detective Anthony Vargas.

Jack spun on his heel and strode to the Impala as quickly and inconspicuously as he could.

Chandler was pacing back and forth beside the car.

"Get in, get in, get in." Jack's words snapped like a machine gun as he hurried to the driver's side. "Vargas is right behind me."

Chandler jumped into the passenger seat. "Oh, man."

There was no time to pull away, so instead Jack just kept his head down, pretending to fiddle with the radio. Detective Vargas stepped out onto the sidewalk, marched over to his car—directly in front of the Impala—and stopped. If he turned to his right…

Jack held his breath.

Vargas just stood there by his car door, staring across the street.

"What's he doing?" Chandler whispered.

"Shh…"

Vargas crossed the road and headed to the burrito stand.

Jack sat up, started the car, rolled back two feet, and pulled out—all the while keeping his head turned away from Vargas.

Once they were clear, Chandler looked back and grinned. "You were awesome!" He held up a huge fist.

Jack knuckle-bumped his friend. "I don't know if I asked the right questions."

"What? You did great with Lori and Betty." Chandler's face fell. "What happened after I left?"

"Lori saw Chambers, Stacy's boss, and called him over. I thought I'd be busted if he got suspicious, but remember how you gave me a hard time about this T-shirt?"

"Yeah…"

Jack grinned. "Well, this T-shirt saved me. Chambers thought I was a cop! He was annoyed at giving up time, but I got two clues off him. He worked late with Stacy that night. He also admitted he argued with her, after I remembered something. I figured out what it was about, too."

"Clue me in, I'm lost."

"Remember when Jeremy said Chambers wanted something right away?" Chandler nodded. "After you went to the coffee shop, Lori said she and Chambers had a meeting with Right-A-Way Shipping. So, I realized, when Jeremy heard Leland arguing with Stacy, it wasn't because he needed something right away. It was something about Right-A-Way Shipping, their client. We need to take a closer look at them. And at Chambers."

17

IT'LL COST YOU

"Hey, Mom!" Jack called out as he and Chandler walked through the front door.

"Hi, honey." Mrs. Stratton came out of the study and gave them both big hugs. "I've been worried sick about you since what happened in the park."

"I'm fine, Mom." Jack gave her hand a reassuring squeeze. "If I'm going into law enforcement, I have to get used to that kind of thing."

His mom's gaze shifted to Chandler. "How could someone ever get used to that?"

"That's what I've been saying to him, Mrs. Stratton," Chandler said.

Jack headed upstairs. "I just need to use my computer to look some stuff up. I shouldn't be too long."

He and Chandler planned to spend the rest of the afternoon going over everything they could find on the Internet about everyone mentioned in Jack's notes.

They started by looking for information on Leland Chambers. It wasn't hard to find. Soon Jack's monitor was covered with business articles, several social media pages, and even a scathing review that Chambers had left for a Mexican restaurant. But none of it seemed to have any relevance to the case.

"How about we take another look at Nina's Facebook?" Chandler said. "Maybe Two Point reached back out to her?"

Jack opened a new tab. But besides pictures of some "cute outfits" Nina had picked up shopping—and more photos of things she'd still like to buy—there was nothing new.

Jack pulled up the H. T. Wells website next. "H. T. Wells is having a memorial run for Stacy next weekend," Jack read. "The proceeds are going to help pay for her funeral expenses."

"Why would her husband need help paying for the funeral?" Chandler wondered. "I thought they owned a house."

"Apparently they were under some financial strain as it was," Jack said, reading the details. "They both had good jobs, but neither of them had been there long—not long enough to really save anything."

"That sucks. You get good jobs, a house and then…boom. Everything is gone."

Jack pulled up Michael Shaw's Facebook page. The last post was a week before the murder. There was a picture of Michael and Stacy at a work picnic for his company, Connect IT. They both looked happy. Stacy beamed at the camera, her eyes sparkling.

But Jack couldn't escape from a different image of Stacy that popped into his head: her body underwater, her dull eyes staring at nothing.

He quickly closed the tab, typed "Connect IT" into the search bar, and went to the web page for Michael's company. Connect IT was a small firm that created software apps for cell phone users. Idly, Jack said, "I think my parents are getting me a cell phone for my birthday."

Chandler didn't say anything.

Jack looked over his shoulder. Chandler's lips were pushed tightly together.

Jack smiled. "I'll take that as a yes."

"Don't tell them I told you." Chandler flopped down on the bed, and the mattress groaned. "How'd you guess?"

"I didn't until I saw your face." Jack laughed. "I was just thinking that this app here would be cool when we're overseas. It's like party chat—we can call my parents and then they can call Aunt Haddie. We get them all on the line at once and save some cash by only making one call."

"Sweet." Chandler grinned. "It's a two-fer." His grin widened. "Actually, for me, it's a zero-fer, because you'll be paying for the call."

Next, Jack pulled up the website for Right-A-Way Shipping. "Ha—you gotta see this. This website looks like someone's kid made it."

Chandler sat up to watch the animated packages flying across the screen and made a face. "Wow, that's really cheesy. I could do better than that."

Jack searched every page of the Right-A-Way website. He made notes as he went and printed out page after page—everything from news articles to their corporate management team bios. All of it was dull and none of it seemed to add up to anything.

Chandler finally sat up and stretched. "Hey, are you getting hungry?"

"No, but my mom will make you something. I just want to check one more thing."

"Knock yourself out, bro. I'll be in the kitchen."

With Chandler out of the room, Jack had a little private sleuthing to do. He pulled up Kelly's Facebook page, and the first thing he saw was that she'd put up a picture of her and Jack. That quickened his pulse. But what he saw next kicked his heartbeat into fifth gear.

She had changed her status from "Single" to "In a Relationship."

Jack quickly switched over to his own Facebook page and followed suit. He typed Kelly a short message to let her know that he was thinking about her, then went downstairs to the kitchen.

Chandler sat at the kitchen table wearing a grin that said it all: he was in heaven and he didn't want to leave. Spread out before him was a plate with a double-decker home-grilled cheeseburger on a toasted deli roll. Pickles, chips, and potato salad were on the side. A huge glass of chocolate milk was at his right hand, and three different types of cupcakes were on his left.

"How are you not as round as a circle, with your mom's cooking?" Chandler mumbled with his mouth full.

"Because I have a little trick called self-control." Jack looked for his mother, but the kitchen was empty. "Mom?"

His mother came up from the cellar carrying a tub of vanilla ice cream. "I thought a small root beer float would be nice for dessert." She smiled.

Chandler's eyes lit up.

"He's got three cupcakes for dessert, Mom." Jack thrust his hand at the food. "He's going to gain five pounds from this meal alone."

"He's a growing boy."

Jack nodded. "He's growing, all right. Sideways."

"Shh. Be nice."

Be nice, Chandler mouthed with a playful grin before he took another bite of his burger.

Jack's mom brought over a burger for Jack, then left the room, leaving the two boys alone.

"At least skip the desserts," Jack said.

"They're not desserts." Chandler pointed to one of the cupcakes. "They're samples. So they don't count."

"Samples of what?" Jack asked.

"Your mom made a bunch of different kinds of cupcake to see which flavor you liked best for a birthday cake."

"I told you, I don't want a birthday cake."

"Shh…" Chandler pointed to the door as Laura came back in.

"I almost forgot your dessert, Jack." She walked over to the counter and picked up a plate piled with cupcakes. "What flavor would you like?"

Her face fell when Jack grumbled, "None for me, thanks."

* * *

As they drove away from Jack's house, Chandler leaned back in the seat and rubbed his belly. "Wow. Your mom is beyond sweet. So where are we going now?"

"Hamilton Park."

"What, again? It's late."

"Are you scared?"

"Ha ha. Yeah, actually, I am," Chandler said. "Hamilton Park after dark is not my idea of a good time."

"I'll hold your hand."

"Okay, answer me this. Why are we going there *now*?"

"I want to see the park now, same time as the crime. Come on. It's a nice night. It'll take, like, fifteen minutes. If I don't go, I know I'll stay up all night thinking about it, because right now I can't picture what happened, it's like a black void. I want to take some notes."

"Fine." Chandler leaned his face toward the breeze coming in the window. "It is nice out."

A short while later, Jack parked by the entrance of Hamilton Park, leaned over, and opened the glove compartment. Chandler yawned and stretched as he got out. Jack moved some stuff around, frowning.

"What are you looking for?" Chandler asked.

"A flashlight." Jack got out and opened the trunk. He rummaged around and found a small one shoved in the bag holding his jumper cables. He clicked it on and off to be sure it worked.

"Where to?" Chandler asked.

Jack pointed. "H. T. Wells is across the street there. If Stacy was walking home, she would have come this way."

"But her car was at Ford's Crossing," Chandler said.

"Say someone did rob her. They could have taken her keys and stolen the car. Then they drove it over there, crashed it, and ditched it."

Chandler had a habit of thinking with his eyes closed. They were closed now, and his head tilted to the side. His lips moved too. "Wait!" He held up a forefinger. "You're saying she left her car at work and walked home? How come?"

"Car problems?"

"Then how did the car get to Ford's Crossing?"

"Good point," Jack conceded. "I'm only trying to think outside the box. What if she had planned on going back to work? What if she was taking a break?"

"I don't think she'd take the big loop around the edge," Jack said.

"Why not? If she was just taking a break, like you said, she might have gone anywhere."

"True. But if she was heading home, then she'd take the middle path on the right. That'd be the best route to her house. Besides, it goes past bench thirteen, and if we're assuming she was killed near where we found her, that's got to be the path she took."

"Yeah, I guess so," said Chandler.

The park wasn't as deserted as Jack thought it would be. As they walked, they saw a few homeless people, some sleeping on benches, others walking around. Then headlights appeared in the distance, on the loop road that circled the park.

"The park's closed to traffic," Jack said. "It must be cops."

"Aunt Haddie told me they're increasing park patrols. Just remember to stay below the radar. The last thing we need is a cop asking us what the hell we're doing," Chandler muttered.

As the headlights faded away, the park was quiet. Earlier, the sound of cars from the street had provided a comforting background noise, but now all they heard were crickets and their own footsteps. The leaves in the trees hung frozen, without even the slightest breeze to move them. Jack and Chandler felt like trespassers in the darkness…as if something wasn't happy about them being there.

Up ahead, leaning against a light pole, was a woman smoking a cigarette. "Hi, boys," she purred as they approached. Her tone of voice, the five-inch heels, the Dolly Parton wig, micro skirt, and skintight top—it all left no doubt as to her profession.

Jack kept his eyes down. As the son of a prostitute, he'd spent his formative years around them. Most people would look at a prostitute and see nothing more than a hooker; Jack saw that too…but he also saw the girl who'd read him *Green Eggs and Ham* and the young woman who occasionally sang him a lullaby. The disconnect made him uncomfortable. Sometimes the prostitutes—when they were sober—had been caring and nice to him, though most of the time, they'd steal from their own mother to get a fix. Even now, their faces still haunted Jack's dreams.

And this woman was bringing back feelings that he didn't want to remember.

"You want some action?" She strolled away from the pole. "How about a group discount?"

"No," Jack said curtly. The offer made his skin crawl.

"How 'bout a dollar then?" She followed them. "Just a couple of bucks so I can get a burger?"

Jack knew not to give her money. Her pimp could be nearby, or she was just trying to get him to take out his wallet. But when he glanced at her, he noticed her black eye. She had tried to cover it with makeup, but hadn't been entirely successful. She was only a few years older than Jack. Or maybe she was younger. It was hard to tell.

Jack pulled two dollars from his wallet and set them down on a bench without stopping. "Here you go."

The woman snatched the money off the bench and strolled away without a word. Chandler looked as though he wanted to say something, but he kept his thoughts to himself.

As they neared the center of the park, they heard the fountain. Up ahead, the moon's faint light reflected off the water spraying into the air.

"We're almost to thirteen, I think," Jack said as they passed another bench. This one had a homeless man sleeping on it. Two full trash bags sat on the ground next to him. His hand rested on them both, guarding them even as he slept.

Without warning, the man opened one eye and watched them suspiciously. As if passing a junkyard with an unchained dog, Jack and Chandler both moved to the far side of the path and quietly walked by.

"Glad you brought the flashlight." Chandler pointed to the ominous darkness stretching ahead of them. The streetlight that should have lit this area was out. Jack flicked on the flashlight and shined the beam up the pole and they saw the light's broken shards of glass silhouetted against the night sky.

Jack peered around. "If I was going to ambush someone, this would be the place. No one would see you. You'd only be visible for a minute when you got to the top of the hill."

"That sounds like something a predator would do. Do you know if she was raped?"

"They don't know."

"Are you sure you want to do this for a living? I don't know if I could handle it every day."

"Someone has to." Jack walked away from the paved path.

"Where are you going?" Chandler asked.

"I want to look around."

"Now? We couldn't do this during daylight?"

"No. I'm trying to understand the victim. See what Stacy saw. Understand what she was thinking."

"You know this is creepy, right?" Chandler hurried to catch up.

"We found her body over there." Jack pointed down to the pond.

"Like I could forget."

"The path bothers me."

"The path to the pond? The killer…" Chandler looked quickly around, then lowered his voice. "Whoever killed Stacy made that path when he dragged her body to the pond."

"I know, but that's not the path that's bugging me. Remember, there was another one." Jack panned the light across the woods until it landed on an opening in the brush. He walked toward it.

The hum of the patrol car broke the silence. "Cops," Chandler said. "They're coming back around."

Jack snapped the flashlight off. "Get down here so they don't see you."

"Hey, it's dark! You know, if we go home, that would be another way to solve the problem of them seeing us." Chandler hurried down the slope beside Jack.

"The moon's bright enough. Shut your eyes for a minute, you'll get used to the dark." Jack looked around. "There's no reason for anyone to come this way. You saw the state of things down by the pond—even the trash was ancient. If Robyn hadn't found the handbag, they wouldn't have located the body for a while."

Chandler took a step closer to Jack. "What are we doing here again? Can't we come back in the daytime?"

Jack waited until the sound of the patrol car disappeared, then he turned the flashlight on and pointed it at the top of the hill. "The killer dragged her over the hill and to the pond." He traced the path beside the trees with his circle of light. "But where did he *start* from? Was he walking along the path behind her, or waiting here?"

"Okay, I changed my mind. This is *super* creepy," Chandler said.

Jack walked toward the trees.

"Now where are you going?"

"To the trail. The one you were going to explore before we found the body."

The trail ran into the woods and was hidden by the hill. Branches pulled at Jack's shirt and the undergrowth got thicker, but then the bushes gave way to a little clearing. As Jack shined the light around at the dense brush cover, he had the feeling of being in a small nest.

"Wait," Chandler said. "Shine the flashlight back over there again. Directly across."

Jack followed Chandler's outstretched finger to some bushes on the opposite side of the clearing. As the flashlight's beam swept over the brush, Jack realized that someone had made a little lean-to shelter. Its backbone was a stout branch stretched between two trees at waist height, and its angled side was made of thin branches that someone had woven together. Leaves covered the outside, camouflaging it.

"We made one of those in Boy Scouts," Jack said.

"Ours didn't look as good." Chandler chuckled at the memory.

They walked over to it. "There's a blanket." Jack shined the light under the branches. The blanket was neatly folded into a square. Jack lifted one corner; the ground underneath was dry. "Someone's definitely sleeping here."

Chandler accidentally kicked a beer can with his foot, and when it rolled over, he saw that someone had cut it open and placed a candle inside. "Listen…whoever that is could still be around. Are you done?"

What if the killer was camped here? Jack stared out into the dark woods. It was a warm evening, but the skin on the back of his neck felt cold. He scanned the shadows but didn't see anyone.

Somewhere off to the left, a branch snapped.

Chandler ducked down. Jack shined the light toward the sound.

"Crap," Chandler whispered. "This is probably some crazy homeless guy's bed."

Jack ignored him and headed toward the sound.

"No, no, no," Chandler whispered through clenched teeth. "No chasing crazy people in the woods at night. That's like a top-ten rule."

Jack stopped and swept the flashlight beam in a wide arc, but the woods appeared empty. He snapped off the flashlight.

"Hey!" Chandler jumped. "Turn it back on, Einstein."

"Shh." Jack closed his eyes tightly and let them adjust. When he opened them, he started to move. At the base of a large maple tree, he stopped and listened.

The woods were quiet. Even the faint car noises were blocked by the trees. The canopy of leaves hid the moon, but soft shafts of light streamed down in places. A deep, earthy smell rose up.

From behind him came a loud snap followed by a thud. "Get back here or I'm gonna beat you," Chandler grumbled.

"If someone was here, they're gone now," Jack said. He turned the flashlight on and walked back. "Do you want to hold the flashlight?"

"No, I'd just like to see. Why the hell did you shut the light off?"

"If someone was out there, they could see me because of the flashlight. I was just trying to even the odds."

They followed the trail back out of the woods the way they came in, but Jack stopped before they climbed back up the slope. He stared back at the pond and tried to drive the picture of Stacy lying under the murky water out of his head. "They dumped her like trash," he said.

Chandler nodded.

They walked back to the paved path and turned toward the parking lot.

"I can't wait till we get NODs," Jack said.

"What's a NOD?"

"Night vision goggles."

"Aren't those NVGs?"

"That's what noobs call them," Jack said. "The guys in the field call them NODs. Night Optical Devices."

"How do you know this stuff?" Chandler stopped at a bench.

"Google. Aren't you reading? Lingo is how people block access to outsiders—in any field. I'm not getting into the Army and looking like a dope because I don't know what NOD means."

"Hey, you!" A man came storming toward the bench carrying two green trash bags. "Get the hell off my bench!"

Chandler immediately jumped up, while Jack spun around and assumed a defensive position—right foot back, knees bent, hands up.

The man was a little shorter than Jack, about five eleven, and wore a long coat despite the summer heat. He gave them both an icy glare as he scurried down the slope and stopped next to the bench. His black hair shot out in all directions and yellow teeth snarled beneath a bushy, unkempt beard.

"That's my bench." He pointed to where Chandler had just been sitting.

"Sorry," Chandler mumbled. He brushed off the back of his pants.

"Do you sit here all the time?" Jack asked.

"What the hell kind of question is that?" the man grumbled.

"I was—"

"Nobody can just sit in one place all the time. You've got to get up once in a while." The man pointed toward the dark area of the path. "I had to move over here since that smart-ass broke my light."

A group of three men in running outfits jogged over the hill and raced toward them. Jack, Chandler, and their new friend didn't speak as the runners sped by and disappeared over the next hill.

"Were you here last Thursday?" Jack asked.

"Yeah." The man's lip curled to reveal yellowed teeth. "Why?"

Jack stepped closer, trying not to make a face as the man's body odor stung his nose. "Did you see anything that night?"

"It'll cost you." The man stuck his hand out. "Man's gotta eat."

"He's not going to pay you to answer questions," Chandler said.

"Then he's gettin' no answers." The man stepped back. His trash bags crinkled and shook.

Jack pulled out a five-dollar bill. "How do I know you're telling the truth?"

"Honest Murray. That's what everybody calls me. Why would I lie?"

"To get five bucks," Chandler muttered.

Jack held out the bill and Murray snatched it from his hand. "A woman was attacked at the next bench," Jack said. "Did you see anything?"

"Nope. Keep your nose out of other people's business and it won't get broke. I live by that."

"You sure you didn't see *anything*? It happened just right down there." Jack pointed.

Murray raised himself up on his toes. "It's dark. I didn't see nothing."

"Did you *hear* anything?" Jack's patience had come to an end.

"Nope. I saw nothin' and I ain't heard nothin' neither."

"That wasn't worth five bucks."

"You want me to lie? You paid for the answers and I gave them. No take backsies."

"Do you know anyone who says they saw anything?" Jack asked. "You know, you're a sharp guy, maybe you overheard people talking, or someone told you something?"

The man glanced around nervously and shook his head. "Nope."

Jack stood straighter. He was sure that Murray knew more than he was letting on. Despite the odor, he moved closer. "You can tell me," Jack said. "Somebody else saw something. It's worth another buck."

Murray cast a nervous glance over at Chandler. Jack held his hand low and motioned for Chandler to move back. Chandler huffed but he walked a few feet away.

Murray held out his hand and waited until Jack gave him the dollar. Then, like a kid sharing a secret, Murray leaned in close, his eyes darting around. He put his face next to Jack's and whispered, "Lonny said Vlad was really mad. He thinks Vlad saw something."

"Vlad?" Jack kept his voice down.

"Yeah, Vlad. He's scary. Lonny said he got even scarier."

"Who's Lonny?"

"My friend. He's at the shelter tonight."

"Does Lonny *know* that Vlad saw something?"

Murray shrugged. "All Lonny said was, 'I *think* Vlad saw the guy.'"

"Where do we find Vlad?"

Murray's eyes bulged. "Don't talk to Vlad! You can't, no one can. Only Lonny, but even he…" He backed away. "Don't say I said nothin'!"

Jack held up his hand. "I won't say anything."

"You can't. Snitches get stitches. I didn't tell you nothin'."

"You didn't say a word." Jack slowly shook his head.

Murray exhaled. "I don't want him to get mad at me."

"I won't say anything," Jack assured him. "Can you just tell me what Vlad looks like?"

Murray shook his head. His whole body trembled. He stepped back again.

"I need to know what he looks like," said Jack, "so…I can avoid him."

"Oh." Murray seemed to relax. "Why didn't you say so? He's my size, but he has big shoulders." Murray held his hands out wide. "He wears an old camouflage jacket. He's Spanish or maybe some kind of Native American. Long black hair. Real long, down to the middle of his back. But don't say I said nothin'." Murray's eyes scanned the darkness.

"I won't. Where does he normally hang out? So I don't go there accidentally," Jack added quickly.

"Do you know the old maintenance building on the east side?"

"With a big chain-link fence around it?"

"That's the one. It's all closed up. Vlad's around there at night."

"What about during the day?"

Murray's voice rose. "Vlad only comes out at night. That's why we call him Vlad."

Chandler walked over. "Like Vlad the Impaler? Like Dracula the vampire?"

Murray nodded nervously. "Be sure you stay away from him. Everyone does."

"We will," Jack said. "Thanks."

Murray clutched his bags to his chest and sat down on his bench.

Jack handed Chandler the flashlight. "Come on." He hurried off to the east.

"The car's back that way," Chandler said, jogging to catch up.

"I know," Jack said. "I want to make one more quick stop before we head back."

Chandler stopped abruptly. "Don't even say it. You're out of your mind if you think I'm hunting Dracula with you."

18

DRACULA

"I'm out of my mind for letting you talk me into coming here," Chandler muttered.

The old maintenance building had seen better days; the roof sagged and weeds grew everywhere. It was surrounded by a rusted chain-link fence and the gate was closed with a chain wrapped around a thick metal pole.

Jack counted as he inhaled. "One. Two. Three. Four." He counted again as he exhaled.

"What are you doing?" Chandler asked.

"Breath control. Navy SEALs do it before a mission. It calms them down."

"What—are you freaked out?"

"Kinda. Aren't you?" Jack pulled the gate open as far as the chain would allow. The creaking metal sounded incredibly loud, like a horror-movie sound effect, but undeterred, he started to squeeze through.

"Hold on there, Captain Crazy." Chandler's hand on Jack's arm tightened into a vise grip. "I'm nervous enough being in Hamilton Park at night and talking to scary homeless people. There's no way I'm going into that…dungeon, to try to find a guy they call *Vlad.* C'mon, that's just buggin'."

"It's just a nickname."

"People get nicknames for a reason. Remember Farty Frank?"

Jack laughed.

"It's not funny, Jack." But Chandler let him go, and Jack shimmied through the gate.

"Come on," Jack said. "Farty's one of the funniest nicknames ever."

"I'm just giving you an example. Forget him. Boomer? They call him Boomer because he likes to smash stuff. Maybe they call this guy Vlad because he likes to suck people's blood. How do you know Dracula didn't kill Stacy?"

"Well…I don't. But I need to talk to him. I don't want to, but he might know something. Besides, I have to learn how to do this. I'm not going to run away just because I'm scared."

Chandler pointed to his chest. "I am. So call me a chicken and put feathers on my butt."

"Come on. You heard Murray. The guy only comes out at night."

"Yeah, because he's crazy," Chandler huffed.

Chandler spun in a circle. "What is wrong with you?" he whispered fiercely. "Whenever I go out with you, I end up with two choices and they both suck. Now I have to pick between going into Dracula's lair or walking home and leaving you here?"

The two friends stared at each other through the fence. Jack knew Chandler was just being smart and cautious, but Jack also knew he'd have to go to the edge if he was going to find out who really killed Stacy. So he didn't blink.

"You're right. Wait here. I'll be back in a minute."

Chandler rattled the chain-link fence separating them. "Do you see all the No Trespassing signs? If we get busted for anything before basic training, they'll kick us straight out of the Army before we even start. Why are you doing this?"

"This guy—"

Chandler grabbed the fence with both hands and the whole thing shook. "I'm not talking about him. I'm talking about *you.* You're going full throttle. You keep pushing this hard, you're going to blow up."

"I'm fine."

"No." Chandler shook his head. "There's something more. It's like you're trying to prove something."

Chandler was right about that. Jack had been looking for justification his whole life. Not for his actions, but for his being. Some proof he wasn't worthless.

But Chandler was wrong if he thought Jack was going to stop.

"Give me the flashlight." Jack held out his hand.

"No. It's dark out here too."

"You've got the full moon for a night-light, you big baby." Jack waggled his hand, reaching. "Give it to me."

Chandler passed the flashlight through the fence. "Fine. I hope it goes out."

Jack left Chandler behind and approached the building, listening carefully to every sound. He shined the light along the front of the one-story brick building. The little windows, which resembled the slots in a cabin, were made out of thick glass. He couldn't see through.

On one side of the building, two cement steps led up to a metal door. He looked back over his shoulder at the gate, where Chandler stood with his back to him, arms crossed.

Jack wiped his dry lips with the back of his hand while a hundred reasons not to go into the building scrolled through his head. But none of those objections could drive from his mind the question he needed answered: Did Vlad witness Stacy's murder?

The soft voice of reason whispered in his head, *Walk away.* Most people would heed their own advice, but Jack was haunted by that phrase. "*Walk away*, like she did," he muttered softly. "Give up on you, like she did."

Jack's whole body trembled, not with fear but fury, as he climbed the steps. His hand had just touched the doorknob when he heard the gate behind him rattle. The attacker, revisiting the scene? He turned and swept the flashlight toward the gate. He heard Chandler curse and mutter. When he saw Chandler, the reluctant vampire slayer, stuck halfway through the gate, he smiled.

"Another fine mess you've gotten me into." Chandler huffed and puffed as he pulled himself through the opening.

Jack suppressed a laugh. "Thanks for the backup."

"I didn't feel like explaining to Aunt Haddie that Dracula ate you."

"Dracula doesn't eat you, he sucks your blood out and turns you into a vampire." Jack shined the light in Chandler's face.

Chandler squinted and pushed the flashlight toward the door. "Oh, that's so much more comforting."

"Boy, you sure are crabby when you need a nappy."

"Yes, I'm tired and hungry because you dragged me all over the park."

Jack reached into his pocket. "Here."

"What is it?" Chandler's eyes lit up. "A candy bar?"

"It's a protein bar. That's to keep you quiet." Jack turned back to the door. "I haven't tried the door yet. I bet it's locked."

To his surprise, when he turned the knob, the door creaked open.

"Great," Chandler muttered. "Better and better."

"It's a small building. We'll just take a look inside."

Just inside the door was a room empty except for a pile of crud in one corner. Old floorboards ran the length of the room to a dark open doorway, but whatever lay beyond it was past the reach of the flashlight's beam.

Jack slipped inside, and Chandler, still muttering, followed. The room was musty, and a faint smell of oil hung in the air.

A crinkling noise made Jack jump.

Chandler held up the protein bar with a huge chunk gone. "This is pretty good," he whispered. "Chocolate chip?"

Jack shook his head and walked softly forward. "Hello?"

"Shh!" Chandler snapped.

"We want him to come out."

"*I* don't. Anyway, he's not here. Let's go."

Jack moved toward the open doorway. "Why would the door be unlocked? I want to check the rest of the building."

"Bad idea," Chandler grumbled, but he wasn't going to let Jack go in alone.

The next room had two tables, plus some shelves built into the walls, but otherwise it was as empty as the first room. The third room was just as uninteresting.

There was one door left to check, a closed metal door that looked like it led to a closet. Jack's flashlight beam reflected off the handle.

"Probably an electrical room," Jack said. "I'm sure this one is locked." He grabbed the handle and pulled, and the rusty hinges creaked open. Jack smiled sheepishly. "Okay. Not locked." He shined the light through the doorway on metal stairs leading down.

Chandler looked over Jack's shoulder. "Great. You keep guaranteeing that we're not going to get into any trouble. Boy am I reassured now."

Sweat rolled down Jack's back. He peered into the cool, damp darkness that swirled up from below and stung his nostrils with mildew.

"No way," Chandler whispered fiercely. "Jack, seriously. This is crossing so many sanity lines I can't tell you. What if the guy we're looking for is the killer?"

"You can wait here. If something goes south, go get help."

"That plan sucks."

Impatient, Jack leaned forward and yelled, "Hello?"

Chandler's fist flew out and delivered an emphatic criticism to Jack's shoulder. "Shh!"

"What?" Jack shrugged. "I don't want to sneak up on him and freak him out."

"You're freaking *me* out. Come on."

"No. We're here, and we're going to check it out." They descended the stairs to a cement basement that was surprisingly clean and dry. A large metal box stood against one wall, its lid secured by a huge padlock. "That's electrical." The flashlight beam swept the rest of the room and stopped on a sleeping mat in the back.

Chandler moved closer to Jack.

If it weren't for the fact that it was on the ground, it would have looked like a freshly turned-down bed with the top blanket folded back. Nothing more than two blankets on the floor and another on top. The flashlight reflected off metal and sparkled. Near the head of the "bed" was a stack of aluminum cans, meticulously arranged.

Jack moved closer.

A crinkling behind him made him spin around.

Chandler put the last bit of the protein bar in his mouth and stuffed the wrapper in his pocket. "Sorry."

Jack shined the light on the stack of cans. "It's a little stockpile," he whispered. "They're not open."

The flashlight focused on the single can at the top of the pile, a soda can, slit down the middle. A candle had been placed inside.

"Look," Chandler whispered. "That's the same kind of candle we found in the encampment, near where…you know…"

The flashlight blinked twice and shut off. Jack chuckled nervously.

"Jack. If this is a joke, I'm going to kill you. Turn the flashlight on." Chandler's voice was low and strained.

"The batteries are dying. Calm down."

"Shake the flashlight!" Chandler's voice rose.

Jack shook the flashlight and tapped the side with his hand. It lit for one brief moment, but then they were plunged into darkness again. "It's okay," said Jack. "We'll just feel our way back up."

Somewhere in the darkness, a man growled.

For a frozen moment there was no sound, except each other's ragged breathing.

Then the door at the top of the stairs clanged shut.

19

I'M LOOKING

Footsteps descended the metal stairs. Jack moved blindly in the dark toward the wall.

"Stop!" yelled a man's voice.

Jack froze, but only for a second. He tried to calm his breathing as he snuck toward the wall again. "I just wanted to ask you a question," he said.

"Why are you here? You're not police."

"Listen." Chandler's voice was loud. "Our friends are waiting for us outside."

Jack winced. He knew what Chandler was trying to do, but starting off with a lie was not the best way to begin a conversation.

"That's not true. I watched you come here. You drive a blue Impala."

Damn.

Jack heard Chandler's sneakers slide along the cement.

"Stop moving," the man said. "I'm looking."

"Jack?" Chandler's voice was even, but Jack heard the fear in it.

"Are you afraid?" the man asked.

Jack felt his heartbeat shift up a gear. Sweat poured down his back. He took another step, and at last his hand touched the wall.

"Stop moving," the man repeated.

"You can't see me." Jack took another step forward as quietly as he could.

"I can hear you," the man said. "I'm looking. Are you afraid of the dark?" The question hung in the air.

"I got locked in a supply closet when I was a kid," Jack said. "The light was on a timer. It shut off Friday night at five o'clock." He continued forward with one hand against the wall, talking fast and loudly to mask the sound of his footsteps. "She didn't come and get me until three twenty-seven Monday morning. It was this dark the whole time."

Jack stopped and listened.

"Why did she lock you in the closet?" the man asked.

Jack tried to figure out where the voice was coming from. It echoed off the walls, but he guessed the man was at the base of the stairs. He started talking and moving again. "She wanted to go out, but there was no babysitter, so she locked me in there. I don't know how long it took, but if you spend enough time in the dark, it stops scaring you."

"Oh, yeah, how long will that take?" Chandler muttered.

Jack stopped and listened. His heart pounding in his ears was the only sound he heard.

A flashlight turned on. Jack's breath stuck in his chest. Hollow dark-brown eyes stared at Jack from only inches away.

"You could trip in the dark." The man marched around Jack and walked past Chandler, who looked ready to bolt. "I told you I was looking. For my flashlight. Found it. I have another light over here."

The man lit the candle in the can. In its flickering light, Jack scrutinized him. He appeared to be in his thirties, but his face was weathered and worn. A long black ponytail hung down his back, and he wore an old camouflage jacket.

The man set the homemade lantern down on the stack of cans. "Are you on assignment?"

Jack's mind raced for an answer to the odd question. "On assignment?" Jack repeated, hoping for more information.

"I heard you outside. You two are in the Army. Are you on assignment?" the man asked again.

Jack hesitated and finally replied, "We enlisted."

"Yeah, Army. Thanks for the light." Chandler gave Jack a look that screamed: *Should we run?*

Jack shook his head slightly. He looked at the man's jacket. "Were you in the Army?"

"Marines. I'm still in. I'm on special assignment." The man snapped to attention and put his hands at his sides. With his shoulders squared, he looked powerful. "Names. Now."

"Chandler Carter, and he's Jack Stratton," Chandler blurted.

The man stepped in front of Jack. "Stratton? I had a teacher named Stratton. Ted Stratton. Math."

Chandler looked like a man who'd just been pardoned; his whole body relaxed. "That's Jack's dad."

Jack held his breath. The fact that this was an old pupil of his father's brought him no comfort. *Please don't be some crazed ex-student my dad flunked. Please don't be.*

"Really?" The man scanned Jack like a drill instructor looking over a fresh recruit. His eyes looked as cold as the cement, and almost as lifeless. "He talked about you. You're the son he adopted." The man seemed to relax somewhat. "Tell him Alex Hernandez said hi. Third-period calculus."

Alex Hernandez? Jack had heard the name before, and he struggled to remember where.

Alex reached out and took two cans from the stack. "Soda?" When he held out the can, the candlelight flickered off his gold wedding band.

Anne. Jack gasped. Anne Hernandez's story was infamous in Fairfield. A new bride, murdered. Brutally. Jack absently took one of the cans and tried to remember details. *Her husband was a soldier…*

Jack's breath came in strained puffs. There had been a lot of local coverage, and he had watched a TV show about it years ago. The details were long forgotten, but the images were still raw in his mind. The show had included a reenactment, and actual pictures…serving up fresh nightmares for months. And right now, in this dark cellar, those nightmares felt all too real.

Alex stepped forward and set the cans on the floor. Jack cautiously picked up one. Chandler looked down at the other can as if it were a grenade. When Jack glared at him, Chandler scowled back and picked up the can, leaving as much distance as possible between himself and Alex.

"Your dad brought a picture of you into class," Alex told Jack. "The day after you came home." He arranged the remaining cans to fill the gaps. "Wait…was it your mom who locked you in the closet?"

"No. No." Jack shook both his hands in front of himself. Some of his soda spilled. "Sorry," Jack muttered as he wiped at the puddle with his sneaker. "That was my…" He struggled for a word. He never called his birth mother anything close to the word 'mother.' "That was a different lady. Before I was adopted."

Alex nodded. He looked up at the ceiling. "I forgot to lock the door. You two shouldn't be down here. I could lose my command. You need to return to the Tock."

Chandler nodded. "You're right." He motioned to Jack. "Come on. Back to the Tock we go."

Jack waved Chandler off. "Can I ask you a question? A woman was attacked Thursday night near the pond. Did you happen to see anything?"

"I was downrange, but I didn't get that mission." Alex put the palms of his hands against his eyes.

Chandler was waving frantically and pointing toward the stairs.

Ignoring him, Jack continued, "Did you see anyone near the fountain? Talk to anyone?"

"No. I don't talk to people. I don't engage. My mission is strictly FO."

"So you're a Forward Observer? Recon? Then you must have seen or heard something? You have a bed over there. We found your lean-to."

"Outpost. That's my outpost. I already reported in. That's my mission: watch and report in. Check my report. I only saw a few messengers."

Chandler grabbed Jack's shoulder. "We'll do that. Let's go look at his report, Jack."

"Wait." Jack pulled his arm free. "Near the fountain? You saw a messenger?"

"It's in my report. He was fast. They wear civilian clothes but they're wired to their RO in the Tock. You need to leave now."

"What did the messenger look like?" Jack asked.

"It's in my report. Blue shorts. Bright-green sneakers. Tall." Alex stepped forward and snapped to attention. "You need to go."

Jack held his hand up, palm out. "I just have one more question. Where—"

The veins in Alex's neck stood out as he drew in a deep breath. "GET OUT NOW!"

In the confined concrete space, the bellow was so loud it caused Jack's ears to ring. Alex shifted his weight. He looked ready to charge. He was almost Jack's height, and when he squared his shoulders, he looked strong.

"Sure thing." Chandler grabbed Jack's arm and backed up. "Thanks for the soda."

Jack hesitated, but Chandler pulled again, and finally Jack started to move.

Alex picked up the candle and watched as Chandler dragged Jack toward the stairs. In a clear, calm voice he said, "I warned you." Then he blew the candle out and enveloped them in darkness.

Chandler shoved Jack ahead of him and up the stairs. Jack's hand hit the metal door and he pushed. The door creaked open. Pushing and pulling each other, they rushed through the rooms and outside. As they hurried toward the fence, the door behind them slammed shut with such force that one of the thick windows on the wall cracked. They both jumped.

Chandler pushed the gate open so Jack could squeeze through. "I told you that was a crazy idea."

Jack pulled himself through and then tugged on the gate for Chandler. "I totally agree. Going in there was stupid. Sorry. Do you know who that was?"

"Dracula? He said his name was Alex Hernandez. Oh, snap—*that* Alex Hernandez?" Chandler's hands went to the sides of his face and his eyes went wide at the realization. "His wife was the lady who got slaughtered?"

"Yeah. I didn't know he knew my dad."

"So Dracula is off-the-rails nuts. He thinks he's still on active duty. Did you hear him talking about messengers? Does he see imaginary people?"

"I don't think so. I think I know exactly who he's talking about."

"He's crazy. He said the messengers were wired together to a clock."

"No, he said they're wired to the RO so they could talk to the Tock. RO is marine speak for radio operator. Alex was saying that runners are connected to tactical operations command: TOC. He's talking about joggers out for a run. I think Alex believes that the joggers wearing headsets are carrying radios."

"You know that's officially crazy."

"Yeah, textbook definition. But he did see a runner near the fountain."

"So? There have to be fifty runners a day in that park."

"Not with bright-green sneakers like I saw on Leland Chambers. Whaddya say we take another look at Stacy's boss?"

20

FRIENDS

Tuesday morning, Jack sat in the Impala outside H. T. Wells. Chandler was helping Mr. Emerson again today, so Jack was alone. He watched the crowd walking up and down the street until he saw the person he was looking for: Betty Robinson, stepping out of the building for a smoke break.

He hopped out of the car and caught up to her just as she lit a cigarette. "Excuse me, Mrs. Robinson? Jack Stratton. We met the other day."

"Yes, I remember."

"I have a favor to ask."

Betty exhaled, and the smoke coiled out like a snake. "What is it?"

"The man they arrested for Stacy's murder—I don't believe he did it. I'm trying to find out who did. You're Stacy's friend. I'm hoping you'll help me again."

"Is the man they arrested a friend of yours or something?"

"Not exactly. But I know him, and I'm pretty sure he didn't do it. I could really use your help."

Betty eyed Jack up and down. "Okay. I'll listen, but over there." She led Jack over to the farthest corner of the building. Betty flicked a long ash onto the ground. "Why do you think I can help?"

"I read your bio on the website. You've been at the company twenty-five years. You started as a receptionist. You probably know more about this company than the owner."

She smiled.

"I need you to look up a report."

She took a long, slow drag. Smoke slowly drifted up as she studied Jack with the interest of a fisherman scrutinizing a bobber. "What report?"

"The Right-A-Way Shipping report that Stacy was working on. You trained her, so you must have access to it."

A strange look passed over Betty's face. "I'm not giving you company material, if that's what you're asking."

"I don't even need to see it. But if something's wrong with that report, I need to know."

Betty took another long drag of her cigarette. "You think Leland Chambers had something to do with Stacy's murder, don't you?"

Now it was Jack's turn to stare. He didn't know how much he should say. But his hesitation caused Betty's expression to sour.

"If you're asking me to help you, you'll have to trust me," she said.

Jack sighed. "Okay. Stacy and her boss argued the night she disappeared. And I figured out it was over that report. When I asked Mr. Chambers about it…" Jack searched for the right word. "It bothered him. A lot."

"That explains things," Betty said. "Leland came to my office with his panties in a twist after talking with you. He wanted to know what I told you Stacy and I talked about that night."

"What did you tell him?"

"Nothing—because you didn't hear that from me. After that, he made a beeline for the only other person who could have told you anything about that night."

Jack knew who that was, but he tried to appear cavalier. "Who?"

"The only other person in the building that night was a janitor named Jeremy." She looked at Jack carefully, as if to identify whether the name rang a bell. "I'm not sure what Jeremy said to him, but Leland fired him."

"Fired him?" A heaviness settled in his stomach. "For just talking to me?"

Betty smiled. "So you did talk to him. And yeah." She dropped her cigarette and ground it into bits with her heel. "Look, Leland is a complete scumbag and sleaze, but he'd have to slither even lower to be a murderer. So what if he got worked up about a report? That's no motive for murder. Hell, I hate my job, and I hate Leland, but he's still breathing."

"But he admitted going for a run in the park around the same time Stacy went missing."

"He admitted that?"

"Yeah. And someone saw him close to where Stacy was killed, too. All I'm asking is for you to look at the report, check if something is in there. If Chambers did have a motive, maybe you'll find it in that report."

Betty turned away and stared at the park.

"Stacy was your friend," Jack said.

Betty's eyes narrowed. "And she's dead. Now I remember, Stacy talked to me about that report that night too. So you think that report may be the reason she was killed, and now you want me to poke my nose into it?" She took out her cigarette pack but glanced at her watch and returned the pack to her pocket. "I need to think about it. It was nice to see you again, Jack. But try not to make this a habit." She turned and walked back to the entrance to the building.

Jack got back in the Impala and headed east. He wanted to question Alex Hernandez more—to find out if he'd seen anything else that night. As he stopped at a red light, he glanced up at the sun, wondering whether Dracula would be in a better mood during the day.

"Hey, Jack!"

Jack turned his head to see Kelly rushing out the front door of a clothing store, waving to him like a whirligig in a hurricane.

Jack pulled over at the corner and hopped out. Kelly rushed over and gave him a quick kiss, while Courtney and two other girls exited the store and walked up behind her.

"Hello." Jack pulled her in close. "What are you up to?"

"We were shopping." Kelly turned to her friends. "This is Leesa and Stephanie."

"You're technically *still* shopping." Courtney tipped her head toward Bottega Maria on the corner. "All your bags are still on the counter, and you haven't paid. You'd better hurry back before the clerk decides you've abandoned her."

"Oh, crud!" Kelly groaned.

Jack looked back at his double-parked Impala. "I'll wait here. Go get your stuff."

"I'll be, like, a minute."

"Take your time."

Stephanie and Leesa accompanied Kelly back into the store, but Courtney called after them, "I'll keep Jack company."

Kelly waved over her shoulder and disappeared inside.

Courtney's foot bounced and she looked like she was having an internal debate. "Hey, Jack, I don't want to dump this on you, but…"

Jack leaned against the Impala and waited for her to continue.

"Don't say I said anything, okay?"

"You haven't said anything."

Courtney rolled her eyes. "Just promise you won't say something."

Jack crossed his arms.

"Warner has been bothering Kelly. Texting her and calling her a bunch of times."

Storm clouds were forming in Jack's eyes.

"She's upset. I think… I think he's been following her too."

Jack straightened up. "What's he drive?"

"His father's silver BMW Z4."

"Where does he live?"

"You're not going to talk to him, are you?"

Jack's jaw clenched. "Why did you tell me if you didn't want me to do anything? Kelly's upset. I want her un-upset. So I'm going to have a little chat with Warner."

Courtney bit her lip nervously.

"What's his last name—"

Kelly, Stephanie, and Leesa came hurrying out of the boutique. Kelly had two shopping bags in each hand. "I bought a sweet outfit for Friday."

Jack forced a smile. "Can't wait." He reached for the passenger door handle on the Impala. "Can I talk to you for a second, Kelly?"

"Oh, no!" Leesa grabbed Kelly's arm. "Hair and nails! We're late. We'll lose our spot."

Kelly shook her head. "You guys go."

"You have to come!" Stephanie grabbed Kelly's other arm. "You're paying."

Kelly looked pleadingly at Jack.

"Go," Jack said. "I'll call you later."

Kelly blushed. "I miss you."

As the four of them hurried down the sidewalk, Courtney turned around and mouthed, "I'll call you."

Jack hopped back in his car and pulled out. As he drove down the street, he kept his eyes peeled for a silver BMW.

***

Jack entered Hamilton Park through the eastern gate. The park looked much prettier during the day than it did at midnight, but even though everyone seemed to be enjoying a beautiful summer day, Jack was on edge. In the same way a carpenter could stand in the middle of a finished home but still picture the framing and joists behind the walls, Jack watched the smiling people chatting away and playing Frisbee, knowing the dangers that lurked unseen there. Drugs, prostitution, homelessness faded during the day, but they weren't gone. Just harder to see.

Jack had only gone a little way when he saw Michelle walking across the park.

"Michelle!" he called.

She turned and waved, then ran over to him. "What's up, my brother?"

"What are you doing out here by yourself?" Jack asked.

"What? I went to the Y."

"You shouldn't be walking in the park alone."

Michelle looked around, confused. "It's during the day. It's fine. And I'm on my way home."

"I don't care. The park's dangerous. Come on." Jack motioned for her to follow him.

"Where?"

"I'm walking you home. Come on."

Michelle made a face. "You sound like Aunt Haddie." But she fell into step beside him. "Are you all right?"

"Yeah."

"Not a good day?"

"Nope."

"Do you want to talk about it?"

"Well, for starters, I found out I got someone fired."

Jack told her about Jeremy. He always found it easy to talk to Michelle. She listened intently, as she always did, and only asked an occasional question.

As they walked, Jack talking and Michelle listening, Jack found his eyes drawn to a man in the distance, walking toward them. Something about the man seemed off. Maybe it was his crisp tan pants and bright new shirt. But as Jack kept an eye on him, he changed his mind—it was the man's walk that stood out. He was tall but his stride was hitched, like he was forcing himself to walk slowly.

Jack stopped.

"What's up?" Michelle asked.

Jack pressed a finger to his lips. He felt as if he were watching a bad actor who had been given the simple task of walking across the stage and nodding.

He was approaching a woman on a bench—a tall, shapely brunette in a sundress. He nodded to the woman, then looked forward again. But his motions were stiff and robotic and not at all natural. When he reached the end of the bench, he took his hand out of his pocket and dropped something.

The bad theatrics caused Jack's adrenaline to kick in.

He's setting her up. Like a spider and a fly, he's drawing her in closer.

The woman rose off the bench and walked nearer to the man. She called out to him, and he stopped. She bent down and picked up what he'd dropped.

The man slowly walked back toward the woman, closer and closer, as she looked down at the object in her hand.

"That guy's up to something," Jack said to Michelle. "Listen, run to the front of the park and get a cop."

"What's going on? I'm not leaving you."

"No. I want you to get a cop. Understand?"

When Michelle turned and bolted for the entrance, Jack started jogging down the path. Neither the man nor the woman saw him approaching.

The woman suddenly jumped away from the man as though she had seen a snake. She ran, but the man's hand snapped out and seized her wrist.

Jack sprinted forward.

"Let go of me!" the woman screamed.

Jack covered the distance in seven long strides.

Glimpsing movement, the man turned toward Jack, but Jack was already lunging. His shoulder caught the man just below his sternum, and the man's breath exploded out of his lungs. Jack's arms wrapped around the man's thighs and yanked his legs out from under him. Momentum carried them across the path.

The man groaned as he landed hard on his back with Jack on top of him.

Jack grabbed the guy's shoulder, rolled him onto his belly, and wrenched one arm up behind his back. His other hand pressed the man's face into the dirt.

"It'll be all right, ma'am," Jack yelled. "POLICE!"

The woman turned and ran.

"Police!" Jack yelled again.

Almost instantly, nearly a dozen police officers appeared from every direction, racing across the grass and out of the woods.

Jack was surprised by the sheer number of cops showing up so fast. "He was attacking her," he said to the one who reached him first. He tilted his chin toward the fleeing woman. "He grabbed her wrist."

The cop yanked Jack to his feet. Jack smiled proudly when a second cop took out his handcuffs. A third officer pointed at Jack and said, "Put your hands behind your head."

"Me? This woman was being attacked."

A couple of officers helped the guy Jack had planted into the ground get up. They didn't cuff him. Instead, they wiped the dirt off his shirt.

"What's going on?" Jack looked around, puzzled. "Why aren't you arresting him?"

The guy he had tackled turned toward Jack. "I'm Officer Barton. Fairfield PD." He pulled out his badge. "You're under arrest for assaulting an officer."

The policeman with the cuffs snapped one around Jack's wrist. Jack felt the cold metal against the scar that circled above his hand. Panic shot through him like electricity through a condemned man and his whole body stiffened.

The cop grabbed Jack's other arm, but Jack held it rigid. "Don't make this harder on yourself, kid." The burly cop tried to bend Jack's arm, but it wouldn't budge.

"Give him your other arm," another cop commanded.

Jack knew what he *should* do. And he wanted to cooperate—but his body refused to obey. Terror seized him, stripping away rational thought, until only raw emotion remained, and the memory of searing heat in his wrist, fiery pain, and the odor of burnt flesh.

The other cops circled closer. "Give me your arm," the policeman ordered again.

A beefy officer stepped in and placed his hand on Jack's shoulder, while another placed his hand on his nightstick.

Jack clamped his eyes closed and forced his arm to bend.

The policeman yanked Jack's arm behind him and up.

In that moment, Jack's greatest fear enveloped him and he pictured the dominoes falling—no Army, no college, no law enforcement. With the click of the cuff, all of his dreams…gone.

21

FACTS

Once again, Jack found himself at the table in the police department interrogation room. The uniformed police officer guarding the door was different, but everything else was as Jack remembered it. The cop looked as if he wanted to be anywhere but here.

So did Jack.

The door swung wide. When Jack saw Vargas's red face, he was surprised the door hadn't slammed into the wall.

Detective Vargas strode over to the other side of the table and dragged the metal chair back. He planted one shiny shoe on the seat and tossed some folders down. "Do you have any idea what I want to do to you right now?"

Several flippant answers came to Jack's mind, but instead he answered, "No, sir."

"Let's start with you explaining why you were in the park," Vargas said.

"I was cutting through. I saw that guy grab a lady."

"A lady? Ha! That's rich. Try a lady of the night. I'm sure that the great Detective Stratton has figured out by now how badly he screwed up our prostitution sting, right? That guy was an undercover cop, and that 'lady' was a prostitute."

Jack ground his teeth.

Vargas laughed. "I did a background check on you." He crossed his arms. "You'd think that with your background you'd know how to pick out a hooker. Your mother was one, right?"

Jack kicked the table back with his leg. He started to stand, but the cop at the door stepped over and placed a large hand on his shoulder. "Settle down."

Vargas just smiled, which made Jack want to lunge across the table at him even more. He knew Vargas was just trying to get to him—and it seemed to be working.

Jack sat back down and tried to control his anger, while in his imagination, he'd already jumped over the table and was going to town on Vargas—slapping that mocking grin off his face.

The cop stayed next to Jack while Vargas kept pushing. "So you were trying to help that woman? Do you know Brittani Roldan?"

"No."

"You've never seen Brittani before today?"

"I have no idea who you're talking about. Is that the girl in the park?"

"She's the hooker you 'rescued.'" Vargas made air quotes. "We both know that's bull. Why don't you just level with me, Stratton. She's working for you, right?"

Jack had to laugh at that one. "Working for me? You think I'm a pimp?" He planted his feet and sat forward. "When do I do that? In between classes at Fairfield High?"

A smirk formed on Vargas's lips. "I would believe that a whole lot more than your 'I'm just a Good Samaritan trying to help' act. Why else would you pick a fight with the guy in the park?"

"Look, I was walking across the park and I thought that guy was attacking that lady. If Stacy Shaw's murder was a sexual assault that went bad, he could have been the guy who killed her."

Vargas laughed hard—but it was a forced laugh, and he overdid it. "You thought he was 'the real killer'?" Vargas made more air quotes. "Oh, that's right. Your friend Jay Martin is really innocent."

Jack felt frustration rise up inside him. That was the truth, but now that Vargas had said it aloud, Jack didn't know that he'd have believed it either. "Jay didn't kill Stacy Shaw. I think someone she worked with may have had something to do with it. I spoke with her coworkers—"

Vargas stuck his hand in Jack's face. "Hold on, Miss Marple. Did you just say you spoke to someone at Stacy's workplace?"

Jack snapped his mouth shut.

Vargas's hand slammed down on the table. "I told you to stay the hell away from anyone who has anything to do with this. Are you trying to screw up my case? Are you trying to get your friend off?"

"No. He's not my friend. But I know it wasn't him wearing that jacket that night."

"You're saying Jay's brother killed Stacy?"

"No, I didn't say that. Two Point stole, or more likely found, her wallet, and then he tried to use her debit card at the ATM. But kill her? No. Tommy's scrawny, and he messed up his wrist when he was a kid. I don't think he'd be able to strangle her."

Vargas's eyes blazed. "How the hell did you know she was strangled?"

"I… When I was in the station, I overheard you and your boss discussing the ME's report," Jack admitted.

Vargas pulled back. His hard expression shifted into neutral. Like a poker player who had just received his hold card, he placed one hand casually on the table and relaxed onto his elbow. He drummed his fingers on the table and silently watched Jack.

Jack felt the tone in the room change. "Detective Vargas, let me explain. You don't know me, and—"

Vargas lifted a hand and held his index finger to his lips. "You're wrong about that, Stratton. I do know you. See, I go by facts. The fact is, you're a bad seed. You're friends with a murder suspect. That's a fact. You visit him in prison and then conveniently find a body hidden in a pond. Fact. Now you tell me that you just happen to know a piece of information that hasn't been made public. Last week you were almost arrested for fighting over some old lady's stolen purse. What was the deal with that? Someone on your crew steals a purse but was going to keep it for himself? Officer Denby said you worked the guy over good. Broke his teeth out. I bet if Denby hadn't caught you, you'd have kept the purse. Maybe that's what happened with Stacy. Jay tried to steal her handbag but she didn't want to give it up."

"I didn't know that junkie. I got the bag back for the lady."

"Do you know her?"

"She's Victor Perez's grandmother."

"Oh, you're friends with Victor Perez, too?" Jack didn't answer, and Vargas smiled without showing any teeth. "Nice company you keep, Stratton. Murderers, drug dealers, prostitutes. You're a regular Boy Scout." He got nose to nose with Jack. "And here's another fact. You just lied to my face."

"What? I haven't lied."

"I asked you twice if you knew Brittani. You said you've never seen her before. But Brittani said she knows you. She said you gave her some money last night. But when I pressed her on that, she closed her mouth and lawyered up."

"That's crazy. I never…"

Jack remembered the hungry prostitute in the Dolly Parton wig from the night before. She must be the same girl caught in the sting. "Wait a minute. She was wearing a wig when I saw her first. You know how prostitutes vary it up for different clients. The look today must be her daytime look, for businessmen. I saw her at night."

"Actually, I didn't know hookers did that, Jack. But you seem to know all about it." Vargas muttered under his breath, "Like a pimp."

"No. I gave her money, but she was panhandling. She wanted a burger so I dropped a couple of bucks on a bench."

"Ha!" Vargas laughed. "You've got a smooth answer for everything, and it always has a 'Saint Jack' feel to it. 'I wasn't stealing. I was really rescuing a little old lady's purse.' 'Why, no, Officer, I did give the hooker money, but just so she could get something to eat, and I got no sexual favors in return. My only reward was her happiness.' Ha!"

Vargas laughed, and even the other cop chuckled.

Jack felt the anger rising in him. He tried to push it down. "Detective Vargas, I can explain. I—"

"Save it, Stratton. I'm done hearing your lies and fairy tales. I've seen your type before. You're nothing but trash that needs to be locked away." He walked over and yanked open the door. To the policeman he said, "Bring him out to the holding bench and stay with him. I've got to go check a few things." Then he turned to glare at Jack again. "Better get used to incarceration, Stratton. You'll be joining your friend in the Bay soon enough."

22

AUNT HADDIE TO THE RESCUE

Jack sat on a wooden bench in the police station, waiting to be charged. He leaned forward with his elbows on his knees and his head in his hands while police officers went about their day.

At the sound of Aunt Haddie's voice, he sat up straight.

Oh no.

Aunt Haddie was standing at the front desk. Luckily she hadn't seen Jack yet, as he was seated off to one side.

Behind the desk was the old police sergeant, Brian Gibson. Brian had a weathered, dark-brown face, cocoa-brown eyes with a friendly sparkle, and a small smile set permanently beneath his white mustache. And beside Brian stood a poised, trim woman in a dark-blue suit. She stood with her shoulders squared and her arms relaxed. A small American flag was pinned to her lapel.

"He tackled an undercover officer," the woman was saying. Jack recognized the woman by her voice, from when he overheard her briefing Vargas after he found Stacy's body: Superintendent Finney. Now he could put the face and the voice together. She seemed unaware that Jack was within earshot. Either that, or she didn't care.

"Who he thought was attacking a woman," Aunt Haddie explained. "Michelle saw the whole thing. If this Detective Vargas insists on going down that path, I want to file a formal complaint against the police department for putting Michelle and Jack, and other innocent children, in harm's way."

Brian Gibson's bushy white eyebrows arched high as he looked down at Aunt Haddie. "Haddie, don't you think that's going a little far?"

Aunt Haddie bristled. "The police obviously did not properly identify themselves, or Jack would never have thought the policeman was a potential threat. Michelle is merely a teenager. I would think that an effort would have been made to keep children away from that situation."

Superintendent Finney gave the slightest nod, conceding the point.

Aunt Haddie continued. "What if something had gone wrong? Weren't other policemen there to keep these kids safe?"

Gibson smoothed the corners of his mustache and glanced over at Superintendent Finney. "Several."

"If this made the papers," Aunt Haddie said, "wouldn't this be a black eye on the Fairfield Police Department?"

"Mrs. Williams." Superintendent Finney's voice was calm and even. "I do appreciate your concern and bringing this information to light." She turned to Brian. "Please wait with Mrs. Williams, Sergeant." Her carefully crafted neutral expression remained in place, but when she turned, Jack saw her blue eyes blazing like pilot lights. She headed straight to Detective Vargas's office and closed the door.

Laying a hand on Brian's arm, Aunt Haddie said, "I'm the one who got Jack involved in this whole situation, trying to do a good deed for somebody. Blame me. But please don't take it out on Jack. Do you know tomorrow marks eleven years ago that they brought him here?"

"I remember. When the kid figured out he couldn't go back to his mom, he went ballistic and tried to escape. It was like someone let a rabid raccoon loose. He almost made it out the door." Brian grinned crookedly. "I think half the cops wanted to open the door and let him go."

"But *you* managed to calm him down."

"Me?" Brian chuckled. "I managed to lure him into an office with a sandwich, that's all. You're the only one who could calm him down."

Superintendent Finney stepped out of Vargas's office and beckoned Brian over. Although Jack couldn't hear what was said, it was obvious that what followed was a one-way conversation: the superintendent spoke and Brian listened. When Finney was done with him, she abruptly retreated back into Vargas's office.

As Brian walked to Aunt Haddie, his small smile was tighter. "You'll talk to his parents?" he said.

Aunt Haddie's chin rose. "I will. Will he be charged?"

"No, ma'am."

Aunt Haddie let out her breath. "Thank you."

Brian turned toward where Jack was waiting. The sergeant, at least, knew that Jack had been listening to the entire exchange. He motioned for Jack to get up and come over.

Jack walked over hesitantly. He expected Aunt Haddie to be furious with him, but the look on her face reminded him of the same warm expression that she'd had when he first met her.

I guess that's what unconditional love looks like.

"Oh, Jackie." She wrapped her arms around him.

"I'm sorry, Aunt Haddie," Jack said. "And I'm sorry you had to come down here."

"Don't you be sorry about that. What else was I going to do after Michelle told me what happened? Let's just get you home. We'll work things out." They headed for the exit.

"Do my parents know yet?"

Aunt Haddie shook her head. "But Detective Clark said he left messages on both their phones."

Jack groaned as he held open the front door of the police station. "I'm dead."

"No you're not. I'll speak to them."

"I'm still dead."

"Let's get you home and we can discuss your demise calmly."

They climbed into Aunt Haddie's station wagon and headed home. Sitting in the front seat beside Haddie brought the heaviness back to Jack's chest. Eleven years later, and here they were, in the same car, pulling out of the same police parking lot.

Jack stared out the window. He fought to push the memories of his past into the shadows where he liked them, but no matter how hard he tried, he couldn't escape who he was. All his studying, all his training—in vain.

"Vargas was right. I am nothing."

Aunt Haddie patted his shoulder. "Don't you *ever* say such a thing, Jackie. We'll get this mess untangled. I'll explain everything to your parents."

"There's no explaining. My father's going to… Can we just forget it happened?"

"You did nothing wrong. Well, you should have called the police first, but"—she pressed her lips together as if she was about to give him foul-tasting medicine—"I do know something that could help soften the news of your being brought down to the police station."

"Name it."

"You know what tomorrow is?"

"Garbage Day."

"Stop calling it that. It's your birthday."

"Same thing. She threw me away. Like garbage. I really don't understand why everyone wants to celebrate that."

"It's a day that I thank the Lord for, because it's your birthday."

Jack chuckled bitterly. "Just because the social worker wrote that date on the form doesn't make it my birthday. I don't know when my real birthday is."

Aunt Haddie shook her head. "Then let *every* day be your birthday. Today's a new day. Besides, the day doesn't belong to you or anyone else. It's the Lord's. He's just letting you enjoy it."

"I'm sure having a blast with this one," Jack muttered.

She whacked his shoulder playfully.

"Ouch! Is that where Chandler gets it from?" Jack rubbed his arm.

Aunt Haddie laughed. She took a right and pulled onto her street. "Your mom would really like to make you a cake, you know."

Jack groaned. "Please tell her not to. Is Chandler around?"

"He's still helping Mr. Emerson. I suggest you go over there and give them a hand."

"Why?"

"Because I'm going to go explain to your father that I just picked you up at the police station. Jackie, I know you were just trying to help that woman. I know, too, that your taking me and Mrs. Martin to the prison to see Jay made you look bad to that Detective Vargas. You've done all you can. You need to leave it to the police. I'll explain all that. But that explanation will go over a lot better if I can add that you're currently helping a widow."

"Right now, every time I help someone, I get jacked up."

"Don't be silly. Jewels in your crown in Heaven."

Jack grumbled, "With the way everything's going, the angels are going to accuse me of stealing those jewels."

* * *

Jack spent the rest of the day helping Mr. Emerson and Chandler install a washer and dryer for Mrs. McDermott. First they had to take the old units down three flights of stairs. Then they discovered that part of the floor was rotted, so they had to rip it up and patch it. Finally they were able to install the appliances that Mr. Emerson had rebuilt.

By the time they were done, it was almost eight and Jack was exhausted. He wanted nothing more than to go home, enjoy his mom's cooking, wash up, and go to bed. But he wasn't ready to face his mom and dad yet, until he'd spoken to Aunt Haddie. Maybe she could give him some idea of just how much trouble he was in.

He drove Chandler back to Aunt Haddie's and followed him inside. They were greeted by the aroma of her baked mac and cheese. His smile vanished when Michelle held the phone out to him.

"Jack, it's your dad."

Chandler gave Jack a look that said, *Good luck.*

I'll need it, Jack thought. *Guess it's time to face the music.*

"Hello?" Jack said.

His father cleared his throat. "Jack…can you explain to me what happened today? I've heard Aunt Haddie's version, and I just got off a call with Detective Clark. But I haven't yet heard a word from my own son. Would you care to fill me in?"

Jack took a deep breath, then ran down everything that had happened in the park. When he finished, there was a long silence.

"Dad? Are you still there?"

"Yes," his father said. Jack pictured him cleaning off his glasses while he gathered his thoughts. "If you believed that man was attacking that woman, you should have gotten the police, not tackled him yourself."

"There wasn't time to get the cops. What was I supposed to do?"

"Get the cops anyway."

"I sent Michelle."

"You should have waited for them."

"Dad, I'm going to be a policeman."

"You're not one yet."

Aunt Haddie had been bustling around and was setting some baked mac and cheese, green beans, and buttered biscuits on the table, along with a pitcher of lemonade. "Suppertime, Jack," she said, loudly enough that his father would hear.

Jack covered the receiver. "It's my dad."

"I know," she whispered. "I need to speak with him." Aunt Haddie held out a hand and smiled.

"Ah, Dad. Aunt Haddie wants to talk to you." Jack quickly handed the phone to her.

"Hi, Ted. I just wanted to assure you that everything is fine. After I spoke with you, I had a long talk with Jack, and we discussed everything you said. I just put supper down for him. He sure did work so hard today helping Mrs. McDermott, poor woman." She gave Jack a wink. "With him being so tired, would you mind if he spent the night?"

There was a slight pause.

"Thank you, Ted. I'll be sure to send him home first thing in the morning, with it being his birthday."

Aunt Haddie listened and nodded.

"Okay. Give my love to Laura."

Jack raised his glass of lemonade in salute. "Aunt Haddie, you're the best."

"I try. I know it was because of me and Mrs. Martin that you got caught between the switches today. Now eat your supper and get to bed. You boys both look like you need it."

* * *

Jack lay on the bed in his old bedroom, staring at the ceiling. Despite his physical exhaustion, he couldn't sleep.

When the clock on the little table flipped to 11:57, Jack decided to give up on sleep. He slid out of bed and went over to the desk in the corner. Turning on the desk lamp, he grabbed his notebook and turned to a fresh page. He wrote *Why?* at the top of the page and underlined it. Then he started writing his questions.

A few minutes later there was a tap on the door, and Chandler stuck his head in.

"What's up?" Jack whispered.

Chandler slipped inside and walked over. "I saw your light turn on. What's up? Can't sleep?"

"You're not sleeping either."

Chandler looked down at Jack's notebook. "What's with the why?"

Jack tapped his pen on the notepad, then dropped it. "I've got a problem with whys. That's what my therapist said, anyway. Why did my mother throw me away? Why did she keep me so long? Why, why, why. I hate why. I want answers. So she told me to write down the whys. That's what I'm doing."

"What about?"

"Stacy Shaw. There's a lot of things that don't make sense to me."

"Aunt Haddie said you should let it go and leave it to the cops."

"I know. But there's nothing wrong with writing on a piece of paper. That won't get me arrested."

"True."

"I mean, why was Stacy Shaw's car at Ford's Crossing?"

"I still figure she was heading home and crashed. What we don't know is why she would go into the park after," Chandler said.

Jack tapped the page. "That's number four on my list. Number five, why was Stacy's phone in the car and not in her handbag?"

Chandler scrunched up his nose and closed one eye. But his train of thought was derailed by an enormous yawn. "We can get answers tomorrow. You should go to bed."

"Did you come in here to tell me that?"

Chandler grinned. "Yeah. I know you. Let it go. You're getting all wound up. Go to sleep."

"I will."

Chandler walked back to the door. "I almost forgot. Happy birthday." He grinned.

Jack didn't. "It's not until tomorrow."

"It already *is* tomorrow." Chandler pointed at the clock; it was after midnight. "Think about it. Eleven years ago, you got to meet me. Best birthday present ever, huh?"

Jack chuckled. "Go to bed, Mr. Humble."

Chandler yawned. "'Night."

Jack picked up his pen, turned back to his notebook, and sketched out the crime scene. When he couldn't remember a detail, he closed his eyes until he could picture it. He was thinking, tapping the pen against the page, when somewhere inside the house he heard a girl's scream.

Jack raced to the bedroom door. Another terrorized shriek came, definitely close by, echoing down the hall. He ripped open the door just as the scream trailed off.

In the bedroom directly across from Jack's, a girl cried out, "GET OFF ME!"

Jack grabbed the door handle, but it was locked. He lowered his shoulder and slammed into the door. Wood splintered, and broken pieces flew as the door smashed open.

Replacement lay in her bed. Jack ran over to her. Her green eyes were filled with terror, and her whole body was rigid. "GET OFF ME!" she shrieked again.

Jack looked frantically around the room for her attacker, but there was no one. He gently touched Replacement's arm. "Are you okay?"

Chandler and Michelle charged into the room. Michelle immediately raced over to Replacement and wrapped her arms around her. Replacement's eyes were open, but by now Jack didn't think she was actually awake.

Aunt Haddie appeared in the doorway and exchanged a knowing look with Michelle.

"Shh," Michelle whispered, rocking the girl in her arms. "It's okay. I'm right here."

Replacement shook her head and blinked rapidly. She looked at Michelle as if she'd never seen her before. Then she burst into tears and buried her face in Michelle's shoulder.

"Come on, boys." Aunt Haddie ushered Jack and Chandler out of the room. She pulled the door closed, then frowned when she saw the broken lock.

"Sorry." Jack rubbed the back of his neck. "She was screaming for help, and it was locked."

"That's okay." Aunt Haddie patted his cheek. "Always the white knight. I'm sure you and Chandler can fix it."

"Me?" Chandler pointed at Jack. "Just because he doesn't know how to turn a doorknob, I…" Chandler trailed off when Aunt Haddie's eyebrow rose. "I mean, yes, ma'am."

Jack tipped his head toward Replacement's bedroom. "What's wrong with her?"

They all heard the muffled sobbing continuing, and Michelle's reassuring murmurs.

Aunt Haddie shook her head. "Night terrors. Poor little angel. She's been through hell." Aunt Haddie's eyes teared up. "She'll be okay. The good Lord willing, she'll be okay. You boys go to bed now." She kissed them both and then went downstairs.

Chandler walked back to his room.

"Sorry about the door," Jack called after him.

Chandler stopped. "I shouldn't have said that. It wasn't you I was mad at." His muscles tensed and his eyes smoldered. "She's such a good kid. Who'd hurt someone like that? Some people are just evil." He went into his bedroom and closed the door.

Jack did the same. When he turned off the desk lamp, the darkness seemed even deeper now than it had before. He lay down on the bed. Still unable to fall asleep, he interlaced his fingers behind his head and thought about a woman he'd never met. *Who was Stacy Shaw?* Someone's daughter. Someone's wife. Jack knew he wasn't just trying to prove Jay was innocent. He was doing something more—trying to catch the person who'd killed a young mother looking forward to a new life and the baby that never had a chance.

The killer waited for her. He rushed her in the dark. Then he dragged her into the woods.

Jack heard his heart thump loudly.

Chandler's words made his stomach tighten. *Some people are evil.*

Just before he slipped into sleep, he realized: *I'm hunting a monster.*

23

SPIRIT DAY

Jack and Chandler walked out the back door of Aunt Haddie's the next morning, and there was Replacement, sitting on the steps with her head in her hands. The samurai-style ponytail on top of her head drooped down her shoulders.

"What's the matter?" Chandler asked.

"Nothing," she mumbled. Her eyes looked like they had cried a lot last night, and maybe weren't far from it right now.

Chandler squatted down and eyed her suspiciously.

She made a face. "Today's Fairfield Town Spirit Day at the community center, but I don't have anything to wear that says Fairfield."

"Ask Michelle! She has lots of stuff," Chandler said.

The ponytail danced back and forth as Replacement shook her head. "Nope. She has *two* Fairfield shirts. She's wearing one and she's letting Moisha wear the other."

"I'm sure she didn't realize..." Chandler patted her shoulder.

"I know that." She pouted. "And I know Michelle would give me her own shirt if I asked, so I'm *not* asking."

"Does it have to be from middle school?" Jack asked.

Replacement didn't look up. "No. Just anything with Fairfield on it."

Jack pulled off his Fairfield High T-shirt and held it out to her. "It'll be huge on you, but it's Fairfield."

She stared up at him, blinking, not reaching out for the shirt.

Jack sniffed the shirt. "I just put it on. It's clean."

Her mouth dropped open, and slowly she reached out for the shirt, her eyes glassy and out of focus. She suddenly rose to her feet, clutching Jack's shirt to her chest, and bolted inside.

"You're welcome, kid," Jack muttered.

Chandler laughed at Jack. "You gonna go out half-naked, or do you want me to run upstairs and get you another shirt?"

"Nah. I got a clean shirt in the trunk."

Chandler smacked his arm as they walked to the car. "I bet she never forgets that."

"What's the big deal?" *Why did she keep staring at me like that?* Jack shrugged. "It's just a shirt."

Chandler shook his head. "Sometimes you're clueless."

"What?"

"I probably shouldn't say anything, but—Michelle told me that Replacement has a huge crush on you. Besides, you remember what it was like. How many people do you think would do something like that for her?"

"You, for one." Jack opened the trunk, grabbed a clean gym shirt, and pulled it on.

"You know I would. We're fighting evil, man." Chandler smiled. "I probably shouldn't tell you this either, but Michelle said Replacement thinks you're like Batman. But"—his chest puffed up—"she thinks *I'm* like Superman."

"That's cool," Jack said, getting into the Impala.

Chandler eased his length and girth into the passenger side. "That's cool? You wouldn't rather be Superman?"

"Are you kidding me? Think it through. Clark Kent has a nine-to-five job. He digs a chick who thinks he's a hopeless loser, and she has the hots for his alter ego."

"Yeah, but Superman can't be hurt by bullets."

"So what? Bruce Wayne is cool all the way around. Boy billionaire. Babes abound. Catwoman. He doesn't work. Sweet cars. Sleeps all day and fights crime at night. *And* he has a butler. There's no contest."

"Superman can fly," Chandler said. "Case closed."

Jack laughed and rolled down his window. He felt it in the air—today was going to be a scorcher. Now he just had to put off talk of Garbage Day as long as possible.

"This isn't the way to your house," Chandler said. "What now? Almost getting arrested, twice, wasn't enough?"

"Five minutes."

Chandler sighed. "A lot can happen in five minutes."

Jack drove to Morton's Hill and parked the Impala across the street from Stacy Shaw's pretty little yellow ranch with flowerboxes in the windows. The grass was long and needed a cut.

Jack settled back into his seat and stared at the house. After a minute, Chandler shifted uncomfortably.

"What?" Jack asked.

"You're parked sorta close."

"Close to what?"

"The house." Chandler pointed. "In the movies, they always park far away. Or in a van with dark windows."

"It's not a stakeout."

"Then why are we here?"

"I'm thinking."

"You can't do your thinking at home?"

Jack ran his knuckle along the door panel. "No. You're supposed to try to get inside the victim's head. I guess that's what I'm doing."

"Aren't you supposed to get into the *killer's* head? Like FBI profiling and all that jazz."

"Yeah, sure. But I figure you should also get to know the victim. Like the guys who spot counterfeit bills. They don't look at the fake bills; they study the real ones. That way, when they see a counterfeit, it sets off alarms in their head."

"Do you have any alarms going off?"

"I just keep wondering why she walked back to work and not here. If she hadn't walked through Hamilton Park, she'd be alive right now."

"That's creepy." Chandler suddenly sat bolt upright. "Oh no…"

Michael Shaw, wearing shorts and flip-flops, was stalking across his yard, straight toward the Impala.

Vargas's warning echoed in Jack's head. *If I catch you within ten yards of anything to do with my investigation…*

Jack stomped on the gas. The engine revved, but the car didn't go anywhere—it was in park.

"Go, go!" Chandler urged.

Jack shifted into drive, but the engine sputtered and died. "Crap."

"Hey!" Michael called out.

Jack slammed the transmission back into park and started the car again.

"Hello?" Michael yelled, advancing quickly.

Jack started to put the car into drive, but his hand hesitated on the gearshift. "This is our chance to talk to him," he whispered.

"No way. Just go." Chandler's hand twitched as though he wanted to move the gear himself.

Jack shut off the engine and got out of the car. He called out to Michael, "I think something's wrong with the carburetor." He walked over to the hood, looked through the windshield at Chandler, and pointed to the driver's side of the car. "When I tell you, start it up."

Shooting Jack a cautionary look, Chandler slid across the bench seat and behind the steering wheel.

Jack lifted the hood and propped it open. "I hope we didn't wake you up with the car noise."

Michael walked over. "Nah, I was up. I just didn't know what you were doing out here." He frowned, and his ruddy complexion went a little paler. "There've been reporters all over the place this last week."

"Give it a little gas," Jack called to Chandler while he fiddled with a lever. "Reporters? Why?"

Michael stared at Jack, his eyes becoming even redder, and blew his nose. Jack saw this as an opening to ask him some questions about Stacy, but he struggled for the right words to get him talking. "Are you famous or something?"

"No." Michael cleared his throat. "Do you want me to call someone for you?"

"I think I can get her going."

Michael exhaled. "Maybe I can help." He leaned his head forward and rubbed the back of his neck. "Is it stalling?"

"Yeah. It's been doing that lately."

"It could just be some bad gas." Michael sneezed, then blew his nose again. "Damn pollen."

"Allergies?"

"Yeah. Pretty severe this time of year."

"Yeah, those can get pretty bad." Jack then called out to Chandler, "Okay, try to start it now!"

Chandler started the engine and held the gas down while Jack adjusted the carburetor.

"Ease off," Jack called out. He looked over at the house, scanning for anything that might have a bearing on the case, but he was drawing a complete blank.

Out of the corner of his eye, he saw Michael watching him. With a greasy finger, Jack pointed behind Michael's house. "I used to cut through your yard to go sledding up on Morton's Hill."

"Oh, yeah. The realtor told us that kids do that." Michael smiled. "My wife and I…" His grin quickly soured. "There's a big tree up the top. She wanted me to put a swing up there for…" He cleared his throat. His eyes glistened. He rubbed them with the back of his hands. "I gotta get some sleep."

Jack felt bad for the guy.

"Look, I'll call a tow for you guys," Michael said.

"Thanks, but I think I can make it home." Jack grabbed the rod and closed the hood. "Sorry again for being loud."

"Don't worry about it. Like I said, I was up."

Jack walked over to the driver's side as Chandler slid over. "Have a good day."

"You too."

Jack waved, and so did Michael.

As they drove away, Chandler exhaled loudly. "That freaked me out. Did you talk about anything?"

"No." Jack rubbed the side of his face. "I couldn't ask him about…you know. I just felt bad for him. I guess I've been thinking of the guy like a piece in the puzzle and not a person. But when I saw him face-to-face…"

"He looked bad. Like he hasn't slept in a while," Chandler said.

"Looked like he'd been crying, too. Sucks."

Chandler looked out the window. "Of course he'd be crying! I'd go out of my mind if someone I loved was murdered."

24

ON BORROWED TIME

Jack sat at his computer while Chandler lay on Jack's bed, tossing a baseball into the air and catching it again. Jack's mom and dad weren't home, which came as a relief to Jack. He hadn't faced either of them since almost getting arrested. He didn't want to see the disappointment in their eyes. Or hear about his birthday.

"Nina's going out with Bobbie G tomorrow," Jack said, reading from Nina's relentless Facebook posts.

"She just wants to tick off Two Point."

"Probably."

Jack had been hoping Facebook would allow him to find out more about some of the people involved in the case—especially Leland Chambers—but it seemed that social media wasn't a great source of information except for Nina.

He clicked over to the *Fairfield Times* website to see if anything new had been reported. Sure enough, the lead headline read, "Grand Jury Set to Convene in Stacy Shaw Homicide."

Chandler read over his shoulder. "What does that mean?"

"It means we're running out of time." Jack opened his email app.

"What's the plan now?"

"Remember those two business cards Stacy had in her handbag? I'm sending them emails to see if Stacy had an appointment or anything."

"Sounds like a long shot."

"It is, but maybe Stacy was heading there. Luisa's Luxe Hair Studio is across from the park on Holland Street, and it's open till nine."

Chandler shook his head. "I bet they don't tell you diddly. Some random guy sends an email asking if a murdered woman had an appointment? And you think they'll respond? The fertility clinic won't say a thing. They have all those privacy laws and the whole patient confidentiality thing."

"I know," Jack said, "but Detective Clark says you should follow up on every lead. The serial killer Son of Sam was caught because of a parking ticket."

"Sounds to me like you're running out of ideas."

"Thanks for the encouragement."

The front door opened. "Are you upstairs, Jack?" his mother called out.

"Hey, Mom," Jack replied. "Be down in a second."

Chandler headed for the bedroom door. "I still can't get over Nina. Bobbie G was seeing Evy. No good's gonna come of that."

Jack got up too, but then stopped in the doorway. "Wait a minute." He spun around and jumped back on the computer, pulled up one of the Facebook pages he'd been looking at, and checked the relationship status. *Single.*

Jack hurried out of his room and down the stairs.

"I didn't think you'd be home this early," his mom said. "Happy birthday." She kissed his cheek, then gave Chandler a hug. "Did you boys eat breakfast?"

His mom didn't even mention the incident in the park. But she did give Jack a questioning smile, and he knew she was searching his face for any hint that his disgust for Garbage Day had lessened. But it hadn't.

"We're good," Jack said. "Hey, can I borrow your car?"

"Is something wrong with yours?"

"Nope. I'm just…doing a test. I'll fill up the tank."

"You don't have to do that." She walked over to her handbag and pulled out the keys. "I won't be needing it. Tracy Dillard is picking me up to go to Foal Brook High. We're giving them a hand with their new record-keeping system."

"Great. Thanks, Mom. I shouldn't be that long."

"You can have it the whole day." She gave him the keys. "Will you be around for dinner tonight?" Her voice rose, and her hands pressed together as if she were praying.

Jack knew what she was really asking: *Would you like a birthday dinner, and a cake?* He shook his head. "I don't think so."

His mom smiled, but Jack read the disappointment in her eyes.

"Hey, do you know when Dad will be home?" he asked.

"He's teaching a summer class. Did you need him for something?"

"I wanted to ask him about an old student."

"Who?"

"Alex Hernandez."

His mother's hand flew to her chest. "Oh, no, please don't tell me he did something…"

"No…Do you know him?"

She fiddled with the cross on her necklace, a sure sign she was upset. "He was your father's student, oh, a dozen years ago. Where did you see him?"

"I ran into him in Hamilton Park."

"How did he know who you were?"

"Ah…he heard my name."

"It's surprising he remembered after all he's been through."

"So you know that he's…kinda nutty," Jack said.

His mom frowned. "I don't like that word. He's troubled. He's been through so much trouble already."

"You mean his wife, Anne? She was murdered, right?"

His mom pinched the bridge of her nose between her thumb and forefinger. "Yes. It was horrible. Poor Alex just snapped. Your father tried to help him, but…"

"Dad tried to help the guy? Really?"

His mom nodded. "Your father does a lot of things he doesn't take any credit for." She folded her hands and stood up ramrod straight, as if she were about to give a presentation. "And Jack, your father wants to talk to you about what happened at the park. He deferred last night to Aunt Haddie, but—"

"Can you get him to defer for my birthday?" Jack smiled hopefully. "Better yet, permanently?"

His mom smiled. "I'll try for the latter, but don't get your hopes up. And Jack, please call me if you change your mind about tonight. I'd love to make you something special for dinner."

"I'm all set, Mom. We gotta run. Love you." Jack gave her a peck on the cheek, plus an extra hug because he knew she was hurting a little over his so-called birthday, and nodded to Chandler to head out.

"I love you too. You're not going to do anything risky today, are you?"

Chandler waved from the doorway. "I'll keep him out of trouble."

"Thank you, Chandler. Oh, and Jack, if you see Detective Clark, be sure to let him know that you met Alex."

Jack stopped just beyond the door. "What?"

"He knows Alex too. Detective Clark watches out for him." She rubbed her hands together and looked off into the distance. "It's just so sad. To lose your wife would be hard enough, but she was expecting. Their first child."

Jack felt the hairs on the back of his neck rise. *Stacy Shaw was pregnant, too.*

25

FOLLOW ALL LEADS

Jack backed into the parking space of a convenience store so the front of his mother's car would face the road to the Shaws' house. The store had been a fixture in the neighborhood as long as Jack could remember. Originally, it had been a house, but the walls downstairs had been knocked down to fit in all the chips, beer, and soda.

"This isn't a car," Chandler grumbled as he tried to get comfortable in the tiny bucket seat. "It's a shoebox with wheels." He had the passenger seat on Jack's mother's compact as far back as it would go, and his knees still touched the dashboard. "Why couldn't we take the Impala?"

"Because Shaw would recognize it. Put your hat on." Jack pulled down the rim of his cap.

Chandler glanced at the Boston Celtics logo on the hat Jack had given him. "Your dad is consumed by Boston sports."

Jack grinned. "Born and bred in Beantown. It's in his blood."

Chandler looked around. "So, what are you hoping to see?"

"If Michael leaves his house, he has to come right by us."

"I get that, but why are you interested in him in the first place?"

"This morning I saw something on his Facebook profile that bothered me. It's probably nothing, but it makes me want to look at him. He changed his Facebook profile to Single."

"Hmm, that could be interesting. But we should look at some other possibilities. Did he change it, or was it already set to that?" Chandler asked.

"What do you mean?"

"Lots of people have no clue how Facebook works. Maybe he set his page up years ago, before he got married. Or maybe he never knew you could set it to Married, or he never bothered. When was the last time he updated?"

Jack was a little ashamed of himself for not asking these questions, but all the more impressed with his outwardly-seeming reluctant accomplice. "I don't know. I didn't check."

"And anyway, didn't the police rule him out? Didn't they say he was four hours away, someplace that sounds like Skinny Lady or something?"

Jack chuckled. "Schenectady."

"Whatever. My money's on Dracula. Prime suspect. A crazy homeless guy who sleeps right where Stacy was killed. He thinks he's still in the military. Maybe he thought she was the enemy or something."

"Maybe," Jack admitted. "But he was so convincing."

"He was just as convincing when he said he checked in with field command." Chandler whistled the theme from *The Twilight Zone*. "The guy's out there—wearing tinfoil on his head crazy."

"True."

"What about Leland Chambers?" Chandler said. "If you believe Dracula, he saw Chambers running through the park wearing those bright-green sneakers. He's Stacy's manager, and that janitor said they argued."

"Yeah, he's definitely a possibility. But I've got nothing to go at him with until I hear back from Betty."

"Isn't she a suspect, too?"

"What makes you think that?"

Chandler sat up and bumped his head on the ceiling. "I'm so scrunched." He took off the hat and rubbed his head. "She was the last one to see Stacy alive. What if she's not telling the truth?"

"I never thought of that. She is a big woman."

"Did you see her hands? They're, like, my size." Chandler held his up, then popped his hat back on and pulled down the brim.

Jack laughed. "They're nowhere close to your giant mitts. Wait a minute." Jack took out his notebook. "Betty didn't give off any red flags, but there was something she said about her husband"—Jack flipped through pages until he found what he was looking for—"Bruce. Betty said he dropped her off after work and then went back out."

"Did she say why?" Chandler asked.

"To run a few errands."

"That seems kinda strange late at night. And why did he drop his wife off?"

Jack shrugged.

Chandler tapped on the roof. "My money's still on Vlad."

"Before you place your bet, there are other suspects too," Jack said.

"Like who?"

"Jeremy. He was nearby. He's physically strong enough, and he had a crush on Stacy."

"What? How did you get that?"

"When I asked him how Stacy looked, he said *pretty*. And just how he acted when he was talking about her. He liked her—a lot."

"You could be right," Chandler said.

"And there's still the two obvious choices," Jack muttered. "Two Point, for one. Say it was a robbery gone bad. And yeah, his hand is screwed up, but I've been thinking about it. There are other ways to strangle someone." He shifted in the seat, reaching for Chandler's throat to demonstrate. "If he pinned her down and grabbed her like this—"

Chandler knocked his hand away. "I get it, so you can use someone else for your strangulation demo. You said two choices. Who's the other?"

Jack stared out the windshield. "Jay."

"What? Isn't he the guy we're doing this for? He wasn't even in the park."

"We only have Jay's word for that. And…he *had* met Stacy."

"Say what?" Chandler did a double take.

"Jay delivered furniture to the Shaws' house."

"No way. So he knew Stacy."

"He met her," Jack said. "He was in her house. And H. T. Wells is only two blocks down from where he works."

"That doesn't look too good," Chandler said. "Still, I think the cops should be looking at Vlad."

"So you've said. And call him Alex."

"I didn't mean anything by it."

"I know, it's just…" Jack shrugged. "He kinda gave me the whole Ghost of Christmas Future type of thing. You know? Like, under the right circumstances, if the right things happened to me, could I end up just like him? Could that be me? Listen, if something were to happen, you know, to one of us—"

"Nothing's gonna happen," Chandler said. "I've got your back. Don't talk about stuff like that." In an obvious effort to change the subject, he added, "So how long are we supposed to sit here and wait for Michael Shaw?"

"As long as it takes, I guess."

Chandler groaned.

"Do you know what the Army's gonna be like?" Jack reminded him. "Job one is hurry up and wait. Same thing with being a cop. I have the patience for it. You're like a bad doctor—no patients."

"That is the lamest joke I've ever heard. There's no way I'm going to sit in this sardine can all afternoon pretending to be a cop. Especially if you keep telling jokes like that."

"It's good prep," Jack said. "My dad's made me read every book in the library on police work—and I'm talking interlibrary loan, too. And now that we're going into the Army, I think he cleared the library out of books on military strategy and survival. You're reading those books he gave you too, right?"

"They're going to cover all that stuff in basic."

"Some of it. Some they won't. They can't cover everything."

"It's the teacher in him," Chandler said.

"And the overprotective dad. Thanks, by the way."

"For what?"

"Coming with me. Having my back."

Chandler's expression changed. He looked serious. "What if they don't let us serve together? I thought they kept family separated."

"They won't know we're foster brothers. On paper, you and I are as different as yin and yang."

"In looks, too," Chandler said.

"But back to back. I've got you covered." Jack held up his fist to knuckle-bump Chandler's. "Besides, I could never show my face again if something did happen to you."

"Hey!" Chandler sat up so quickly the whole car rocked.

"What did you see?" Jack stared down the road.

"No, not that." Chandler waved his hand dismissively. "This is a stakeout, right?"

"Kinda."

"Is it or isn't it?"

Jack didn't know where the question was leading, but he figured Chandler was up to something. "Is."

"Great!" Chandler reached for the door handle.

"What are you doing?"

"Getting some doughnuts. This place has Krispy Kremes!"

"Stay in the car," Jack snapped. "You just ate."

"Come on." Chandler's outstretched hand almost hit the driver-side window, his reach was so long. "You said we need to do what cops do."

Jack laughed. "They don't sit there eating doughnuts."

"I would."

Jack laughed again.

Chandler's smile vanished. "Incoming." He pointed.

Jack looked down the road and saw Michael in his silver Toyota, then quickly looked away. "Just act cool."

"Always do." Chandler grinned.

The Toyota passed them.

Jack put the compact car into drive. As the gears tumbled into place, something inside Jack shifted too. He felt the warm glow of adrenaline rush through his veins, and a determined grin spread across his face. He pulled out onto the road and accelerated. The compact's little engine whined in protest.

"Speed up," Chandler said.

Jack broke into his best Scottish accent. "I'm givin' her all she's got, Cap'n."

"What's this car have under the hood for power? Hamsters?" Chandler scoffed. "Stop fooling around; you're going to lose him."

Jack looked down at the red-lined tachometer on the dashboard. "The lawnmower engine in this thing is about to blow a rod. My foot's flat on the floor. Unless I strap a rocket on the roof, this is it."

It took three blocks of weaving in and out of traffic, but they finally caught up with the Toyota. They followed it west, out of Fairfield.

"I think he's going to the highway," Jack said.

"Are you too close?"

"I don't know." Jack slowed down.

"No! You'll lose him."

Jack sped up again.

"Don't get right behind him," Chandler cautioned. "You're supposed to leave a car or two between us and him."

"You're driving me crazy. You're the worst backseat driver ever."

The Toyota took the ramp onto the highway.

"He's hitting the highway." Chandler's big hand swept up and thwacked the ceiling. "This thing will have a hard time at fifty."

Jack stepped on the gas, and they zipped up the ramp. Traffic was light, but the other cars obscured their view of the Toyota.

"You lost him." Chandler craned his neck and peered ahead.

"It's a highway. He can only go straight. I'll find him." Jack kept his foot pinned to the floor and glared at the speedometer.

"I should get out and push," Chandler grumbled.

Jack moved into the far left lane of the three-lane highway in order to pass a slow-moving tractor-trailer in the center lane—apparently the only vehicle on the road that was slower than they were. "I still don't see him," he said. "But the next exit isn't for, like, ten miles."

"It'll take us that long to catch him," Chandler said. "Oh, man!"

They'd passed the tractor-trailer and the silver Toyota was right beside them, in the far-right lane. Chandler turned his head down and away, pretending to fiddle with the radio.

Jack sped up.

"What are you doing?" Chandler hunched up his shoulders. "You're not supposed to pass him."

"I got this."

The little car shook as it strained to go faster.

Chandler looked around. "I think the wheels are going to come off this thing."

"Trust me." Jack looked in the rearview mirror. Michael was still on the far right, and the middle lane was clear. Jack slowed down.

A minivan behind him flashed its lights to signal Jack to move out of the left lane. Jack just slowed even more, and the minivan pulled into the middle lane to pass them. Jack used the minivan to block their car from the view of the Toyota, then switched over to the far-right lane, a couple of cars behind Shaw.

"See." Jack held his hand out as if he had just served up the Toyota on a platter.

"Sweet, but don't get us jammed up."

"I won't."

"One call to the cops and we're *screwed.* The Army doesn't want troublemakers."

"You sound like Aunt Haddie."

Chandler smacked his arm. "Yeah, just this morning she said that to me." He cleared his throat and broke into his best Aunt Haddie impression: "Now, Chandler, you need to stay out of trouble or you're *screwed.*" He stretched the word out.

Jack laughed. "I meant 'troublemakers' sounds like Aunt Haddie. But fine, you sound like my mom. Okay?"

"Like your mom has ever said 'screwed' either." Chandler held up his index finger. "Listen, I'm one hundred and ten percent as serious as a heart attack. I cannot, and will not, get jacked up in this. The Army's my ticket to college."

"You won't."

They followed the Toyota for the next ten miles. Chandler shook his head. "This guy's probably just running an errand. Getting a TV fixed or his tires rotated."

Just when Jack started to wonder whether Chandler was right and they were wasting valuable time following this guy around, the Toyota's right turn signal started blinking.

Chandler pointed. "He's going to Darrington."

The Toyota took the off ramp and Jack followed, with a van between them. At the end of the ramp, both the Toyota and the van took a right, and Jack rolled through after them.

"Can you see him?" Jack craned his neck and drifted toward the middle of the road.

The Toyota and the van both took a right.

"The stupid van is going everywhere Michael is," Chandler said.

The Toyota took a hard left. So did the van.

Suddenly, the Toyota slammed to a stop. The van skidded up right behind it, turned a little to the left to avoid a collision. Jack jammed both feet down on the brake pedal to keep from rear-ending it. Everything on the front seat shot forward and onto the floor, while Chandler braced himself against the dashboard.

Chandler whispered, "Wow, that was close." They looked at each other and said in unison, "Amen!" as Aunt Haddie had taught them to do in narrow escapes. Of which there had been quite a few over the years.

Jack leaned over and looked out the window to see Michael storming over to the driver's side of the van.

"What the hell! Are you following me?" Michael yelled.

"What? You just stop," the van driver said in a thick Spanish accent.

"What's your problem?" Jack wasn't listening to the words so much as he was trying to read Shaw's body language, but it wasn't hard to read the classic signs of aggression and testosterone, with maybe some paranoia mixed in: he was leaning into the driver's window and shouting, "Why are you following me?"

"No. I no follow you! We working there." He pointed just ahead, to a house on the right.

Michael screamed at the van driver for a while, and then the passenger door of the van opened and it turned out there had been a second man in the van all the time, rather powerfully built and wearing a scowl that would strip paint. When he got out and started walking around the front of the van, Michael stomped back to his car.

Chandler craned his neck, but he couldn't see both sides of the action. "What's Shaw doing?"

"Getting back in his car."

Michael yanked the door open and jumped in. As he drove away, the van didn't move.

Jack laid on the horn.

"Don't beep! He'll see us."

"We're losing him."

The van driver flipped Jack off and drove away.

"Now Michael knows we're following him!" Chandler said.

"No, he doesn't. You need to act normal if you're undercover. And blowing your horn at someone stopped in the road is normal."

"Normal people cut someone slack after a crazy guy gives them a brake job then goes all psycho on them. That's what *normal* people do."

"Whatever. But you're right, Michael did go psycho."

Chandler said in Aunt Haddie's voice again, "Oh, yes, child, that man's got temper issues."

Now that the van was out of the way, Jack followed Michael at a distance. It was past noon and the traffic was heavy as the two cars wound closer to downtown Darrington. Jack's knuckles were white and sweat ran down his back as he tried to keep Michael's car in sight, but not too close, while at the same time navigating through traffic.

Finally, the Toyota pulled onto a side street and stopped in a parking lot behind a white two-story colonial.

"What is it?" Chandler asked. "A house, or a business?"

"I'll drive around and see if there's a sign," Jack said.

Jack circled around the block. Sure enough, mounted on two white posts was a large green sign with gold letters: *Tate, Wolfe and Rice. Experts in Civil Litigation.*

Jack parked in a lot across the street where they could see Michael's car. Fifteen minutes later, Michael hurried out of the law office, smiling, and got back in the Toyota.

"Wow, quick change," Chandler noted as Jack pulled out and followed Michael again. "Now he looks all happy."

"Yeah. Why?"

They continued to follow the Toyota, but always kept at least one car between them. It looked like Michael might get back on the highway, but he drove right past the entrance.

"I guess he's got someplace else to go," Jack said.

When they reached the downtown business district, the Toyota pulled into a parking space by the curb with no open spaces around it.

Jack slowed down. "What do I do now?"

"Just keep going," Chandler said.

They drove past the Toyota, and Jack saw a space farther down the street.

"Do I park?" Jack asked.

"Er…"

"Do I park?"

"Ummm…"

"Do I park?" Jack nearly shouted.

"How do I know?" Chandler blurted.

Jack zipped into the parking space and put the car in park. He glared at Chandler. "If I ask something, you need to answer me."

"What if I don't know the answer? You want me to make something up? Ask me again."

"What?"

"Ask me again." Chandler lifted his chin.

Jack rolled his eyes. "Do I park?"

"Blue."

"What?"

"See. My answer makes no sense because I don't know the answer."

"Then tell me that," Jack said.

"I did. I said I didn't know if you should park."

"You didn't say *I don't know*. You just went, ah… um… errr…"

"So what if I did?" Chandler's finger poked the dashboard.

"Sorry. Look, I'm not trying to be a jerk, but we need to get our communication down. Pretty soon we're not going to be asking where a parking spot is, we'll be asking where the guy who's trying to shoot us is."

"That's a good point," Chandler admitted.

Jack glanced in the rearview mirror. "Here he comes."

They both lowered their heads as Michael walked down the sidewalk and past the car.

"Where's he going? What should we do?" Chandler asked.

Jack thought for only a moment. "We follow him."

"So you did hear my whole don't-get-us-arrested speech? The guy flipped out once already. And why are we following him anyway? For all we know, this is nothing more than a wild goose chase."

Jack ignored the question and got out of the car. "You wait here."

"What?" Chandler said.

"You don't blend in. You're a giant."

"But you're the one he's seen already."

"He saw you too," Jack said.

"Not as well. I stayed *in* the car, remember?" Chandler pointed at himself. "I should go."

"I don't want you to get jammed up," Jack said.

"Back to back. It's settled."

"Okay. You follow him, and I'll follow both of you from the other side of the street. If he gets someplace and starts coming back, we'll switch sides."

Chandler nodded. He got out of the car and followed Michael down the sidewalk. Jack crossed the street and kept pace.

The lunchtime rush was in full swing. Office workers rushed down the street and darted into restaurants in the daily scramble called "lunch hour"—though it was only a half hour for many of them. Like contestants on some warped game show, they had to race out of the office, find a place to eat, order, scarf it down, and then scurry back to servitude.

Even in the lunch crowd, because of his size, it was easy to keep an eye on Chandler as he moved down the sidewalk. Jack kept his head tipped slightly down and tried to walk casually.

Michael, and then Chandler, passed by a busy bistro. The outside tables were packed; Michael had to slow down considerably and Chandler was getting too close to Michael.

Jack was about to try to signal Chandler to back off when Chandler knelt and tied his shoelace. The people behind him looked irritated by his sudden stop. They moved around him and looked down with a scowl as they passed.

Michael picked up his pace, got to the next corner, and stopped at the crosswalk light, which was red. Then, suddenly, he turned around.

Jack's breath caught in his throat. Chandler was still walking, heading straight toward Michael.

Damn. If he recognizes Chandler…

Michael stood with his hands at his sides, staring back down the sidewalk in Chandler's direction. Chandler walked right up beside him, as casual as could be, and waited for the light to change. Jack stood on the other side of the street, holding his breath.

Michael started to walk again—back the way he had come.

The crosswalk signal turned green, and the herd of people who had bunched up on the corners began walking, including Chandler and Jack. When they passed each other in the middle of the crosswalk, Chandler wiggled his eyebrows. "Close one," he muttered.

Jack nodded and continued across the intersection.

Michael was already a good distance away, moving back toward his car. As Jack followed, Michael approached the bistro again. He slowed down and kept his head turned toward the tables. It seemed to Jack like he was looking for someone, scanning the diners.

As Jack watched, Michael homed in on one table where two women were sitting, a blonde and a brunette. The brunette was talking animatedly, her back to Michael. But as Michael walked past, the blonde glanced in his direction.

Michael's pace slowed even more. He stared back at the blonde until he passed the table, and then swiveled his head forward and picked up his pace again until Jack had to hustle down the street after him.

Jack reached his car, hopped in, and started the engine, waiting for Chandler. In his rearview mirror he saw the Toyota pull out and ducked his head as it drove past. A few seconds later, Chandler jumped in.

"Go!" he panted.

Just as Jack was about to pull out, a car rolled up beside him and stopped, blocking them in.

"What the hell?" Jack said. He honked his horn.

The woman driving scowled and pointed to the parking space behind Jack.

"She's parallel-parking behind us," Chandler said.

"You've got to be kidding me. Move, lady."

As soon as the woman backed up enough for Jack to squeeze through, he pulled out.

"He's stopped at the light," Chandler said, craning his neck out the window. "It's only three cars ahead of us. But there are three cars ahead of him. I hope it's not a quick light."

But it *was* a quick light and only four cars got through before it changed back to red. Michael got through; Jack and Chandler were stuck.

Jack laid on the horn. He let fly with a steady stream of swears.

"Now *you* sound like Aunt Haddie," Chandler joked.

"Shut up." Jack stuck his head out the window, searching the cars and traffic ahead. "We'll never find him now." Jack rubbed both hands down his face. "This sucks. The first time I tail a car, and I lose him. Damn."

"Maybe he's going back to Fairfield?"

"No. The highway's to the left. He went straight."

When they finally made it through the intersection, they drove straight, peering down the side roads, but the silver Toyota was nowhere in sight. Jack rolled to a stop at another light.

"Well, where to now?" Chandler asked.

The light turned green, and Jack hesitated. The car behind him beeped.

"You gonna go?" Chandler said.

Jack stomped on the gas and banged a U-turn. Horns blared all around.

Chandler grabbed the dashboard. "Hey! What are you doing?"

"Did you notice anything when you followed Michael?"

Chandler took off his hat and wiped his brow. "No."

Jack headed back the way they'd come. "Well, I did. I betcha he's sleeping with the blonde."

"What blonde?"

"Remember that café with the tables outside?" Chandler nodded. "And the way he doubled back?" Another nod. "There was a woman, a blonde. The way she looked at him as he passed. And he looked at her, and slowed way down. They know each other but didn't acknowledge it. Not a wave or anything."

"Then how do you know they know each other?"

"It's like when we got kicked out of the Charlie Horse."

"Because of you," Chandler added.

"Yes, but…before the act began, I told you that the hypnotist and the guy in the red shirt were in cahoots."

"And you were right. The whole thing was a setup. The guy in the red shirt was a plant."

"Yeah. Well, that wasn't just a lucky guess. The hypnotist was mingling around the club, and I watched him. Him and that guy—they exchanged a look. Just like Michael and the blonde. I'm telling you, they know each other."

Chandler leaned up against the door. "You think Michael's having an affair because of a look?"

"Not *just* a look. Think about it. He drives all the way from Fairfield, gets out of his car, walks down the sidewalk, turns around and walks back, then just leaves? Why?"

"True. That's weird."

"He has to know her. She was what he wanted to see. It fits. It's why I wanted to follow Michael in the first place."

"How could you know Michael was having an affair?"

"I didn't. It was a hunch."

"I don't know, Jack. It seems sort of weak. Even if he is having an affair, that doesn't make him a killer."

"Statistically, seventy-eight percent of the time, when a woman is killed, it's by someone she knows. Michael would be the prime suspect if they hadn't lost focus and arrested Jay."

"That doesn't mean Michael killed her."

Jack paused. "No. But right now, we just need to get the cops to look at other suspects—to actually get back to investigating instead of locking in on Jay. We bring the cops proof of an affair, and they have to look more closely at Michael—he has a possible motive for killing his wife."

Chandler raised an eyebrow.

Jack leaned over the steering wheel and stared out over the hood. "Or maybe I'm just getting desperate."

He pulled into a parking space across from the bistro. "Good, the blonde's still here," he said, pointing her out to Chandler. "I want to see where she goes." He shut off the engine. "Same deal as before? I'll start behind them, you cover this side of the street?"

"Okay." Chandler held out his hand and they knuckle-bumped.

"We've got good timing. They're paying the check now."

As the two women left the café, Jack casually followed them down the block. They were just chatting away, completely unaware of Jack. The brunette's hands flew in all directions, and once in a while, Jack heard her loud laugh.

They took a left at the corner and headed toward a modern glass and steel building set back from the road. Floor-to-ceiling windows looked out on the trees that surrounded the building on three sides.

As the women went inside, Jack turned back and met up with Chandler. "Let's go get the car."

"Don't you want to check out the building?" Chandler asked. "From a distance," he added quickly.

Jack grinned. "Yeah, but we can do that from the car."

A few minutes later they were parked in the building's lot. The big windows meant they had a direct view into the interior—a typical cubicle farm.

Chandler exclaimed, "Hey, the girl at the front desk—"

"The chatty brunette," Jack finished.

Chandler's hand shot out. "And there's the blonde. See, walking near the big plant on the left?"

Jack leaned against the steering wheel. The blonde sat down at a cubicle and disappeared from view.

Jack rolled down his window, and Chandler followed suit. A cool breeze blew through the open windows, bringing with it the smell of freshly cut grass and the scent of roses from the bushes behind them.

Chandler played with the rubber seal around the window. "Why didn't Michael talk to the blonde?"

"I don't know. Maybe he wants to lie low. Everyone knows the cops always look at the husband. Put yourself in Michael's shoes now. Would you want to get caught with another woman and have the cops look harder at you?"

Chandler nodded, considering.

"And what if he *did* do it? What do people do after they commit a crime?"

Chandler made a face. "A crime like killing your wife? I'm sure I wouldn't know."

"You have to try. Remember when I stole that case of soda?"

"Yeah, I remember." Chandler frowned. "I got grounded for a week because I was there."

"Sorry. Again," Jack added. "I was only seven, by the way."

"It was still stupid. I told you it belonged to the store. Who just leaves a case of soda on the sidewalk?"

Jack waved his hand. "Whatever—that doesn't matter. The point is, I knew it was wrong. So I hid the case in the shed, and then I couldn't sleep all night. I kept thinking that Aunt Haddie knew I'd stolen the soda. I thought the store owner and the police were watching me. I went out to the shed to check if it was still there three times that night. And finally I confessed. The guilt and fear of getting caught drives you crazy."

"Like 'The Tell-Tale Heart,'" Chandler said.

"Poe, right?"

"Yeah. But that's if Michael is guilty. And we don't know that yet. You're jumping to a lot of conclusions."

"Maybe," Jack said. "But consider how Michael reacted to the van. He thought they were following him. He's acting suspicious, just like I did when I felt guilty. And if he really thinks he's being watched, he's not going to run around with his mistress out in public. He'd keep a low profile."

"I still don't know, Jack. If he's feeling guilty about something, it's probably the fact that he's having an affair. Maybe she's married."

Jack made a face.

Chandler's fingers drummed the dashboard. "And why drive all the way up here just to walk by her?"

"Because he's too paranoid to stay away? Cheaters think everyone else cheats, too. So Michael may worry that she's stepping out on him. You add that to paranoia from his wife's murder, and it's a recipe for crazy."

"You know what?" Chandler crossed his arms. "I agree with almost everything you think, but that doesn't give us any proof of anything. Right now, even the affair itself is pure guesswork. All you have to go by is a look."

Jack's hands balled into fists. "I can't think of any way to prove it."

"Betcha the brunette knows." Chandler nodded in the direction of the receptionist.

"Probably. Girls talk."

"Hey!" Chandler turned in his seat to look at Jack. "Go to that detective and have them get a wiretap."

Jack laughed. "Oh, they love me down there at the precinct. 'Wiretap'? Sure."

"Yeah. Just joking."

"Besides, on what grounds? As you pointed out, all I can say right now is that Michael and that woman looked at each other. I'll sound like an idiot."

Chandler exhaled.

Jack closed his eyes. The sweet scent from some nearby rosebushes drifted through the open window.

Chandler cleared his throat. "Are you taking a power nap? What are you doing?"

"Thinking." Jack sniffed, then opened his eyes. "That just gave me an idea." He started the car.

"What idea? The wiretaps?"

"Nope." Jack grinned. "But I think I can prove they're having an affair."

Chandler looked doubtful. "You can prove this from a distance, I'm assuming?"

Jack didn't answer.

26

DELIVERY

Forty-five minutes later, Jack pulled the car into the parking lot again—but this time with a half dozen balloons floating up from the backseat. One drifted forward, and Chandler shoved it back, annoyed.

"I thought that credit card was just for an emergency," Chandler said.

"This *is* an emergency. Grab me a pen out of the glove compartment, would you?"

Chandler searched the glove compartment and handed Jack a chewed-up pencil.

"Keep looking. There's a pen in there somewhere."

Chandler threw the pencil on the floor and moved around papers and protein bar wrappers until he found an uncapped pen. "You ready to explain what the balloons and flowers are for?"

"They're bait," Jack said. He pulled the cap off the pen with his teeth, and wrote something on the little card that came with the balloons.

"What are you writing? You don't know her name," Chandler said.

Jack smiled. "I don't need to know it. Here's the message: *I need to see you. I miss you. Love, Michael.*" He grinned and shoved the card into its little envelope.

Jack drove the car right up to the front door of the building, took the bouquet and the balloons from the backseat, and headed inside. Chandler, grumbling and shaking his head, waited in the car.

The lobby was open and airy, filled with tropical plants and a waterfall wall that flowed into a small koi pond. With the summer sun streaming through the windows, it felt like a rain forest, despite the air-conditioning running so high it created a breeze. The contemporary reception desk, a sweeping curve of glass, metal, and smoky plastic, reminded Jack of *Star Trek*.

The brunette raised an eyebrow as Jack approached.

"Hello." Jack smiled. "Delivery."

"Who's it for?" Her voice was nasal.

Jack reached into his pocket and turned it out: empty. Awkwardly, he shifted the balloons into his other hand, then searched the opposite pocket and pulled out several scraps of paper.

The brunette tipped her head to the side and smirked.

Jack shrugged sheepishly. "I'm sorry. I just got the address." He took out the envelope. "There's a card, but no name on it."

The brunette snatched the card out of his hand, then proceeded to read what Jack had written on the inside and smiled knowingly. "I know who it's for. Thanks." She waved her hand as if she were shooing away a fly, then turned and placed the flowers and balloons behind her.

Jack had to force himself not to run back outside.

"Well?" Chandler said.

"She took the bait."

Jack drove to a spot at the far side of the lot, where they watched the events unfold, like two kids watching a crime thriller at a drive-in movie.

The brunette receptionist was walking through the cubicle farm, balloons floating behind her. Like gophers popping their heads out of their holes, several employees' heads rose above cubicle walls as they stood to watch the parade pass by. Most were no doubt looking around to see who would be the lucky recipient of the gifts; one woman gave a dismissive wave of her arm when the receptionist passed her by.

The longer the brunette walked, the faster Jack's heart beat.

As Jack had hoped, she stopped at the blonde's cubicle and held out the flowers and the balloons.

Chandler pounded Jack on the back. "Bam!" he cheered. "Back left pocket, baby!"

Jack clenched both fists and held them high. "They have to be having an affair!"

"You were right. The receptionist knew exactly who to give them to."

The blonde stood in her cubicle, her phone pressed against her ear. She was slowly twisting back and forth with a bright smile on her face.

"You think she's calling Michael?" Chandler asked.

"Guaranteed," Jack said. "Look how happy she is."

The blonde stopped twisting.

"Uh-oh…" Chandler said. "Looks like this is the part where Michael says, 'I didn't send you any flowers.'"

The blonde covered the phone and turned to the receptionist. The brunette looked like an orchestra conductor gone mad. Her hands flew out in all directions.

"Maybe we should go," Chandler said. "You got your proof."

"Not yet," Jack said. "Right now we don't know if she called Michael Shaw. We're just guessing. And I'm not talking to Clark unless I'm a hundred and fifty percent certain. But if Shaw comes here and talks to the blonde, it will prove that he knows her. Then we've got him."

"Or he gets us. Do you realize you're luring a man back here who you think could be a killer?"

"It's not like we're in danger," Jack said. "You can't really see us from the office building. And we'll see Michael coming from a mile off."

"So that's the plan? We're just going to sit here and see if the psycho shows up?"

"That's the plan." Jack grinned.

Chandler didn't.

* * *

The minutes ticked away. Cars came and went, but the silver Toyota was nowhere to be seen. Jack drummed his fingers on the steering wheel.

"How long are we gonna stay here?" Chandler asked.

Jack turned to answer him, but his mouth clamped shut as the Toyota came into sight. Jack pointed, and they both watched the car zip into the parking lot and stop right at the front of the building.

Michael got out, and the blonde and the brunette both came out to meet him. Michael paced back and forth, and Jack heard him yelling, though he couldn't make out what he was saying.

Suddenly the brunette looked in Jack's direction. Jack thought the car was pretty well hidden, but her eyes narrowed. She shouted something and thrust her hand out—pointing straight at Jack.

"Oh, hell no," Chandler muttered.

"Uh-oh… Our cover's blown. Let's go." Jack started the car.

Michael was already running toward them.

The tires on the little car squealed as Jack shot out of the parking space. There was only one exit from the parking lot, and Jack drove straight for it.

But Michael got there first. He blocked the exit, and his expression dared them to come closer. His face was bright red and his hands were clenched into fists. In between the string of profanities that flew out of his mouth, Jack picked out the words *bloodsuckers* and *TV trash.*

"He's nuts," Chandler warned.

"He thinks we're reporters." Jack cut the wheel and headed back into the parking lot.

"What are you doing now?" Chandler said.

"There's another way out of here." Jack pointed.

"That's called a sidewalk!" Chandler shouted.

"It's got a handicapped access ramp."

"It's still a sidewalk, Jack," Chandler repeated, his voice rising.

Jack kept going, steering the tiny car up the ramp and then down the sidewalk. One wheel hugged the top of the curb while the other crushed the grass along the edge. As they dropped off the sidewalk onto the road outside the parking lot, metal scraping on the curb, Jack checked the rearview mirror to see whether anything had fallen off.

"No, no, no." Chandler leaned away from the window. "Incoming!" he warned.

Michael had grabbed a rock, and now he heaved it at the car. The stone just missed the hood and bounced harmlessly into the street. They heard him screaming behind them.

"He's running back for his car," Chandler said.

The streetlight ahead turned yellow.

"Go!" Chandler yelled.

Jack laid on the gas and took a hard right. The little car's engine whined. For a moment Jack thought they were in the clear—until he looked in his rearview mirror and saw the Toyota running the red light.

"Not good." Jack cursed.

Jack passed a Buick and took a left. The Toyota stayed with them. Michael screamed something. Spit flew against Michael's windshield as he ranted and gestured at Jack to pull over.

"I knew it." Chandler smacked his forehead. "I knew something like this would happen."

"I'll lose him." Jack took a right and headed down a narrow two-way street.

"In this wind-up toy? I don't think so."

Michael was right on their tail.

The light ahead turned yellow.

Jack didn't slow down.

"Jack…"

A huge black SUV barreled from left to right toward the intersection ahead of them, but Jack still didn't slow.

"The SUV's jumping the red light." Chandler put his huge hands on the dash.

"There's a passenger-side airbag. Sit back or it'll break your arms."

"Stop the car and it won't go off!"

Jack's knuckles tightened on the steering wheel. "He'll stop."

"You won't make it."

"I might."

"Might?" Chandler's voice shrilled.

The compact zipped in front of the huge SUV. The SUV driver laid on the horn and slammed on the brakes.

Jack didn't see the BMW taking a right.

Chandler screamed. So did Jack, but he kept the gas pedal pinned to the floor. The BMW just missed the rear bumper, and Jack's little car with the *I Love My Math Teacher* bumper sticker sped through the now snarled intersection, to the accompaniment of horns blaring and people cursing.

Jack looked back. Michael had skidded to a stop behind them, on the other side of the intersection.

"What the hell is wrong with you, Stratton?" Chandler roared. "You could have killed me, you, and everyone else back at that intersection."

"How am I going to kill them in this tin can? Sure, *we'd* die, but this car would've bounced off the SUV without even denting it. And the light was still kinda yellow."

"You know, it's not too reassuring that you care so little about us dying."

"We didn't."

"Unacceptable risk. Learn that term." Chandler smacked the dashboard with his fist. "I'm not taking them, and neither are you. You need to be responsible."

"I am responsible," Jack said.

"No, you're not. If you haven't realized it about yourself yet, let me explain it to you. You're the wild child of the family. I'm the responsible one."

"I'm not that wild."

Chandler laughed. It was deep and real. "So says the crazy man who just gunned it through an intersection in a toy car." He mimed driving, holding his hands out and making a high-pitched whine.

Jack laughed.

After several minutes of weaving down side streets, Jack headed toward the highway. "I think we lost him."

"I hope so. He looked nuts. What now?"

"I'm going to talk to Detective Clark. The police will have to look at Shaw now."

27

NOT YOUR CASE

"You *what*?" Detective Clark glanced across the lawn of the police station and took a long drag of his cigarette.

"I didn't break any laws," Jack said defensively.

Clark jabbed the air with his cigarette. "Before we get into breaking laws, did you miss the part where Detective Vargas told you that this is an ongoing investigation?"

"But—"

"But nothing." The old detective's wrinkles became even more pronounced as he scowled. "And it's not my case."

Jack felt his frustration rising. He respected Detective Clark and valued his opinion, but right now the detective's dour expression hurt Jack. "It's wrong to just sit there. I had to try to do something. I tried to explain to Detective Vargas, but he didn't listen. So I decided to look into it myself." Jack squared his shoulders.

Clark sighed, but his scowl remained. "You may as well tell me what you found. Start at the beginning."

Jack took out his notebook.

"You took notes?"

Jack nodded. "I went to H. T. Wells and started asking around."

"You can't do that, Jack."

"There's no law against talking to people."

"There is one about hindering a police investigation."

"I'm just trying to bring you other possibilities. Vargas is locked in on Jay, when he should be looking at other people too."

"Such as?"

"Stacy's manager, Leland Chambers. He argued with Stacy that night. Over a report. For the Right-A-Way Shipping company."

"Where did you get that?"

"The custodian, Jeremy. And Betty Robinson corroborated. When I questioned Mr. Chambers about the report, it really got under his skin, and he had Jeremy fired."

"That's interesting."

"I thought so."

Clark pulled out his own notepad and started to take notes. "Go on."

"I also found someone in the park you need to look at. Alex Hernandez."

Clark's expression soured. "I know Alex."

"Well, the night of the murder, Alex was in the area right next to where Stacy's body was found. He calls it an outpost."

Clark lowered his notepad. "Wait a minute—he spoke with you?"

"Yes. He answered a few questions."

"Do you know how unbalanced he is?" Clark took another long drag. His face glowed almost as brightly as the end of the cigarette.

"I do now."

Clark ran his fingers through his hair. "I've already spoken with Alex. Detective Vargas interviewed him too. Alex cooperated fully."

"I thought you said you weren't part of this investigation."

Clark's scowled deepened. "I said it's not my case. But when you work law enforcement, it's all hands on deck. Besides, if there's an issue with Alex, they call me in. How was he after you spoke to him?"

"Agitated. He got really upset. Was he a suspect in his wife's murder?"

"No. He was overseas at the time." Clark looked around. "I'll have to go talk to him again. Where did you see him?"

"In the basement of the old maintenance building at Hamilton Park. He told me he saw a messenger that night, in civilian clothes. I think he was talking about a jogger, and based on his description of the shoes, that jogger was Leland Chambers."

Clark flicked his ashes. "Alex thinks that all joggers are messengers. There were several in the park that night—we talked to a few. We interviewed Chambers too."

"I think you should be looking at both Alex and Chambers." Jack's eyes lit up. "*You* gave Alex the key to the maintenance building."

Clark sucked on his cigarette so hard Jack was surprised it didn't burst into flame. "Alex didn't tell you that."

"No. You did."

Clark's forehead creased.

"You weren't surprised when I said I talked to him inside the maintenance building."

Clark exhaled until the last puff of smoke drifted out of his mouth. "I didn't give him the key, but I do overlook the fact that he has it." He clicked his tongue. "I feel bad for him after what happened to his wife. I worked her murder."

"My mother told me." Jack shook his head. "Did you catch the murderer? Is he in jail?"

"No."

"So whoever murdered Alex's wife could have murdered Stacy Shaw. It's the same MO. Anne Hernandez was pregnant, wasn't she?"

"They're not in jail because they're dead." Clark watched a group of police officers walk into the station. "Being a cop is a ticket to hell, Jack. Sometimes you have to see things people shouldn't see. Anne Hernandez was killed in a home invasion. Two junkies were looking to stick up a drug dealer at home. But they got the wrong address. They tortured Anne for hours, trying to get her to give up where the dope was." He snuffed out his cigarette and took out another. "It was one of the worst crime scenes I've ever seen. Once she was dead, they stole her car, took what money she had, and bought a load of heroin. We found them the next day—OD'd." Clark cupped his hand around his cigarette as he lit it. "And Alex…he never went home again. His old house is right across the street from the maintenance building, but he won't go there—won't leave the park. He believes Anne's still alive and had the baby. He thinks it's his mission to stay and watch over them—from a distance. Recon."

"But you don't think he had anything to do with Stacy Shaw's death? Even with his camp right there?"

"No, I don't." Clark rolled his shoulders. "Did you find out anything else?"

"I followed Michael Shaw to Darrington. First he stopped by a law office."

"Did you get the name?"

Jack flipped through his notebook. "Tate, Wolfe, and Rice."

Clark wrote the name on his pad. "Continue."

Jack explained everything that had happened, from Shaw's Facebook status to following him to the bistro, to baiting him to the blonde's office. He took his time going over each step.

"Is that everything?" Clark eyed him suspiciously. "You're not leaving anything out?"

"That's everything."

A muscle in Clark's jaw twitched. "Hold on a second." He took out his phone.

"Who are you calling? Detective Vargas?" Jack felt a mix of vindication and pride wash over him. "You're going to have him look at Michael Shaw, right?"

"No, I'm calling your father."

Jack's mouth fell open. "What? Why?"

"Why?" Clark looked at Jack as if he had four heads for even asking the question. "Ted? Hi, it's Derrick. I'm sorry to bother you, but I need you to come down to the station. It's about Jack." Pause. "Yes, he's with me now." Pause. "No, nothing like that." Another pause. "Fifteen minutes sounds good. Thanks, Ted."

Clark clicked off the phone and took a drag of his cigarette.

Jack stood there, shocked. "Why would you do that? Why not look into the information I gave you?"

"I told you this is an ongoing investigation. If you want to stick your neck out, you have to be ready to face the consequences. Are you ready to do that?"

"You're going to screw me up getting into the Army? If I don't go to the Army, I've got no shot at being a cop!"

Clark shook his head. "I'm not jeopardizing that. Look, like you said, you didn't break any laws—from what you told me. But this isn't a game, Jack." He closed his notebook. "Do you know what you've figured out? Nothing. Detective Vargas has everything you gave me."

"What? How?" Jack shook his head. "Vargas wasn't looking into this. He's focused on Jay."

Clark looked at the sky. "You rushed to a judgment about the police and Detective Vargas. You thought because Jay confessed to finding the wallet that we'd just stick a bow on it, have a few drinks, and pat each other on the back. Well, you're wrong, Jack. It doesn't work that way. *We* don't work that way."

"But you're not even looking—"

"We've had an APB out for Tommy Martin since the day Stacy went missing. We know what we're doing, Jack. We just don't make everything public knowledge, especially to someone we think is his friend."

"But what about the other suspects?"

"Detective Vargas interviewed everyone at H. T. Wells. We canvassed the park with more than a few dozen officers and interviewed anyone who might have seen or heard anything. We brought in Michael Shaw for questioning too. Right at the start."

"But you didn't know about the affair."

"Yes, we did, Jack. Shaw told us about it, first thing. He was ashamed, but he came clean."

"He *told* you about having an affair?"

"Shaw made it sound like it was over but he told us everything."

"I don't understand."

"Jack, having an affair makes him a scumbag, but it doesn't make him a murderer."

"But it's a motive."

"It could be. But a good portion of the population has affairs, and they're not killing each other."

"Maybe he took out a big insurance policy on Stacy?" Jack suggested. "That would give him motive."

"I'm not sure if he had any insurance. If he did, it wasn't much." Clark flipped his notebook closed. "Michael Shaw was in Schenectady for work. Do you know how we know that?"

Jack didn't say anything. He wanted to find a hole to crawl in and die. He stared at his worn sneakers.

"We investigated every lead. We pulled cell phone records for both Stacy and Michael. We even pulled the surveillance footage from that hotel. Michael's car didn't leave the parking lot. Detective Vargas even drove up to Schenectady and interviewed the damn concierge who was on duty that night."

"I didn't know."

"There's a lot you didn't know. Do you want to? Do you want to know what's really going on?"

Jack forced himself to look Clark in the eye.

"Then let me tell you. Up until twenty-four hours ago, we had an airtight case against the guy who killed Stacy Shaw—Jay Martin. But Jay and his family played you. They know you want to be a cop. They got you to pretend that you are one. They got you to run around and taint witnesses. Jay came up with the bull crap story 'It wasn't me, it was my brother dressed in my clothes,' and you bought it. I warned you. You should've listened to your head and looked at the facts. The facts say Jay Martin killed Stacy Shaw. I believe them. You should too. You got played, kid."

Jack's head spun.

"You're a good guy, Jack. You meant well. But this isn't your job; it's mine. You've got a lot to learn."

Jack nodded. His chest felt as if a boa constrictor was crushing it. "Yes, sir." He hung his head.

Clark moved closer. "Listen, I won't let this screw up the Army. I'll run interference with Detective Vargas. But I need you to stay the hell out of this now. Putting your old man on you is the only way I know to keep you away."

Jack stared at his feet. He'd gotten it wrong. He didn't just feel foolish—he felt worthless.

On top of that, now he had to deal with his father.

28

TROUBLE

Jack watched his dad pace back and forth across the kitchen floor. For the past ten minutes that was all he had done—pace. Detective Clark had told his father everything outside the police station. Jack had repeated it in the car. Now all Jack could do was wait.

His mother sat at the other end of the kitchen table. Once again the Stratton family kitchen resembled a courtroom more than a dining area. It was a too-familiar situation for them all, because of their wild, quick-to-anger, high-maintenance, impetuous, rebellious son, Jack. Ted was the judge, ready to lower the boom, while Laura acted as the defense attorney begging for mercy for her client, who sat silently on the witness stand.

Ted took off his glasses and cleaned the lenses, staring at the floor. When he finally looked up, he didn't try to hide his disappointment.

"Jack, I'm unhappy with your decisions on many levels. And the worst part is that you put Chandler's future in jeopardy."

"What? I never said Chandler was there."

Ted leveled his gaze at Jack. "You didn't have to. Thick as thieves. If you're around, I just need to look for his shadow." He sighed. "Chandler needs that tuition reimbursement program. I can't believe you'd risk that for him."

"But Dad—"

"You should have come to me. You're still under this roof, even if you just turned eighteen."

Jack tried to stifle his groan.

"Your mother got a cake. She made a special dinner that's now sitting in the refrigerator—"

"I didn't want anything. I hate this cursed, rotten, worthless day."

"We don't usually see things from polar opposite positions, but you must know that to me and your mom, this is a very blessed day."

"I know. I just don't see it that way. I think about today and I just see *her* walking away from me. She wouldn't even turn around."

"Is that the reason why you've been acting like this? Are you trying to prove your worth by solving this crime?"

Jack rubbed the back of his fist with his other thumb. What could he say? He wasn't trying to prove that he wasn't trash because he was trash. He hated the fact but he accepted it.

"Maybe you need to stop looking at yourself that way. You're looking back. You're watching her, and your past. Turn around, and you'll see all the people waiting for you—Aunt Haddie, Chandler, Michelle, your mom. Looking forward might be a lot less painful."

Jack stared at the floor. He knew his father was right, and he could jeopardize his future trying to change the past.

"What concerns me are your decisions," his father continued. "You had many other options. You could have come to me, your mother, Detective Clark—"

"I went to Clark and he finked me out."

"He didn't. He had an obligation to tell his superiors and to call me. He should have, and he did. That was the right thing to do. He didn't want to, but he did it."

"That's *my* argument, Dad. I didn't want to help Jay. I don't like him. But it was the right thing to do. So I did it."

"But you had other options. You went at it all wrong."

"What other options? I went to Clark, but the cops weren't doing…I didn't *think* the police were doing anything."

"But they were."

These words had finality; they hung in the air and shot down any argument Jack could think of. He put his head in his hands.

Ted felt for his wallet in his pocket. "I need to get ready for night school. We'll finish this discussion when I come home."

He kissed Laura, then picked up his wallet and keys from the table and marched across the kitchen. He hesitated at the door. "I love you both." He didn't look back.

"That went better than I expected." Laura squeezed Jack's hand.

"It was a suspended verdict. I'll get a life sentence when he comes home."

"I'm sure your father will have calmed down by then. Would you like me to heat something up for you?"

"No thanks."

"Do you want to talk about it?"

"There's nothing to talk about." Jack let his arms flop down on the table. "The police have been looking at other suspects. Vargas has been doing his job. I was wrong."

His mother laid a gentle hand on his forearm. "I don't see it that way."

"Because you're my mom."

"No." She gave his arm a squeeze, but it was not just out of affection; there was urgency, too. "I *love* you because I'm your mom. I believe you're *right* because you're Jack."

Jack sighed. "I was wrong, Mom. It's that simple. I have no idea who killed Stacy Shaw."

"Just because you haven't figured it out yet doesn't make you wrong." She crossed her arms. "I don't think I've sat down and watched a movie or TV mystery in the past seven years that you haven't solved before the end."

"That's different, Mom. Watching a crime show doesn't make you a detective any more than watching *The French Chef* makes you a cook."

"No. It doesn't. But it's a step in the right direction. So are all those books you read. So was the citizens' academy class you took. How many times did you take that class?"

"Four," Jack admitted. "They let you do ride-alongs."

"Someday you're going to have a name plate on your desk that says 'Detective Jack Stratton.'"

"But what about now?"

"Right now solving this murder is someone else's job." She held up a hand and lowered an eyebrow. "You can't investigate this murder anymore, Jack. After you go into the Army, graduate college, and the police academy, you'll be equipped to investigate anything you want. And I'm sure you will be spectacular at it."

"Thanks," he muttered.

"All your father and I ask is that you stay out of the way of the investigation. Call Detective Clark if you think of something."

Jack nodded.

"Good. Now, please, will you let me heat something up for you? You have to eat."

Jack smiled at his mom. He knew she couldn't be blind to his mistakes any more than his dad was, but here she was, just trying to take care of him. Still being a mom. "Yeah. Thanks, Mom. I'm going to go up to my room, but I'll come back down for it."

"I'll bring it up to you when it's ready."

Jack only picked at his food, sitting at his computer. His throat felt thick and his whole body felt heavy. He knew he wasn't coming down with anything; it was just his body's way of registering his mind's sensations of failure and shame. He picked up his notebook and glared at it. "Stupid," he muttered, and tossed the notebook across the room and into the wastebasket in the corner. "Chandler was right. I never should have started helping in the first place."

Defeated, he pulled up his email, and was surprised to see that he had received responses from both the fertility clinic and the hair salon. He opened the email from the fertility clinic first. Chandler was right again; they didn't answer his question. Their reply was a terse one-sentence response: "Per policy, we do not comment on pending litigation."

Jack opened the email from Luisa's Luxe Hair Studio. They didn't answer his question either—although they did include a coupon code for a discount on a Brazilian hot-oil treatment.

Jack stared at his computer. *What am I doing? I can't believe I opened those thinking I'd find something. I'm done.* He shut down his email and then his entire computer. *I can't look at anything related to the case. I can't think about the case. I can't get involved in the case, or I'm toast. Besides, the cops have it under control.*

He was leaning back in his chair and staring at the ceiling when his mother knocked on the door, holding the phone. She covered the receiver and said, "There's a Betty Robinson on the phone who wants to speak with you."

Betty Robinson? Why would she be calling? Jack had agreed to stop investigating the case, but if Betty had new information…

"Thanks, Mom." He took the phone from his mom and waited for her to go back downstairs before answering. "Hello?"

"Hi, Jack. It's Betty Robinson. You asked me to call you if I saw anything in that report for Right-A-Way Shipping."

"Did you did find something?" Jack's heart skipped a beat. "And?"

"Yes. You were right—Leland was hiding something. One of the IT guys got me an old version of that file from the backup tapes. It was archived the night Stacy disappeared. Stacy had made several notes about discrepancies. It took a lot of digging to sort through what's going on, but—well, the short story is…it looks like Leland's embezzling."

"No way. How?"

"By overpaying the insurance premiums. I guess he has a contact or a partner over at Right-A-Way, and they've been issuing the refund check to a shell company owned by Leland's brother-in-law. It didn't trigger any flags because the payment to Right-A-Way is legit; it's just too frequent. He's working the scam with other companies, too. He did it again this week."

"Have you told anyone about this?"

"I'm calling Detective Vargas next. And I'm going to our CFO in the morning. I wanted to tell you first because…well, you earned it."

Jack said quickly, "If you don't mind—please don't mention to Vargas, or anyone else, that I had anything to do with your research. I'm already in hot water."

Betty chuckled. "I think I can understand why—you've got a way about you. Don't worry. I won't mention your name. But in my opinion, your digging turned up something really interesting."

Jack exhaled. "Thank you."

"Don't mention it. If that son of a bitch murdered Stacy to hide what he was doing, you can bail me out after I kill him. And Jack…I still don't understand exactly how you're involved in this, but I'm glad you've stepped up. You probably saved a bunch of people's jobs."

"You have too, Betty. You stuck your neck out. Thanks again."

Jack hung up and stared at his notebook splayed in the wastebasket. He had known something wasn't right with Leland Chambers—and now the police would have to look harder at him. Maybe it would lead to something more. Chambers might have had motive. But…

Thinking about his list of whys, Jack realized that Leland's embezzling answered several of the questions on that list, but not all of them.

He walked over to the trash can and stared down at the notebook.

Walk away.

Jack straightened back up and his shoulders slumped.

It's not my case.

This time, he listened to that voice in his head and left the notebook in the trash.

Leave it to the police.

He took his plate and headed downstairs. As he washed his dishes, he felt the headache that had been percolating for hours begin to pound. He opened the medicine cabinet and grabbed the aspirin bottle.

Betty said Chambers ran the scam again this week. If he killed Stacy, wouldn't he take a break and lie low?

He could step away from his investigation, but apparently he couldn't keep his mind off the case.

Chandler was right about the emails—the doctors won't give up any information.

He set the aspirin bottle down absentmindedly. *Privacy laws shouldn't—*

Jack stopped, the aspirin forgotten. He ran back up to his computer and read the email from the clinic again.

Pending litigation.

They said they couldn't comment because of pending litigation—not privacy laws.

"What litigation?"

The telephone rang. Thinking it might be Betty again, Jack ran downstairs to answer it. It wasn't Betty.

"Jack?"

It took him a second to place the voice. "Two Point?"

"Gotta talk. Meet me at the ball courts."

"Why?"

"I'm here now. Come on. It's important."

"Listen, Two." Jack tried to lower his voice so his mother wouldn't hear him. "I've almost gotten arrested—twice—all trying to help you and your brother. You've been jerking me around. Go ahead and sell J-Dog out, but I'm done listening to the lies."

"I'm not lying, I swear."

"You did before."

"Not now, I want to come clean. You gotta believe me…"

Jack didn't say anything. If he thought Two Point had anything remotely worthwhile to say, there still remained a decision to make about whether he should be involved.

"Listen, man, something bad happened to Jay."

Uh-oh.

"He got stabbed this morning."

"What happened?"

He heard Two Point's breath catch in his throat. "It's bad."

Jack's shock shifted to anger. "That's on you."

"I know. I know. Look, if you come…If you come with me, I'll talk to that suit you know."

"You'll tell them it was you who found the wallet?"

There was a long pause. "Yeah."

"If you're playing me…" Jack threatened.

"I'll tell them it was me. I swear. On my father's grave. I swear. But you gotta come with me."

Jack debated. He wanted to believe Two Point, but he'd been burned before. *Still…*

"Fifteen minutes."

He hung up and set the phone down on the table, then spun it in a little circle.

His mother walked into the room. "You certainly are getting a lot of calls. Birthday wishes?"

"Kinda."

"I'm going to watch a movie. Do you want to join me? I'll let you pick."

"Ah, no. Actually I'm going to take a ride."

His mother's eyebrows rose and she clutched the cross at her chest. He felt an answering wave of anxiety rise up at her familiar, anxious gesture, but then she surprised him with a totally unfamiliar gesture, a wink.

Stopping at the door she said gently, "I trust you, Jack. And… your father didn't say anything about you being grounded. But just be careful. Okay?"

29

THE TRUTH WILL SET YOU FREE

Two Point was pacing back and forth along the trees that screened the basketball courts at Hamilton Park, his hands thrust deep in his pockets. When he saw Jack get out of the Impala, he stopped.

Jack had left his house feeling a thousand times better than when he had entered it, a few hours earlier, about to face the judge and jury known as Ted Stratton. But the sight of scrawny, nervous Two Point, with his low-slung pants and gangsta pretenses, infuriated him.

"You ever lie to me again," Jack stalked forward, "and I'll knock your teeth down your throat and drag you in to the cops myself."

Two Point took a step back. "What the hell, Stratton? I said I'd tell them it was me."

"Well, start talking."

"If they have pictures of me, it musta been at the ATM. No cameras in the park."

"They have a picture. I've seen it. It only caught part of your face, and Jay's jacket. Where did you get the wallet?"

"I found it."

"Where? Describe it."

"You know the fountain? It was close to there. Um, between some hills. It was pitch-black—"

"Where the light is out?"

"I don't know. It was, like, *dark* dark. But I saw something sparkly. I walked over and it was a handbag."

"It was just lying there?"

"Yeah. I figured someone dropped it. You know, some drunk chick or something? I took the wallet out and tossed the handbag."

"Where?"

"Into the woods."

"Did you see Stacy Shaw?"

"No."

"What about anyone else?" Jack leaned in. "Was there anybody around?"

"Nobody. Nope."

"Nobody at all. Not even on the way out?" Jack's voice had dropped down to a low rumble.

"Some gutter bum."

"Describe him. How tall?"

"I dunno. My height, I guess. It was dark, so it was hard to see. And I wasn't trying to memorize him or nothin'."

"Think." Jack growled.

"He had a green Army jacket." Two Point nodded. "Yeah. And a ponytail."

Alex Hernandez.

"Was he walking away or toward you?"

"How would I know? I saw him earlier in the parking lot. Only one car there—slim pickins for me."

"Okay, then what?" Jack asked.

Two Point wiped his forehead and sighed, as if all this telling the truth stuff was absolutely exhausting. "I looked through the wallet. The lady had written a PIN on her library card, so I thought she might use the same one for everything. I decided to try the ATM." Jack wasn't totally sure, but Tommy might have been looking a little ashamed here. "It didn't work. After that, I went to hide my stash and I went home."

"But…" Jack prompted.

"But I screwed up. When I went to my stash, I forgot the wallet was in the pocket of Jay's jacket, and you know the rest. The cops found it and blamed Jay."

Jack looked around the courts and the parking lot. It was a nice summer night, and the courts were busy. Jack didn't want to be spotted with Two Point.

"You're gonna go with me, right?" Two Point asked. "No cop's ever gonna believe me. J-Dog don't trust them either. He's right. They're not doing anything. They're not even looking for the guy who really killed that lady."

"And who stabbed Jay?"

"It was just random," Two Point whined. "Just some guys at the Bay, took out some knives, and *whoosh whoosh*"—he slashed the air.

"He got stabbed because you put him in there! You served up Jay on a silver platter!" Jack started to pace. "The cops have the ATM picture, showing a guy in Jay's jacket. The wallet's in Jay's jacket. Her blood on his shoes. To protect *you*, Jay confesses and says, 'Yeah, it was me. I stole it.' They don't *need* to look for anyone else. *You* gave them everything."

"But I never even saw the lady. Maybe the cops planted something on me, you ever think of that? They planted evidence. How else did blood get on my shoes?"

"She cut her foot open, you idiot. You must have stepped in her blood on the hill when you found the handbag. All they need is a trace, with DNA testing."

"You have to tell the cops the truth," Two Point begged.

"I don't *have* to do anything," Jack snapped. But something Two Point had said a moment ago was nagging at him.

"Wait a second…You went to your stash, but you didn't put the wallet there. So you went to your stash with something else. What was it?"

"Nothing."

Jack grabbed Two Point's shirt and yanked him forward.

"What the hell?"

"Shut up and listen. I'm in no mood. Victor said you've been boosting from cars. The night Stacy was killed, did you rip off a car in the parking lot?"

"Maybe."

"Maybe, nothing. Yes or no?"

"Yes."

"What kind of car was it?"

"Green."

Jack waited.

Two Point's shoulders crept up. "What? It had four doors."

"Make? Model? Plates?"

"Aw, c'mon, man." Two Point shifted his weight from one foot to the other so fast it looked as if he had to run to the bathroom.

"What did you steal?"

"I don't remember."

Jack's eyes blazed and he shook Two Point so hard his teeth rattled.

"Okay, okay. Just a GPS."

"Do you still have it, or did you pawn it?"

"I haven't touched any of my stash since this all went down. In case the cops were following me."

"Where's your stash? Take me there."

"What? I'm not telling the cops I was stealing—"

"Yes you are."

"I can't. The cops would know I violated my probation. What do you want with the GPS anyway?"

Jack's hand tightened into a fist.

Two Point shook his head. "No way, Stratton. I'll tell them I found the wallet, but I'm not taking you to my stash. You can threaten me all you want."

Just then there was a rustle from behind the nearby trees, and Replacement walked right up, planted herself between the two men, and turned her back to Two Point. "It's in the Grangers' shed. I've seen him put stuff there. Behind some paint cans in the back. In a milk crate."

"Shut up, you—" Two Point started to say, but Jack yanked him forward so they were nose to nose.

"Get this straight," Jack growled. "This kid is Chandler's replacement. In fact, we call her *Replacement*. You know what that means? It means what you do to her, you do to Chandler. You give her any lip, ever, for anything whatsoever and I swear the whole neighborhood will put you in a box. Do you understand me?"

Two Point nodded.

Jack turned to Replacement. "Thanks, kid. I guess your sneaking around isn't all bad. But right now I think you should head home."

Replacement looked up at Jack, eyes wide and cheeks flushed. Then she dashed back into the trees.

Jack looked after her for a second, in amazement, then turned back to the business at hand. "This is how this works. *Shut up*. I'm not explaining. You're giving me what you took from that car in the parking lot. And that will back up your story. Got it? Let's move."

* * *

The Grangers were an elderly couple, the husband in a wheelchair. They must not have entered the shed in years, and judging by the rusty creaks the door made when Two Point pulled it open, their hearing must be pretty much shot.

Two Point walked straight to the corner.

"You'd better pray it's here," Jack said.

Two Point reached behind some old paint cans and pulled out a green milk crate filled with an assortment of loot: a car stereo, cell phones, CDs, some expensive-looking sunglasses. On top of it all was a GPS.

"No way," Jack said. "It looks like this day isn't that cursed after all."

Two Point handed Jack the GPS. It tipped forward and a stream of water poured into Jack's palm. Two Point looked up at the basketball-size hole in the roof. "Crap. Rain got in it."

The GPS looked new, except for the water, which was still leaking out. There was a sticker on the back.

LIBERTY CAR RENTAL. SCHENECTADY, NEW YORK.

A sharp current surged through Jack's body, and he turned to Two Point. "Off to the cops we go."

"Right now?"

Jack grinned as he took hold of Tommy's skinny arm and half dragged him to the Impala. "Right now is the best time in the world to do the right thing."

30

YOU DO THINK I'M STUPID

Jack strode through the doors of the police station—Two Point in one hand and the GPS in the other, like a treasure hunter with his prize—and marched up to the front desk.

"Detective Clark, please. Jack Stratton."

The desk sergeant called the detective, and after a few minutes, Detective Clark pushed through a door, a storm cloud over his head that looked about to dispense lightning and thunder.

"Before you yell at me, just listen for one minute," Jack said firmly. "This is Tommy Martin. Jay's brother, the one with the APB. He stole this GPS"—Jack placed it on the desk—"from a car in Hamilton Park the night Stacy was killed. There's a sticker on the back—it's from Liberty Car Rental in Schenectady. I believe Michael Shaw rented that car."

Clark's eyebrows were raised so high, Jack thought they might disappear into his receding hairline. He couldn't tell whether this was a good or bad sign. He took a deep breath.

"I think he rented a car and came back and killed his wife."

Detective Clark looked down at the GPS as though it were a pipe bomb. When he looked up at Jack, the pleased smile Jack expected was not to be seen.

"Wait here." Clark walked over to a man in a suit. Jack thought he recognized him from the night Jay was arrested. The two spoke briefly, then Clark handed him the GPS and said to Jack, "Come with me." Motioning for two uniformed officers to follow him, he led Jack and Two Point down the hall toward the interrogation rooms.

Jack wasn't eager to go back there. "Can we talk in your office?" he asked.

"You." Clark pointed at Two Point. "In there." He motioned for one of the cops to accompany Two Point into a room. "Make sure you pat him down," he added.

Two Point looked at Jack, eyes wide and full of fear. Jack tried to offer a reassuring look back, but the officer pulled the door shut.

Clark walked to the next interrogation room and held the door open for Jack.

"I'll take that as a no," Jack mumbled as he entered the room.

"Up against the wall," Clark said calmly.

"What for?"

"Just do it."

Jack assumed the position. Clark patted him down, then gestured for Jack to sit in the chair.

"Start right after you left me." Clark's words popped with clarity.

Jack was confused and tired. Detective Clark's face was crimson, and the vein at his temple throbbed. Jack had thought the detective was going to be so happy he'd solved the case…maybe Clark would suggest the town hold an official Jack Stratton Day. The last thing he'd expected was for Clark to look as if he was about to explode.

"I got home. My dad picked me up after you called him, and he gave me a long lecture. Then Tommy called. He'd heard Jay was in the hospital and he wanted to confess."

"And he offered you the GPS as proof?"

"No. I was asking how he found Stacy's wallet—"

"Jay Martin stole Stacy's wallet."

"No, he didn't. Tommy found it. Right near where I found her body. The thirteenth bench. It was in the handbag. Tommy took the wallet and threw the handbag into the woods. Robyn, the homeless lady, found it there."

"How'd Tommy get the GPS?"

"Tommy's been stealing from cars around Hamilton Park, and he stole from a green car that night. The way I figure it, Michael Shaw rented a car in Schenectady and drove back to Fairfield. He only used the hotel as an alibi. So he parks and waits in the woods to kill his wife. Tommy comes along and boosts the GPS from the rental car."

Jack leaned back in his chair, crossed his arms and legs, and attempted a grin. "Proof."

Clark's vein continued to throb. "Wait here," he said. He and the policeman left.

It took Jack a second to realize why the cop didn't wait with him this time. He was eighteen and no longer a minor.

Jack waited.

And waited.

After at least half an hour of waiting, he tried the door. Locked.

Jack pounded on the door until a policeman opened it up.

"Where's Detective Clark?"

"He'll be back when he gets back. Keep it down or we'll have to come in and restrain you."

"Restrain me?"

"Yes."

"You said, 'when he gets back'? Did he leave? Like leave the station?"

"Just wait here," the cop said gruffly. He shut and relocked the door.

Jack went back to the table and sat down. He didn't know what Clark was up to, but he did trust him. He folded his arms on the table and laid his head down.

* * *

The door to the interview room opened. Jack sat up and rubbed his eyes.

Vargas strutted in with a look of disgust on his face. A uniformed policeman followed him. The policeman stood against the door while Vargas walked over to the table and set down the evidence bag with the GPS inside.

"Nice try, Stratton. It didn't work."

"What do you mean?" Jack asked, confused. "It was filled with water, but you can check the memory card or something, right?"

"I'm not talking about that," Vargas snapped. "You do think I'm stupid, don't you? I'm talking about your ruse."

"My ruse?"

"You think slapping a fake sticker on this GPS and a false confession is going to screw up my case? It won't."

Now Jack was completely confused. "Fake sticker?"

"Clark believed you, you know. He drove all the way out to Schenectady. He checked with Liberty Car Rental and had them pull all the car rental records. Michael Shaw didn't rent a car, and they're not missing any GPSs."

Jack stared blankly at the table. His heart went so cold his chest hurt. "I don't understand."

Vargas put one hand on the table and leaned down so he could put his face right near Jack's.

"That can't be right," Jack stammered. "Did you check the travel records on the GPS? Did you pull the memory card?"

"The damn thing's filled with water. Our IT guys said the memory card is ruined. No one's getting any data off that thing, which I'm sure you know."

"I don't get it," Jack muttered in disbelief.

"What? What was that?" Vargas laughed. This time it was real. He laughed hard. "Oh, you are priceless. I think Clark might be right. You may just be a gullible boob. The sticker's fake."

"There has to be another explanation."

"Get real, Stratton. And what's Shaw's motive for killing his wife?"

Jack sat up. "Maybe he killed her for the money?"

"Money? If he planned to kill her for money, he did a lousy job. Do you know how much life insurance they had? None."

Jack rubbed the back of his neck with his hand. "Maybe he… Maybe he just went crazy? It doesn't make sense."

"I'm with you there. Your theories are crazy. Michael Shaw was in Schenectady the whole night. You know how I know that? Facts. Michael Shaw called Stacy from Schenectady on his cell phone. There's a record of that call, and it bounced off the cell tower in Schenectady."

Jack sat for a moment, racking his brain. "I think I can explain that. There's this phone app. Shaw works for the company. It can call—"

Vargas kicked the chair across the room. "Shut up, Stratton!" he roared. "I just brought a grieving widower back in here today because of you!" His lip trembled—Jack thought it was from anger until he looked at Vargas's face. The detective's eyes were moist.

"And I leaned hard on him. I *accused* him," Vargas continued. "Do you know what Shaw did? He cried. Real tears. Do you have any idea what that felt like for me? No, because Boy Wonder seems to think that his *hunches* are better than anything the police—highly trained professionals—could ever come up with. But I did it because it's my job, so I had to re-interview him because of you and your damn fake evidence. You made that necessary. You're trying to frame a man whose wife was murdered, you piece of garbage."

"No." Jack shook his head and ran his hand through his hair. "The sticker's not fake. It's not. Shaw could have—"

"Shut up. There's always an answer with you, but not anymore."

"But why would someone put a fake sticker on a GPS? Listen—"

"You have the right to remain silent." Vargas took out his handcuffs. "I suggest you use it, because I don't want to hear anything else come out of your mouth."

He held the handcuffs out to the policeman at the door. As Vargas continued to read Jack his rights, and the other cop put the cuffs on, he felt as if the whole world had shifted. His head spun and his breathing was labored.

Vargas picked up the chair he'd kicked over. "I'm charging you," he said, "for impeding a police investigation."

Jack's breath hitched.

"You were warned to stay away from the investigation by a law enforcement official, yet you continued to impede *my* investigation." He tapped his chest with his thumb. "I'm also charging you with being in possession of stolen property."

Were J-Dog and Two Point playing me all along?

Jack's mouth ran faster than his spinning head. He spoke before he thought it through. "If you think I faked the GPS and the sticker, how can you charge me with stealing it? Wouldn't it be mine?"

Vargas's chair scraped across the floor as he shoved it into the table. "Congratulations on flushing your life down the toilet. You could have gone into the Army like you said you wanted. But no. You chose the wrong path. Now no Private Stratton. No Detective Stratton. Now you are, and forever will be…just Jack."

The door shut with the finality of a coffin lid.

31

CONSEQUENCES

His father hadn't spoken a word since picking Jack up at the police station. But as they drove home, Jack saw the strain in his face.

When they reached a red light, his dad finally broke the silence with a sigh. "You disobeyed me."

"I'm sorry, Dad." He was having trouble with his voice and had to clear his throat. "I'm really sorry."

"Why? What was going through your head? Was there anything going through your head?"

Ted looked at his son, and Jack was shocked by how haggard, tired, and old his father looked. This was a disaster. How could he have been so off-base?

Jack ran down everything that had happened, as much for himself as for his father: the phone call from Tommy, the GPS, talking to Clark, getting arrested. "But I'm telling you that sticker's not fake. It's not, Dad. It has streaks on it from the water, too. I looked when Vargas brought it back in."

"But the car rental place isn't missing any GPSs. And there's no record of Michael Shaw renting a car."

Jack leaned his head against the window. "I can't explain it. But Dad—"

"Right now, we need to let things cool down." His father sighed again, but this time it was longer, sadder. "Even if we do manage to work things out, I think you need to rethink going into the Army."

The words cut Jack to the core. "What? Why?"

"The Army is all about following orders, son."

Jack's shoulders slumped.

"It's your decisions lately, Jack. Time and again you're just rushing in. You act without thinking of the consequences."

"I had to do something. What was I supposed to do?"

"You should have called the police, how many times do I have to tell you that? You put yourself in a dangerous position, and others as well."

"I'm going into the Army. That kinda puts me in a dangerous position twenty-four seven."

His father frowned. "Smart-ass comments won't help."

"I'm sorry. It doesn't matter now anyway. With this on my record, the Army won't take me now."

"I spoke with Detective Clark. He thinks if we let things cool down, he might be able to get Vargas to drop the charges."

Jack sat up. "Hold up. What did you just say?"

His dad leaned back. "Jack, I said they *might* drop the charges. I don't know if you fully understand the gravity of the situation."

"No. Wait." Jack shook his head rapidly, as if trying to knock a thought into place. "You said smart-ass."

"What?"

"Dad." Jack's face lit up. "That's what the homeless guy said to me."

"What?"

"The homeless guy who sleeps at that bench." Jack's palm smacked the dashboard. "He said some smart-ass broke the light."

"I'm not following."

"He's a witness."

"What are you talking about? A homeless man? Your mother said you spoke with Alex—"

"No. I talked to this other homeless guy in the park"—Jack flipped frantically through his notes in his mind—"Murray. He saw the killer."

"He saw the murder?"

"No, he wasn't there that night. But he saw the killer."

"You're not making any sense. If he didn't see the murder, how did he see the killer?" His dad shook his head. "Jack, start at the beginning."

"Dad, we need to go to the park."

His father looked at him as though he'd just lost his mind. "Are you listening to yourself? Are you listening to me? To anyone?"

"Dad, if *I* figured out there's a witness, then whoever the killer is may have figured it out too. If the killer realizes they left a witness behind, they'll go after him. Murray's life is in danger."

"Then we call Clark."

"No. He's not going to send someone out to protect a homeless guy, certainly not on my word. Dad, I feel it in my gut. We have to go now."

"Jack...please listen. There's still a chance, a very slim one, that you can salvage your career. Your dreams. But if you do this, there's no going back."

"But Dad, that man's a witness. I'm sure of it."

His dad's voice was stern. "No more going off half-cocked. Start by explaining it to me."

Jack took a deep breath. "The light fixture. It didn't dawn on me until just now. The light where Stacy was attacked was broken. The way the homeless guy said it—I think he meant somebody broke that light *on purpose*. This wasn't a random act of vandalism. It was the murderer, Dad, planning his crime. He probably tampered with her car, too, so she'd be forced to walk home. He planned it all. And if Murray saw him break the light, he knows who the killer is—or at least what he looks like."

"Jack, the last few days you've been 'sure' about a lot of things that turned out to be wrong."

"Please believe me, Dad. I need someone to believe me."

His father stopped at a red light. He took off his glasses and rubbed his eyes. "I know you're upset about today, and right now you may think that you're right." The words stung Jack. "But if you decide to do this, I won't be able to shield you from the consequences."

"I'm not asking you to shield me. Are you saying this is my decision?"

"You're eighteen now. You need to make your own choices, and face your own consequences. I can't do that for you. But as your father I have to remind you: You could be giving up everything you've worked for. Everything."

"I know. But I know I'm right."

"Jack!" His father rarely raised his voice, but he did now. "There are still consequences."

That brought Jack up short. "If I prove Jay didn't kill Stacy, how can I get jammed up?"

"Let me put it another way. Suppose you prove that Detective Vargas is wrong in front of his boss and all his colleagues. Do you think he'll congratulate you? Or will he pursue charges, if he thinks you still impeded his investigation?"

Jack looked out the window.

The way to Hamilton Park was to the right. The way home was to the left. Jack's father looked both ways, and then turned to Jack. "Since you first came to us—eleven years ago today—you've wanted to be a policeman. Are you willing to risk losing that for Jay Martin?"

Jack paused, but he didn't need time to think about his answer. "Wrong's wrong. It isn't just about Jay. Not anymore. I didn't even know Stacy, but…the person who killed her left her in a pond like trash. Like I was." Jack swallowed.

"Jack…"

"Yeah, I could close my eyes and go on with my life, and become a police officer, and everything I've ever wanted—but does that mean an innocent person rots in prison and a killer goes free? And if something happens to that homeless guy tonight, I'll never forgive myself."

The light turned green. Jack's dad hesitated. He took a long time to decide, while various scenarios spun in Jack's mind…his parents proud of him, graduating from police academy…and then, Vargas putting him in a cell…

Finally his father exhaled, straightened up in his seat, and turned toward Hamilton Park.

"Thanks for believing in me."

His father sped up. "That's what dads are for."

***

As they walked into Hamilton Park, the wind blew in gusts and the air was sticky.

"It's going to rain soon, so let's find him fast," Ted said. They didn't see anyone else. As the wind picked up, Jack kept turning his face toward the sky, waiting for rain.

They reached the bench where Jack and Chandler had seen the homeless guy the other night, but he wasn't there. Then they headed to bench thirteen. He wasn't there either.

"Are you sure this is the right place?" Ted asked. "The light is working."

Jack looked up. "They must have fixed it. But it's the right place."

His father took off his glasses and wiped them. "Let's try the shelter. He probably went before—"

"Evening," said a voice. Jack and his father jumped as the homeless man walked toward them out of the darkness. "Didn't see me, did ya?"

"Nope." Ted popped the end of the word and his eyebrows lowered. "That's why we jumped."

The man grinned. "Murray Pratt."

"Nice to meet you. Ted Stratton. This is my son, Jack." He reached out to shake Murray's hand, but then thought better of it.

Jack spoke as calmly as his pounding heart would allow. "Murray, you remember me? We talked a few nights ago. You said that a smart-ass broke your light, is that right?"

"He sure did." Murray nodded emphatically.

"So you spoke with him?" Jack held his breath.

"Not really. He walked over and started throwing rocks at my light. I asked him what the hell he was doing and he told me to get lost. I told him that that's where I sleep, and you know what he said? 'No one wants to sleep with the lights on.' Then he broke my light."

"What did he look like? Was he white? Black?" Jack asked.

"A white guy. Big. Taller than you. Light-brown hair."

"It wasn't Vlad or any of the other homeless guys around here?"

"Nope."

"Would you recognize him again if you saw him?" Jack asked.

"I think so," Murray said.

"Would you be able to tell the police what you just told us?" Ted asked.

Murray shifted his weight from foot to foot. He looked nervous. "I don't know."

"It would be a big help to a lot of people. I'd be personally grateful and—"

"How grateful? Money grateful?"

"Possibly." Ted smiled. "Tell you what, I'll buy you dinner. All you have to do is tell the police what you just told me."

"Really?" Murray eyed him suspiciously.

"Really." Jack's dad raised his hand in promise.

"Deal," Murray said.

A rumble of thunder echoed through the park.

Ted shrugged. "No time like the present. How about the Waffle House near the police station?"

"I love waffles."

"Right after you talk to the cops," Jack added.

As the three of them headed back to the car, Murray kept talking about what he wanted to order. Jack's dad just kept nodding and saying, "That sounds good, Murray. Get that."

When they rounded the top of a hill, Murray pulled up short.

"Everything all right?" Ted asked.

The color had drained from Murray's face. "No. You know…I can't."

"What's the matter?" Jack asked.

"No." Murray took a step back. "Snitches get stitches," he muttered.

"You're not snitching," Ted said. "This man murdered—"

"What?" Murray looked back and forth between Jack and his father as if they might grab him. "I thought he just broke the light! You think he's a killer?" He took another step back. "I didn't see nothin'."

"Murray, you could already be in danger." Ted stepped closer. "If that man realizes that you could identify him—"

"I'm not identifyin' nobody."

"The police can protect you."

"Get away from me!" Murray spun on his heel and hurried away.

Jack started after him, but his father grabbed his arm. "Let him go."

"But he knows. He saw the guy!"

"I'll talk to Clark."

"But what if Murray chickens out? He knows, Dad. He saw him."

"And right now he's scared. We can't drag him to the police station."

"*I* can."

His father shook his head. "You can't *legally*. After everything that's happened, you still think you can bust in and save the day? I don't know what to do with you." He started back to the car.

"So we're just going to let him walk away? What about Jay? What about Stacy?"

"Jack, you're really trying my patience." He reached for his phone and made a face. "Shoot, I left my phone on the hall table. We'll go home and I'll call Clark. That's final."

As Jack stood there, fuming, the first drops of rain fell. He glared at the sky. "I hate this cursed day," he grumbled, and stomped toward the car.

They walked in silence. By the time they crested a hill and the parking lot came into view, wind was whipping, shaking the nearby trees. Then something caught Jack's eye.

"Damn."

His dad frowned. "Don't swear."

Jack pointed at the silver Toyota parked in the far corner. "That's Michael Shaw's car."

His dad stopped walking. "Are you sure?"

"First car I ever tailed. I'll never forget what it looks like."

Ted stared across the parking lot. "Why would he be here now?"

Jack scanned the park. "Dad, why else? He's here for Murray. He knows Murray saw him break that light. Murray's in trouble."

Ted frowned in thought. "Even if you're right…why wait until now? If Shaw wanted to hurt Murray, he could have done it anytime."

"Because I stirred things up," Jack said. "When Shaw thought he was safe, killing Murray wasn't worth the risk. But Vargas brought him in again today and questioned him. Because of the GPS. It made Shaw scared. Now he's trying to cover his tracks."

"We need to get the police."

"There's no time." Jack walked back into the park.

"What? No." His dad grabbed Jack's arm. "Haven't you learned anything? We need to get the police."

"But Murray's out there. And Shaw might be with him already."

"Shaw could have a gun! Jack…are you going to risk your life for Murray?"

Jack felt the warm glow of adrenaline sweep through his system. "I have to, Dad." He stepped backward. "*You* need to go get the police."

"I'm not leaving you."

"I'm faster. I'll run back to the bench."

"We go together."

They started running, but before they were halfway, Ted was huffing and had to slow down.

"Dad, let me go on ahead. Trust me."

His dad stopped and placed his hands on his hips. He ground his teeth in frustration. "If you see Shaw, run. Do you promise me?"

Jack nodded.

"Go."

He was already gone, pushing against the wind, the rain stinging his eyes. At the top of the next hill, he saw the bench. He raced down the hill, skidded to a stop, and peered through the thick rain. No one was in sight.

Jack cupped his hands to his mouth and yelled, "Murray! Murray!"

The storm howled in response.

Jack ran down a side path, calling for Murray, but after a few minutes, he decided to start back toward his dad. Maybe he'd find Murray on the way. They could search together…

From the direction where he had left his dad came a voice, cutting right through the wind and rain: "Stop right there!" Jack had never heard his father sound so commanding.

His feet flew over the slick pavement. At the top of the hill, he froze.

Below him, his father was standing on the grass just off the path, his legs planted shoulder-width apart. Michael Shaw stood about fifteen feet away, with something in his hand, a cane or a thick branch? In a heap at Shaw's feet, rain pelting his matted hair and filthy rags, lay Murray, not moving.

"Stop hitting him and step back, now," Ted ordered in his sternest teacher voice.

Shaw straightened up.

"Move away from him!" Ted walked forward. "Just back away. We can work this out."

Shaw looked dazed.

In a flash of lightning, Jack saw the gleam of what Shaw held in his right hand. A tire iron.

Shaw started toward Ted.

"Dad! Look out!" Jack skittered down the wet grass.

Ted took a step forward, fists raised.

It was a lopsided matchup: the hulking man, wielding a heavy tool, versus the short, stocky scholar.

Shaw screamed in rage and charged.

Jack's hands clawed the air as he raced forward.

Shaw swung. The tire iron swept toward Jack's father's head.

Jack dove between the two men. Jack's back took most of the impact. The base of his skull took the rest. His momentum carried him into Shaw and his weight drove the man back, but Shaw remained on his feet while Jack collapsed to the ground.

The rain sparkled and the world spun. Jack's tasted the tang of metal in his mouth—blood.

Shaw stared down at Jack in disbelief. His lips pulled back so far all his teeth showed. "You!" he shrieked. Gripping the tire iron in both hands, he raised it high over Jack.

Ted slammed into Shaw's ribs and threw all his weight into it, at last toppling the bigger man. Shaw's feet slid out from under him on the wet grass and he tumbled backward, dropping the tire iron. The two men rolled, and Ted, summoning up All-

State high school wrestling skills from twenty-five years ago, came out on top and firmly pinned one of Shaw's arms to the ground with his knee.

But Shaw's other hand was free, and he was the stronger of the two. Jack, on hands and knees, fighting to get breath back into his lungs, watched Shaw take a swing. His first blow glanced harmlessly off Ted's shoulder.

The second broke Ted's glasses on his face, the frame slicing into the skin above his right eye. Then an uppercut caught Ted under the chin and knocked his head back. He fell off Shaw and onto his side.

By now, Jack had managed to stand, and so had Murray. Blood ran down the side of Murray's face and into his beard. He locked eyes with Jack for a split second, then turned and fled over the hill, his rags flapping against his arms and legs.

Jack looked at his father through blurred eyes. Shaw's huge hands circled his throat. For the first time ever, Jack saw terror in his dad's eyes.

"Run, Jack!" his father ordered.

Jack processed the order to run, but he was still dizzy from the blow to the head. He stumbled and crashed back down to the ground, helpless, and saw Shaw leaning all his weight forward, trying to crush his father's throat. Ted's fingers clawed at Shaw's grip. His face was turning blue as Jack watched in horror.

Do something! Jack rose to his feet, using his own rage to push himself up. "*Shaw!*" he bellowed. He still had a voice. Jack tried to put at least a tire iron's weight into it. "Let him go."

His father's back arched, and his eyes bulged in his head.

A shrill, ear-piercing whistle cut through the storm. A red baseball hat bobbed over the horizon. Again and again the whistle shrieked, closer and closer.

Robyn dashed over the hill, blowing her whistle for all she was worth.

"Shut up!" Shaw released Jack's father and stood up.

But Jack's father didn't move.

"It's over, Shaw. Give up," Jack said. "You murdered your wife! The police know everything. The phone app. The broken light."

The ghost of a shadow flickered in Shaw's eyes. He put both of his hands over his ears and stumbled backward, walking away and shaking his head like he was trying to drive the memory back to the darkness.

Robyn ran up beside Jack, who had reached Ted's side. Her whistle quieted. Tears poured down her face. She was furiously huffing, but the only sound coming out was a strained wheeze.

Jack was trying to keep one eye on Shaw and one on his father, who still wasn't moving. Robyn was kneeling at his side and watching him closely, holding his hand and wiping the blood off from where the glasses had cut him.

"The police are on the way."

Shaw's eyes fixed on the tire iron lying in the grass. He marched over and picked it up.

"Michael. Stop," croaked a hoarse voice. Jack's father. "Please, stop."

Jack's heart skipped a beat. *Thank God, he's alive.*

Michael Shaw looked bad, like he hadn't slept in days. He appraised Jack's father, then eyed Jack and Robyn. Jack realized he was trying to figure out whether he could finish them all off—and he'd still have to track down Murray too.

Shaw raised the tire iron over his head.

Jack's vision blurred, but he tried to focus on the large blur in front of him. He balled his right hand into a fist.

One punch.

He might have one good punch left in him. One good punch might buy them a few more minutes; Robyn could run and get the police… He instructed his left shoulder, the only good one at this point, to cock back and was just about to release the safety off his fist—

"Here! Over here!"

Everyone turned to look. Alex Hernandez stood atop the hill near the road, his black hair streaming around him, his arm pointing at Shaw. Murray flapped down the hill with him, followed by a policeman in full orange rain gear and heavy boots, sweeping his flashlight over the group.

Ted, Jack, Robyn, Alex, and Murray all pointed at Shaw from different directions.

The cop drew his gun, keeping the flashlight on Shaw.

"Freeze! Hands where I can see them!"

Jack managed a faint smile.

Sweeter words he'd never heard.

32

LIKE YOUR OLD MAN

Jack lost track of how long he was in the emergency room, where he'd been poked, pricked, X-rayed, and prodded. Now he waited in one of the visitor's chairs in a small examination room, itching to find out how his father was.

A doctor walked in and introduced herself. They shook hands and she quickly scanned his chart.

"How's my dad?" Jack asked.

"He's fine. He'll have a sore throat for a few days, and a sore body. We stitched up a cut on his face. It's mainly in his eyebrow, the scar shouldn't be too noticeable. He's getting dressed and will be with you in a minute—"

Jack's dad hurried into the room, still putting on his shirt. The left side of his face was bandaged; his right eye had a deep black circle under it and was swollen shut. Jack cringed when he saw the bruises around his throat.

They hugged, and then Jack's dad turned back to the doctor. "You said nothing's broken?" he asked hoarsely.

She smiled. "Young bones. He's got a nasty bump on his head and a dislocated shoulder. You'll both need to take it easy for a little while. I'll leave instructions with the nurse."

She lost the smile and cleared her throat. "There's a detective outside who wants to speak with you. You can use this room."

After the doctor left, Detective Clark walked in. He looked at Jack's father and shook his head. "This is what I get for assuming at least one of you could be a responsible adult?"

Ted scoffed, "Don't be so dramatic, Derrick."

Clark brushed his gray hair back and his scowl darkened. "Dramatic? You both almost got beaten to death by a murderer with a tire iron and *I'm* being dramatic?"

"It's my fault," said Jack.

"No, it isn't," the older men said at once.

Ted continued. "I'm responsible. And there's a very good reason for my actions."

Clark crossed his arms and waited, but Jack was beginning to think that he wasn't really all that mad at them.

Ted cleared his throat, and rasped, "Jack realized there was a possible witness."

"Murray Pratt?"

"Yes, Murray. I decided that before speaking with you, I should go and warn him that his life was in danger."

"It's the 'before speaking with me' part that I have a problem with, Ted."

"Seriously, Derrick? What was I going to do—tell you some homeless man in Hamilton Park 'might have seen something'?"

"Yes."

Jack's dad huffed. "You can't work off that. You need facts. Something more concrete."

"No. We would have canvassed the park again, asked different questions. It's standard procedure."

"Well, I thought—and Jack thought," he added loyally, "Murray's life was in immediate danger…and that it was the right thing to do."

Jack jumped in. "And then, when things got hairy, Dad realized he didn't have his phone on him."

Clark looked back and forth between Jack and his father. His gaze stopped on Jack. "Now I know where you get it, kid. Apple doesn't fall far from the tree."

Jack smiled at Ted.

Clark's harsh face softened. "You did save Murray's life."

Jack replied, "Well, if it wasn't for Murray getting help, and Alex getting the police…"

"You were right about Michael Shaw, too. He killed his wife, and then lost it. Paranoid as hell. I don't think he's slept since he killed her."

"He confessed?"

"Yes. To everything. After we confronted him with the evidence, he gave us every detail. I personally think it was you who drove him over the edge." He winked at Jack.

Jack's dad laughed. "Jack can have that effect on people."

Clark leaned against the wall. "During his confession, Shaw kept talking about this guy who was following him around, showing up at his house, shadowing him and his mistress. He thinks you're some avenging spirit sent to torment him for killing his wife. Then we pulled him in for the GPS, and I guess that was the last straw."

"How come Liberty Rental didn't have a record of him renting a car, or of the GPS being stolen?" Jack asked.

"Shaw swiped a driver's license from one of the other sales reps at his company, and then returned it without the guy knowing. He used a prepaid credit card that he'd been using to hide his affair from his wife. And he used that same card to buy a new GPS to replace the one Tommy stole. The rental car company had no idea. But the linchpin was that phone app, Jack."

Jack struggled not to look too pleased.

"You were right on the money. Shaw left his own cell phone at the hotel in Schenectady. The phone records show that Shaw's cell phone received a call from an unknown number one minute before he called Stacy. We traced the unknown number to an over-the-counter burner phone purchased with the same prepaid credit card. With that app he rerouted the call, making it look like he had an ironclad alibi."

"He really planned this thing in detail," Ted said.

"Right down to where he was going to attack her," Clark said. "I've no doubt he even walked Stacy through the park a few times so she'd take the same way home."

"Monster," Ted mumbled.

Jack wanted to know every detail. "What about her car?"

"He pulled the starter relay fuse to disable it, so she'd have to walk. Afterward, he drove her car away from the body so we'd be looking for evidence in the wrong place.

And he staged an accident where he knew the car would be found right away. He needed to firmly establish that she went missing during the time he was in Schenectady with his perfect alibi."

"With all the security cameras nowadays, how come none of them caught him walking back into town?" Ted asked.

"He dumped the car right next to the main electrical lines. Then he stayed on the path underneath the lines until they reached Hamilton Park. I'm telling you, this was all carefully planned."

Jack shook his head. "But why? I don't understand. What was the motive?"

"That law office you followed him to? They were handling a civil suit against the Darrington Fertility Clinic. A few years back, Stacy Shaw had undergone a botched procedure there, which doctors believed had left her sterile. Then she got pregnant."

Jack shook his head. "I still don't get it."

"The clinic was about to settle with the Shaws for two million dollars."

"He murdered his wife and child for two million dollars." Jack stared at the wall.

His dad put his hand on Jack's shoulder. "That man is pure evil. And if not for you, he would have killed again. You saved Murray's life."

Jack nodded absently, a little dazed by the puzzle that was still raveling and unraveling in his mind. "How is he?"

"He'll be fine. Concussion, a few stitches," Clark said. "He gave us a statement, and so did the homeless woman, Robyn." Clark wiggled a finger in his ear. "My ears are still ringing from when she insisted on demonstrating how loud her whistle goes."

Jack chuckled, remembering the alarm whistle, then the red cap cresting the hill, and finally little Robyn herself.

Ted suddenly tipped his head to the side, as if decoding an urgent message from his subconscious. He said to Jack, "You know, her Red Sox hat—"

Jack talked fast. "That's great, everyone's okay. That's the important thing. Right?"

"I'm proud of you, Jack." Clark grinned. "Hell, even Vargas was impressed, though he'd never admit it."

Jack looked down; his dad smiled proudly.

"Oh, hey, what about J-Dog? I mean, Jay."

"Good news: he's being transferred to Fairfield General Hospital. All charges against him are dropped."

"Tommy?"

"After all his family went through, the superintendent plans to pull some strings. For his cooperation, I think he'll be looking at some community service. If he keeps himself clean, he'll be able to work something out."

Clark, who had elected not to take the third chair in the room and had been standing the whole time, squared his shoulders and raised his voice a couple notches.

"Now. The night's not over. We need to discuss what you two did. I specifically told you both that this was dangerous and you should back off. You kept going. There are consequences for that."

Jack was too surprised to say anything.

"Wait a second," Ted said. "How would it look if you charged Jack after all he's done?"

"We're not going to charge him. But the wrath you two are about to face is far worse than prison." Clark walked over to the door, opened it, and stood aside.

In the hallway, Laura Stratton was speaking with the doctor.

Jack could count on one hand the number of times he'd seen his mother truly angry. As she fumed in the hallway, Jack realized he might need to start using both hands to count.

His father's mouth fell open. "You called my wife?"

33

YOU THINK I'D MISS THIS?

Two Weeks Later

Jack parked the Impala at the end of Kelly's long driveway. The Dawsons were having another picnic, and once again Jack was invited. He didn't know whether that was a good thing.

Well before he reached the door, Kelly ran around from the back of the house, straight to Jack, and wrapped her arms around him. "Hey! I didn't think you'd come."

He gently pulled her long hair to one side, closed his eyes, and took a deep breath at the back of her neck. *Jasmine? Vanilla?* He held it in as long as he could.

"You think I'd miss this?" Jack grinned. "I didn't want to wait a whole day to see you again."

They were right on the edge of a kiss when a pack of guys, including Warner, Preston, and Archer, walked out of the backyard. Warner said something, and they all burst out laughing.

"If they ask you to play football, say no," Kelly whispered. "Just tell them your shoulder's still healing."

"No can do, sorry. It's a guy thing."

She pleaded, "My brother is just doing this because of Dad, and"—she huffed. "Warner and I—"

"Were a thing." Jack shrugged. "Past tense."

"Not for him. I heard him tell Preston that he was gonna really bust you up if you played again."

"I kinda figured that when Preston called me and suggested another game."

Kelly's mouth opened, but she closed it when her brother strode up.

"Glad you could make it, Jack," Preston said with a Ken doll smile.

Warner sneered, opting for silent sarcasm.

"I'm actually looking forward to it." Jack handed his keys to Kelly.

As they walked across to the backyard, Kelly squeezed his hand and mouthed, *Don't.* Jack just smiled.

"Same teams as last time?" Preston asked. "With you we have nine, but Hayden can sit out."

"It's okay, Preston, I'm glad you've got eight guys. I figured I'd take you up on your offer."

Preston looked confused. "What offer?"

"Last time, Archer said it'd be okay if I brought some friends." Jack hitched his thumb down the street toward two approaching cars. "Just a few guys I grew up with."

A rusted brown van pulled up, followed by a gray sedan. All six foot six of Chandler got out of the van first. The driver's door opened and Gino, an even six feet tall but almost three hundred twenty pounds, got out next. Then the van side door slid open, and Bobbie G and Anthony got out and stood next to Chandler. Bobbie G was a little smaller than Chandler but outweighed him by forty pounds. Anthony's enormous biceps, covered in tattoos, bulged as he crossed his arms.

"What's up, Jack!" Estoban jogged up from the sedan and knuckle-bumped Jack. Two other big guys followed him, along with Michelle, Makayla, and Lori.

Jack surveyed the group of guys—they were as large as an NFL team. "Thanks for coming," he said with a smile. Then he turned to Warner, who was noticeably paler. "Well, let's play some football."

Michelle, Makayla, and Lori joined Kelly and her girlfriends on the sideline as the two teams lined up. Warner's team got the ball first, and on each of the first three plays, they all ended up flat on their backs, groaning in pain. On the fourth play, Archer wisely just threw the ball away.

Then Jack's team got the ball. Estoban, their quarterback, huddled up the team. "I say we let our host score the first touchdown." He turned to Jack. "Jack, fake like you're going left, then cut back behind me and I'll toss the ball to you. Stick close to the sideline."

Chandler leaned in. "Jack's got a bull's-eye on his back and a bum shoulder, so no one let the other team get near him. Got it?"

Everyone nodded.

Chandler cracked his knuckles and grinned at Jack. "We've got your back."

As planned, Estoban tossed the ball to Jack. Jack bobbed left, then right. He cut quickly in front of Preston before he had time to react—then he made sure to run the ball right past the ladies on the sideline, grinning the whole way. He made it look good, but the truth was, with his friends guarding him, Jack could have walked down the field and scored.

After they had regrouped for first down, Jack tossed the ball back to Archer, who held onto it and yelled, "Time-out! Hold on a second." Still holding the ball, he ran over to his jacket. He took out his phone and held it up to his ear. Then he turned back to the guys. "Sorry, guys. I totally forgot—something. I have to go."

One of the other kids ran over to Archer. "I… I was supposed to help you with that, right?"

Archer looked puzzled at first, and then quickly nodded. "Yeah. Sure. Yeah, we gotta go."

"We should just call it then," muttered two other guys from Warner's team, walking off the field.

"Come on, guys," Warner whined.

"Hold up, Warner." Jack strode over to him. Warner looked off to the side. Jack lowered his voice and leaned in. "Are we done?"

Warner scrutinized the grass. "You mean with the game?"

"All the games," Jack growled. "Look, this is how we're going to handle this. I'm dating Kelly now. You got a problem with that, tell me, and we'll settle it right here, right now."

Warner swallowed. He looked over at Preston, but there was no help there.

Jack straightened up.

Warner's shoulders slumped. "I get it. I'm done."

"Game's over then." Jack strutted over to his crew like a pirate on a captured frigate. "Looks like we won, boys!"

Cheers, jeers, and high fives were quickly exchanged.

"Hey, Jack," Lori called out as she ran up to him. "Nice touchdown."

"Thanks."

"I haven't gotten to tell you yet. Guess who got indicted a few days ago?"

Jack broke into a wide grin.

She nodded. "Yep. Leland Chambers did the walk of shame—in handcuffs and everything. Do you know how many employees he's made miserable over the years? He had it coming."

"Speaking of which, have you heard from Jeremy?"

"He's doing great. He came back home. After it came out what Leland had done, they reinstated him, and Betty made sure they gave him a few extra weeks' vacation."

That was the best thing Jack could have heard, along with the news that Betty was now director of finance.

Lori left to get some lemonade, and Chandler, Michelle, and Makayla walked over to Jack. "The girls want to go get some ice cream," Chandler said. "You coming?"

"I'll catch up with you. I gotta say bye to Kelly and swing by home before I come over."

"We're watching the game at Estoban's later, right?"

"I have one stop to make first."

"You'll be late."

"I won't."

"Wanna bet?"

Chandler reached for his wallet, and Jack laughed. "Get outta here."

As Jack's friends piled into their vehicles and drove off, Kelly appeared beside him. "Well, that was a blowout."

"I'm glad Preston quit before Chandler started to really play."

She laughed. It was light and happy.

Jack smiled.

"Thanks for saying something to Warner."

"Who?" Jack pulled her close.

She grinned and kissed him. Their heads shifted, and so did their hands. Jack's breathing sped up, but Kelly pulled away. She cast a quick glance at her house and tipped her head seductively.

Jack kissed her again.

She pressed into him and then, after another intense round, she pushed back. "You're so bad," she purred.

"Can you come over tomorrow night? My mom's having a belated birthday thing for me."

She nodded. "Can I bring a present?"

Jack's breath hitched. "It might be difficult wrapping yourself. Maybe just put a bow on top of your head."

She giggled.

Jack held her around the waist. “Seriously, you don’t have to get me anything. I’m just doing it for my mom.”

“I want to.” She bit her bottom lip. “Besides, you just gave me an idea.” She pouted. “I’m just bummed I have to wait until then.”

“Maybe we could go out tonight? I’m watching a game with the guys, but that’ll be over by eight.”

Kelly bit her lip and slowly twisted back and forth. “I’ll convince my mom.”

Jack leaned in.

“No, no, no…” She wagged her finger. “I’ll never let you go if I kiss you again.”

“So kiss me again.”

She took one step forward, and Jack took a step back.

“Tonight.” He grinned roguishly. “Tonight you’ll kiss me and I won’t let go.”

She nodded.

Jack walked to the Impala with a swagger in his step.

34

BROKEN REEDS

Jack carried two bouquets of flowers into Hamilton Park. It was a beautiful summer day. Walking down the path and then into the woods, he took in a long, deep breath, enjoying a momentary feeling of peace. The sun hung low in the sky, and the darkness under the canopy of the trees was lit from the side by the sun's rays across the water.

Jack walked down the embankment to the broken reeds. He swallowed and looked back up the hill behind him, where new grass had already begun to grow up in the path of destruction. Then he looked out across the water. He realized that the memory of her would always haunt him, spur him on when he couldn't go on. Something like this, he'd never forget.

And he couldn't help but wonder what might have been. At this moment, would Stacy have been shopping for her baby? Buying toys for the nursery?

A gentle breeze stirred the lily pads. The water sparkled and Jack followed the line the sun made to the other side. As the sun dipped lower, the whole pond glittered a bright gold and white.

Jack unwrapped the flowers and laid each bouquet onto the water. He bowed his head and prayed.

Then he whispered, "You aren't trash."

THE END

THE DETECTIVE JACK STRATTON MYSTERY-THRILLER SERIES

The Detective Jack Stratton Mystery-Thriller Series, authored by *Wall Street Journal* bestselling writer Christopher Greyson, has over 5,000 five-star reviews and over one million readers and counting. If you'd love to read another page-turning thriller with mystery, humor, and a dash of romance, pick up the next book in the highly acclaimed series today.

AND THEN SHE WAS GONE

A hometown hero with a heart of gold, Jack Stratton was raised in a whorehouse by his prostitute mother. Jack seemed destined to become another statistic, but now his life has taken a turn for the better. Determined to escape his past, he's headed for a career in law enforcement. When his foster mother asks him to look into a girl's disappearance, Jack quickly gets drawn into a baffling mystery. As Jack digs deeper, everyone becomes a suspect—including himself. Caught between the criminals and the cops, can Jack discover the truth in time to save the girl? Or will he become the next victim?

GIRL JACKED

Guilt has driven a wedge between Jack and the family he loves. When Jack, now a police officer, hears the news that his foster sister Michelle is missing, it cuts straight to his core. The police think she just took off, but Jack knows Michelle would never leave her loved ones behind—like he did. Forced to confront the demons from his past, Jack must take action, find Michelle, and bring her home... or die trying.

JACK KNIFED

Constant nightmares have forced Jack to seek answers about his rough childhood and the dark secrets hidden there. The mystery surrounding Jack's birth father leads Jack to investigate the twenty-seven-year-old murder case in Hope Falls.

JACKS ARE WILD

When Jack's sexy old flame disappears, no one thinks it's suspicious except Jack and one unbalanced witness. Jack feels in his gut that something is wrong. He knows that Marisa has a past, and if it ever caught up with her—it would be deadly. The trail leads him into all sorts of trouble—landing him smack in the middle of an all-out mob war between the Italian Mafia and the Japanese Yakuza.

JACK AND THE GIANT KILLER

Rogue hero Jack Stratton is back in another action-packed, thrilling adventure. While recovering from a gunshot wound, Jack gets a seemingly harmless private investigation job—locate the owner of a lost dog—Jack begrudgingly assists. Little does he know it will place him directly in the crosshairs of a merciless serial killer.

DATA JACK

In this digital age of hackers, spyware, and cyber terrorism—data is more valuable than gold. Thieves plan to steal the keys to the digital kingdom and with this much money at stake, they'll kill for it. Can Jack and Alice (aka Replacement) stop the pack of ruthless criminals before they can *Data Jack?*

JACK OF HEARTS

When his mother and the members of her neighborhood book club ask him to catch the "Orange Blossom Cove Bandit," a small-time thief who's stealing garden gnomes and peace of mind from their quiet retirement community, how can Jack refuse? The peculiar mystery proves to be more than it appears, and things take a deadly turn. Now, Jack finds it's up to him to stop a crazed killer, save his parents, and win the hand of the girl he loves—but if he survives, will it be Jack who ends up with a broken heart?

JACK FROST

Jack has a new assignment: to investigate the suspicious death of a soundman on the hit TV show *Planet Survival.* Jack goes undercover as a security agent where the show is filming on nearby Mount Minuit. Soon trapped on the treacherous peak by a blizzard, a mysterious killer continues to stalk the cast and crew of *Planet Survival.* What started out as a game is now a deadly competition for survival. As the temperature drops and the body count rises, what will get them first? The mountain or the killer?

Hear your favorite characters come to life
in audio versions of the
Detective Jack Stratton Mystery-Thriller Series!
Audio Books now available on Audible!

Novels featuring Jack Stratton in order:
AND THEN SHE WAS GONE
GIRL JACKED
JACK KNIFED
JACKS ARE WILD
JACK AND THE GIANT KILLER
DATA JACK
JACK OF HEARTS
JACK FROST

Psychological Thriller
THE GIRL WHO LIVED

Ten years ago, four people were brutally murdered. One girl lived. As the anniversary of the murders approaches, Faith Winters is released from the psychiatric hospital and yanked back to the last spot on earth she wants to be—her hometown where the slayings took place. Wracked by the lingering echoes of survivor's guilt, Faith spirals into a black hole of alcoholism and wanton self-destruction. Finding no solace at the bottom of a bottle, Faith decides to track down her sister's killer—and then discovers that she's the one being hunted.

Epic Fantasy
PURE OF HEART

Orphaned and alone, rogue-teen Dean Walker has learned how to take care of himself on the rough city streets. Unjustly wanted by the police, he takes refuge within the shadows of the city. When Dean stumbles upon an old man being mugged, he tries to help—only to discover that the victim is anything but helpless and far more than he appears. Together with three friends, he sets out on an epic quest where only the pure of heart will prevail.

INTRODUCING
THE ADVENTURES OF FINN AND ANNIE

A SPECIAL COLLECTION OF MYSTERIES EXCLUSIVELY FOR CHRISTOPHER GREYSON'S LOYAL READERS

Finnian Church chased his boyhood dream of following in his father's law-enforcing footsteps by way of the United States Armed Forces. As soon as he finished his tour of duty, Finn planned to report to the police academy. But the winds of war have a way of changing a man's plans. Finn returned home a decorated war hero, but without a leg. Disillusioned but undaunted, it wasn't long before he discovered a way to keep his ambitions alive and earn a living as an insurance investigator.

Finn finds himself in need of a videographer to document the accident scenes. Into his orderly business and simple life walks Annie Summers. A lovely free spirit and single mother of two, Annie has a physical challenge of her own—she's been completely deaf since childhood.

Finn and Annie find themselves tested and growing in ways they never imagined. Join this unlikely duo as they investigate their way through murder, arson, theft, embezzlement, and maybe even love, seeking to distinguish between truth and lies, scammers and victims.

This FREE special collection of mysteries by *Wall Street Journal* bestselling author CHRISTOPHER GREYSON is available EXCLUSIVELY to loyal readers. Get your FREE first installment ONLY at ChristopherGreyson.com. Become a Preferred Reader to enjoy additional FREE *Adventures of Finn and Annie*, advanced notifications of book releases, and more.

Don't miss out, visit ChristopherGreyson.com and JOIN TODAY!

You could win a brand new
HD KINDLE FIRE TABLET
when you go to
ChristopherGreyson.com
Enter as many times as you'd like.
No purchase necessary.
It's just my way of thanking my loyal readers.

Looking for a mystery series mixed with romantic suspense?
Be sure to check out Katherine Greyson's bestselling series:
EVERYONE KEEPS SECRETS

ACKNOWLEDGMENTS

I would like to thank all the wonderful readers out there. It is you who make the literary world what it is today—a place of dreams filled with tales of adventure! To all of you who have taken Jack and Replacement under your wings and spread the word via social media (Facebook and Twitter) and who have taken the time to go back and write a great review, I say THANK YOU! Your efforts keep the characters alive and give me the encouragement and time to keep writing. I can't thank YOU enough.

Word of mouth is crucial for any author to succeed. If you enjoyed the series, please consider leaving a review at Amazon, even if it is only a line or two; it would make all the difference and I would appreciate it very much.

I would also like to thank my wife. She's the best wife, mother, and partner in crime any man could have. She is an invaluable content editor and I could not do this without her! My thanks also go out to: my two awesome kids, my dear mother, my family, my wonderful team: Maia McViney, Maia Sepp, my fantastic editors—David Gatewood of Lone Trout Editing, Faith Williams of The Atwater Group, and Karen Lawson and Janet Hitchcock of The Proof is in the Reading—my fabulous proofreader, Charlie Wilson of Landmark Editorial, my fabulous consultant, Dianne Jones, and the unbelievably helpful beta readers.

ABOUT THE AUTHOR

My name is Christopher Greyson, and I am a storyteller.

Since I was a little boy, I have dreamt of what mystery was around the next corner, or what quest lay over the hill. If I couldn't find an adventure, one usually found me, and now I weave those tales into my stories. I am blessed to have written the bestselling Detective Jack Stratton Mystery-Thriller Series. The collection includes *And Then She Was GONE, Girl Jacked, Jack Knifed, Jacks Are Wild, Jack and the Giant Killer, Data Jack, Jack of Hearts, Jack Frost,* with *Jack of Diamonds* due later this year. I have also penned the bestselling psychological thriller, *The Girl Who Lived* and a special collection of mysteries, *The Adventures of Finn and Annie.*

My background is an eclectic mix of degrees in theatre, communications, and computer science. Currently I reside in Massachusetts with my lovely wife and two fantastic children. My wife, Katherine Greyson, who is my chief content editor, is an author of her own romance series, *Everyone Keeps Secrets.*

My love for tales of mystery and adventure began with my grandfather, a decorated World War I hero. I will never forget being introduced to his friend, a WWI pilot who flew across the skies at the same time as the feared, legendary Red Baron. My love of reading and storytelling eventually led me to write *Pure of Heart*, a young adult fantasy that I released in 2014.

I love to hear from my readers. Please visit ChristopherGreyson.com, where you can become a preferred reader and enjoy additional FREE *Adventures of Finn and Annie*, advanced notifications of book releases and more! Thank you for reading my novels. I hope my stories have brightened your day.

Sincerely,

CPSIA information can be obtained
at www.ICGtesting.com
Printed in the USA
LVHW030307050321
680570LV00009B/58/J

9 781683 990031